CW00447564

RUTHLESS HEIR

RUTHLESS DYNASTY BOOK 1

SASHA LEONE

Copyright © 2022 by Sasha Leone

All rights reserved.

No part of this book may be reproduced in any form or by any electronic or mechanical means, including information storage and retrieval systems, without written permission from the author, except for the use of brief quotations in a book review.

PROLOGUE
GABRIEL

5 years ago...

The mark she left on my forearm throbs as I wipe a splash of blood from my jaw.

This is all her fault.

"Your blood or his?" Tytus asks, pulling his scarlet blade from the body twitching at his feet.

"His... of course," I growl. The corpse I just created is already deathly still. "Do you think I've gotten that careless?"

"I wasn't so sure."

With a wry grin, my oldest friend looks over my shoulder, towards our final destination. I reluctantly follow his gaze.

My pounding pulse quickens at the sight of the dark building looming just ahead. By now, its heavy wooden doors are all too familiar. So are the countless black windows. Same with the tall shadowy clock tower.

Even at night, with its empty halls and abandoned classrooms, the sight is enough to make me sneer.

Westwood High.

"Just because this stupid school treats its students like children doesn't mean I've become one. A year of classes isn't going to change who I am."

A monster.

"You don't think it might have softened your edges just a little bit?"

"Fuck no," I grumble. "If anything, it's made me sharper. Angrier. More—"

"Reckless?"

He's not wrong, but I've had enough bullshit for one night.

"Let's do this," I grunt.

Turning my back to Tytus, I step over the dead guards and reach for the silver handle on the large arched doorway.

This will be the last time I ever open this fucking door again. I should be thrilled. But the cool steel knob only makes the lingering burn mark on my forearm burn all the hotter.

It's a maddening reminder of why I'm here; of why I have to leave; of why I've failed.

Her.

Bianca Byrne.

When I'm through with that brat, she's going to wish we never met.

But first, I've got a mess to help clean up. A mess that I helped create.

A mess that she made even worse.

"It's just that mark on your arm," Tytus shrugs, playfully shoving me aside to pull open the door for himself. "It's got me thinking. The old Gabriel would have gone blind with rage if someone had done that to him. Hell, if you were still the cold-blooded kid I remember, we might be breaking you out of juvie tonight, instead of back into your high school."

"It's not my high school anymore," I remind him, ignoring the rest. As hard as it's going to be, Bianca needs to stay out of my mind. That spoiled princess has occupied too much of my time already. "... Not that it ever really was."

That's the truth. I never belonged here. And no number of lies could ever change that.

Gritting past the lingering ache in my arm, and the metallic taste of blood on my tongue, I step past Tytus and storm inside.

I'm immediately met by my own demonic reflection. The nightmarish vision shimmers back at me from just behind the immaculate glass of Westwood's pride and joy. The trophy case.

It's enough to stop me in my tracks. I've been pretending to be someone else for so long now that even I'm a little shocked by what I see.

This is definitely not someone who belongs here.

Not with these tattoos, so black that they might as well be endless voids. Not with the drying blood dripping from my face, or with the strong calloused fingers wrapped so tightly around a glistening crimson blade.

Dark locks of wet hair fall over my furrowed brows. Steam rises from every inch of my exposed skin. My broad shoulders lift and fall as I heave with the adrenaline of a fresh kill.

And then there are my eyes.

They glow against the pale moonlight like fractured emeralds. A cursed mixture of hazel and green that could belong to the devil himself.

How did they ever let me into this place?

"So, you're telling me the girl didn't even get a spanking?" Tytus taunts, jogging to catch up as I rip my gaze from the trophy case and barrel into the dark hallway ahead. "If it was me, I would have punished her right—"

"Shut up," I snap.

There's no room left in my life for Bianca Byrne. I'm already walking on a razor's edge. One more false step and I could be the next fucker with a blade against my throat.

There can be no distractions.

"Why? You can talk to me, Gabe. There isn't anyone left here but us."

"That's not true."

I regret my choice of words almost immediately. Despite my failure, despite my anger, despite my shame, I'm still in control of what happens here tonight.

Well, some of it.

Not everyone in this building needs to die. But I won't be able to save anyone if I'm preoccupied with the girl who's become my biggest failure.

"Did we forget to kill any of the guards?" Tytus asks, confused.

"No," I mumble, correcting myself. "But you never know who could be listening..." In the distance, I can hear the faintest echo of a desperate voice pleading for his life. We're right on time. "Did you cut the phone lines?"

"Of course," Tytus nods. "And I have the jammer drone hovering about a hundred feet above the clocktower. Even if Drago and his crew have left anyone alive, they won't be able to call for help until long after we're gone."

"Good."

"Is there anyone else we need to worry about?"

"No." I quickly lie, but my gaze stays vigilant. Anyone could be hiding in these tall, deep shadows; listening, waiting to expose all of my lies.

If they're smart, they'll keep hidden until after we've left. Because if they don't, not even I will be able to protect them.

"This way."

Clenching my fists, I lead Tytus towards the gymnasium.

The closer we get, the louder the terrified wails become.

I recognize the anguished voice all too well.

The bastard is finally getting what he deserves.

"Are you ready?" Tytus asks, as we turn around the last corner.

"Always," I sneer.

Ahead, the big royal blue doors of the gymnasium stand out like a sore thumb against the plain grey walls. It doesn't matter how thick they are, though. Agony seeps out into the hallway like a chilled greeting.

Drago has started his interrogation, and his victim is already wailing for mercy.

He won't get any.

Not from him, and definitely not from me.

With a single shove, I push my way into the gymnasium.

For a second, the pleading howls stop, and the only sound is the slow creaking of the gym doors as they shut behind us.

"Nice of you to join us," Drago says from up ahead, breaking the silence. He doesn't bother to turn around. The man understands our blood lust well enough to trust that we would never leave a threat un-gutted.

"Didn't think you'd show up," Roz quietly teases as we join the group.

Everyone has gathered around the collapsible bleachers at the far side of the gym. Everyone except one poor, damned soul.

"How could we miss this?" Tytus smiles back.

"You weren't busy at the burn ward?" Roz smirks, her sharp eyes cutting through the darkness towards me.

By now, everyone knows what happened this morning.

"Are you two done?" I sneer, brushing by them to take my place at Drago's side.

"He's just upset because he's going to have to leave his girl behind," Tytus whispers to Roz.

"He's upset because he failed," Drago interrupts. His deep, gravelly voice slashes through the stale gymnasium air like a whip.

We all go quiet.

"I'm not upset," I try to reassure him. "I'm pissed off."

"Same thing," Tytus jokingly coughs, unable to help himself.

Drago doesn't seem to mind. He's always liked me best when I'm angry. But being furious about a failure is different than being enraged with everything else.

I've never failed this badly before.

And it's all her fault.

Bianca Byrne. Daughter of the don who killed my mother. Princess of an empire that belongs to me.

She was my target. My prey. My chance to prove myself. But the stubborn brat wouldn't budge, no matter how hard I pushed her.

And now, I'm going to have to wait to make her pay for it.

But this isn't over. Not by a long shot.

Someday, I will get my revenge. No matter what it takes. She will be punished. And I will enjoy the *hell* out of it.

Until then...

"... I'm so sorry. It won't happen again..." a shivering voice drifts down from the darkness above our heads. "I promise. Just let me go. Please... just let me go!"

The tense silence surrounding us is shredded by the return of the pathetic groveling. This time, though, the whimpers coming from above aren't directed towards Drago.

They're directed at me.

"Look him in the eyes," Drago orders me.

He doesn't have to ask twice.

With a twisted sneer curling my lips, I look up at the man who was first responsible for getting me into this gilded prison.

Albert Winchester.

He's hanging from the rafters, a noose tied around his throat. The only thing keeping his neck from snapping are the half-folded bleachers—they pin his shins against the wall, crushing his legs, but keeping him alive... for now.

"Hello, Principal Winchester," I nod, venom lacing every word.

"...My dear boy... please," he croaks. "Talk some sense into your father... He's gone mad... I promise, I—"

"Shut the fuck up," I roar, all of my pent-up rage fuming out into the empty gymnasium. Still, even in the heat of it all, my forearm throbs, and my attention drifts back to what happened this morning.

No. Fuck off. That's over. You'll deal with Bianca later. Stay focused.

"I'm not the boy's father," Drago reminds the disgraced former principal, his deep voice eerily calm.

"Of course. Not officially," Winchester coughs. "I'm sorry, I was just—"

"You were just shutting the fuck up," I remind him. "We didn't come here to listen to you apologize, Winchester. We came here to stop you from doing something very fucking stupid."

"I know it was stupid," Principal Winchester sobs, his head dropping for a moment, before the tight rope around his neck reminds him that he can't afford such a luxury. "I was desperate. I should have come to you first."

"Why didn't you?" Drago asks.

Looking down at my boss's bloody hands, I see a familiar coin dancing through the slits of his fingers. An ancient Slavic silver piece. He'll leave it here after this is all done. A calling card to our enemies and our friends; a wicked reminder of what happens to those who dare cross us.

"I was scared," Winchester rasps, his voice shaking almost as intensely as his limbs are. But even that trembling pauses when he sees Drago look over to his second-in-command, the despicable Kuba Krol. It only takes a stern nod from our fearsome leader to seal Winchester's fate. "No, wait!"

But the cruel bastard Krol doesn't take orders from anyone other than Drago.

Pulling down on a wall-mounted lever, the dark serpent closes the folding bleachers another few inches.

The cracking of Winchester's shins is barely audible over his ear-splitting wails.

It makes the hair on the back of my neck stand up. But it's not because of the gruesome scene. I've witnessed worse.

It's because of the noise.

We're not alone here.

There's at least one more person cowering somewhere in these shadows—probably just around the corner of one of the blackened hallways outside, or under the littered desk of her shabby basement office. Someone who couldn't be talked out of coming to do her job here tonight, no matter how obvious I tried to make my subtle hints.

It's someone who doesn't deserve to die. Someone whose death might almost make me feel bad, if I wasn't already growing numb again.

My forearm throbs as I clench my fist and look up at the grown man crying above me.

"That's enough," Drago commands.

Just like that, the bleachers stop moving.

"Please, please, please…" Winchester whines. Cowardly tears trickle down his red cheeks, mixing in with the blood dribbling from his lips.

"*Gabryjel* wasn't here to hear your confession earlier," Drago says, his tone remaining cool and callous. "Why don't you repeat what you told me. Remind us why you're here tonight."

"Because I did something stupid," Winchester sniffles.

"And what was that?"

"I betrayed you."

"How so?"

I already know the story, but Drago's cruelty is on full

display. He loves playing with his food before he tears it to shreds.

"I... I..." The pain is visible in my former principal's mangled face, but everyone in this room—him included—knows that this will only get worse if he doesn't comply. "I tried to sneak back into my old office," he admits. "I was going to decrypt the secret file that got Gabriel into Westwood. The file that holds all of his secrets..."

"And why were you going to do that?" Drago pushes.

"To cut a plea deal with the cops."

Once more, Winchester drops his head, but this time, he lets the rope dig into his raw throat until he's coughing up blood. Anything to look away from Drago's soul crushing glare.

But he doesn't only have to worry about my boss anymore. The reminder of what he's done sets off an eruption inside of me.

"Cut him down," I growl through gritted teeth. "Let me kill him with my own hands."

"You'd have to get through me first!" Krol shouts from his place by the wall.

But I'm done with being teased, especially by someone as despicable as Krol. The sneer I shoot him is filled with pure hatred.

"I'll kill you both if I have to," I bark back.

"Easy now, young prince," Drago growls. "You'll get a chance to redeem yourself... eventually. But it won't be tonight."

"At least let me make the creep suffer a little bit," I press.

"Don't blame him for your failure, *Gabryjel*," Drago warns me. "This is nobody's fault but your own—even if this whole farce was really over months ago. If anything, you should thank Mr. Winchester here for ending it all now, before you could make a further fool of yourself. It was already getting painful."

"Painful?!" I snap. The rage pulls my glare away from Krol, away from Winchester, and towards the man who once saved me from a life of destitution. The man who adopted me from the streets, who forged me for power, who promised me the world—but only if I did his bidding. "Look what that bitch did to me this morning," I sneer, holding up my forearm so that he can see the red and torn skin that cuts through my black tattoos. "She needs to pay. So does her father. So does everyone who's benefitted from their brutal reign."

My fists are clenched so hard that I'm suddenly not so sure if the blood dripping from my palms is mine or someone else's anymore. When I get like this, there's no controlling myself.

My fury is endless.

"You want revenge on a teenage girl for burning your arm with a bit of coffee?" Drago asks, raising a dark knowing brow in my direction.

"I want revenge on her father for murdering my mother—because that's what Ray Byrne did, right? He killed my mother."

"That's right," Drago nods, before turning to look back up at the hanging Principal. Winchester is sobbing. Blood and tears cascade down his crooked body as he fades in and out of consciousness. "And the girl was supposed to be our way into his inner sanctum—it was supposed to be how you got your revenge; how you earned your inheritance; how you fulfilled your destiny, and how I fulfilled mine. But instead of making her your slave, you made her your enemy."

"It was a stupid fucking plan," I blurt out.

"No. You just failed," Drago shrugs, unbothered by my outburst. "I will say, though, I'm almost impressed with the girl." Out of the corner of my eye, I notice him take a quick glance down at my flexed forearm, almost like he can see it throbbing. "Ambushing a man like you... hell, even if she doesn't actually know who you really are, there's no denying your nature, or how you look, or how much older you are than her. For a sixteen-year-old girl—especially a sheltered princess

—to confront the almighty *Gabryjel*... hmm, it could be mistaken as admirable. Still, her courage is telling. If our enemy's weakest link is that fearsome, our revenge won't be so easily taken."

"It wasn't an ambush," I grumble, my raging mind forcibly pulling me back to that maddening moment in the hallway earlier today.

There's just no fucking way Bianca did that on purpose.

Over the past year, I've stalked her closely enough to know her routine. She gets a hot cup of coffee from the cafeteria almost every single morning. She also takes that very same route to her first class nearly every single fucking day.

It's why I was passing by that same way. At that exact same moment. It had become part of my routine too. A part of my day that I came to dread, because it represented my growing failure.

I was supposed to seduce her.

Instead, I made her hate me.

Every day, I got the same loathsome look from those crystal blue eyes. I received the same shock of brilliant auburn hair as she turned her chin up at me. I felt the same stab in my chest as she stormed away.

You aren't good enough for me. And you never will be.

Fuck. Maybe I'd just learned to dissociate from it all. Maybe I'd shut off my mind just to cope.

Maybe that's why I was distracted.

Maybe that's why she was too.

Because the more I allow myself to think about it, the more confident I am that her little ambush was just an accident.

As tough as Bianca Byrne pretends to be, as hard as she tries to act, for as much as I've put her through—both on purpose and... by accident—I've always been able to see the truth hiding behind her hateful blue eyes, because I can see them glaring at me every time I close my own.

She's a sheltered little princess from a big ruthless family.

Her father may be a savage brute, but he's also managed to shield his naïve little daughter from the most twisted truths of our cruel world.

If I get my way, I'll shatter that shield and shove her face right into the depravity of it all. Into the darkness. Into the fires of hell. I'll make sure she sees it all before I put an end to her spoiled reign.

"Please... please..." Principal Winchester's whimpers leak through the stale, tense gymnasium air, and I'm yanked out of my own thoughts for just long enough to turn my anger back towards him.

"Why are you stretching this out?" I ask Drago. "We know what he was doing. Kill the rat and let's move the fuck on with our lives!"

Really, I just want to see Winchester dead. The man has screwed me over more than just once now, even if this is the first time he was truly trying to.

"I want to know if he's told anyone else about you, or our plans," Drago says, his tone encased in ice. "He can't die until we know if there's anyone else we need to go after."

"We should go after his replacement next," I sneer.

Principal Ryerson.

That's the fucker who called Bianca's parents after our little incident this morning. He sent her home and took away my last chance to amend my yearlong fuck up—not that I had really had any chance to.

I was just too fucking angry. Hell, I still am. At Bianca. At myself. At Principal Ryerson. That asshole should have stayed out of it, just like we paid this asshole to.

Shit. But would Winchester really have done anything different from his successor?

Yeah. He might have tried to blackmail Bianca into doing something disgusting, just like he did to those other girls...

Fucking hell.

For some reason, the thought fills me with a whole new wave of rage. But this sudden onslaught of white heat is different to what I was feeling before.

It's more protective.

She's mine to torture, and no one else's.

"Please, Gabriel..." Winchester mumbles. "I've only ever tried to help—"

But I've had enough. All of my fury—in both its new and old form—turns to focus entirely on him.

"Shut up, you disgusting fucking predator," I sneer. "Maybe you should have kept your dick in your pants around your underage students, then you would have never been fired in the first place. You would have never been charged either. And then you would never have had to even think about crossing us to make a plea deal with the cops!"

In response, Winchester coughs up some more blood. But the formerly dignified middle-aged man isn't done speaking yet, even if the smartest thing for him to do now is shut the fuck up.

"My boy... I'm sorry for all that's happened to you... I... I tried to help..." A deep sigh escapes his dripping lips. "Your mother, she was—"

Before he can finish—hell, before I can even interrupt him —a thunderous crack fills up the dark gymnasium.

The sound is so loud and close that it makes me jump back.

"What the fuck..." I mumble, looking up.

My ears are still ringing as I slowly realize what just happened.

Out of the corner of my eye, I see Drago standing up straight, his right arm extended. In his hand is a smoking gun. The barrel is pointed up at Albert Winchester.

A fresh bullet hole has appeared between the former principal's all-white eyes.

Dark blood gushes from the wound. It stains Winchester's pale face, before pouring down onto the bleachers.

"What happened to keeping him alive until he answered all of our questions?" I grumble through the ringing in my ears.

"He'd talked enough," Drago sneers, the first bits of emotion gnawing through his scarred face. "You three stay here and clean up this mess. If you can, make it look like a suicide. Krol, come with me. Everyone else, meet us back at the base."

With those simple commands, Drago shoves his smoking gun under his belt. Then, he drops the blood-stained silver piece from his fingers. The Slavic coin clangs against the hardwood, rolling on its sides as he marches away.

Krol follows closely behind, as does everyone else.

Before long, it's just Tytus, Roz and I. We stand side-by-side in the empty gymnasium, staring up at the dead body.

No one moves until the coin stops spinning.

"How the fuck are we going to get that fucker down?" Tytus finally complains, breaking the stunned silence.

"The same way they got him up there," Roz shrugs.

"And how are we going to make a man with rope burns around his throat, and a bullet hole in his forehead look like someone who committed suicide?"

At that question, the two look at the only one of us who has any personal knowledge of the dead man.

Me.

"We just have to give the authorities an excuse," I grumble, still reeling from what just happened.

Why the hell did Drago shoot him?

Winchester was about to say something about my mom... but what?

"An excuse for what?"

"An excuse to rule this a suicide," I sigh, trying to focus. "They'll have to shut down the school... Parents will demand an explanation. No one on the board will want to admit that this kind of thing could happen here. Same goes for the cops and the security firm who's men we massacred outside. We only need to do enough to let them write this all off as a violent murder-suicide—the dying breaths of a disgraced member of their community—no matter how contradictory the actual evidence is. The people who live in this sheltered area would never dare face a problem like this head on, not if they don't have to."

That seems to work for both Tytus and Roz.

Without another word, they nod, then immediately get to work.

But I'm frozen in place, glued to the floor by a whirlwind of uncertainty.

What the hell is going on?

I'm in danger of losing myself to the darkness, when something snaps me out of it.

My forearm.

The burn mark pulls me back down to earth.

Fucking hell.

That girl.

"It was a stupid plan, anyways," I hear Tytus suddenly shout from the far wall. Pulling on the lever, he extends the bleachers out so that Roz and I can recover Winchester's mangled corpse.

"Yeah," Roz shrugs, clearly trying to comfort me. "Drago just doesn't understand these spoiled rich girls. He thought they'd be like the women we all know and love—you know, the street walkers who crawl over themselves just to get in your line of sight."

"There's only one girl in my line of sight," I sneer. "And she's lucky I haven't already pulled the fucking trigger on her."

Neither Roz or Tytus seem to hear me.

"Hey, those street walkers crawl over themselves to get to me too, right?!" Tytus shouts up at Roz.

"Yes, yes. You're very handsome," she assures him, and I can practically hear her eyes rolling. "Isn't he, Gabriel?"

I don't answer.

But It's not because I'm angry at either of my only two friends. Instead, I quickly turn my back on them because I hear something quietly stir by the gymnasium doors—they click shut before I can see who opened them.

My hackles immediately rise, and I drop everything to race out into the dark hallway, switchblade drawn.

"Where are you going?" Tytus shouts after me.

He doesn't get a response.

"I didn't see any faces, I swear..."

The tiny, terrified voice is the first thing I hear when I push through the creaky gym doors. It comes from a shadow-filled corner to my right.

But I don't look over.

I recognize that voice.

Rosa.

The school janitor.

Out of the corner of my eye, I can just make out her silhouette. She's cowering on the floor, head tucked beneath her legs, shaking like a leaf.

Fuck.

Why hasn't she tried to escape already? I purposely led Tytus away from her office so she wouldn't be caught up in this shit.

"Leave," I command, disguising my voice with as much disdain as I can possibly muster. Then, before she can obey me, I turn and push my way back into the gym.

But my nerves are frayed.

Maybe I really am a failure. All of a sudden, I can't even bring myself to kill a measly janitor. Innocent or not, she's a witness. She should be dealt with.

No, I think, shaking my head. *I can't do that.*

Rosa doesn't deserve to die. She's always been kind to me. I've seen pictures of her kids. I've heard about how her husband wasted away into nothing earlier this year, before tragically dying of cancer. It's why she's working double shifts, night and day. She needs to make up for the lost income, and pay the hospital bills.

I've always wanted to help. But I couldn't risk the possible attention.

That's not a problem anymore. I'll make sure to fill her desk up with cash before I disappear forever. Maybe then, she'll be smart enough to leave and never come back.

Just like I should.

"Is everything alright?"

Tytus is immediately there to greet me when I re-enter the gymnasium.

"Yeah," I mumble, pushing forward, hoping that he'll follow me back into the gym instead of stepping outside for a quick inspection of his own.

"Don't worry, brother. You'll get your chance," Tytus sighs. "Ray Byrne will pay for what he did. And then you'll be able to do whatever you want with his sweet little daughter."

I can feel his depraved smirk as he brushes by my shoulder, returning to the problem of Winchester's corpse.

"You two love birds done necking in the halls?" Roz shouts down at us. She's still standing at the top of the bleachers, knife it hand, ready to get this over with.

But I know this isn't over with.

And it won't be for a very long fucking time.

You'll get your chance.

Whether Tytus is right or wrong, it doesn't matter. One thing is certain.

I'm not going to be able to get Bianca Byrne out of my fucking mind anytime soon.

That long auburn hair. Those crystal blue eyes. The smooth

olive skin dotted with pale freckles. The hatred. From the moment I first saw the spoiled princess, she's haunted me like a fucking ghost, taunting me every time I close my eyes, every time I look into the darkness. Every time I think about my past. And my future.

Her father made me an orphan.

She made me a failure.

They both need to pay.

Still, the thought of ever having to deal with that tiny fucking firecracker again makes my hands ball into fists. It makes my heart clench into stone. And it makes my forearm throb so hard my entire body aches with rage.

Fucking hell.

I hate how tightly my future is tied to her and her family.

My freedom. My inheritance. My self-worth. It's all trapped beneath the overbearing weight of the Byrne mafia empire.

There's no moving on. Not until I've won. Not until I've risen up and crushed her beneath my heel. Until I've destroyed her so entirely that she vanishes from my mind forever.

That day will come.

It has to.

And when it does, I'll be ready.

Will she?

1

BIANCA

Present day...

"They're ready for you."

Uncle Maksim's deep voice seeps through the thick protective wood of my bedroom door. His usually calm tone is laced with urgency.

"Fuck," I mutter under my breath. "You don't want to go in my place?"

Looking over my shoulder, I raise my brow at Rian. The giant lion of a man is leaning against the wall by the door, intense blue eyes glaring down at his phone screen.

"Oh, I'll be coming with you," he smirks. Shaking away all of his troubles back home, he slips his phone into his pocket and turns to open my bedroom door. "Isn't that right, Uncle Maks?"

"Your presence has indeed been requested," Uncle Maksim nods. But his demeanour remains serious. Deadly serious. "You're to advise your cousin on the matter at hand."

Rian might be young enough to think all of this violence is

good fun, but Uncle Maksim knows better. You can see it in his stony face.

None of this is meant to be enjoyed.

Not that there's any chance I'm about to enjoy a second of it. I may be even younger than my mighty cousin, but I know just enough to understand how unprepared I truly am for all of this —even if I wish I wasn't.

"I don't need to be advised," I stubbornly huff. Lifting myself off my bed, I suck in a deep breath and prepare myself for the shame to come.

"That shiny new scar over your eyebrow begs to differ," Rian points out.

"Getting into one measly bar fight doesn't suddenly make me useless," I respond. "How many fights have you been in? A hundred? A thousand?"

"Enough to handle you," he chuckles, turning his broad back to me.

There really isn't anything I can do but reluctantly follow him into the hallway.

"It's like being in high school all over again," I mumble, quickening my pace to keep up with my two brutal chaperones.

"How many bar fights did you get into in high school?" Rian asks, never one to let anything I say go unchallenged.

"More than you," I lie, desperate to keep up with my older cousin. "But that's not what I meant."

"Than what did you mean?"

"It's this whole process," I sigh. "The over-protective measures. The lockdown. The confinement. I'm an adult now. I'm supposed to be able to take care of myself. But suddenly, it's like I'm sixteen again."

"Your dad gave you way more freedom than this when you were sixteen," Rian reminds me. "Hell, I remember visiting from out east and spending an entire night on Venice beach with you and Mel."

"He didn't always give me that much freedom," I recall, a knot forming in my gut. "Didn't I tell you about that time my high school closed down for like a month because they found the former principal hanging from the gymnasium rafters?"

"You might have mentioned it," Rian shrugs, unbothered by the gruesome image. He's witnessed far worse.

"Well, Dad did some digging and found out that he probably didn't commit suicide," I grumble. "But a murder on school property meant it wasn't safe for his precious little princess anymore. It didn't matter that I'd overheard descriptions of far worse shit just around this house; that we're supposed to be this savage mob family, rulers of a brutal mafia empire. My fearsome father didn't care. I was pulled out of school for the rest of the semester and put on house arrest for like two months."

"Sounds like something you would have enjoyed," Rian says. "Didn't you hate school?"

He's not wrong.

A chill stakes down my spine at the mere mention of my old school.

So many bad memories...

... And they all seem to stem from the appearance of one asshole.

"No. I enjoyed going out with friends," I spit, suddenly angry at myself for daring to remember that bully—especially at a time like this. "I enjoyed being free. I enjoyed doing stupid shit like spending an entire night on a dirty, dangerous beach with my two rough and tumble east coast cousins."

"That was fun, wasn't it?"

"It was, until Uncle Aiden found out about it."

"My father would have never found out if you didn't let it slip at lunch the next day," Rian returns.

"Will you never let that go?"

"Maybe for Christmas one year."

Even through all of the overwhelming pressure that's been weighing me down lately, I can't help the little grin that lifts the corners of my lips.

"How generous."

"Call me Rian Claus."

"No, thank you."

"Suit yourself," Rian shrugs, purposely slowing down just enough that I absent-mindedly run into his mountainous back.

"Keep moving, bozo," I say, giving him a push forward.

"Or what, you're going to come after me with a broken bottle?"

"Well, now that I've gotten a little practice, maybe I'll actually be able to draw some blood this time."

"Wait, you didn't even cut that asshole from the bar?"

Ahead, Uncle Maks silently plods along. I'm sure he's listening—men like him always do. But I'm also certain he's already been briefed on the whole story.

It's why we're heading downstairs, after all.

"I got one punch in before the bastard's goons pulled me away. The broken bottle didn't come into play until after it collided with my forehead."

Together, we turn a corner. Then, suddenly, the air shifts. Just like that, the playful lightness floating around my cousin's broad shoulders turns heavy. His shadow darkens. His fingers clench into fists.

"If I was there, it would have been a massacre," he growls.

"Then, it's probably better that you weren't," I note, my stomach twisting as I remember where we're headed... and why. "Yesterday, I overheard some info on the incident. One of those frat boys was a senator's son. You killing him would have opened up a world of chaos."

"Is that why Uncle Ray hasn't done anything about it yet?"

"Dad's doing plenty," I warn him. Rian might be a crown

prince, the oldest son of the underworld king who rules all underworld kings, Aiden Kilpatrick, mafia royalty of the highest order, but right now, he's on the west coast. That's Byrne terrain. Here, Dad is boss. And there's no room for dissention. Not even from family. "He's doing *this*." I say, nodding forward.

Rian knows all about the horrors currently playing out in the dark basement below our feet. He knows what we're about to witness.

He knows Dad would never let a threat go unanswered.

But that doesn't mean the two men always see eye-to-eye.

Reaching a familiar winding staircase, we begin our descent into hell.

The cellar.

I'm usually not allowed down there. But this is a special occasion—even if we'd all rather it wasn't.

"I still wish I'd been there to fight beside you," Rian huffs, but the thick darkness that had just engulfed him is already evaporating.

He's too excited to stay angry.

"You could have been," I point out. "But only if you'd had the foresight to cause all of that trouble back home a week earlier. Then you'd have been forced to flee to the west coast just in time to catch an invitation to that stupid bar."

"As if I'd be caught dead in a college bar."

When we reach the bottom of the staircase, I look to my left, towards one of the large Palladian windows that line the main floor. It's too dark to see outside, but the black glass casts a perfect reflection.

The sight causes a soft sigh to flutter from my lips.

My new scar is even more pronounced than I feared. Red and loud, it slashes through my eyebrow like a lightning bolt.

"Shit."

"It suits you," Rian says.

His reflection is just as clear as my own, and I can see those intense blue eyes focus in on my half-healed wound.

"What suits me?" I ask, playing dumb.

"The scar. It's about time you got one, I guess. Welcome to the mafia."

"I've always been a part of the mafia," I rebuff. "But that doesn't mean I like being disfigured."

"It makes you look like the villain you've always wanted to be." Placing one of his giant hands on my shoulder, Rian leads me away from the window and back onto our path. "Maybe we'll finally get you a tattoo next."

"A tattoo would be fun," I admit, trying my hardest not to lift a hand up to my throbbing scar. "But I never wanted to be a villain."

"You've always wanted to be like us, Bianca," Rian says. "You never hid it. We're villains. It's just how it is. Someday, you'll learn to love it."

"I already do," I quickly correct him. "That's why being on lockdown is so frustrating. I want to be out there, fighting with you. Going to that creep-filled bar was a huge mistake, but I don't regret what I did. That douchebag was slipping pills into people's drinks. I couldn't just let that happen. It's not how I was raised. I mean, even villains have codes... right?"

"Sure, but you're not on lockdown because of the bar fight," Rian is eager to remind me. "You're on lockdown because of a far more serious matter, or have you forgotten about the kidnappings?"

"*Attempted* kidnappings..." I stubbornly try to correct him.

"No. Not all of them failed."

That's Uncle Maksim's deep voice. Just up ahead, he's stopped in front of the heavy metal door that leads down into the forbidden cellar.

Into hell.

"What?"

Suddenly, Rian has transformed again. But this time, it's not just rage lifting his hackles.

It's fear.

"Don't worry, nephew. They didn't take any of our people," Maksim quickly assures him.

That drops Rian's tensed shoulders a bit, but it doesn't unclench his fists.

"Then who?"

"Yesterday, Congressmen Olsen's daughter was successfully taken." With a deep breath, Maksim pulls open the heavy cellar door, and a cold, metallic gust rushes up from the darkness below. "... We found her body this morning."

The reality check is so harsh that neither Rian or I know how to react.

"Fuck." Rian grumbles.

"But... But Congressman Olsen... he's a politician. What does he have to do with us?" I try to reason. "Are you sure its connected?"

Maksim only nods. "He's on our payroll. And now, he's going to be on our asses to find the killers."

"They still haven't found out who was behind the attempts back east," Rian whispers, his hand reaching into his pocket. "I was just talking to—"

"Is that the real reason I'm still on lockdown?" I interrupt, unable to keep the words from slipping out. It's already been a week. Usually, shit gets figured out much faster around here.

"You were put on lockdown because of the attempted kidnappings in New York," Uncle Maksim sighs. "Clearly, whoever is behind this was trying to start with easier targets. The Italian families may work for us, but they don't have as many resources as we do. Some bastards must have taken them for easy practice."

"And they still failed," Rian barks.

"But only barely," Maksim replies, steely eyed. "Two

Italian princesses were nearly stolen in a matter of hours. And it was only by pure luck that the second one managed to escape."

"You think the kidnappers got frustrated and decided to come out west and try an even easier target?"

"The coincidence is too glaring to ignore."

"Fucking hell," Rian growls. "Let me loose, Uncle. I'll burn this entire fucking coast to the ground and bring you the charred remains of those responsible."

"That's exactly why we can't let you loose," Uncle Maksim replies "We don't want a repeat of what happened back east; of what you did in Manhattan."

"That was an accident."

"I'm sure it was, but we can't afford accidents right now, nephew. We have the blood of a sitting congressmen's daughter on our hands. Even if we didn't kill her, he'll find a way to pin it on us if we don't find the real culprits."

"So, let me help."

"No. Your duty is much more precious."

Slowly, Uncle Maksim's heavy eyes fall on me. The implication is clear, and Rian instantly understands. As do I.

"I'll whip the bastards downstairs into shape," my cousin nods, his back straightening as he accepts his responsibility.

Me.

"They've already been whipped into shape," Uncle Maksim says. Turning his back on us, he slips through the open cellar door. "Your job will be to keep them in line."

"Understood."

Shutting our mouths, we follow Uncle Maksim down into the darkness. The further we descend, the more suffocating it all becomes.

This is worse than I thought.

Maybe I do need protection, after all...

By the time I finally see light up ahead, I realize that I've been holding my breath. My first exhale billows like smoke from my lips. A shiver crawls over my skin.

It's freezing down here.

"Wait here," Uncle Maksim orders, when we reach the bottom of the stairs. "I'll go ahead to make sure everything is... proper."

His footsteps echo through the frigid hall as he disappears ahead. A second later, the sound of another heavy door being opened fills the basement. In the distance, I hear an exchange of mumbles, then more footsteps. Soon, though, everything goes quiet.

"Do you smell that?" Rian asks. Turning his nose up, he sniffs the air.

I smell it too. Thin metallic strands of warmth that slither through the cold.

"Is that..."

"Blood." He confirms. "The ritual is complete. The process has ended. Your bodyguards have been chosen. Now, it's up to me to make sure none of the survivors are anywhere near as incompetent as your last brood."

"They weren't incompetent," I hear myself whisper. "They were just busy flirting with some college girls."

"That's incompetence of the highest fucking degree," Rian snaps, anger rising over him once again. "They were on the job. They should have only been worrying about you. But they failed at that. Now, they won't have to worry about anything ever again."

A bolt of dread lashes through me at Rian's jarring words—that strong sting is closely followed by a wave of guilt. It's the same red-hot guilt that I've been trying to supress ever since that night at the campus bar.

My bodyguards.

I wasn't even thinking about them when I slipped out from under their protective circle. All I cared about was confronting those disgusting frat boys who were clearly slipping pills into people's drinks.

If I was thinking straight, I would have ordered them to act for me. But I'd been drinking. And I thought I could handle myself.

I was wrong. And my recklessness sealed the fate of everyone who was tasked with protecting me.

Is that their blood we smell?

"What happens if you don't think any of these new bodyguards are good enough?" I hear myself ask.

"Then I'll do what I have to do," Rian states, his voice gravelly with a growing bloodlust. "I'll fucking show them who's in charge here."

For all of the happy memories I share with my cousin, there's never been any hiding how brutal he can be.

Still, being down here with him, in the cold, unforgiving darkness of this forbidden cellar, while he's preparing to unleash his beastly side, makes me realize just how different we really are.

I've never felt so helpless.

Hell, I'm afraid. Of the darkness. Of the blood. Of this side of Rian. Of this side of my family.

To some extent, everyone I know or care about is a monster.

So, why do I feel so much guilt? So much weakness?

Why can't I flip a switch and become a beast?

What's wrong with me?

"Rian, I—"

I'm not even sure what I'm about to say, but before I can finish, the sound of footsteps reappears in the distance, echoing through the cold hallway like a hammer.

"Everything is set up," Uncle Maksim's voice rumbles through the darkness ahead. An instant later, his broad silhouette slips back into the dim light. "This way," he says, beckoning us forward.

We do as we're told.

"How do they look?" Rian asks, already taking the lead.

"Rough. But that's to be expected, especially after what they've just been put through," Uncle Maks replies, before looking back over his shoulder at me. "I apologize for the mess in advance, Bianca."

"I'm sure I've seen worse."

"I can't imagine you have."

My gut clenches at his response.

Sure, I've been sheltered from the worst of my family's dealings. But I've still seen some shit.

What could be worse than the carnage I've already witnessed?

Trying to take a deep breath, I gulp in a mouthful of stale metallic air. It's nauseating, and the further we walk into the underground hallway, the stronger it gets.

Shit. Maybe Uncle Maksim is right. Maybe this is different.

Something about It definitely feels different.

What's changed?

Did I just get too reckless at the bar? Are these recent kidnappings just that serious?

It's hard to tell. All I know for sure is that my hands are shaking by the time we pass a half-open door. The stench of blood that seeps from the room is almost powerful enough to send me to my knees.

I don't want to look. But the scar above my eye suddenly flares up, and my head twitches to the side, pulling my gaze towards the slit.

Inside, I see what nightmares are made of.

Corpses.

Everywhere.

Piled up onto one another. Hacked to shreds. Spilled of their organs. Brain matter torn out and splattered over the crimson concrete.

For one dreadful moment, I meet a pair of pale dead eyes. They look oddly familiar, but my mind won't let me make the connection.

Somewhere behind the door, I hear weeping. It's faint, but loud enough to lodge itself deep into my mind.

"Don't look at what's in there," Rian says, his voice low and guttural. The warmth of his hand snaps me out of my nightmare. "That door should have been closed."

"No," I hear Uncle Maksim sigh. "Her father insisted it stayed at least partially open."

"Why?" Rian asks, shocked.

"A lesson," Uncle Maksim says, before stopping in front of a fully closed door up ahead. "Your father wants you to know how dangerous this world truly is. How brutal. He needed you to see the consequences of your decisions, if even just a sliver of it. There's no hiding you from it anymore, Bianca"

"That's cruel," Rian growls.

"That's life," Uncle Maksim replies. Pursing his lips, he looks me square in the eyes and nods. "Are you ready?"

It feels like I'm being choked. Like there are a pair of bloody hands wrapped around my throat. But after a moment of dread-filled shock, I force myself to fight through it.

It's not like a have a choice. This is my life.

This is my world. No matter how dark and disturbing it is. I need to live with it. One day, I might even need to rule it.

"Yes. I'm ready."

Isn't this what I always wanted?

"Very well. It's time to meet your new bodyguards."

The heavy metal door creaks open against Uncle Maksim's hand. He steps in first. Then Rian.

An electric heat jumps over their big bodies, rushing past them to prick at my skin. With a final deep breath, I follow my cousin inside.

The stench of blood isn't as strong here as it was in the other room, but it still burns the hairs in my nostrils.

"I'm sorry you had to see the mess we made in the other room, dear."

Dad's commanding voice cuts through the suffocating air.

Wrapping my fingers around my wrist, I try to keep my limbs from shaking too much.

Be strong, Bianca. Show these men that you belong.

Stepping aside, Uncle Maksim and Rian open a path for Dad to greet me.

"I'll be alright," I say, looking up at his deep brown eyes. For a split second, they shimmer with concern. But that concern is quickly glazed over by a familiar, savage strength.

He is always strong for me. It's my turn to be strong for him.

"I know," Dad nods.

Behind him, I can feel the heat of the men who've been brought here to protect me. I can't see them, though. Not yet. Dad's big body blocks off my view—that is, until he too steps aside, revealing the line of bloody, shirtless beasts standing before us.

The gruesome sights sends another shock of fear through me. But I bite down on my tongue and try to appear fearless.

"You've all done well to survive this ordeal," Dad says, addressing the troops.

While he talks, I force myself to stare down the line of beaten bodies.

These blood-stained men have gone through hell for the privilege of protecting my fragile little life. The least I can do is acknowledge their existence.

I promise myself to look every one of them in the eyes. No matter how hard that is. Because, if I've learned anything from that stupid bar fight, it's that their lives are just as much in my hands as mine is in theirs.

"But this is only the beginning," Dad continues. "From now on, you only have one goal in life. To protect my daughter. Bianca Byrne. A princess of the Kilpatrick empire. Heiress of my west coast kingdom. Future of the underworld. She is all that matters."

Gritting my teeth, I begin my self-appointed task.

These men have already fought for you. Killed for you. Look them in the eyes, Bianca.

But that's easier said than done. And not just because of my own fears. There are physical barriers too.

Eyelids have been swollen shut. Skin has been dyed dark shades of cracked crimson. Bones have clearly been broken.

Still, every last man in the line holds their chin up high. Being sworn into my family is a rare honor. I can't imagine any of them are taking this moment for granted—even if the truth is this only means they will now have to protect me.

A sheltered princess who got her last bodyguards killed.

"My nephew, the great Rian Kilpatrick, will be your leader," Dad announces. "Impress him and your opportunities will be endless. The young man isn't just a seasoned soldier in his own right. He's also first in line for his father's throne. One day, all eyes in the underworld will look up to him for leadership. You are the lucky few who get to follow him first."

Not one of the bloody men dare move an inch as my father addresses them. No one sways. No one coughs. No matter how badly injured any of them are, they only stare in our direction and listen.

In return, I do as any royal should—I silently greet them back with the same stoicism.

Or, at least, I try.

One by one, I move down the line. Black eyes. Brown eyes. Blue eyes. I meet them all. Puffing out my chest with fake courage.

But even I can feel my brave face drop when my gaze lands

on the intense pair of eyes glaring at me from the middle of the lineup.

No.

Just like that, all of the fake courage in me disintegrates.

In between all of the black and brown and blue, shine a devilish pair of hazel-green eyes. They slash through my soul and dig into my gut like a jagged blade.

I've seen those eyes before.

Without warning, my heart starts to twitch wildly behind my chest. My limbs begin to shake. Black spots pierce my vision.

The otherworldly hazel, sprinkled with specks of emerald green flakes, framed by endlessly dark black rims.

They practically glow—even through his blood-drenched black hair; through the purple bruises on his swollen cheeks; through the crimson cuts that litter his bearded face; I can see those eyes.

I *know* those eyes.

How could I ever forget them?

After all of these years, they still find a way to haunt me.

Gabriel Corso.

My bully. My tormenter. The bane of my teenage years.

He's dead center in a lineup of men who have been hand-picked to protect me from the darkest threats this depraved world has to offer.

But he is the darkness and the depravity of this world. Fully formed in a sinfully wicked body of hard muscle, deep scars, and heavily tattooed flesh.

He is exactly what I need to be protected *from*, not what I need to be protected *by*.

So, what the hell is he doing here?

2

GABRIEL

This is the moment of truth.

All that I've worked for. All that I've sacrificed. All that I've suffered. It was so that I could end up here, in the lion's den, standing before these despicable monsters.

In front of her.

Bianca Byrne.

The one who got away.

Fucking hell.

It takes a conscious effort to keep my hackles from rising. My fists from clenching. My anger from taking over.

She's looking right at me. Those haunting crystal blue eyes. Shit. I've never forgotten those stupid eyes. They shimmer with such hate... and so much fear.

Silly girl. You're the one in control here... for now. Take advantage of it before I rip that power away from you forever.

"Is that understood?"

Ray Byrne finishes his speech with one last boom.

"Yes, sir!" I shout in unison with everyone else.

Keeping my gaze focused straight ahead, I try to subtly

study the girl who's fate will soon rest in my hands. But I don't dare make a single movement.

I can't afford to give away my hate.

Still, I feel the slightest twitch take over my brow when I spot the bright red scar cutting through her left eyebrow.

That's new.

... And concerning.

"Good. Maksim, you take them from here. Rian, you can stay if you want to. Bianca, come with me."

Thankfully, Ray Byrne doesn't look at his daughter as he turns away. If he did, he might see the twisted look of fear and confusion contorting her deceptively pretty face. He might also see what the cause of that fear and confusion is.

She sees me. She fears me.

But she won't tell anyone.

And I know why.

She's too stubborn.

I'm *her* problem. And she's the kind of girl who desperately wants to be independent.

The plan is to take full advantage of that naïve stubbornness. It's the only reason I thought this stupid scheme might work in the first place.

But that wound...

I've been in enough fights to know a battle scar when I see one.

The Bianca I know—the one I've obsessed over, studied, stalked—she wouldn't have a scar like that. She wouldn't be *allowed* to have a scar like that.

Shit. Maybe I've underestimated her.

"Coming," Bianca's soft little voice drifts through the harsh stale air as she forcefully shakes the dread from her pretty little face and turns to follow her father out into the black hallway.

And then just like that, she's gone.

But even if I've survived the moment, I'm suddenly not so confident in my plan anymore.

The scar.

It changes everything.

It changes *her*.

Biting down hard on my tongue, I keep a sneer from warping my lips. For the time being, I need to force Bianca from my mind.

Because that scar over her eye isn't the only problem that's appeared in this suffocating cellar.

A notorious mafia prince has also entered the equation.

Rian Kilpatrick.

Fuck. That bastard is going to be my boss. He'll be watching my every move.

How the hell am I supposed to get close to Bianca with that Irish lion watching over me?

"We'll get you boys cleaned up in a moment," the infamous Maksim Smolov says. "First, though, I will assign your shifts."

With a simple nod, the old Russian is handed a tablet by one of his assistants. But for all of the savage wisdom and brutal experience he notoriously possesses, he appears to struggle with the new technology.

"Fucking hell," he grumbles, sliding his fingers across the screen as the pale glow lights up his sunken cheeks.

"Here, let me help, Uncle," Rian quickly steps in, sensing his elder's frustration.

"Very well."

It doesn't take long for Rian to figure out what the problem is. With a few quick swipes, the young lion seems to break into the device and find what he needs. But instead of handing the tablet back to his uncle, he only looks over at the old Russian to ask for permission to continue on his own.

"May I have the pleasure?"

Maksim hardly hesitates. "They are your crew now," he nods.

Studying the screen for a second longer, the lion of a man steps forward. "Shifts will be allotted in three-day segments," he starts. "You will work for three days straight, then you will get three days off. But you will always be on call. Those of you who are not assigned to the direct protection of Bianca on a given day will still be on the Byrne compound—specifically, you will stay in the guest house we have set up for you. The accommodations are comfortable, but I warn you: do not get comfortable. A single fuckup by any one of you will result in the termination of you all."

The harsh reminder is well served, and I feel a few of the men stiffen up at the underlying threat in Rian's words.

We all know what happened to the last crew.

"We have vetted each and every one of you a thousand times over. We know your pasts. We control your future. We have witnessed your savage loyalty. We have studied your every move. The process has been long and hard, I know—even if I haven't been here for all of it. But let me assure you, the rewards for your success are great. My uncle was right. I will be king someday. And I never forget a face, or a loyal soldier. Do you hear me?"

The self-important ass.

Still, I join the shout of "Yes, sir!" that fills up the cellar in response.

"Good," Rian nods. "Kelleher, Chiesa, Veratti, Idah, Giles and Egen. You will have the first shift. Come with me. The rest of you, follow Maksim to the guest house. Get cleaned up. And get ready."

With that, the lion turns his back on us and steps out into the hallway. The six men he named quickly follow after him.

I watch them go, unsure of how to feel about the fact that I wasn't put on the first shift.

Didn't they see how I ripped those men to shreds in the other room? The adrenaline still pulses through my veins, disguising the pain that ravages every inch of my steaming body.

Fucking hell. I already want to fight again.

But that's not going to happen. Not today. Hell, probably not until I finally put my vicious plan into action.

And even then, it will hardly be a fight.

No. That will be a massacre.

"With me," Maksim orders, after Rian and his new unit's footsteps have faded down the black hallway.

Shirtless and bloody, I jump to the front of the line and follow the old Russian general into the darkness.

The men I will eventually betray all follow in my scarlet footsteps.

I feel no guilt about what I will do.

All that matters is what I deserve.

Everything.

Hot rain washes over my bruised face as I sprint away from the compound.

No matter how sure I am that I'm not being followed, I still look over my shoulder, ever-vigilant.

Anyone could be hiding in these shadows.

The moon was out when I first left the Byrne's guest house. But it's long since been hidden by black rainclouds. Above, there is only darkness.

This is where I belong.

Lifting my hand to my brow, I wipe away the water and the blood cascading down my forehead. The shower I took earlier was only barely long enough to wash away the guts and the brain matter, and nothing else.

Sure, I could have cleaned myself more thoroughly. But there was no time to waste.

I had to prepare for my escape.

My bunkmates were all asleep when I finally managed to sneak out of the bathroom window. Even the toughest among them was exhausted from a long and brutal day. But I never sleep. And I've had far more brutal days.

Not that today was a walk in the park.

There were moments when I actually doubted myself. When I doubted this stupid plan. When I thought I might actually die like some of the others. But I persevered. I always do.

It's why I *will* taste victory. No matter how outnumbered I am.

Slipping through the shadows of the palm trees that surround the compound's tall concrete walls, I try not to get lost in what's already happened.

My focus needs to remain on the task at hand. On the future.

Still, something tugs at me from the past.

Fucking hell.

Every step I take away from the Byrne mansion is accompanied by a flash. A vision that rattles my swollen skull and punches me square in the chest.

Bianca.

After all these years, I finally saw her up close again, and it's fucking with my mind.

Somehow, she's gotten even more dangerously stunning since high school. And that scar above her left eye...

Shit.

My heart twitches violently as I trudge through the muddy dirt path that winds secretly through the black forest.

The palm trees are quickly disappearing at my back. The harshness of the real world is slowly remerging all around me.

Overgrown branches scrape at my swollen cheeks, dirty rain pours over my eyes.

But still, I can see her face. That twisted look of shock. That newfound hint of maturity on her once completely virgin appearance.

The scar.

That fucking scar.

Why am I so fixated on that stupid scar?

Is it because it changes everything? Because it might just force me to re-evaluate what I think I know about Bianca Byrne?

Fucking hell. She's supposed to be fake tough. A bratty princess who would crumple at the first sign of real adversity.

But the sheltered daughters of mafia royalty don't get scars like that. And now that I think about it, they aren't brought down to look over their new bodyguards after we've just massacred their old ones in hand-to-hand combat, either.

What the hell has she become?

My chest twists again as I break free from the thick vegetation and burst onto the wet sand of a lonely beach.

In the distance, deep over the black ocean, three quick bolts of lightning slash through the darkness. For a split second, the jagged white strips illuminate two dark silhouettes.

They're waiting for me by the ragged shore.

Before I take another step forward, I fill my lungs with the wet air and fight away the disturbing tightness in my chest.

But Bianca's scar won't leave my mind, and neither will the crystal blue eyes that glare out from beneath it.

It's infuriating.

Grab hold of yourself, Gabriel! The scar doesn't matter. She hasn't changed enough to change anything. And neither have you!

Bullshit! A demon shouts from somewhere in the darkness beneath my skull. *You're just jealous someone else got to mark her before you!*

As if! Another demon screeches in response. *It's not that. You're furious because someone touched your prize. Your girl.*

Before I can silence the voices myself, a deafening crack of thunder rips down from above.

Just like that, all is quiet. At least, internally it is. Outside, the wind howls and rugged waves crash against the ragged beach ahead.

Sneering through the lashing rain, I latch onto the forced silence and claw my way through the storm, towards the black silhouettes waiting for me by the raging shoreline.

"You're late."

Drago's voice is just as cutting as ever. Somehow, it seems completely unaffected by the harsh weather.

I hear him loud and clear.

"I had to wait until everyone was asleep," I grumble.

"You sure you didn't just get some shut eye for yourself?" Krol spits.

"How about I shut your eyes for fucking good?" I snap at him. I'm not in the mood for this asshole's attitude. Not after what I just went through.

"Try me, b*oy*," Krol challenges. Before he can step forward, though, Drago raises his arm, putting a quick end to our petty bickering.

"I'm sure you've had a long day," Drago says. "But we are not the people to take out your frustrations on."

"You should have brought Tytus with you instead of this animal," I sneer.

It's been months since I last saw my best friend. Same with Roz. If Drago had really wanted to reward me for all that I've done so far, he would have dragged them out here instead of Krol.

But that's not his style.

"Tytus is busy," Drago says. "As is Rozalia."

"And you aren't?" I snip at Krol.

"I'm never too busy to see you, *boy*."

"Enough!" Drago booms, just as another crack of thunder blankets the black sky.

"Rian Kilpatrick has been made head of my brigade," I growl, when the roar has settled. "He'll be watching over me whenever I'm near Bianca."

Behind him, a shock of lightning cracks through the black horizon. It somehow drapes Drago in even more darkness.

But I don't need to see his weathered face to picture it. This is new information to him. And he takes a moment to process it.

"You will have to win his trust," he finally says.

"I have to win everyone's trust."

"Yes. But Rian Kilpatrick is different." Through the darkness, Drago's black eyes slowly come into focus. They are darting back and forth. He's thinking. Planning. "... We might have to take him too."

"Take Rian Kilpatrick?" Krol's disbelief is loud and wild.

Mine is much quieter and controlled. But I'm just as shocked.

It's rare that we agree on anything.

"How do you capture a lion?" I ask, trying to hide the skepticism from my voice.

"By becoming part of his pride."

"I can't imagine I'll ever get that close to someone who's supposed to be my boss," I tell my real boss, subtly reminding him of what he's told me countless times before.

My adoptive father has never been one to get too close to anyone. Not even me.

"You must try," Drago insists. "If we're smart we could turn his presence into a positive. The young man has a special skillset that I could make good use of."

"And what skillset is that?"

"Your job isn't to question me, *Gabryjel*."

"My job is to find answers."

For a second, Drago pauses, and it almost looks like he might let something slip.

But then those black eyes glaze over, and I know I'm not going to hear anything I haven't already heard before.

"I will tell you later."

"No," I shake my head, fed up. "Tell me now. I'm not going to be able to sneak out again. Not anytime soon. Hell, the only reason I could tonight was because I'm already covered in enough cuts and wounds and bruises to disguise my perilous little journey. From now on, they'll be keeping track of every blemish. They'll be no hiding anything from them."

Another crack of thunder shakes the air as Drago considers my request.

Before long, though, he comes to his conclusion.

"You'll just have to trust me, son," he says, shaking his head as he reaches a hand out towards me.

That hand lands on my shoulder. It's cold and final.

"Drago, I—"

"He said no, *boy*!" Krol barks.

My swollen knuckles clench, but somehow, I manage to keep myself from lashing out. I've killed enough men today.

Instead, I look into my adoptive father's eyes, and try to pry the truth out of him.

But his face is made of chipped stone, and his eyes are too black to decipher.

Fuck.

"Here, take this," he says, imploring me to ignore his rabid dog Krol.

Dropping his frigid hand from my shoulder, he reaches into his pocket and pulls out a tiny Ziploc bag. Through the rain and the darkness, it looks empty. But I immediately understand what's inside.

"The tracker," I mumble, taking the bag.

"Trackers. Plural. Slip them under your fingernails. When you get close enough to the princess, flick one her way. It will melt into her skin. Then, we'll be able to follow you both."

"They have scanning devices around every door," I'm quick to remind him.

"Rozalia has been hard at work," Drago smiles in response. "These are her newest inventions. Undetectable. She's a smart one, that sister of yours."

"I thought you told me to stop calling her my sister," I mumble, placing the bag into my soaking pocket.

"That was before I decided to marry you off to someone else."

"Bianca."

Just like that, the Byrne princess is back at the forefront of my mind. Behind Drago, another shock of lightning gnaws through the dark horizon.

"That's right," Drago nods. "Have you seen her yet?"

"Yes."

"And?"

"I'll break that fragile little princess into a thousand tiny pieces."

In response to my ruthless declaration, Krol's sour mood finally seems to sweeten. A cruel chuckle escapes his slimy lips.

I don't pay him any mind. Another fight has taken hold of me. A battle to rid myself of those crystal blue eyes.

"Be gentle," Drago says. "Remember, she needs to survive long enough to become your bride."

"And then she needs to be in good enough condition to carry and birth your heir," Krol adds.

"I know the fucking plan, *Krol*."

"Just making sure, *boy*."

Hot rain lashes between us and I find myself dangerously close to breaking. I've always wanted to give Krol a taste of his own medicine...

"Go now," Drago orders, sensing my weakness.

It takes me a second to hear him, but when I do, I know it's best that I listen.

"Fine," I grumble, prying open my fists.

I'm about to turn my back on Drago and leave, when I suddenly remember what I spotted above those crystal blue eyes.

"What is it?" Drago asks, reading me like a book.

"Nothing," I stubbornly sneer, shaking my head even as Bianca's image crackles behind my forehead.

"Speak, my son," Drago quietly insists. His voice is so low that I'm not even sure I actually hear him over the rain.

Maybe he didn't even speak at all. Maybe I just want to get to the bottom of this.

"Bianca... she had a scar above her left eye," I finally allow myself to utter. "How did it get there?"

With all of my remaining strength, I try to hide any emotion from my face, even if I'm not sure what emotion might leak out.

Anger? Jealousy? Pain? Joy?

It's all a confusing mess. But my entire life has been a confusing mess. Really, I should be used to it by now.

"A bar fight," Drago shrugs.

"With who?"

"Some frat boys at a campus bar."

The fist I had just pried open clenches shut again.

"When?" I growl.

"While you were training with the Byrnes."

"Who gave her the scar?" I ask, nails digging into the already torn skin along my palms.

"Like I said, some frat boy."

"Tell me his name."

"No," Drago sneers, clearly fed up with my insubordination. "The kid belongs to an important family. We don't need that kind of attention. Whatever delirious ideas your exhausted mind is concocting, snuff them out now. Leave here. Go back to the Byrne compound. Get some rest."

"Tell. Me. His. Name."

I've lost control. Thunder cracks over our heads. The sky shakes. But I don't budge.

Drago doesn't take too kindly to my resistance.

"Remember your place, *Gabryjel*," he warns me, stepping forward so that I can see the scars that cross his cheek and the paleness of his dead right eye. Even Krol shuts up in the face of the dragon's impending eruption. "Remember what this is all for. You aren't actually a bodyguard. Not a protector. You're a kidnapper in disguise, a predator doing whatever it takes to get close to his prey, a selfish killer pretending to be selfless."

His fury builds with every word, until suddenly, it vanishes.

Lightening slashes through the sky behind him one last time before he turns his glare away from me. Without another word, he brushes past my shoulder and walks back towards the thick wall of forest that borders the ragged beach.

My fury doesn't follow him. It remains raging inside of me. Burning even hotter as Krol leaves his place to chase after his master like the obedient dog that he is.

Before he can brush by me, though, he stops and leans in close to my ear.

"Kevin Porter," he whispers, his wretched breath curling against my swollen jaw as he burrows the name into my skull.

Instantly, I know who that name must belong to. And I know what Krol must be doing.

But it doesn't matter. I've already lost myself to the rage.

Kevin Porter.

That must be the fucker who scarred Bianca.

Fuck.

I know I should let it go; keep my head down and do my duty. Pretend to be who I'm supposed to pretend to be.

But how can I?

Someone marked her before I could. Someone cracked my fragile prize. Someone didn't know what is suddenly blindingly clear to me.

She's mine.

And no one's allowed to fuck with her but *me*.

It's not even just about pride, or even silencing the raging inferno swirling around those haunting blue eyes.

It's about doing what's right.

Sure, I'll leave this stormy beach. Head back to my barracks. Lay down in that cot they've allotted me and prepare for my first shift in two days.

But I won't sleep until I've made that frat boy pay for what he's done. Until I've planted the first seeds in the back of everyone's mind about what the fucking deal is.

Bianca Byrne belongs to me.

So, get the fuck out of my way.

3

BIANCA

"Why the hell didn't you tell me right away?"

Rian's arms are raised in disbelief. His greyish blue eyes are wide and wild. His jaw is on the floor.

He can't believe what I've just told him.

Shit. I can hardly believe it myself.

"I... I wasn't sure if I was right. I mean, what are the odds?"

Closing my eyes, I try to fight away the cosmic hazel-green glare that has been eroding my sanity ever since I saw it in that suffocating dungeon three days ago.

My demon has returned.

... Or, at least, I think he has. My mind is so mixed up I've been seriously considering that he was nothing more than a fever dream.

"Well, you were right. Gabriel Corso is on my list. He was in the cellar. That was him. Unless he goes by some other name?"

"No," I sigh, rubbing my forehead. "That's his name—though, there were rumors at school that it was a fake."

"Why would a high school kid have a fake name?"

"I don't know. For the same reason he had tattoos. To make himself seem cooler."

"Sounds like some typical prep school bullshit," Rian mumbles, shaking his head.

I hate that I've brought my problems to him. He already has enough shit to deal with.

But Gabriel's first shift is today.

Could I really risk encountering that demon alone?

My heart sinks as conflict slashes through it.

Shit. Maybe I should have kept this all to myself. I already managed to do it for three days.

Yet here I am, folding just before the big moment.

Like always.

"It probably was bullshit," I agree with Rian, trying to brush aside my concerns.

"Either way, I'll look into it. But I can't imagine something like that slipped past Maksim and your father during the vetting process. That shit is intense, trust me."

"I do trust you," I sigh, but just the mention of Dad makes the hair on my forearms stand up. "That's why I've told you all of this. Please, though, Rian, don't tell my dad."

The way Rian stares at me in response is almost enough to make me hang my head in shame. It's like he's looking at a naïve little child. One who doesn't understand anything, let alone know what she wants.

"Bianca, I don't think you quite grasp the magnitude of this situation. We're supposed to trust these people to protect you. If one of them was a problem for you in high school, and we somehow didn't know about that, then we're going to have to get rid of the whole group."

"No!" I rasp, bolting up from my bed.

But Rian isn't budging. "I'm going to tell your dad, Bianca. At the very least, I need an explanation as to why someone you just described to me as your high school bully was allowed to become your bodyguard."

"Dad was never allowed to know about him," I plead,

remembering the rule Mom had put into place the first time I came home crying over some mean boy or girl. "Neither was Mom. She was too afraid of how they would both react. You know what my parents are like, Rian. Yours are the same. They are capable of so much destruction."

"I'm well aware of what we're all capable of. But if your father doesn't know about your connection to this boy, then it's all the more reason to bring it up to him."

"Please, Rian. Dad's already got enough on his plate. Or have you forgotten about what happened to the congressman's daughter?"

Shit. That's so manipulative. But I'm getting desperate. Asking for help from my cousin is one thing, but dragging these stupid teenage problems to my dad will set me back years.

"What happened to the congressman's daughter is *why* we need to be extra careful," Rian counters.

"Fine, then talk to Uncle Maks. I'm sure he was intimately involved in the vetting process."

"And what if this connection between you and Gabriel is news to him?"

"Then kick Gabriel out onto the streets," I posture. "Replace him with another guard."

Rian's demeanour immediately darkens at the suggestion.

"That's not how it works," he tells me.

Those sharp blue eyes nearly overflow with concern. It's like he's worried about telling me too much.

I don't blame him, not after how I've just acted. But I'm nothing if not stubborn.

"Then how would it work? Just get rid of him," I shrug

"You can't do that," Rian sighs, shaking his head. "These guards are all connected. They've come up together, fought together, killed together, survived together. They are a team. If one fails, they all fail. If one is dismissed, they are all dismissed."

"Alright, fine," I give, dropping my shoulders. "But how hard can it be to find another dozen fit loyal men to protect me?"

"Let me be clear, Bianca," Rian says, stepping forward so that his shadow engulfs me. "When I say dismiss, I don't mean fire. After what we put them through, these men have become connected by blood. By the fabric of their very being. In the mafia, we don't let men go. We don't fire them. We terminate them. We wipe them off the face of the fucking earth. All of them. I know it. They know it. And I think you already knew it too."

He's right. To some extent, I did know that.

Still, the brutal confirmation cuts through me like a scythe. Hell, even the scar above my eye starts to ache as I swallow a ragged breath and try to fight my way out of the darkness Rian has just plunged me into.

Fuck. I really am naïve. This darkness is part of my inheritance. I should be welcoming it, not running from it.

But that's so much easier said than done.

"I... I don't want that," I admit.

"Neither do I. These are good men," Rian quietly responds. "Well, good might be a stretch. They are the wretches of society. Vicious demons. The stuff of nightmares. But they are ours. They are loyal. And they will do whatever it takes to keep you safe."

"Even Gabriel?"

"That's what I'm going to go find out right now."

"You're going to go talk to him?"

"How could I not? I'll bring it up with Uncle Maks first. But even if he knows about all of this drama, I'll still have a little chat with the asshole who hounded you in high school."

A dark weight pushes down my shoulders as Rian turns his back to me and heads for my bedroom door.

"Wait," I hear myself say. Even through the heaviness surrounding me, a stubborn flame has managed to rise up through it all.

"What?" Rian stops and looks back over his shoulder at me.

"Send Gabriel to me."

The shock lifts his entire face. Hell, even I'm stunned by what I just asked for.

"You want to see him?"

"I want to show him who's boss."

The prideful smile that crosses my cousins face in response fills me up with a red-hot determination. There's no backing down now. I've made my choice. This is what being an adult is all about. Facing down your demons. Confronting them head on. Crushing them beneath your heel.

It's time to grow up.

I'm ready. Right?

"That's what I like to hear out of my little cousin," Rian nods. "You'll be a fearsome warrior princess yet. I'll go fetch the bastard."

His words of praise fan the stubborn flames lashing around inside of me. Hell, the fire gets so hot that I can't help but open my big fat mouth again.

"One more thing," I hear myself call out, just as Rian reaches out to open my bedroom door.

"Yes," he asks, not bothering to turn around this time.

"Send him in alone."

My words might as well be a whip, because they twist Rian around like he's just been lashed.

"Bianca, let's not go overboard. We—"

"Please," I ask, letting a bit of my desperation slip out.

That desperation is enough to pull back my cousin's protective curtain just enough to allow him to seriously consider what I'm asking.

But as he ponders my proposal, so do I.

Is this what I really want?

... Or am I getting dangerously ahead of myself?

"We'll see," Rian finally nods. Then, turning back to the door, he opens it up and steps out into the hallway.

"Thank you."

With that, my door is closed, and I'm left to process what I just did.

Fuck. Have I gone mad? Is this just cabin fever? Or has this lockdown finally forced me to take the first step down a path that has always been there, waiting for me?

The path that leads to my destiny.

Someday, I'll be the queen of a ruthless empire. Sooner or later, I'll need to learn how to deal with the problems that come with that kind of power.

What better way to start than by confronting the demons of my past?

Shit.

No one said it was going to be easy.

Taking a deep breath, I try to prepare myself for what's to come.

Those green-flecked hazel eyes that I saw in the basement haven't just been silently stalking me for the past three days—if I'm being honest with myself, they've been haunting me ever since they first appeared in my life, then suddenly disappeared, all those years ago.

All of these years, I've been asking myself the same question. How could a single gaze stick with me for so long?

I've never settled on an answer. But now, I wonder if it isn't because there was no closure with Gabriel Corso.

After Principal Winchester's death, a good portion of the

student population never returned to school. Gabriel was chief among them—at least, he was in my mind.

But unlike the others, who I still saw on social media and around town, I never heard or saw anything from Gabriel ever again—well, except for some twisted rumors.

Now, suddenly, the heart-melting, impossibly infuriating bad boy is back. And he's grown into a beast of a man who has already killed for the privilege of getting close to me.

So, the question has shifted. It's no longer about why I can't forget him.

No.

Now, there's only one thing I want to know. One thing I *need* to figure out.

What the hell is he doing here?

The fateful knock at my door comes long before I'm ready for it.

Not that I'll ever be ready for this.

I've spent the last twenty minutes cursing my very name, all the while seriously contemplating if I have enough time to run to the bathroom and puke out my nauseating anxiety.

Well, there's no time for that anymore. I'm going to have to swallow my dread. Confront it head on. Just like I wanted.

Fuck. Maybe I don't actually know what I want.

"Come in!" I try to declare, but my voice is half shattered from anxiety and it cracks like a coward's squeal as I frantically look around for a better place to stand.

I'm still trying to decide on my perfect spot when the door creaks open and Rian's face pops in.

He doesn't say a word, but the expression on his face is loud enough.

Are you sure about this?

Yes, I silently nod, lying through my teeth.

For a second, the lion just pauses, like he isn't quite ready for this either. But that indecision doesn't last long. It never does with him.

Before I can reconsider and beg Rian to send Gabriel away, the lion's head disappears. The door closes.

Then, it's pushed back open.

That's when I see him.

Gabriel Corso.

He was no hallucination. He's real.

And he's here.

"I'll be waiting outside," I hear Rian say, but I can't see him. I can't see anything but the dark prince standing in my doorway.

Gabriel takes a long step inside, and the door swings shut behind him.

Just like that, we're alone. In my bedroom. My childhood bedroom. The same bedroom where I spent many restless nights hating myself for being unable to get the cocky popular kid out of my mind.

"Princess," he says, half-bowing so that a wavy lock of pitch-black hair falls over his right eye.

"Gabriel," I reply. My voice is raspy, but surprisingly steady.

"You look... well."

"Well what?" I hear myself immediately respond, confrontation pushing out every word.

The smirk that lifts his thick red lips makes my racing heart stop in its tracks.

"You look good," he clarifies.

Instantly, I recognize how foolish I just sounded. I've already made my first mistake. A hot wave of shame threatens to flush my cheeks and sabotage my position.

Fuck.

"Alright," I mumble, unable to think of anything clever to

say. That's mistake number two. Everything is already falling apart. "You look like you've been through hell."

Shit. That was too much. The lack of subtlety is like a bull-horn in the quiet bedroom—even if it is true.

Gabriel may have the face of a Greek god, but the sharpness of his cheekbones have been dulled by swelling; the smooth golden tan of his olive skin has been interrupted by cuts and bruises. And I'm sure the same could be said of his jawline, if it wasn't hidden under a short, thick brush of jet-black facial hair.

The beard is new; it adds a smack of maturity to his cocky smirk.

I hate it—no matter how well it frames his face... and those fucking eyes.

"I have been through hell," he nods, his smirk faltering ever so slightly. "But it was worth it."

"To become my bodyguard?"

"To become part of this family."

"You. Are not. Part of my family," I suddenly snap.

The fucking gall of this man.

My little outburst wipes another millimetre off of Gabriel's cocky smirk, but even as his lips drop and he tilts his head slightly to the side, I swear he's still smiling. Mocking me.

"Did I do something wrong, princess?"

"Stop calling me princess."

"What would you prefer?"

"My name is Bianca."

"Bianca Byrne."

Even without the smirk, the knowing glint in his stunning eyes is enough to confirm he's fucking with me.

"Yeah, Bianca Byrne. Sounds like the name of some second-rate comic book character, right?" I sneer, reminding him of one of his schoolyard insults. "Like I'm in the running for worst comic book character of all time, right? Isn't that something you once told me?"

Gabriel's head tilt becomes more pronounced as he stares into my eyes, then right into my soul. But instead of looking like a lost puppy, he looks like a fucking wolf sizing up its prey.

"Did I?"

"Yes, you did," I nearly hiss.

The motherfucker is testing me. I've pulled him in here to see him grovel, but he's just as cocky and irreverent as ever.

He must know that I don't have the heart to doom a dozen men to their deaths just because I hate him. He must think he's safe.

I fucking hate that he's right.

"Well, then I apologize, Bianca. You know how kids are."

The apology slips out of his blood red lips like a quickly forgotten breath. It's so casual, in fact, that it almost doesn't register.

"Kids *are* cruel," I admit, before throwing in a warning. "But adults are crueler."

"I'm well aware."

"What else are you aware of?"

"That you probably hate me for how I treated you in high school. That you probably called me in here to gloat one last time before you put me and my whole crew to death. That you think your father doesn't know who I am, or how we're connected, and you're afraid to tell him because you think it will keep you locked away in your little gilded cage forever. I'm aware of all of that, Bianca Byrne. And so much more."

Each word he says is like a knife twisting into my chest. This is not a man here to beg for his life. This is a man who's been through hell and knows that I've never even been close to the inferno.

This is my old bully all grown up.

"Well, I do hate you. So at least you got one thing right," I spit. But the desperate frustration in my voice makes every word a raspy mess.

"Can't we put our differences aside, princess?" Gabriel asks, the ghost of his smirk returning to haunt my every thought. "This family is bigger than that."

"If you ever become part of my family, I'll kill myself."

"As your personal bodyguard, I just couldn't allow that to happen."

"You'll do whatever I say."

"No," Gabriel shakes his head. To my surprise, the dark wolf takes a step towards me. He smells like fresh rain. But even that surprisingly crisp fragrance isn't enough to keep me from shuffling backwards in fear—not that there's anywhere to go. The back of my knees quickly catch the edge of the mattress. My gut drops. "I'll do whatever I need to do to keep you safe."

"I don't feel safe around you," I rasp.

It feels like I've been plunged beneath the dark waves of a nightmare. This was a bad idea. I'm not ready for this. For him. For the darkness.

"Then tell your dad about me. Doom a dozen good men to death. That shouldn't be hard for you. I mean, what's a dozen good men to a mafia princess, right? Your empire is built on blood and bones and—"

"Rian!" I shout, my cowardly mind clawing at the walls, screaming to escape.

Just before my cousin can burst in and save me, though, Gabriel takes a long step back.

By the time Rian pops inside, the two of us are far enough apart that no one could ever guess what just happened—especially as I desperately try to wipe the fear and shock from my face. It's an instinct I can't fight against. No one should be allowed to see me like this. Not even my cousin. Not even if Gabriel just did.

"Is everything alright?" Rian asks, stepping up beside the dark wolf.

Rian is wider and more muscular, but Gabriel is taller, with the kind of lean, athletic build that makes me believe he could wrap a blade around my throat in the blink of an eye.

A fight between these two titans would drown the world in blood.

"Everything is fine," Gabriel replies for me.

But Rian isn't going to listen to that bullshit. He already knows about Gabriel.

"I didn't ask you," my cousin growls, brushing by the wolf to get a better look at me. "Bianca?"

Before I can gather myself enough to give a straight answer, a commotion in the doorway whips the rooms attention away from me.

"We have a fucking problem."

It's Uncle Maksim.

Immediately, I can tell something is wrong. My uncle's usually stoic demeanor has cracked just enough to see the blood-red fire raging behind his eyes.

"What?" Rian asks, straightening up as he senses the same urgency I do.

Looking towards Gabriel, Uncle Maksim steps forward. "You. Prepare the men," he commands. "We're leaving. Now."

Gabriel hardly even hesitates. "Where to, sir?"

"That is not for you to know. Gather the men from the guest house too. We need a full detail. The princess is being transported to a safer location."

"What? Why?" I croak, the dread of what just happened colliding with the new anxiety of what's to come.

Before Uncle Maksim answers me, though, he makes sure to step aside and fling his arm towards the doorway. "Go!" he orders.

Gabriel doesn't need to be told twice.

The savage wolf gives me one last hard look before turning away. In the blink of an eye, he's gone. The door slams shut behind him.

"What is it?" Rian and I both quickly ask.

"We've been framed," Maksim growls.

"What the hell are you talking about?" Rian asks.

But Maksim doesn't respond by looking at Rian. Instead, he turns his attention to me; to the scar throbbing above my eye.

"The kid who gave you that scar. He was a state senator's son. Kevin Porter. This morning, they found his head swinging from a lamppost outside of the bar where the fight happened... the rest of his body was propped up by the front door."

The air is sucked out of the room.

"No fucking way," Rian grumbles.

I'm too shocked to even curse.

This wasn't supposed to happen. Our men were ordered to stay far away from that brat. But if I didn't know better, I'd say that the gruesome murder sounds exactly like something we'd do to send a message to an enemy.

We've been framed.

"I told Uncle Ray we should have put our own secret security detail on the kid..." Rian barks.

"We did," Maksim sneers. "Yet somehow this still happened."

"Fuck. How long do we have until every cop in the state is knocking down our door?"

"Not long. I'll hold them off for as long as possible. But while the cops are around, the bulk of our army can't be. And that puts Bianca at risk. Someone out there is still trying to kidnap mafia princesses. You need to be protected, child."

"Uncle Maks—"

"No. Don't talk. Listen. I've already put the backup plan into action. You'll be meeting your cousins at an undisclosed location. From there, we will escort you all to the island. Our army will meet us there. No one will be able to get in. You will be safe."

My stomach drops. The heaviness that had just been

weighing me down seems to get a hundred times heavier, and a hell of a lot darker.

Whatever independence I was trying to forge by confronting Gabriel hasn't just backfired spectacularly, it's been coupled with a direct shot to my chest.

This lockdown is about to get a whole lot more intense.

I know the island Uncle Maksim is talking about.

He's right. There's no chance anyone will be able to get onto it.

But no one will be able to get off of it, either.

I'm trapped.

4

GABRIEL

What the fuck was I thinking?

Even as I pack into the back of the black van with a half-dozen other men, rifle slung over my shoulder, Glock loaded and stuffed beneath my belt, switchblade strapped to each ankle, I know the foolish answer to my questions.

I wasn't thinking.

I was acting.

I was trying to intimidate Bianca into keeping her pretty little mouth shut.

But it wasn't so I could hold onto my life.

No. The truth is even more cowardly than that. And it rages around in the back of my skull like a fucking grenade as the van door shuts behind me and the engine rumbles below my feet.

Shit. I've never cared much about living or dying. All that's ever really mattered to me is getting what I deserve; what I want; what I need.

And in that precarious moment, spent two feet away from the crystal blue eyes that haunt me even now, I only wanted one thing. Hell, I only needed one thing.

Her.

And I was willing to do whatever it took to get my way.

That's the truth.

Fucking hell.

My chest stirs as the armored van peels out of the Byrne compound, rattling the metal floors and shaking the truckloads of ammo we've each brought along with us.

But our firepower is only the start.

Before I jumped into the back of this van, I helped load three others with more weapons and ammo than I've ever seen in my life—and that's fucking saying something.

I can still smell the metal and the oil.

It lingers just beneath another scent. A scent that has joined those unescapable blue eyes... and those plump pink lips.

Blood rushes below my waist as I remember how close I was to her. Close enough to smell her. Close enough to *taste* her.

I'd never been so tempted in my entire life.

Fuck. Her vanilla scent still swirls around my head, even as I desperately try to singe it away so that I can concentrate on what matters right fucking now.

I need to figure out what the fuck is going on. And fast. Because whatever it is, it's big.

We're essentially moving an army's worth of firepower.

And with it, we're towing along a fragile little princess who's heir to the most powerful mafia empire on the west coast.

That vanilla scent caught on the wind while I was loading the last van. When I looked over my shoulder, I saw that lion Rian Kilpatrick, and his eagle-hawk of an uncle, Maksim Smolov, accompanying a still shaken Bianca to the black escalade that was parked behind the very van that I'm in now.

Fuck.

I take a deep but subtle breath and try to calm my nerves.

When Maksim barged into Bianca's bedroom, I thought that I had been made.

He looked furious. And his fury immediately fell onto me.

I was just about ready to fight my way out of there.

Fortunately, it was a false alarm.

Still, my little meeting was cut short before I could sink my claws any further into the princess. But it wasn't a complete loss.

I still got close enough to flick one of Roz's tracking devices in her direction.

"Do you know where we're headed?"

The sudden question comes from Seamus Giles, the man to my right. He's a big Irish lug with a tiny little voice. Over the course of our training, I've learned that he's a man who asks too many questions. That should have disqualified him long ago. Yet here he is. Bugging me.

"Why would I know?" I grunt.

"I saw you go up to Bianca's room with Rian Kilpatrick earlier," Giles whispers, as if it's some big secret and he's doing me a great favor by keeping it quiet. "I figured he was grooming you for some important position."

"No," I shake my head. "He just needed someone to unclog her toilet."

"Don't they have maids for that?"

"What do you—"

Before I can get another word out, a skull-rattling blast erupts somewhere outside. A split-second later, the van is lifted into the air, and every man is thrown to the ceiling.

Somehow, Giles gets there first, and I only hit my head against his gut, instead of the hard, bullet proof interior.

There's no time to be thankful, though, because we're thrown around again.

The van is flipping.

Fucking hell.

Grabbing onto the strap of Giles' rifle, I pull myself into his body so that he takes the brunt of the contact as we twist and turn.

It feels like a chaotic eternity before the rolling finally stops. Then, just like that, we're all tossed into one final pile of bodies and weapons.

Groans replace the sound of shearing metal inside the van. Outside, a gunfight has already erupted.

"Shit," I curse, pushing myself off Giles' twisted body. "Are you alright?"

When he opens his mouth to respond, only blood pours out.

The poor bastard's eyes are wide open, and I spot a familiar realization in them.

The big lug is desperately trying to move. But he can't.

Behind me, I hear the surviving members of my crew cough and curse as they crawl over each other to open the slanted van door. Just before they can manage it, though, I pull out my gun and put a bullet right between Giles' eyes.

"What the fuck was that?!" someone shouts, after the sound of the gunshot has faded.

"Gabriel, you asshole!" someone else adds.

I hardly pay them any mind.

"He was paralyzed," I growl. "Better to put him out of his misery quickly. There's a battle to be won. Now, which of you fuckers is going to join me?"

I don't wait for any answers. Pointing my gun up at the mangled handle of the dented van doors, I fire, and they bust open, flinging us into a world of shit.

Immediately, I feel a bullet whiz past my ear. Then I hear it lodge itself into some unlucky bastard behind me.

It only serves to piss me the fuck off.

I'm not here to die.

I'm here to reclaim what's mine.

And she's in trouble.

"Protect the princess!" A voice calls out through the chaos.

I'm way ahead of him.

Climbing my way out of the busted van, I shoot at everyone and anyone I don't instantly recognize. That leaves a lot of corpses in my wake. But I don't give a shit.

Only one thing matters.

Her.

Somewhere behind me, another explosion shakes the air. The blast nearly knocks me off my feet, but I manage to stumble over to the now-bullet riddled Escalade that Bianca was in earlier.

Ducking down, I take cover so that I can reload. But not before I take a quick glance inside.

It's empty.

Shit.

Where the fuck are you, princess?

My answer comes quickly enough. Just as I'm ready to go again, I hear a shrill scream come from somewhere up ahead. It's a woman's scream, and there's only one woman in this entire entourage.

Pouncing out from behind the smoking hood of the black Escalade, I make sure my gun is properly loaded by putting three quick bullets into the nearest motherfucker.

He falls to the ground, instantly dead, and I hurdle over his corpse, racing in the direction of the screaming.

I've been in countless battles before. All of my life, I've been surrounded by endless violence. Still, something about this moment feels different.

It feels more urgent.

A primal instinct has been unleashed within me. The

corners of my vision fill with a deep red, blocking out everything but the way forward.

Another scream cuts through the chaos and into my ears, and I know I'm close. Then, suddenly, I spot a flash of auburn hair up ahead. It flickers through the chaos, before disappearing around a dark corner.

Bianca.

It's hard to say how many men I kill before I reach that corner, but my hands are slippery with blood by the time I take the sharp turn.

I see her.

Up ahead, completely out of place amongst the grime and dirt of the dark alleyway, is the Byrne princess.

She's being manhandled by a group of three soon-to-be dead men. They're violently trying to drag her into the black tunnel at the end of the alleyway.

Something inside of me snaps.

It only takes a single bullet to down the man in the rear of the group. But I can't stop with just one shot. Unloading my clip into his corpse, I propel myself forward, directly into the line of fire.

Fortunately for me, Bianca is putting up a fight. She kicks and screams and bothers the remaining two men just enough to keep them from getting a straight shot at me.

Still, some of their bullets get awfully close, and at one point, I have to drop my gun and hit the ground just to avoid getting shredded.

Without a wasted movement, I roll forward, tearing out the switchblades strapped to my ankles.

"Oh shit!"

Those are the last words of the first man I decapitate.

"You fucking bastard!" yells his doomed friend.

Whipping his gun around, he points the barrel directly in my face. But before he can shoot, the stubborn damsel who's hair he has bunched up in his other fist manages to flail hard enough to twist his entire body.

The act seals his fate.

My first blade plunges into his skull through his right eye. My second through his left. He doesn't get the privilege of realizing he's dead before I grab both handles and rip them from his bloody sockets. Scarlet tears gush down his cheeks as I cross the dirty blades through his throat, so that his severed head hits the ground long before his body does.

My lungs burn as I take a second to stare down at the carnage.

Then...

"You."

Bianca's voice is almost a whisper.

When I look over at her, my heart drops.

Her olive skin has gone pale. And her immaculate hair is ripped and frizzy. But I don't see any wounds... or detect any hostility behind her exclamation. That's good news.

You.

"That's right," I respond, savoring the way she stares at me.

For the first time ever, I don't see any hate in her gaze.

And what a fucking gaze. The beauty in those crystal blue eyes shine out even through the fear; they're made even more stunning against the crimson brush strokes splashed against her soft skin.

Is that the blood I just spilled for her?

"Rian!"

Her undivided attention quickly snaps away from me, lifting up over my shoulder just as I feel a presence at my back.

Whipping around, blades raised, I get ready to kill again. But Bianca wasn't lying.

It's her cousin.

How did I not hear him coming?

You were distracted.

"Bianca! Are you alright?" There's an unexpected panic in the lion's voice.

Hell, I guess he's human. That's good to know.

'I... I think so," Bianca croaks, her gaze dropping as if to check to make sure she's telling the truth. When she's sure she is, those crystal blue eyes lift again.

But they don't move back towards her cousin. Instead, they fall onto me.

"He... He saved me," she mutters, as if it's almost impossible to believe.

"I know," Rian responds, looking over his shoulder at me, suspicion and gratitude mixing behind his own blue eyes. "Thank you."

"Just doing my job," I grumble, slowly becoming aware of the jealous fire rising in my core.

He's touching her.

"The job isn't done yet," Rian points out. Helping Bianca back to her feet, he hands me his gun.

That's when the blood finally rushes from my ears. Behind us, I hear the battle still raging. Though, it's instantly clear there aren't many soldiers left.

The gunshots are sparse. But distant enough that Rian and I both have the same thought.

Whoever ambushed us, they're retreating. This battle is nearly—

Before I can even finish my thought, I hear an all too familiar sound.

A bullet whizzing past my ear.

I blink, and when my eyelids reopen, Bianca is gone.

"NO!"

Somehow, Rian processes what's just happened before I can, and he whips around, pulling out another gun from beneath his belt.

The lion is already firing back down the alleyway when my gaze falls onto the body writhing at my feet.

Bianca.

Blood leaks from an unseen wound, staining the alley floor, as she buries her face into the cold, dirty cement below.

The sight stuns me.

For the first time in my life, I'm not sure how to react, or what to do.

But that hesitation doesn't last long, not after a nuclear bomb erupts inside of me.

My vision red with blood-lust, I turn around, and start to shoot... but the clip is empty, and nothing comes out.

Rian handed me a neutered weapon.

Fuck.

"Get her somewhere safe!" the lion roars.

Up ahead, blocking the entrance to the alley way are at least six men. No one challenges them from the rear.

That means all the rest of our men are either dead or gone.

It's just Rian and me.

"Go!" he yells again. Each shot he takes is a ticking time bomb. That's a Glock 19 in his hand. It only holds nine rounds. The second he's out of ammo, we're fucked.

"I'm on it," I hear myself say.

There's no time to waste. Ignoring every instinct in me, I resist the urge to fight to the death, to charge the enemy in a suicidal rage.

Instead, I sprawl out over the bleeding princess at my feet. Wrapping her up in my arms, I use my body as a human shield, and race ahead, precious cargo in tow.

"... Rian?"

Bianca's voice is so tiny and faint that I'm surprised I can even hear it through all the noise. Yet, somehow, it cuts through everything, floating directly into my ear.

At my back, the lion roars.

Instinctively, my embrace around Bianca tightens. She's so warm.

"I'll get you to safety, princess," I promise. "Then, I'll fix you up."

"I'm not a princess..."

Barreling into the black tunnel at the end of the alleyway, I'm temporarily blinded. But then I spot a sliver of light just up ahead, off to the right.

That's where we head.

Anything to get away from the men back there. Men who don't seem to want anything but blood.

They shot her... What kind of fucking morons shoot at something so valuable?

Pushing forward, I try to keep an eye on both the princess in my arms and the light that will lead us out of this darkness.

But while Bianca's pale face only seems to get paler, the light up ahead never seems to get bigger.

Then, suddenly, I do something I've almost never done before.

I trip.

It's like an anvil is dropped over my head, and I plunge downwards into the cold blackness. A second later, my knees hit the hard ground. The wave of searing pain that follows quickly shocks me back awake. It hurts like hell, but I'm comforted when I look down.

Bianca is still in my arms. I didn't drop her. I won't let her ago.

And I don't, not even after I finally realize why I've fallen. My leg. The flesh just above the back of my knee is on fire.

Fuck.

I've been hit.

When the hell did that happen?

"Gabriel Corso," Bianca suddenly whispers. A weak little cough follows.

For some reason, her voice pierces my fucking chest. The pain is almost as sharp as the throbbing wound on the back of my leg.

"That's not my name," I hear myself say.

Maybe I've already lost too much blood, but the unplanned confession hardly even stuns me.

Still, my hands shake around her as Bianca whispers up at me once more.

"What is your name, then?"

The question isn't real. She's falling into a dream. A dream she won't ever wake up from if I don't do something soon.

But not even that brutal truth stops me from giving her an honest answer.

"I... I'm not sure," I mumble, before shaking my head clear. "It doesn't matter. Are you alright?"

"What's happening?"

"You were shot." Keeping one hand fastened against the small of her back, I search her body for a wound.

"Really? It doesn't hurt..."

She really is delusional. But so am I.

This is dangerous.

"It will later," I assure her, leaving out the part where it will only hurt later if she manages to pull through.

Finally, I find the source of her blood. It's spilling from a wound high up on her shoulder. That's a good sign. It means no internal organs were hit. She might survive... as long as she doesn't bleed out first.

The thought hits me like a hammer.

No. She won't die. I won't allow it.

I've worked too hard to get this close to her. She's mine, and there is no escape. Not in life. Not in death.

I've finally touched her.

And I only want more.

There's no concern for my own injury as I strip away the strap of her blood-soaked tank top, revealing her fresh wound.

"I can't feel anything," Bianca sighs.

Shit. I know exactly what that means. I'm losing her.

The princess needs a shot of electricity. Fast. Something to jolt her awake from the growing darkness before it consumes her forever.

Raising a hand to her pale face, I give her cheek a light slap.

It doesn't do anything.

Those sharp crystal blue eyes are fading. Her bottom lip starts to tremble.

My mind goes blank.

Everything feels so out of my control. Like I'm stuck in a dream. But I don't fight back as my eyes gently close, and I lean forward, towards the sleeping princess.

With her fragile jaw cupped in the palm of my hand, I kiss her.

It's like being injected with morphine. Warm and pleasant, her soft lips press against mine.

Then, she kisses me back.

But the act shocks me back to reality. My eyes rip open and I jump up like I've just been hit by lightning.

What the fuck was that?

"That felt nice," Bianca whispers, the faintest smile lifting her porcelain cheekbones.

But when her eyelids close, and that crystal blue disappears, I know my reckless act didn't work.

At least, it didn't work on her.

My fading body, on the other hand, has been shot full of electricity.

Before I know it, I'm back on my feet, unconscious princess fading in my arms. My feet start to move. My lungs start to burn again.

Finally, the light ahead begins to grow.

At my back, I can hear the faintest sound of gunshots. But they don't last long. Someone has won. Everyone else is dead.

There's no point int trying to guess the outcome. All that matters now is us.

And after what feels like an eternity, I finally see what's waiting for us on the other side of the black tunnel.

An empty street, spotted by lamplight.

The moment I step out of the tunnel, I start looking for our getaway car. Anything will do. It just needs to be something I can hotwire.

Bianca needs to get to a hospital. I don't care about the consequences.

Before I can find the nearest makeshift ambulance, though, I hear the squealing of tires.

My first instinct is to turn around and get ready for a fight— not that I'll be of any use with my hands full like this.

I'm not met with a fight, though. Instead, I spot something completely unexpected.

An oddly familiar looking car screeches to a halt five feet away.

No matter how tinted the front windshield is, I immediately realize who I'm looking at—even if I don't understand what the fuck he's doing here.

Tytus.

Rolling down his window, he pops his head out to greet me.

"Why, fancy seeing you here, stranger," he smiles "You look like hell."

I don't know what to say. I haven't seen him in months. And all of a sudden he shows up in an empty street, just when I need him the most?

"Well, don't just stand there," another familiar voice comes from the passenger window. "Get in, loser."

It's Roz.

Her voice slaps me awake.

No matter how confused I am, I'm not in a position to be picky. I need to get in that car.

There's no going back. Not to Rian. Not to the Byrnes.

My short stint as a bodyguard is over. This whole fucking thing has jumped the shark. All I can do now is put my head down and move forward.

The Byrne princess is finally mine.

But only if I can keep her alive.

5

BIANCA

The second my eyelids flutter open, a lifetime of dreams and nightmares are instantly burned away, forgotten forever.

But that's not all I've forgotten.

At first, my addled mind is completely empty. Then, slowly, a gentle ache builds behind my forehead. It's followed by a single, all-important question.

What the hell happened?

No answer appears before me. Still, I can feel that something is different. A massive change has occurred. The weight of the world has shifted, and it hovers directly above my body, threatening to come crashing down at any moment.

My first instinct is to move, to try and evade the invisible menace.

That's a dumb decision.

Before I can move anything more than a finger, my entire skull erupts in agony.

The pain is enough to jerk me around and plunge my face directly into the pillow that props up my head.

It takes a moment before the suffering retreats enough for

me to think straight. But when it does, I get the first hint of where I am.

A bed.

But who's bed?

Another deep breath confirms that it's not mine.

Still, the subtle scent wafting off the pillow is oddly familiar. It doesn't help ease my painful confusion.

Where the hell am I?

A dozen or so deep breaths later, and I've finally gathered the strength to turn myself around again.

At first, the world is blurry. All I can make out are shades of white and grey. Slowly, though, it all comes back into focus.

Not that there's anything to focus on.

This is a bedroom alright. But it has almost no defining features.

The sprawling space is essentially empty. White walls hold no artwork or photographs. Soft corners are vacant of furniture. Even the carpet is a fuzzy looking shade of light grey.

Strangely enough, the void has an almost comforting effect on my pounding head. There's no overload of new information. No nooks or crannies or shadows to flinch away from.

Still, there are some lines that stand out from the monotony.

Along one of the walls, I recognize the outline of a door. It's shut tightly. On an adjacent wall, two thinner shuttered doors indicate a closet. Just beside that, there is one last door. Unlike the others, it isn't shut tight; through the open slit, I can just make out a white marble sink.

That must be the bathroom.

If I didn't know any better, I'd say this place almost looked like some kind of futuristic, high-class hospital room. Still, I'm not ready to get comfortable just yet. I've been to hospitals before. The best that money can offer. None of them have looked anything like this.

As gently as possible, I try to remember what happened to me.

What am I doing here?

The question echoes around in my throbbing head as I mindlessly search the empty walls for answers.

But there's nothing.

And suddenly, the reality of what that really means hits me.

There is nothing.

Not even windows.

That's when I feel the first strike of fear. It's also when I first notice I've been dressed in a soft silk nightgown. Who's nightgown is this?

What the fuck is going on?

Even if this place is easily twice the size of my bedroom back home, I'm instantly beset by claustrophobia.

And what I hear next only makes it all a thousand times worse.

The jarring sound of a door being unlocked.

Unlocked.

Fuck.

Immediately, my heart starts to pound against the inside of my chest. Panic washes over me.

Why the hell am I locked in here?

Have I been caught? Kidnapped like the congressman's daughter?

None of those questions are answered as I rip my terrified gaze over to the opening door.

Because the man who steps inside is just as much a mystery as whatever the fuck has happened to me.

It's Gabriel fucking Corso.

That's not my real name.

The confession flashes through my throbbing skull like a strike of lightning as I watch him enter.

Was that from one of my dreams? Nightmares?

Or did he really say that?

"Finally." It's the first word out of his mouth. A taunting hello that's so flippant, I almost short-circuit.

"Finally?" I hear myself croak in response.

"You've been out for almost two days straight, princess. That's pretty dramatic, if you ask me."

I don't have the energy to snap back at him.

All I can do is shut my eyes and brave the throbbing storm swirling around just behind my skull.

I haven't woken up. I'm still lost in a nightmare.

"What is this?" I manage to ask, even as every inch of me begs for relief.

Pinching my nose, I open my eyes again.

Gabriel has shut the bedroom door behind him. He's leaning against the wall beside it. Like he's not sure if he should get any closer. Not yet.

"This is a bedroom," he states.

"No shit," I rasp. "What the hell am I doing here?"

"Recovering."

"Recovering from what? Where's my family? What are you doing here?"

"Your family is working. I'm doing my job."

"Your job is to waltz in here and tell me I'm being dramatic?"

"My job is to come in here and tell you the truth."

"And what is the truth?" I ask, wanting to break down and just beg him to stop being so fucking smug.

Something is wrong. Something is seriously fucking wrong.

Gabriel shouldn't have the gall to act like this around me. Especially if I just escaped some kind of serious danger. Mom would be here. Dad wouldn't leave my side. Rian wouldn't either. And they definitely wouldn't leave me in the care of a brand-new body guard—especially after what I've already told Rian.

"The truth is this, princess: two days ago, your uncle Maksim ordered us to escort you to a new secure location. It didn't go well. We were ambushed. Everyone died. Well, everyone except the two of us. I managed to save you. So, you're welcome. You did get nicked by a bullet, though. It tore open a small wound on your shoulder. There was a lot of bleeding, but it was all for show. You probably would have survived even if I hadn't dragged you out of there and helped stemmed the loss."

"I... I was shot?"

"Barely," Gabriel smirks. "And you weren't the only one, so don't feel special."

Stepping forward, the dark wolf reveals a slight limp. Then, just to make sure I get the idea, he rolls up his pant leg and shows me the thick bandage wrapped around his upper knee.

"You were shot protecting me?"

Gabriel shrugs in response. "I might have been a bit dramatic about the whole thing too," he chuckles. "It wasn't a bullet that got me—at least, not an entire one. Just some shrapnel. Look, by the end of that battle, we were both a little delirious from blood loss... But you were the only one who passed out."

Rolling his pant leg back down, Gabriel starts to walk towards the bed. My first instinct is to flinch away—even as bits and pieces of what he just told me resurface from the recesses of my mind.

He's telling the truth. If only just a slice of it.

"What happened to everyone else?" I ask. Slowly, I begin to remember the chaos.

There was an explosion. Car crashes. Gunfire.

"You aren't a very good listener, princess. I told you. We were the only survivors."

Gabriel is right. He did already tell me that. But I barely processed it. Now, though, it hits me like a fucking mac truck.

"Rian," I gulp, a desperate grief appearing deep in my gut.

"He's fine." Gabriel is surprisingly quick to assure me.

"You just said everyone died?"

"He wasn't there."

"He... he was in the car with me," I hazily recall.

My skull throbs as I'm bombarded with flashbacks of being rushed into the back of that black Escalade.

Did anyone explain to me where we were going and why?

I can't quite remember.

But I can see Rian sitting beside me.

"Well, it's good to see you didn't hit your head too hard before I swept you off that grimy alley floor and saved your life," Gabriel grumbles, the smirk wiped from his face.

"Where's Rian?"

"Working."

"How did he escape if no one survived?"

"I guess I lied when I said everyone else died."

"What else are you lying about?"

No matter how weak my voice is, that question seems to cut Gabriel somewhere sensitive. Limp or not, he lunges forward so quickly that the gust of his massive body nearly blows me off the bed.

Suddenly, he's towering over me, hands pressed into the mattress, forearms bulging with a barely restrained fury.

"Is that something you really want to know, princess?"

"Yes."

Despite the fear that has just crawled down my throat, I can't help my stupid, stubborn nature. Especially not as I get a whiff of the dark wolf who's supposed to be so terrifying.

Gabriel may be a killer, but he smells like soft rain and fresh earth.

It makes me less afraid of him.

But a whole lot more afraid of myself.

Because no matter how hard I try to hold his stunning gaze, my eyes keep dropping down to his blood red lips.

For some reason, I can practically taste them; I can almost feel the way his dark stubble would brush against my sensitive cheeks.

What the hell is wrong with me?

"The truth is too much for you right now," Gabriel says, and when I force my gaze back up to those insane hazel-green eyes, I catch them rising too. Almost like he was sneaking a look at my lips.

"No. It isn't," I respond, each breath getting deeper as a disturbing reality starts to sink in.

Gabriel is up to something.

But what?

Am I his captive? Is he working with the kidnappers who killed the congressman's daughter?

Or is it somehow even worse than that? He could be lying about Rian to protect me. I haven't even asked about Dad or Uncle Maksim.

I could be the last one left.

"Don't go all doe-eyed on me, princess," Gabriel scoffs, pushing himself back from the bed. "It won't work."

"Work for what?" I snap, disgusted. The further back he retreats, the better. That way, I won't get lost in those stupid, endless hazel-green eyes, or that strangely comforting scent.

"You have no idea what's coming your way," he warns, avoiding my question.

"Then tell me."

"Why?"

"Because you work for me. And I can take it."

That's a lie and we both know it. No matter how tough I've tried to be in the past, I've always been protected from the darkest truths.

And now I'm starting to think it was for the best.

I don't feel ready for any of this, whatever the truth is.

"No. You can't," Gabriel says, his gaze dropping against some heavy weight.

"Try me," I challenge him.

For a tense moment, he hesitates to respond. But that hesitation doesn't last long.

My stomach drops when the dark wolf turns his back on me. Instead of heading for the door, though, he stays put. Crossing his arms, he grabs the bottom of his shirt. Then, he pulls it off.

The sight steals my breath away.

Fucking hell.

The dark wolf's back is a wall of perfectly built muscle, draped in a gothic mosaic of black tattoos. Somehow, he looks even more powerful now than when I saw him shirtless and bloody in the cellar back home.

"What do you see, princess?" he growls, his voice sharp and deep.

I don't answer.

How could I?

A disturbing pressure has appeared in my core, and I'm too busy uncurling my toes to come up with a convincing lie.

This man could crush me.

"Nothing," I manage to mumble.

"Answer me, and I will tell you what you need to know. What do you see?"

Fuck.

"I see..." *Don't say muscles. Don't say muscles.* "I see a man."

"What about the man do you see?"

"... That he likes tattoos. That he's covered in tattoos," I stubbornly resist.

"And why do you think he's covered in tattoos?"

"Because he wants to look cool," I blurt out, instantly regretting it.

I feel like a stupid, immature teenager all over again, getting bogged down in gossip and rumors and excuses for why I don't like the popular kid.

"No, princess," Gabriel chuckles. His voice is so deep it seeps into my bones. "That's not the reason."

Tossing his shirt to the ground, the dark wolf turns around and moves towards the bed. There's something about the look in his eyes that freezes me. And I can hardly even bear to breathe as he leans forward and takes my wrist.

His touch is burning hot, and I immediately try to jerk away. But that only tightens his grip.

"Let me go," I croak, trying to pull away again.

This time, Gabriel doesn't just tighten his grip. No. This time, he tugs me forward, then wraps my arm under his.

With all my strength, I crank my head to the side so I don't faceplant into his broad, steaming chest.

"Open your hand," Gabriel orders, his already deep voice dropping a register.

Behind his back, my fingers are curled tightly into a fist.

"No."

I'm shaking like a fragile little leaf. This is bad. He doesn't have to confess anything to me anymore. I know the truth. I'm alone here. I have to be.

No one would dare treat me this way if there was even a chance my fearsome father or cousin could do anything about it.

"Do as I say, princess, and I will give you what you want."

"I want you to let me go," I beg, even as the swirling pressure in my core deepens.

"Then that's what you shall receive."

My skull still pounds as I try to think up a way out of this. But part of me knows that even if I had all of my wits about me, there would be no escape.

Whatever's happening, I'm not in control.

Gabriel is.

"Fine," I mumble, a deep anguish unclenching my fingers.

When my hand is finally open, Gabriel presses my palm against his searing flesh.

Instantly, I feel the scars.

Angry and raised, they rise out from under his black tattoos like burning mountains.

It doesn't take long for me to understand what Gabriel is getting at.

The tattoos, they're not to look cool. Fuck no. They're to cover these scars.

What has this man been through?

"You couldn't see the scars, could you?" Gabriel asks, his voice deep, yet surprisingly quiet.

"No," I weakly admit.

"Now you know they're there," he says. "Do you see what I mean? Before, you couldn't see the truth, even though it was staring you right in the face. You couldn't see it because you didn't want to see it. But I've ripped back the veil for you princess. I've shown you the truth. It doesn't feel very good, does it?"

"No. It doesn't," I softly admit.

How did he get these scars? My mind runs wild with the dark and dreadful possibilities.

"Feel that knot twisting in your gut?" Gabriel continues. "Remember that feeling when you ask me for the truth. Remember how much it hurts. Remember that you can't handle it."

His hot skin pricks the tip of my fingers as he forces me to feel the agony of his past. Suddenly, though, he drops my hand.

For a moment, there's nothing forcing me to keep touching him. Yet my hand doesn't move. Because the pinpricks of his scars slowly dissolve away, vanishing in place of a simmering heat.

I don't realize how cold I truly am until the warmth of his

body starts to wash up my fingers, down my wrist, over my arm, and into my core.

Biting the inside of my lip, I desperately try to burn away any sign of my arousal. But it's no use.

It's not the man, I tell myself. *It's the body. Who wouldn't be attracted to this body?*

Opening his mouth, so I catch the slightest glimpse of his thick wet tongue, Gabriel leans forward.

My racing heart freezes as he silently reaches towards my throat. I'm too stunned to move. Too confused with my body's reaction to fight back.

But he doesn't wrap his fingers around my neck.

Instead, his beefy forearm brushes up just beneath my jaw as he reaches for the strap of my nightgown.

Pinching the soft silk, he gently pulls it down my shoulder.

Not even the warmth of Gabriel's body can disguise the gust of cold air that washes over my exposed skin in response.

"You're a fast healer, princess. I'll give you that," Gabriel says.

Suddenly finding myself able to finally move again, I gaze down at my shoulder.

To my surprise, there's a shiny new wound there.

It looks like it's been slathered in some kind of cream—numbing, maybe? Because I can't feel it at all. Hell, I can't even feel the transparent bandage that's been placed over top of it.

"You did that?" I ask, my hand dropping down Gabriel's broad back an inch. "You treated my wound?"

"I didn't want you to hurt anymore, princess."

My hand drops further down his back as my body melts under his heat.

"I'm not hurt."

"That doesn't mean you shouldn't rest," with a deep breath, Gabriel leans back, and my hand falls completely off of him.

"Sleep, princess. Rest. Recover. You'll learn everything in due time. Now, do you have any other questions?"

He's teasing me. The moment got too tender. Gabriel couldn't have that.

But I'm nothing if not stubborn.

"Yes," I whisper, dragging my gaze away from the treated wound I didn't even know was there. "I have another question: stop calling me princess."

This is getting too intimate, too dangerous. I need to remind Gabriel of what we are.

Enemies.

This whole encounter has only solidified it. Whatever's happening, one thing is clear.

He's toying with me.

Like a wolf playing with his food.

"That's not a question," Gabriel points out, pushing himself back off the bed, away from me.

"And nothing you just told me was the truth," I respond, keeping my gaze drawn downwards. "You're trying to distract me. Stop it. What is this, Gabriel? Am I your hostage? Is my family dead?" Slowly, I manage to lift my eyes from the mattress and onto him. It's a long journey, filled with temptation and dread.

But it all ends when I meet those cosmic hazel-green eyes.

"What did I tell you about—"

"Tell me," I interrupt. "I order you."

My demand doesn't go over well.

"No. You don't get to order me around anymore," Gabriel booms, his blood red lips somehow twisting into a half smirk, half snarl. "Now, it's my turn to show you who's boss."

"I will never listen to you."

"Wrong. And I'll prove it to you right now. Stand up, princess. Stand up and take off that pretty little nightgown. Get naked for me. I order it."

A shock of fear trembles down my throat as I stare up at those ruthless hazel-green eyes.

"Or what?" I gulp, my bravery undercut by terror.

The snarling half of Gabriel's lips respond by twitching into a fully depraved, disturbingly sinful smirk.

"Or else I'll punish you."

6

GABRIEL

There it is.

The trembling lower lip. Softer than any pillow. More delicious than any delicacy. The most tempting sin.

She's intoxicating.

Even after I spent an hour scrubbing her down, cleaning her wound, washing blood and guts from her long auburn hair, Bianca still retains that vanilla scent of hers.

It's baked into her flesh. It's seared into my mind.

I *need* another taste.

"Everyone is dead."

The tender realization cascades down her face in a single tear.

It's not the kind of response I was expecting. And my deranged lust is almost stifled by the tenderness of my captive's sorrow.

She was being so strong—I could nearly see the queen I never thought she could become. Nearly.

"I never said that," I remind her.

"You didn't have to," Bianca whispers. Lifting her chin up at me, she exposes the shimmer in her crystal blue eyes. "You would never treat me this way if any of my family were still around to make you pay for it."

"I'm not a coward, princess. I do what I want, no matter the consequences."

"There's no way you *wanted* to be my bodyguard."

"I wanted you."

The revelation stuns us both. And a thick silence swirls between us as I wonder if I can shove that declaration back down my throat.

"Why?" Bianca gulps.

"It's a long story," I grumble, my gaze wandering down to her newly exposed clavicle.

Fuck. My cock is already throbbing.

Sure, Bianca was naked when I mended her earlier. She had to be. But I had lost enough blood to be foolishly chivalrous.

I looked only where I needed to look. I felt only where I needed to feel. And as soon as she was washed, I draped her tender innocence in that old nightgown, protecting her from my savage lust.

But now she's awake, and a primal desire rushes into my cock, pumping it full of hot, beastly blood.

"Do we not have time?" Sniffing away the tears, I watch as Bianca physically forces herself to be brave.

It's almost admirable.

Almost.

The way she wipes her nose makes her look as innocent as any lost doe.

Is she trying to manipulate me?

Or am I just softer than I fear?

"We have as much time as I say we do."

"And you want to spend it torturing me?"

"Who said anything about torture?"

"You want me to strip for you," Bianca sniffles. "That's torture."

Chewing on my tongue, I start to pace, circling my prey as I decide what to do next.

She's so vulnerable right now.

Sure, I could tell her everything and watch as the brutal truth crushes her. Forty-eight hours ago, I would have jumped at the opportunity. But now...

"And what if I repaid you for your obedience?" I ask, moving around the bed, studying my captive from every angle.

The sight of her fragile little shoulder blades makes me even harder.

"How could you possibly repay me for anything I do?" Bianca asks.

"By telling you what you want to know."

"You'll answer my questions?" Bianca rasps, peaking at me from over her tender shoulder.

"Yes," I reluctantly nod. "We can play a little game of truth or dare."

This is stupid. I should assert dominance over her right away. Shatter that stubborn spirit before she can even think to resist my might.

But my cock is doing all of the thinking now. And it's not sure how arousing another set of tears would be.

"Fine," Bianca says. Sucking in a deep, jittery breath, she rips her gaze away from me, looking forward again. "Let's play truth or dare."

To my surprise, she pushes herself off the bed.

"Well, well, well..." I can't help but smile. "Look at you."

"There, I did as you said. That was a dare. Now, I want a truth from you."

"My dare was to stand up and get naked," I remind her.

"No. You only get one thing at a time."

Before I can pick apart her terms, Bianca's neck snaps down.

A split-second later, she's falling.

But before she can hit the ground, I've lunged over the bed and caught her in my arms.

The warmth of her little body washes over me.

"You stood up too quickly, princess," I say, watching as her eyelids flutter back open. "Are you alright?"

"I... I'm fine," she mumbles, her brow furrowing as she tries to lift the weight I've forced upon her.

But all I see is that red scar above her left eye.

Fuck. It makes me so angry.

Killing the kid who did it to her hardly made me feel any better. It doesn't take back the fact that someone else was allowed to fuck with what's mine.

Even if Bianca may have been asking for it.

"Drink some water, and then we'll continue our game."

There isn't enough mercy in me to stop now. Sure, she needs to rest. But my cock is rock hard. I've waited long enough to get this close to the Byrne princess. I'm going to savor every moment of it.

Placing her back on the side of the bed, I reach over to the nightstand and grab the big glass of water I'd brought in while she was still passed out.

"No," Bianca mumbles, pulling away as I lift the glass up to her pretty pink lips.

"You're going to die of thirst just to fuck with me?"

"How do I know it's not drugged?"

"Because I'm not some loser frat boy," I growl. "Now, drink."

"It's not your turn to tell me what to do," she says, that stubborn fire lashing out, even through her deep and labored breaths.

"Yes, it is. You still aren't naked."

Shaking her head, Bianca rebuffs the water, and I reluctantly place it back down on the nightstand.

"Here," she grumbles, shooing me away with a limp wrist. "Back up and I'll give you your stupid show."

"Don't fall down again."

"I'll do whatever I want to do."

Her fire reaches down my throat, filling my chest with a strange heat, and I take a step back just to keep from being burned.

What the hell is going on here?

That attitude... it's holding up, even under this immense pressure.

It's not something I expected. But it's fucking captivating.

The scar suits her, after all. I want to see what she does next.

"Fine. I'll get you to fucking hydrate with my next turn. First, though, fulfill your dare. Stand up. Strip for me."

"I'll fucking strip for you alright," Bianca grumbles.

Taking a deep breath, she pushes herself off the bed one more time. My entire body tenses as she sways before me.

But she doesn't collapse.

Instead, she reaches up to the right strap of her nightgown and jerks it down. The soft silk doesn't fall down her body just yet, though. Not with those perky tits holding it up.

I can't help but bite my bottom lip as my eyes fall onto what's happened to her nipples. Even through the thick material, I can tell exactly how hard they are.

You and me both, darling.

"Almost there," I growl, my cock twitching beneath my pants, wild with anticipation.

"Yeah, I bet you are," Bianca snips. Then, with a cute little snarl scrunching her button nose, she rips off the rest of the nightgown.

It's hardly graceful. But I don't fucking care.

The sight of her naked form almost sends me flying off my feet.

"Good girl," I grumble, my fingers curling into fists as every inch of me begs to take her.

But I resist the urge.

Not yet.

She's not ready.

Better to build her into something strong than to shatter her into pieces.

Someday, she will have to be my queen—if even only for a short while. For long enough to give me an heir.

"Happy?" Bianca hisses.

"Yes," I quickly respond, almost delirious with lust. I can't stop imagining how tight that little pussy of hers would be. How my cock would disappear between her thigh gap. How I would fill her up with my cum.

I wonder if she's ever been fucked before?

"Good. Then, it's my turn. Tell me—"

"If I can give you some advice," I interrupt, snapping myself out of it. "Start small. I don't want you fainting again."

The warning hits Bianca like a cool breeze, and her flat stomach flexes against the realization of just how desperately fucked she might truly be.

"And if I don't?"

"Then I might have to catch you when you fall."

The faintest pink blush flushes through Bianca's cheeks as she rips her gaze down to the floor—a futile attempt to hide her shame... and her desire.

But there's no hiding how aroused she is. Not anymore. Her tits are on full display. Each one of her supple pink nipples is pitched like a fucking tent.

My tongue slips out and I wet my lips, imagining how good she must taste.

"Ask your question, princess. Before I reconsider my leniency."

A quick look of disgust flashes across her pretty face, before it's forcefully replaced by a mask of stubborn resignation.

"Start small, right?" she whispers, her eyes still planted on the floor.

"That would be wise."

"Alright. Then, how did I get into this nightgown?" she accuses, kicking the soft silk off from around her ankles.

"I put you in it," I easily reply.

"Why?"

"Because you needed something to take off for me."

That rips her gaze back onto me. I meet her fire with my own, straightening my back as her fury warms my very fucking soul.

I fucking love it.

"Why are you so obsessed with seeing me naked?" she hisses.

That makes me smile.

Should I tell her the truth?

That this is about asserting my dominance. That it's about showing off the power I hold over her. That I'm desperate to confirm a lingering suspicion. A suspicion that can only be confirmed by her uncovered body.

"No," I respond, shaking my head. "That's not a follow up to your question about the nightgown. Only one train of thought at a time, princess. Now, it's my turn."

"Fine," Bianca quickly huffs.

"I want a dare."

"That's not how the game works. I get to choose whether it's a truth or dare."

"Not when you're in my domain."

"So, I am your captive?"

"That can be your next question," I chuckle. "But you'll only get that far if you obey my next dare."

"Go ahead then," Bianca fumes. "Dare me."

Running a hand through my hair, I consider what exactly I want. The answer comes quickly enough.

"Get on your knees."

The fear in Bianca's crystal blue eyes only grows as I take a short step forward.

"I just stood up for you," she gulps.

"And you did it perfectly," I tease, pinching my fingers together. "Let's see if you can keep that streak going."

Bianca's jaw flexes and her stomach hardens as she takes my taunts. But her defiance only makes my cock even harder.

Oh, what I'm going to do to that body; to that mouth...

"You're an asshole. You've always been an asshole," Bianca huffs. Still, she does as she's told, stiffly sinking to her knees.

The sight of her kneeling before me is like a shot of adrenaline. My fingers tremble and my eyelids drop halfway down as I draw in a shaky breath.

I want her so fucking bad.

"Your turn, princess" I growl, barely restraining myself. "Truth or dare?"

"I choose a dare."

"Very well."

"Stop calling me princess."

The pettiness of her request nearly snaps me out of my lustful daze.

"That's what you're asking for? Really?"

"Yes."

"For how long?" I tease, lifting a brow at her.

"Forever."

"Deal. My turn."

I already know what I'm going to do next. My cock is about to rip through my pants. I need to loosen them up a little.

"Go ahead, then," Bianca snarls. But I can see a heavy gulp work down her throat as I move towards her. "What do you want?"

"Everything," I answer truthfully. Stopping half-a-foot in front of her, I stare down at the kneeling princess and breathe her in. "But for now, I'll settle for you undoing my belt."

I can practically see the smoke fuming from her nostrils as she fights back against the urge to give into my demand unchallenged.

She's clearly not just angry at me for making her do this.

She's angry because she wants to do it. She's mad at herself. Furious.

She wants me. Just like I always suspected. And she fucking hates it.

"Do I get to keep it?" Bianca snidely asks. But before I can even respond, she's reached up and started to dutifully unbuckle my belt.

"We'll see," I smile, heart pounding behind my chest.

Her thin forearms brush so close to my bulge that it starts to throb. Pre-cum lines the tip of my cock. I want her to see it all.

You're not the only one who's into this, princess. Not by a long shot.

When every buckle has been released, Bianca violently yanks my belt out, before dropping her hands to the floor. Still, she keeps the fine leather griped tightly between her tiny fingers.

"Give it here," I order, gesturing for the belt.

"No. You only get one dare per turn. Your dare was to take it off."

Every inch of me wants to lean down and squish her soft little cheeks between my fingers. I want to squeeze that defiance out of her. Drink it up. But I know that won't do any good.

I'm already wearing her down. And the anticipation is hotter than any use of force could ever be.

"Fine. Then it's your turn. Go quickly."

"I will go at whatever pace I please," she says, deepening her voice, mockingly imitating me.

This fucking girl.

Even naked and on her knees, she fights back.

That scar over her eye is starting to suit her better than I ever expected. But there's no point in fearing that my plan might not work out because of it anymore.

She's mine.

Instead, the scar signals something else—no longer a warning, it's quickly becoming a symbol of the endless opportunity ahead.

Perhaps she's truly tough enough to last as my queen.

"Truth or dare?" I ask.

"I want a truth."

Bianca must know that I would never grant a dare for her freedom. Letting her go just isn't an option, and I think she realizes that the best she's going to get are some answers.

"Ask away, little mouse."

"*Little mouse.* That's almost worse than princess," she grumbles.

"Would you like to change to a dare?"

"No," she defiantly sneers up at me. "I want the truth. Tell me: who the hell are you? Really."

Bending my knees, I crouch down until my gaze is level with hers. The heat swirling around us is intoxicating, but even more tempting than the thought of how I could use her body, is the memory of how her lips tasted.

"I am Gabriel Corso," I lie.

"No," Bianca responds, her voice turning raspy as she feels the same electricity I do. "That's not true." Her brows furrow, accentuating the jagged scar, just as she seems to remember something. "You... You told me it wasn't your real name..."

I can tell that she isn't sure if the memory is from a dream or not, and I let Bianca struggle for just a little bit longer as I wait for her to remember what happened just after my delirious confession.

"What else did I tell you?" I impatiently ask, pushing her towards the answer.

Fuck. I want to kiss her again so badly.

But what I want even more is for her to kiss me back. Just like she did in the darkness of that alleyway.

That won't happen if I take her by force.

"You... You..." Her eyes suddenly go wide, nearly popping out of her head. "Did... Did you kiss me?"

"Yes."

"Why?"

Reaching down, I grab hold of my belt and gently slip it out of her hands.

"Because you were fading on me, pri—Bianca. I needed to shock you back awake, and I didn't have jumper cables."

"So, you kissed me?"

"And you kissed me back."

"No..."

"Yes."

"I... I was delusional."

"So was I. But I know you liked it. Just like how I know you like this. Kneeling naked in front of your master."

"You're not my master," she croaks, a horrible realization dawning on her.

"Not quite yet," I admit. "But we're getting there. And it's my turn."

Bianca is too lost in her own thoughts to fight back as I lift the belt from the floor and tenderly begin to wrap it around her throat.

Even as I tighten the leather, pulling until I've found the perfect buckle, she hardly reacts. Her crystal blue eyes dart back and forth trying to make sense of the searing memory we both share.

The kiss.

Finally, I'm able to snap her back to reality. With a stern tug on her new choker, I cut off enough air to force her to concentrate.

"What are you doing?" she rasps.

"Claiming you."

"Why?"

"That question will have to wait until it's your turn again."

Through the tight leather, I can feel a heavy gulp slide down Bianca's tender throat.

"What do you want?"

"A dare."

"What else could I possibly do?"

Only one thought occupies my mind. It's the only option.

"I want you to kiss me again."

Those crystal blue eyes shimmer with uncertainty... or maybe it's just that my belt is wrapped too tightly around her throat. Either way, it doesn't stop Bianca from blushing.

A pretty pink hue fills her cheeks. Her gaze drops. My hand lifts.

Pinching her chin, I force those crystal blue eyes back onto me.

"Dare you," I whisper.

That's all it takes. She's too competitive for her own good.

Closing her eyes, Bianca takes a deep breath, then leans forward.

The next thing I know, my eyes have closed too.

Our lips meet, and the electricity that pricks the air explodes, rushing through our lips, and into our bodies.

The kiss fills me up with an unexpected feeling. Something that I have trouble grasping as we taste each other with a careful desire.

Bianca's warmth fills my chest and grabs my heart. I just want to wrap her up and protect her from all of this darkness.

But I know I can't do that. Not yet.

"Who are you?" Bianca whispers, when our lips finally fall apart. Her voice is so soft, yet so coarse. And her question is filled with equal parts terror and sincerity.

"I am the man who's committed his entire adult life to

capturing you," I confess. "And now, you're mine. But that's not enough."

"What could I possibly give you?" she rasps, terror overcoming the sincerity.

"Everything," I declare. "You are my key to everything."

It's hard to tell what's sincere and what's a product of the oxygen deprivation.

Either way, Gabriel's belt isn't nearly as suffocating as his words.

What the hell is going on?

Before I can think to use my turn to ask him, the sinfully gorgeous wolf has unbuckled my skin-tight choker and pulled it loose from around my throat.

The heat from his massive bulge brushes past my burning cheeks as he stands up. Taking a step back, he re-holsters his belt, thick forearms flexing with frustration as he tightens the leather back around his waist.

"This game is over," he announces. A low simmering fury paints his features. But it's mixed in with something else. Something I can't quite pinpoint.

Regret? Disappointment? Fear?

It's impossible to tell. But whatever it is, Gabriel isn't enjoying it.

Without another word, the hulking, shirtless wolf turns his back to me and storms away.

Somehow, even through the building tears blurring my vision, I can see the scars hiding beneath his tattoos. I can still feel them against my fingertips.

How did I ever miss them?

"Gabriel..." I croak after him. It feels like I'm lost in a dark ocean, alone, watching a black ship sail away.

Throw me a lifesaver...

"I'll bring you some food," is all he says, stopping briefly at the door. Pulling open the handle, he looks over his shoulder, towards the nightstand. "Drink the water. You'll need all of your strength."

With that, he steps out into the hallway and clicks the door shut behind him. A moment later, I hear the turning of a lock as I'm secured back into this confusing prison.

The walls must be thick, because I can't hear Gabriel's heavy footsteps march away, but I feel his presence leave, abandoning me to the black waters.

It's somehow his most gutting act.

The teasing. The taunts. The dares. The belt.

The kiss.

The tenderness.

It all swirls around in my unhinged mind, clashing against each other as I'm thrown back and forth against the dark waves.

We kissed.

He asked me to kiss him, and that's exactly what I did.

But it wasn't forced. He didn't push me.

He dared me.

And part of me smiled when he did.

None of me is smiling anymore, though.

I'm drowning.

The only consolation to any of this is that Gabriel didn't reach between my legs before he left.

If he had, I'd have been completely compromised.

I'm soaked, aroused in the dirtiest way.

For a moment there, I wanted to spit in his face... but only so he would punish me. Lift me up by the leather choker around my throat, throw me onto the bed, and wreck me.

Not that Gabriel couldn't tell I was turned the fuck on.

He saw my nipples. He felt the way I gave in to the restrained passion of our kiss.

A deep, jagged breath escapes my nostrils as I really process what just happened.

Gabriel Corso and I just fucking kissed.

Somehow, that's even more shocking than the confirmation that Gabriel Corso isn't his real name—or the fact that he's clearly fucking kidnapped me.

From the day I accidentally spilled hot coffee on him, I've been almost expecting the wolf to slip out of the shadows and drag me back to his den. To punish me for marking him.

He always seemed like the type.

But to kiss me? Like that?

To save me from an ambush and fix me up? To act like he cares about my well-being, even if only briefly?

It's enough to pull me to my feet. Otherwise, I might have sunk into the darkness forever.

Lifting my hand up to my throat, I trace the throbbing outline of the mark he's left on me.

Why was that so fucking hot? Why was any of that so fucking hot?

Playing a twisted game of truth or dare with my high school bully sounds like a nightmare. But as I sit down on the bed and close my eyes, all I can imagine are the dirtiest of dreams.

The pressure in my core has gone nuclear. My pussy is soaked. When my eyes open, my hand is between my thighs, fingers on my clit.

There's no stopping it. I start to rub, to play with myself like Gabriel just played with me.

My own hand doesn't feel nearly as good as his, though—at

least, not until I close my eyes again and picture those thick fingers softly pinching my clit, then sliding down to slip inside my soaking little hole.

It doesn't take long before the swirling pressure in my core cracks. A deep warmth races out, ravaging every inch of my body from the inside out.

If my throat wasn't so sore, I'm sure I would be screaming. But all I can manage are a few deep, raspy breaths.

No one has ever dared touch me like that before.

Soon enough, the pleasure blankets me, and I'm pulled out of the black ocean that Gabriel left behind.

But the warmth doesn't last for long. And before I can sink into the afterglow of my orgasm, I'm forced awake; pushed back into the vast, cold bedroom I'm locked up in.

When my eyes open again, all I feel is emptiness... and shame.

What have I done?

A humiliating warmth replaces the cold emptiness as I rip my hand out from between my legs.

I want to slap myself.

How could I fall so easily for such an obvious monster?

Gabriel played me.

Despite our little game of truth or dare, no important answers were given. No great secrets revealed. Only little bits of information were teased to me.

What happened to Rian? Uncle Maksim? Is Dad alright? Mom? Who ambushed us? Why did Gabriel take me?

You are my key to everything.

What the hell does that even mean?

The unknown implication behind his deep, dark words threatens to eat me from the inside out. I'm desperate to know the truth.

But even just the thought of being forced into another

depraved game of truth or dare with Gabriel sends a boulder of dread rolling through my gut.

So, I wipe the possibility from my mind, and instead try to focus on something else. Something more imminently important.

My dry mouth.

I'm parched. And the big glass of water on the nightstand looks almost as tempting as Gabriel's broad chest and muscular back.

But the stubborn side of me doesn't want to give in again. To do what *he* wants.

It's a stupid instinct, and I manage to fight through it easily enough.

There's no point in dying here. Whatever's happening, I need to survive—at least long enough to get answers, if not some fucking revenge too.

The water is somehow still cool as I chug it down. Still, it hardly helps the searing mark that Gabriel has claimed me with.

Not even my rumbling stomach can drag my attention away from the memory of his touch. It was so terrifyingly powerful. So careless. Yet somehow so immensely tender.

Placing the empty glass back on the nightstand, I open up the bottom drawer. Anything to distract myself from the lingering taste of Gabriel's lips, or the horrors of what's possibly happened to my family—let alone what's about to happen to me.

But there's nothing in the first drawer. Nothing in the second, either. Thankfully, the top one is filled to the brim.

It takes me a second to recognize what's inside.

Medical supplies.

Gauze tape, bandages, Neosporin, numbing cream, fresh IV tubes.

Shit.

Did Gabriel bring in an entire medical team just to keep me alive?

No. He said it himself. My injury wasn't that bad. I was only grazed by a bullet.

Hell, the first fucking thing he did when I woke up was make fun of me for being so dramatic. As if I could help how my body reacts to being fucking shot.

Still, it must have been more serious than he let on. I was out for what, two days? That doesn't happen from a scrape.

Unless Gabriel was drugging me.

Reaching across my naked chest, I gently touch the big translucent band aid draped over the red wound on my shoulder.

It's completely numb. I'm at least thankful for that—especially as the scar above my eye gently throbs.

What a hellish month this has been. Two life-altering scars in the span of two weeks.

Maybe Mom was right when she said I needed to take a deep breath and slow down.

Fuck.

Mom.

She was so proud of me for what I was doing at school. It's the only reason I even went through with university. Being an academic was never part of my dreams—but I was willing to put up with it for four years for Mom's sake.

After that, I'd be free. At least, I was supposed to be free.

I was supposed to be able to do whatever I wanted.

And that would have meant becoming more like Dad. A leader. A killer. A tough guy.

But Mom is tough too. And smart.

She knew better. I was going off the rails, trying to be like my old man.

I wasn't ready. I overstepped. Now, I'm more trapped than ever before.

Fuck.

Even that God-forsaken island would have been a thousand times better than this.

At least there, I would have been surrounded by people who cared about me.

No matter how tender Gabriel's kisses have been, he doesn't care about me. Only what I can do for him. What he can use me for.

You are my key to everything.

What the hell does that even mean?

My stomach rumbles again as I look over towards the half-open bathroom door. Shit. I could really use a hot shower.

But for some reason, I just can't bring myself to get off the bed. Without Gabriel here to prod me, I feel completely drained.

All I can do is get lost in my own head.

Gabriel must have tended to my wound all on his own. He would have stripped me naked and washed me off and fixed me up.

Somehow, I know he didn't take advantage of my vulnerability. I'm a virgin, after all. I'd feel if something was different. Right?

But how could a monster be so gentle?

You don't know that he was, an inner voice stubbornly fights back. *He could have easily drugged and raped you. You're a virgin. You don't know how it would feel afterwards.*

But that stubborn voice doesn't feel like it has any teeth. No matter how much of an asshole he is. How much of a monster. Gabriel just doesn't feel like the type.

And I know the type. One of those assholes gave me the scar above my eye. That ugly frat boy had no choice but to spike drinks.

But Gabriel is so different.

In high school, he had to step over mountains of girls just to get to class. And as much as I hate to admit it, he's even more handsome now—if just in a darker and more terrifyingly rugged kind of way.

Slipping onto my back, I rest my gently throbbing skull against the pillow and stare up at the ceiling.

The subtle scent I woke up to floats back into my nostrils, and I slowly realize why it was so oddly familiar.

Fresh rain.

It's Gabriel.

He's used this pillow before.

But what the hell does that mean? Is this empty room his bedroom? Is this his house?

I have no idea where I am. But it seems fitting that someone as mysterious as him would have at least one room without windows.

Where else would he hide his captives?

Suddenly, a disturbing thought tenses my entire body.

Did Gabriel kill the congressmen's daughter?

The thought worms its way down my spine until it's sitting like a fucking mountain in my gut.

Could he have been the one who was trying to kidnap Italian mafia princesses out east?

Maybe he didn't fail at all. Maybe those attempts were just practice. A threat to put the chess pieces into play, so that he could make his move.

You are my key to everything.

His words become more and more threatening every time they rattle through the blackness of my mind.

I didn't think Gabriel was the kind of person to drug and rape a girl, but if he could kill one—and a congressman's daughter at that—even just for practice, then he's truly capable of anything.

Every inch of me jumps when the eerie silence of the empty bedroom is broken by a sound that's already horribly familiar.

Someone is unlocking my door. The handle clicks open, sending a shiver of dread prickling over my skin.

That was fast. Too fast. I've barely even had time to breathe, and my monstrous captor is already back.

What kind of sick twisted game will he make me play now?

8

GABRIEL

The second I see Bianca's big shimmering eyes, a small knot of guilt tightens in my gut.

She hasn't eaten solid food in almost two days now, and I just made her wait another hour—and for what? So I could jerk off until my veins bulged and my toes curled?

No. It wasn't just so I could jerk off. It was so I could control myself when I returned with her food. I needed to free myself of the desire that invaded my mind earlier. I needed to furiously stroke it away. Expel it from my throbbing cock in stream after stream of thick creamy cum.

Sure, I might have clogged the drain in my shower, but it was worth it. My head is clear and my mind is sharp.

In about an hour, I'll be walking into an all-important meeting, and I'm not sure I would have been able to pull myself back out of this bedroom if I hadn't relieved myself first.

Now, at least, I have a chance.

"Eat this," I mumble to Bianca.

The tray I've brought up from the kitchen is filled with all sorts of food. A cold cut sandwich, a bowl of soup I just heated up, some sliced fruit, a pitcher of fresh glacial water, and even some fucking cookies.

Bianca doesn't look like she eats much, but this might have to last her a while.

I'm not so sure when I'll make it back to feed her again. And I'm certainly not letting her out of this room.

She has enough of my respect now for me to understand that giving her even the slightest bit of space is dangerous. She'll take full advantage of any slip up.

It's why she kissed me back, after all.

"I'm not hungry," Bianca stubbornly lies, yanking her bedsheet up to her shoulders so I can't get another look at her delectable little body.

It's for the best. Even just the glimpse of her naked collarbone has me half-hard again.

"Sorry, I couldn't hear you over your rumbling stomach," I tease, clenching my fist in a futile attempt to divert blood from my already growing cock.

"You must be hearing things," Bianca quickly replies. "Maybe you're losing your mind?"

If only she knew the half of it. I've been through so much over the past month. But somehow, none of it compares to that fucking kiss we just shared.

It threw everything upside down.

Nothing in my life has ever felt as real as that one burning moment. It was too much.

I had to pull away. But here I am, back at the scene of the crime—like a fucking psychopath.

"The world has lost its mind," I grumble down at her. Her plump lower lip is trembling again.

Fucking hell...

"You don't need to tell me."

"Then what do I need to tell you? That you're not going to survive this if you don't eat?"

"You need to tell me what '*this*' is first."

"*This* is none of your business."

"Excuse me?" Bianca croaks. "How the hell is this none of my business? Am I not involved in my own kidnapping?"

"Who said you were kidnapped?"

"You really have a shit memory, don't you?" my fiery captive sneers. "Or was I dreaming when you said that you'd committed your entire adult life to capturing me?"

"*Kid*napping someone is different than *capturing* them," I respond, unable to help myself. "Unless you think of yourself as a child?"

"Fuck your semantic bullshit. I don't want to hear it."

"What do you want to hear?"

"The truth. I want to know what the fuck is happening."

"No you don't," I warn her.

"Try me."

"Eat," I insist, turning my back to the bed. "If all of that food is gone by the time I return, then I will take it as a sign you're serious about playing with the big boys."

"... You should have died in that cellar," Bianca hisses in response. "The second I recognized you, I should have told my father and watched as he cut your throat."

The sudden savagery in her voice yanks my gaze back over my shoulder.

"You should have," I quietly agree, my eyes tightening into slits as I consider the levels of depravity this little princess could be capable of. Fuck. I can't wait to test her limits. "... But then who would have given you your first kiss?"

Just like that, the ruthless mask is torn from her face, revealing the scared, fragile girl beneath it all.

The guilt returns to my gut. The dark curiosity fades away.

"I... I've been kissed before," she mumbles, her plump bottom lip dropping.

My cock lifts in response. Those thick pillow lips would have to stretch so thin to fit me inside...

"You've been kissed like that before?" I meet her.

"I...I..." The truth of my taunt hits her like a speeding train, and she can't even finish her thought.

It's clear to me that she can't think straight while the searing memory of our kiss runs wild through her mind.

Welcome to the club, honey.

"That's what I thought," I say. Running a hand through my hair, I turn back towards the door and head for the hallway.

"Where are you going?" Bianca calls after me.

"Now *that* is none of your business," I smile, stopping in the doorway for one last look at my captive princess.

She looks like a fucking angel. Perfect in every way. So innocent. So fragile.

So broken.

My heart sinks as I realize that I don't actually like seeing her broken like this. Maybe I've gone too far again.

It's that fire of hers that really turns me on. The warrior queen hiding behind the sheltered princess. That's what I want to uncover.

I'm just not so sure I'll be able to rip it out of Bianca without shattering her first.

Still, the thought occupies my mind, and for a moment, we just stare at each other, unsure of what to do next.

But then I snap to.

I've got shit to do. Important fucking shit.

Like doing whatever I can to keep her safe.

Because I'm not the only one after the Byrne princess. But I might be the only one who's determined to keep her alive.

Slamming the bedroom door shut behind me, I sever our glance.

Still, those shimmering blue doe-eyes linger in my mind. Even as I step down the cold, lonely hallway ahead.

Bianca isn't the only one in this house who's unsure about what the hell is happening.

Drago hasn't been honest with me. Not completely.

And I'm about to go find out just what the fuck he's hiding.

———————

"Be careful, Gabe," Tytus warns. "You know how Drago deals with dissention."

"Who said anything about dissention?" I grumble. "I'm just looking for answers."

"We've already told you everything we know," Roz points out, racing to keep up with us.

"What you know isn't enough," I tell her. "And it's definitely not the full story. Why the hell would Drago be so reckless with Bianca's life? I've spent years trying to capture her alive. And he just orders an all-out attack on her motorcade? She was fucking shot, Roz. No matter how we all feel about Bianca Byrne, someday she'll be my wife. The mother of my heir. The key to my kingdom..."

"*Our* kingdom," Roz corrects.

"You know what I mean."

"It wasn't supposed to be an all-out attack," Tytus jumps in. "Just an ambush. But I guess Krol got excited. You know how that bastard can be."

"I swear to god, if Drago tries to pin this shit on Krol..."

"He will. As he should," Roz says. "Everyone—including us —were following Krol's commands. He led the operation. He gave the orders. He told us not to leave any survivors."

"No survivors?" I growl, fists tightening as I march forward down the vast, overgrown subterranean tunnel.

"Except you and Bianca, of course," Tytus is quick to recover.

The deeper we descend into the darkness of this abandoned subway route, the brighter my rage becomes.

Roz and Tytus are my friends. Hell, they're more than just friends. They're my adopted family. If anyone was supposed to have my back, it's them.

Instead, they followed Krol's every command, staying just far enough away from the ambush to ensure there wasn't a single friendly face to help me the fuck out.

"I'm sorry we weren't there until the end," Roz says. "We were just following orders."

"Orders to come in after the battle and pick up the two corpses with tracking devices on them?" I snidely ask.

"We're not lying when we say there wasn't a bounty on your head," Roz tries to assure me.

"Or on hers," Tytus adds.

Fuck. I believe them. Up until two days ago, I usually didn't question my orders much either.

But then Bianca started bleeding, and we shared that first delirious kiss...

"It's alright. I'm not angry at you two," I try to assure them, even if I am frustrated as fuck. "It's Drago I'm pissed at. It's Krol I want to kill."

"Well, then let's stop here and take a second to calm the fuck down," Roz warns. "Fighting those two isn't going to settle anything."

"I'm not going to fight anyone," I lie, entirely ready to split Krol's skull open.

"Then what are you planning to do?"

"I'm planning to get answers."

"And if they don't give you any?"

"Then I plan to keep the Byrne princess completely for myself," I growl, knowing full well that no matter what happens next, I will be keeping Bianca anyway.

"You know Drago won't let you do that," Roz mumbles.

"I'm well aware."

"So what will you do when he tells you to fuck off?"

"I'll tell him to come find me."

"Fucking hell," Tytus grumbles, stopping just ahead of me. Turning around, the giant blocks me from continuing forward. "You know you're putting us in a world of shit too? What do you think will happen to us if Drago finds out we helped you dissolve Roz's trackers?"

"I don't want to stand around in this depressing fucking tunnel all day, Ty," I bark. Still, I stop in my tracks before I can crash into his hulking body.

Tytus and I have fought before. It's not pretty. There's no point in getting into it here. Especially not with Bianca waiting back home for me.

No one knows about the place I'm keeping her. The grey house is my little secret. A piece of property that I've managed to keep hidden from everyone else—even Drago.

"He won't believe that we don't know where you're keeping her," Roz says from behind me.

"But you don't know," I remind her. "After you helped me, you dropped us off in the middle of nowhere, remember?"

"It doesn't matter what the truth is," Roz sighs. "Drago won't believe it."

Her breathy voice swirls through the darkness as I stand between my two oldest friends. They're right to be worried. Both about the plan going awry and of Drago's wrath.

"I'll make sure nothing happens to you guys," I say.

"We can look after ourselves," Roz and Tytus both reply at the exact same time.

"It's you we're worried about," Roz says.

"We're worried you've become a little too obsessed with the girl," Tytus adds.

That sets a fucking nuclear reactor off inside of me. "Look, it wasn't my idea to involve Bianca fucking Byrne in all of this shit," I remind them. "We were barely adults when Drago came up with this stupid fucking plan. When he made me fake my age and go to a fucking preppy California high school to play popular kid in a desperate attempt to get close to Ray Byrne's daughter. It wasn't my idea to come back to her either, not after all these years. I'm not obsessed with the girl," I lie. "I'm following orders, just like you two were. Fuck. If I'm obsessed with anything, it's with what she can bring me."

"Everything," Tytus nods. "She can bring *us* everything."

"But only if she remains alive," I huff. Leaning down, I roll up my pant leg, revealing my bandaged wound. It doesn't hurt anymore, but it will leave a scar. A memory that I will have forever. "Only if *I* remain alive."

My point is well served, and I can see the look of determination come across Tytus' rugged face.

"We'll back you up," Roz says from behind me. "You know we always will."

Tytus nods in agreement.

"But don't expect this to go well," Roz warns, referring to the meeting I've requested with our leader, serpent of the shadows, ghost of the old country, the feared Dragomir fucking Raclaw.

"I never expect anything to go well," I grumble.

That draws a stifled laugh from both Tytus and Roz.

"Let's get the hell out of here," Tytus says. Shaking his head, he turns those broad shoulders around and starts moving again.

Without another word, I follow him into the darkness, ready for the fight of my life.

Whatever happens, it will be well worth it.

Bianca is mine. And mine only. Mine to imprison. Mine to tease. Mine to kiss and fuck and impregnate.

Mine to marry.

And mine to protect.

Even Drago Raclaw needs to learn that.

And I'm about to make sure he knows just how fucking serious I am.

9

GABRIEL

"Where is the girl?"

I can practically smell Krol's putrid breath from across the gilded room.

It doesn't matter that Drago's base is set up a hundred feet below the ground, he's done his best to recapture the ancient sense of underworld royalty he was once brutally deprived of.

It's that sense of power that we're all still chasing—even if we are slowly starting to disagree on how we're going to finally fucking catch it.

"She'd be buried six feet under if you'd had your way," I snarl back. Krol always finds a way to get under my skin. But this time is different.

He was in charge when Bianca was almost killed. I'm not going to fucking stand for that.

"I ordered my men to shoot anyone who looked Irish or Italian," Krol shrugs, his withered face stuck half way between a sneer and a disgusting smirk. "I guess you're starting to look like a mick—or maybe more of a wop."

Tilting his head to the side, he mockingly studies me.

"Yeah, I could definitely see how you could be mistaken for a dirty fucking wop."

"I swear to God, Krol," I growl, fists clenching into brutal weapons.

"Try me, little prince."

"You don't have to ask me twice."

I'm only allowed to take one step forward before Tytus lifts his heavy arm across my chest.

My friendly beast stays silent, but I feel his nervous energy. It's directed over to the center of the room, where Drago leans against a large mahogany desk.

"Is that all?" Drago asks, his calm tone undercut by a threatening impatience.

"I'm doing just fine," Krol says. "It's the pretty boy who always seems to have a problem."

Forcing myself to ignore the fucking serpent, I step back from Tytus' raised arm and look towards the man who is supposed to be my adoptive father.

"Who were those men who you sent to ambush us?" I ask, gently trying to divert attention away from Bianca's whereabouts. "I didn't recognize any of them."

"They were expendable contractors," Drago calmly explains. But I've known him long enough to hear the fury bubbling just beneath his words. "They did what they were paid to do. And then they all died like they were supposed to."

"And who told them to shoot the Byrne princess. You or Krol?"

Drago's black eyes dig deep into my soul as he silently challenges me to question him again.

"No one was supposed to kill that bitch," Krol spits. "Or you, for that matter—though, you're making me wish I had put a bounty on your fucking head."

"If you didn't order them to shoot her or me, then that

means you must be fucking incompetent as hell, right? Because we both got fucking shot."

"I heard that the princess was only grazed," Drago says, his deep voice lifting as he stands up from the edge of his desk. "And I barely see a limp on you anymore. From what I understand, you weren't even shot. Am I supposed to think that the fearsome *Gabryjel* Corso is bothered by a bit of shrapnel?"

Fuck. Someone must have let the true nature of our injuries slip. It could only have been Tytus or Roz. They were the only ones there, after all.

Out of the corner of my eye, I see Roz's head drop ever so slightly. I know that look. It was her. But it wasn't on purpose. Sometimes, she can talk too much.

I'm not mad. Not at her. How could I be? Especially after she helped dissolve her own state-of-the-art tracking device from under Bianca's skin, and mine.

Sure, I had to knock Bianca out for an extra day so that she wouldn't feel the intense pain of the process. But it was well worth it to know that I'm the only one in this entire fucking world who knows where she is.

Grinding my teeth, I remember the acidic burn of the neutralizer Roz injected under my skin. I'll be having night-mares about that for the rest of my life.

But at least Bianca won't have to remember the agony.

"Are you listening, *boy*?" Krol barks from his corner.

"Yes," I grumble back, keeping my gaze peeled ahead. *Stay focused, Gabriel.* "But I've decided to no longer respond to my fake name."

Corso.

For as much as I hate the phony last name, it's not the real reason I'm bringing it up now. No. I'm just trying to bide my time until I can figure out how to keep Drago away from Bianca.

"Is your name not *Gabryjel* anymore?" Drago asks, his black brow lifting in my direction.

"It may be. But I don't want to be called Corso anymore. Tell me my real name."

"No," Drago responds, venom lacing his tone. Finally, the fury is bubbling over. "Not until you've earned it."

"Then tell me what to do next."

"Give me the girl."

Fucking hell. So much for biding some time.

"No."

I can practically hear Roz's head snap back up. Out of the corner of my eye, I see Tytus straighten up too.

They both knew I was planning on standing my ground against Drago. But none of us have ever dared to be this direct.

"Excuse me?" Krol immediately responds for his master. "How fucking dare—"

Raising his hand into the air, Drago shuts his lapdog up with a single motion.

But I was never worried about Krol. If push comes to shove, I could kill Krol, even if he'd probably manage to take a chunk out of me first.

Drago, however... Even if I got the upper hand, could I really kill the man who took me in when I had nothing and no one? Could I end or journey together like that? After he's promised me the world?

"Don't let your little crush get in the way of our destiny, *Gabryjel*," Drago quietly warns, his voice shaking ever so slightly—the tremors before an eruption. "This is not a game."

"I'm not playing," I respond, dead fucking serious.

"But are you lying?"

"To who?"

"To me. And to yourself."

"Have I ever managed to sneak a lie past you?" I test him. The truth is, I have, if even just a handful of times over the course of my life. But more often than not, Drago is able to see past my deception.

Not this time. I won't let him. He doesn't need to know of all the games I've already played with Bianca. And of how she's inadvertently playing with me too.

"So, the truth is that your tracking devices got scrambled in the ambush? That's why they aren't sending a signal anymore? The truth is that you no longer trust me with the safety of your captive, because of how Krol handled the ambush? The truth is that you think you know the plan better than I do? That you are willing to put the fate of everyone here in the palm of your hand? That you can handle it?"

All I can do is stand tall and take Drago's accusation with a stony face.

"My answers are all the same: yes," I bluff, hoping that Roz and Tytus can keep the lie going for as long as I can.

"Fine," Drago nods, his sharp black eyes cutting through me. "Keep the girl for yourself. As long as she's safe, it doesn't matter. Not right now. But I'm holding you personally responsible for her well-being. And when the black priests arrive from the motherland, you will reveal your bride to us all once again. Understand?"

"So be it."

Clearly, my lies haven't been accepted as wholly as I hoped. Drago is violently suspicious, but he's being smart enough not to push me. Not yet.

There's no point in starting a civil war before he can reap the benefits of my inheritance.

"Rozalia," Drago says, snidely turning his attention away from me. "Make more of those tracking devices."

"Yes, sir," Roz dutifully nods. "But it might take a while. I'll need to find the specific ingredients."

"Tytus, get your sister what she needs."

"Yes, sir."

"Good. Now go."

With a single wave of his hand, Drago sends my only two allies back into the darkness outside. But they leave behind a sliver of warmth.

Thanks to them, I will have the time I need to figure out my next move.

When the door closes behind them, Drago gestures at Krol. "You wait outside. I'd like to speak to my son alone."

Krol's face twists in disgust at that word. *Son.* He hates that I get the title and he doesn't—even if it wouldn't make sense for him. The lapdog is old enough to be Drago's younger brother.

It's pathetic.

"Sir, I—"

"Leave," Drago orders once more.

He never asks twice, and Krol reluctantly obeys, making sure to brush awfully close to my shoulder on his way out.

When the door slams shut behind him, Drago turns his back to me. Circling around his desk, he opens a drawer and pulls out a matchbox and a Cuban cigar.

"Come here," he says, gesturing me forward.

When I'm close enough, he reaches out and hands me the matchbox. Then, he leans across his desk, cigar in his mouth.

"I'm not a kid anymore," I sneer, realizing what he's doing.

"Clearly," Drago replies, not budging. "You used to love lighting my cigars when you were younger."

"I liked feeling useful."

"I know. And I've always done my best to make sure you knew just how useful you could be. It's why I finally told you about your ancestry. About your bloody history. About your parents and their kingdom and those who ripped it all away. So that you would understand that you are more than useful. *Gabryjel.* You are the only way I will ever become whole again. We will take back what's ours. But not if we fall to in-fighting first."

"You almost had me killed," I remind him. *And Bianca.*

"That was Krol. But it was my mistake to trust him around something so fragile. You know the man well enough. He's like a bull in a china shop. We're just lucky you were there to save the most delicate item."

Drago is trying to comfort me, but all I can see is the gut-churning image of Bianca bleeding out on that alley floor.

"I'm just doing my job," I grumble. Finally, I give in and strike a match, lighting Drago's cigar before throwing the box back down onto his desk.

"This isn't a job," Drago says, after taking a long puff. "This is destiny."

"We won't know that it is until the dust has settled."

"I've already seen enough," Drago says. A smoke ring floats from his thin lips, hovering just past my ear. "You're finally starting to like this girl."

"I'm starting to like the idea of becoming king, and she's the only way that's going to happen," I try to deflect.

"It's true," Drago nods. "But it's always nice to have some kind of affection for your pawns. It makes it easier to spend the necessary time with them."

"But harder to betray," I hear myself mumble under my breath. Immediately, I regret saying the words out loud. They make it sound like I'm having doubts.

I'm not. For this plan to work, I don't have to betray Bianca in the end. She could become my queen...

But first, she needs to survive being my captive.

"I'm glad that you've at least come around to this plan," Drago sighs, taking another puff of his cigar. "Is the girl alright?"

"Yes."

"Are you alright?

"Yes."

"Good. Because I have more work for you."

The announcement doesn't surprise me. Adoptive father or not, Drago has always found ways to put me to work.

"Tell me what to do," I respond, subtly crossing my fingers, hoping that whatever this job is, it won't keep me away from Bianca for too long.

I already crave her like crazy. I need more. More of those crystal blue eyes. More of those soft pink lips, that tender throat, her tight body, those perky tits.

Most of all, I need more of her fire.

It's cold down here in hell. But somehow she manages to make it a whole lot fucking hotter.

"Are you still willing to do whatever it takes to regain the crown that was stolen from you?"

"Yes," I growl.

"Whatever it takes to make those responsible pay for what they've done?"

"Yes," I respond, with far less conviction.

For as little as I know about my past, Drago has let a few details slip.

I know that Polish drug lords killed my father. I know they chased my mother to America. I know they couldn't find her, so in response, they extinguished every trace of our family from the motherland.

I know if they hadn't done that, I might already be king of the Polish mafia—one of the most ancient and feared underground syndicates to ever exist.

I also know that I will never have the satisfaction of getting my revenge on those drug smuggling fuckers, because the Kilpatricks wiped them all out decades ago.

But most clearly of all, I know that my mother survived the purge... until Ray Byrne found her.

Until Ray Byrne killed her.

My fists clench and my chest tightens as I remind myself of what I need to do. Perhaps Bianca will become more than just my captive someday... but after I do what needs to be done, could she ever really become my queen?

"Ray Byrne will die," I assure Drago. "I will make sure of it."

"Good," Drago nods. Finding an ashtray, he rids himself of his smoky cigar.

"But revenge won't keep us in power. Sure, it may fuel us now, but once we have wiped out our enemies, we will still need to rule."

"I understand."

"Do you understand that power is leverage?"

"Yes," I grumble, becoming impatient. *Just tell me what I need to do so I can get back to my captured princess.*

"I knew you would," Drago says, pursing his lips. "It is for that reason that I need you to return to the Byrne family."

It takes me a second to process what I just heard, but when I do, my stomach drops a hundred feet deeper than this fucking underground lair.

Whatever kind of hellish task I was expecting, it definitely wasn't that. Anything but fucking that.

"What?" I blurt out, unable to control my disbelief.

"You need to get close to Rian Kilpatrick. It's absolutely essential to our future struggle to stay in power."

For a moment, my outrage is bottled and a flash of relief passes through me.

"He's still alive?"

"Yes. The lion managed to kill the last of our men and escape."

Shaking my head, I try to rid myself of the warm relief lapping against the inside of my chest.

I'd just assumed he was dead. Fuck. I was dreading Bianca's reaction to the news.

But he's not dead. And that's somehow even worse.

The lion is alive. And probably engulfed with fury about

the disappearance of his cousin. The same cousin he last saw *me* with.

"What the fuck does Rian Kilpatrick have to do with our power struggles?" I foolishly ask. "Drago, this is fucking suicide."

"No. It's not suicide," he shakes his head. "It's necessary."

"They'll kill me on sight!" I shout. "If they weren't suspicious of me before, then they definitely will be now!"

"They'll probably handle you roughly at first," Drago responds. "Hell, they might even torture you a bit. But I have an alibi all lined up for you. As well as a suspect that you can all hunt down together."

"Why would they ever believe me? I was already on thin ice. Ray—"

"They will be desperate," Drago interrupts, lifting his hand in the air to quell me. "They will want answers. They will want a life to end. A villain to disintegrate. And you will have a very detailed description of just the man they're looking for."

"Who the fuck could I possibly use to convince them I wasn't involved in Bianca's disappearance?"

"Me," Drago smiles. "You will lead them to me."

It's another unexpected blow. Drago is running fucking circles around me.

"A trap?" I try to catch up, blinking away the stars in my vision.

"Precisely. Ray Byrne will do anything to save his daughter. And that includes following you into the mouth of the monster."

"You promised me I could kill him," I mumble under my breath, unsure of how to feel. Just a moment ago, I experienced doubt that I could even bring myself to kill Bianca's father. Now, I'm furious that I might not get the chance to decide on my own.

It feels like I'm being pulled apart from the inside out.

"Plans change, *Gabryjel*," Drago says. "Are you willing to change with them, or are you ready to go extinct?"

"I want my revenge."

"You will get everything you ever dreamed of and more. But first, you must trust me. Do you trust me?"

I don't. Not anymore. Not after the ambush. But I know I have no choice here. Not now.

"Yes," I grumble.

"Good. For that trust, you will be rewarded. I may be the one to kill Ray Byrne, but you will be the one who wipes out the last remnants of the organization that betrayed your father."

"The Reca's?" Another unexpected fist punches me right in the fucking gut.

"Yes," Drago nods, the fading smoke from his cigar shrouding his pale face. "The heads of that serpent may have been chopped off long ago, but they still have their disciples. And those disciples remain vigilant. To this day, they still work the docks. They continue their attempts to build and grow and smuggle in enough drugs to rebuild the empire that was taken from them."

"How the fuck do they tie in?"

"They will be made to look like my crew," Drago explains. "You will lead Rian and Ray to those traitorous fuckers. Then, you will personally wipe them from the face of the earth, once and for all—much like they did to your family. Only then will I pounce from the ashes. I will kill the Irish king. And then together, we will take his Irish lion. Rian Kilpatrick is more than just a primal beast, *Gabryjel*. This I've learned. And his hidden talents will come in great use for our future reign."

"How?" It's all I can manage to spit out after being over-loaded by Drago's sinister twist in our master plan. "How will Rian Kilpatrick help us? Why would he?"

"He won't have a choice. And you don't need to know yet. It

will all come in due time, just as all else will. How does that sound?"

"It sounds like madness."

"Indeed it is," Drago smirks, his lips thin and white and crooked. "Are you in or are you out?

Fucking hell.

The tornado of new information wreaks havoc behind my skull as I try to process everything.

Still, through all of the chaos, I know one simple truth.

If I'm going to keep Bianca safe; if I'm going to fulfill my destiny; if I'm going to finally take what's mine, then there's only one way out of this storm.

Forward.

"Fuck it," I growl. "I'm in."

But first, I'm going home to see my princess.

Because before I leave Bianca again, I'm going to make sure she understands the ruthless truth of who she truly belongs to.

Me.

10

BIANCA

The shame kicks in again when I step out of the bathroom.

Ahead, on the nightstand, is the tray Gabriel brought in earlier. It's completely empty. Not even a crumb remains. Not after I got through with it.

Fuck.

The empty bowls and plates stand out like a sore thumb in the empty room. I have little doubt that it's the first thing he'll see when he returns. All that will matter to him is that I did as he ordered.

Even if he's clearly just playing a cruel game with me, it still hurts to lose.

Why can't that asshole just be a regular... well, asshole? Instead of teasing me like this, I almost wish Gabriel would just open his palm and slap me across the face.

It would cement him as my villain, and let the hate that I hold for him fester until I finally understood that there's only one way out of this, whatever *this* is.

I need to kill my captor.

Stepping onto the soft gray carpet, I stroke the ends of my damp hair and mindlessly float back towards the bed. The hot shower I just took hardly helped anything. I'm still a mess.

There wasn't a single second I stood under that steaming water where I wasn't thinking about Gabriel. My thoughts raced back and forth between the satisfaction of killing him and the ecstasy of giving into him.

No matter where my mind ran off to, though, that kiss followed. His thick red lips chase me even now, as I slip back into my soft silk nightgown and sit down on the edge of the bed.

Sighing, I remember who I am. A sheltered princess.

I'm not killing anyone, let alone Gabriel.

Gabriel. Fucking hell.

How long has he been gone now?

A few hours? A day? Longer?

It's impossible to tell in here. There are no clocks, no windows, no indication that anything exists beyond these pale empty walls. There could be no purer form of torture.

Whoever Gabriel really is, he's quickly become an expert at pushing me to my limits.

I am the man who's committed his entire adult life to capturing you. And now, you're mine. But that's not enough.

That's what he said after we kissed. After he'd tied his belt tightly around my throat and marked me.

After I'd finally had enough of his mysterious bad boy shtick.

I asked him who he was, and he was brutally honest, if characteristically vague.

The dark wolf said his life revolves around me.

So why the hell does he seem so hell bent on tearing me apart?

Lying down on my back, I sink into the mattress and stare up at the monochrome ceiling. Almost immediately, I'm overcome with an intense sense of nostalgia.

I've been here before.

Not physically, obviously. But mentally. Lying on my bed, staring up at the ceiling, obsessing over the boy who's made my life a living hell.

Gabriel Corso.

It doesn't matter that it's not his real name. That's who he is to me. The devil disguised as a hotshot prince. He almost looks more like young mafia royalty than any of my cousins do. Even Rian is more polished.

But Gabriel is darker. More terrifyingly put together. Every inch of him screams depraved killer. Yet, there's something so savagely graceful about his every move.

It's why I can't stop thinking about him.

It's why I can't stop craving him.

My fingers are already sliding between my thighs when I hear an all too familiar sound.

Ripping my hand away from its dirty daydream, I snap my attention over to the doorway.

The lock clicks open, and Gabriel steps inside, bathed in all of his ruthless glory.

"You showered?" he immediately asks, head tilting more like a puppy than the dark wolf he is.

The contrast makes me pause for a moment. But only for a moment.

"I felt dirty," I snap back.

The dullness of my captivity is immediately set on fire by Gabriel's presence.

"And you ate, too," he smiles, his intense hazel-green gaze falling on the empty tray. "Good girl."

"I felt empty," I mutter, trying to ignore how my body reacts to the condescending compliment.

Good girl.

Fuck. That shouldn't be so hot. I'm supposed to loathe this man.

"And how do you feel now?"

Sitting up straight, I shoot my meanest glare directly at the dark wolf. He looks like he's just stepped out of some twisted fairy-tale, one where he murdered all of the heroes, just because he could.

"Angry."

That only serves to widen Gabriel's grin. In fact, his thick red lips stretch so far that I suddenly notice something about his face that I never have before—or maybe I just forced myself to forget.

Just behind the short black facial hair that he uses to frame his gorgeous face are two deep fucking dimples.

My heart skips a beat.

"Good. I like it when you're angry. That's when you're the prettiest," Gabriel teases.

The backhanded compliment—combined with the revelation of those fucking dimples—hits me like a slap to the face.

But it's not the kind of slap I was secretly wishing for.

"How fucking dare you..." I hear myself hiss.

"How dare I what?"

"Compliment me."

"Why wouldn't I?" There's that head tilt again. It sends a lock of wavy black hair falling over Gabriel's right eye.

"Because you hate me, and I hate you."

"I don't hate you," Gabriel says, shaking his head. Another strand of his thick black hair falls over his forehead before he pushes them all back with his big tattooed hand.

"Bullshit," I snort. "Why else would you lock me up in here?"

"Because I like you," he taunts.

Before I can snap back at him again, Gabriel shuts me up by reaching down to his waist and unlatching the first buckle on his belt.

"What... What are you doing?" I gulp.

Immediately, the heat of my rage is transferred somewhere else. Directly to the hidden pressure in my core. I've been trying to ignore the constant presence of that pressure all fucking day, but all this man has to do is unbuckle a single notch on his belt, and it returns with a fury.

I really am in deep shit.

"I'm going to show you how much I like you," Gabriel says. Ripping his belt from around his waist, he straps it over his shoulder and steps forward.

My first instinct is to retreat. But my body won't let me. My chest tugs me forward, towards the beast. Under my nightgown, my traitorous nipples are already hard.

"I don't need you to show me anything."

"Are you sure? Does that mean you believe me when I say that I like you?"

"... No."

"Well, then I'll just have to prove it to you."

Stopping at the edge of the bed, Gabriel tosses his belt onto the mattress, then, with one swift motion, he rips his shirt off over his head.

A gust of warm air seems to rush from his body, nearly knocking me over. But the pressure in my core won't let me fall away. Not until I lay my eyes on the sculpted masterpiece that stands before me.

"Stop," I mutter, still unable to pull myself away. But the pressure in my core is slowly being invaded by a pit of dread.

He's fucking with me again. Toying with me.

"Stop? Why?" Gabriel asks. Still, to my surprise, he doesn't move another inch.

"Because I... I don't know what the fuck is going on."

"Would you like to know?"

"Yes!" I exclaim, frustrating cracking my voice.

"Alright," Gabriel nods. "Then let's play another game of truth or dare."

My stomach drops, but the pressure in my core starts to swirl at light speed. I remember what happened the last time we played this twisted game.

"I don't want to play that game again," I whisper, unsure if I'm lying or not.

"You can go first," Gabriel says. "Start as big or as small as you want."

My heart twitches with uncertainty as I stare up at the dark wolf. From this angle, he looks even more princely. Even more powerful. Black hair parted down the middle, hazel-green eyes blazing over golden olive-skin. Even the neck tattoos somehow add to the gothic royalty that emanates off of him.

"Who are you?" I hear myself ask, before clarifying. "No vague bullshit... please..."

Leaning down, Gabriel shoves my feet aside and sits at the edge of the bed. The whole mattress sinks under his weight, and I'm drawn ever closer to the handsome devil.

"My name is Gabriel," he says, before quickly raising his hand to stop me from pointing out the obvious. I already knew that. "My real last name is... well, I don't know."

"How don't you know your real last name?"

"Because I never knew my parents. They were both murdered before I was old enough to form any memories."

Despite the unrestrained power pouring out of the beastly man sitting before more, I feel a shot of sympathy pierce through my racing heart.

"I... I didn't know. I'm... I'm sorry."

My chest aches for him.

For a moment, we both sink into the tender vulnerability of what was just revealed.

Then, slowly, Gabriel leans forward. I can't bring myself to pull away as he gently pinches my chin.

For the first time ever, I don't return his gaze with hate or desperation. Instead, I try to find the boy behind the fractured hazel eyes. The man hiding within those emerald green flecks.

"How could you have known?" he whispers, his thumb brushing across the edge of my bottom lip. "I never told you. I've never told anyone who didn't already know."

Instantly, the mood has changed. There's still a simmering fury bubbling just beneath my skin, but it's taken a back seat to a strange sadness. And a burning arousal.

Gabriel is close enough that I can smell him again. That earthy musk seeps into my very fucking soul as I remember how good those dark red lips taste.

"Your turn," I whisper, my cheeks flushing with warmth.

"I want a truth," Gabriel says, his voice so deep that it rattles my bones. "Why didn't you like me in high school?"

My brows furrow against the shock of his unexpected question.

Where the hell did that come from?

"Because you were an asshole," I remind him.

"Not at first, I wasn't," he quickly replies.

"It's not like it was any big secret," I grumble. "Or maybe I just picked up on the fact that you were trying to use me."

"What could you have possibly thought I was trying to use you for?"

"I don't know... maybe as a punchline to a joke..." I say, before trailing off. Embarrassing memories lurk just beneath my surface. Painful ones too. I don't want to remember them. Not now.

"*Maybe* as a punchline to a joke? So you hated me because of something you thought I'd do?"

"Guys like you never got along with girls like me. And let's not forget about what happened that night in the parking lot..."

"What kind of guy did you think I was?" Gabriel asks, ignoring that second part, for obvious reasons.

His blood red lips lift into an amused smile. The dimples

are back. My heart quivers. It somehow feels so light and so heavy all at the exact same time.

"I thought you were a fake tough rich boy like every other dark haired, tattooed dickwad at that stupid prep school."

"That's funny," Gabriel chuckles, his grip tightening around my chin. "Because I always thought you were a fake tough rich girl."

Lifting his free hand, Gabriel softly traces the scar above my eye with the back of his fingers. The tender act sends a warm shiver dancing over my skin.

"I was," I sheepishly admit.

"But you didn't want to be, right?"

"No."

"Well, you may have underestimated yourself, *myszko*. No one gets a scar like that from being fake tough. And no one marks a man like me without having some fucking balls."

Dropping his hand from my forehead, Gabriel turns his thick, veiny forearm around in my face. It takes me a second to understand what he's showing me, but when I realize what's hiding beneath his mosaic of black tattoos, I can't help but sigh.

Another scar.

But I'm the one who left this one. It's the reason I got suspended the day before they found Principal Winchester's body. I threw hot coffee at the wolf prince himself... or so the rumor went.

"That was just an accident," I sheepishly admit. "You ran into me."

"I figured," Gabriel smiles. "But while you may have accidentally run into me that fateful day all those years ago, you definitely didn't just accidentally run face first into a fight with the frat boy who gave you that scar, did you? You went after him like a fucking hellhound."

"He deserved it," I sneer.

"He deserved a lot worse," Gabriel says.

Suddenly, a terrifying thought lashes through my mind.

"You... Did you kill him?"

Gabriel's dimples deepen as he licks his blood red lips.

"Look at you, putting it all together," he teases.

"He... He was a senator's son," I croak.

Kevin Porter. The senator's son. News of his death is what caused us to flee my home in the first place. It forced us out into the open. Made us vulnerable.

That's when we were ambushed.

That's when I was taken.

Holy shit. Did Gabriel set it all up?

No. It was just a coincidence. It had to be. Gabriel was being possessive. He was laying claim to me.

Still...

"Being a senator's son didn't do him much good in the end," Gabriel growls, and I can practically see the blood on his hands.

My racing heart starts to pound in thick, heavy beats behind my chest.

Gabriel really is the devil.

But could he be my devil?

"Why did you kill him?" I gather the courage to ask.

"Isn't it obvious?" Gabriel responds, his powerful fingers suddenly wrapping around my thigh. Fuck. His hands are so big he practically engulfs my entire leg.

The pressure in my core starts to outgrow everything else— even the dread.

"You killed him because he gave me this scar?"

"I killed him because he touched what was mine."

"I don't belong to anyone."

"Wrong. You belong to me, Bianca. And you have ever since I first laid eyes on you."

Sliding his right hand up my thigh, Gabriel uses his other to slip the straps of my nightgown down my shoulders.

"I'm sick of belonging to other people," I whisper.

"Just because you belong to me, doesn't mean I can't belong to you, as well," Gabriel says.

Placing his palm against my shoulder, he gently pushes me down onto the mattress.

"This doesn't feel like we're equals," I rasp, my toes curling as Gabriel forcefully spreads apart my thighs.

"That's just because you don't know what to expect. But I'll teach you. I can show you how to truly be tough—hell, you're already half way there."

The second his lips press against my inner thigh, every last bit of my resistance melts away. Biting the inside of my lip, I try with all my might to keep from grabbing Gabriel's dark hair, from pulling his lips closer to where I already know they're going.

This is so wrong.

"Why would you help me?" I rasp, my voice cracking as he slowly kisses up the inside of my thigh. "You've only ever treated me like every other man in my life. With kid gloves. Like I'm the most fragile fucking thing in the world."

My voice gets hoarser with every word, but even as my back arches and my toes curl, I know I'm lying.

No one's ever kissed me like he has before. No one's ever choked me like that. And no one's ever put their lips where his lips are right now.

"The gloves are off, baby girl," Gabriel growls, proving me wrong with every approaching kiss. "Let's see just how much you can handle."

Before he can reach my soaking pussy, though, the dark wolf reaches across my body and grabs his belt.

"What are you doing?" I ask, my voice trembling with fear and lustful anticipation.

But Gabriel ignores my question. Instead, he asks one of his own.

"Tell me, *myszko*," he starts, those hazel-green eyes staring up at me from between my open legs. "Are you a virgin?"

"That's none of your business," I gulp. But I know he can already smell the truth.

"It is now." Digging his fingers into the bottom of my nightgown, he pulls. Instantly, the soft silk is ripped from my body, and my naked skin is exposed to him.

"Fine. I'm a virgin," I rasp, as if that will slow Gabriel down. "Happy?"

"Yes."

The dark wolf doesn't slow down as his greedy hands wind up my stomach, towards my rock-hard nipples. My entire body quivers when he pinches my pink nubs between his thick fingers.

"Now tell me one of your secrets," I hear myself croak, my toes curling as I feel Gabriel's hot breath wash against my soaking pussy lips.

"Here's a secret for you... I'm older than you think I am."

"What?" I gasp. But before the weight of his revelation can settle in, I feel his thick tongue slip out from behind his red lips and lash across my pussy lips. "How much older?"

The question comes out in a quiver, even as I finally give in and plunge my fingers into Gabriel's thick black hair.

"Only two years," he says, taking one last deep breath before plunging back between my legs. His tongue finds my swollen clit and I feel like I could explode.

Fuck.

The ecstasy that erupts up from my cunt is like nothing I've ever felt before. Hell, it's so intense it almost hurts. It rises up from my soaking pussy, just as Gabriel palms my tits, sending a burning weight plunging down from my chest.

It all clashes in my core, threatening to rip me to shreds.

"You creep," I rasp. "All of those girls at Westwood who followed you from class to class..."

"I never touched a single one," Gabriel growls. "Because I wasn't there for them. I was there for you."

After one last teasing lick of my swollen clit, Gabriel lets my tits go and lifts his face up from between my legs.

Before I can gather my senses, he grabs me by the hips and violently flips me onto my stomach.

"Gabriel!" I scream, shocked by the sudden savagery.

"Don't call me Gabriel," the dark wolf quickly growls back. "Call me daddy. It's time to test your limits."

Sticking a knee under my legs, Gabriel forces my ass into the air. Then, without warning he whips my bare cheeks with the hard leather of his folded belt.

The sudden shock of pain crackles through my body at light speed. Before I can even process what just happened, before I can even scream for him to stop, to be gentle, I feel the searing warmth that follows the crack.

The red-hot afterglow washes through me like lapping waves, before settling in my core. The molten pressure there only grows more intense.

"That fucking hurt," I mumble, my fingers curled into fists around the bedsheets. "Gabriel, you—"

I'm interrupted by another lash to my bare ass. Again, a flash of pain tears through me. But it's quickly followed by that same searing warmth.

It's fucking addicting.

So much for being treated like a porcelain doll.

"That's not my name," Gabriel reminds me. "Not right now. Not to you. Give in, baby. You'll like it better that way."

"Am I supposed to give in, or am I supposed to—"

Once more, Gabriel's whip snaps across my ass cheek.

"What was that, *myszko*?" he asks.

Fuck. The harshness he puts into that word '*myszko*'... it makes me shiver.

But it's not the only thing making me shiver.

Pressing the leather belt against my throbbing cheeks, Gabriel forces the pain to linger just a little longer. The skin where I've been whipped is already on fire. But just inches away, my cunt is wetter than it's ever been.

"Daddy," I whisper. "Tell me what I'm supposed to—"

Another lash sends a muted whimper rushing from my lips.

"You're supposed to take it," Gabriel orders. "Now, do you want more?"

My fists clench and my toes curl as I consider his question.

Do I want more?

I know I shouldn't, but that's not what comes out of my quivering lips.

"...Yes."

"Yes what?"

"Yes, daddy."

"Good girl."

Another whip sends my feet into the air. But before they can bend sharply enough to drop onto my throbbing ass, Gabriel pushes them back down to the mattress.

Another lash stings my raw cheek. Then another.

"More," I hear myself beg.

"What was that?"

"Daddy, please!"

It feels so fucking wrong to call him that... yet so fucking right. Another lash cracks the molten pressure swirling around in my core. My entire body starts to tremble, but Gabriel doesn't let up.

His brutality makes me cum. An earth-shattering orgasm rips through every inch of my body. It's too intense to take head on. But when I start to squirm against the overwhelming pleasure, Gabriel throws aside his belt and crawls on top of me, pinning me to the mattress, forcing me to surrender.

"That's just the beginning, baby," he growls deep into my ear, even as I continue to shake. "I'm going to burn away every last inch of your innocence. Set you on fire and plunge you into the flames of hell... But don't be scared. I am the devil. And you will find your place by my side. Ruling. First, though, you need to learn to enjoy the pain. And you definitely need to lose that fucking cherry."

Pushing me down with the palm of his hand, Gabriel shoves his hips into my throbbing ass. Immediately, I feel the heat of his massive bulge.

It so huge that just the thought of trying to fit it inside of me is terrifying. But I fight through the fear.

Gabriel is right. This is just the beginning.

I want more. I *need* more.

I need him.

Fuck. I've lost my mind.

"Will you break apart if I fuck you, baby girl?" Gabriel asks, his fingers wrapping around the back of my neck.

The tremors of my first orgasm have hardly left my body, but I'm already desperate for another round.

But how could Gabriel top what he's already done to me?

"There's only one way to find out," I rasp. "Fuck me, daddy."

11

GABRIEL

I'm already tightening the belt around Bianca's tiny wrists before I can even stop to think twice about it.

This is crazy. It's fucking stupid and wrong.

But I don't care.

If I don't stick my cock in Bianca's tight little pussy soon, I'm going to fucking implode.

"Are you comfortable, *myszko*?" I ask, because... well, she doesn't look comfortable. Her sharp shoulder blades jut out as she arches her back and presses her ass into my cock.

"No," Bianca whispers. "But I don't care anymore."

Whatever this is, it's working for her.

And me.

"Good girl," I praise.

A wild whip of pride slashes through me as I sneer down at my prize.

The tender skin on her ass is raw. Her tiny hands are bound behind her back. Her pussy is fucking soaked.

This is what I've always wanted.

Bianca Byrne. The sheltered princess. Tied up in my bed. Begging for my cock.

There's no point in being gentle any more. Something has snapped within us both, split open by the leather of my belt.

"I won't lie to you, baby girl," I say, standing up so that I can rip my pants off. "This is going to hurt. But if you grit your teeth and take the first wave of pain, then I promise we will reach heaven together."

"Fuck heaven," Bianca mumbles. "I want hell."

She's even more depraved than I'd hoped.

"Let's see if you can handle it."

My pants hit the floor and my rock-hard cock whips out. Immediately, I'm on top of Bianca, pre-cum leaving a glistening trail across her plump ass as I lean down and gently bite the bottom of her earlobe.

"Oh my god..."

The princess quivers against the pressure of my teeth. Her back arches sharper still and her shoulder blades dig into my chest.

"Every one of your holes belongs to me," I growl, slipping my tongue into her ear.

She trembles so violently that I have to wrap my forearm beneath her throat just to keep her from rolling out from under me.

"My mouth?" Bianca whispers.

Twisting her head around, I shove my tongue down her fucking throat. "You better fucking believe it," I tell her when I pull back.

"My ass?"

"Every. Hole."

"... My pussy..."

Sliding my knees up between her legs, I pry her open and rub my throbbing head against her soaking lips. "Is your pussy ready for me?" I ask.

My body isn't about to wait around for an answer, though.

Bianca's fingers flare out into my hard stomach as I blindly find her tiny hole with my cock.

"I'm so wet," she mumbles, as if she's surprised by her own arousal.

"That means you're ready."

With a savage thrust, I force my way inside of her.

"Gabriel!" Before she can scream again, I smother her pillow lips with the palm of my hand. "... Daddy..." I hear her quietly correct herself.

"Welcome the pain,," I growl, my thick throbbing shaft sliding deeper and deeper into her little wet hole. "Let it consume you."

It's easy for me to say. There's no pain on my end—at least, not at first. There's only pure fucking ecstasy... until my pelvis hits Bianca's raw ass. By then, she's become so tight that her slick pink walls are practically strangling my swollen shaft.

It feels like I'm being squeezed into oblivion. I've never been inside a pussy this tight before. It's almost suffocating. But I don't flinch.

I welcome the pain too.

"You're so big." Bianca's muffled voice seeps up through my fingers. I tighten my grip.

Her hot breath washes against my outstretched palm as I slide my throbbing cock half way out of her dripping cunt again.

Then, I pound her raw ass with all of my fucking might.

"Your pussy is so fucking perfect," I loudly growl, covering Bianca's yelp with my own grunt. "But I'm going to loosen it up anyway."

Sliding halfway out of her soaking cunt one more time, I rail back down into her plump little ass. Bianca's bound hands tremble against my hard stomach, her outstretched fingers digging into my flesh. It adds another level of subtle pain to the whole experience.

I fucking love it.

"Again," her voice is barely audible. But I can feel every word as they splash against my palm.

"As you wish."

This time, when I pull halfway out, I don't plunge back into her with only one brutal thrust. Fuck no. I'm done taking it slow. She's had her time to prepare. If I don't start dictating the pace, I'm going to explode before I can truly appreciate what's happening.

I'm fucking Bianca Byrne—and a split second later, I'm not even just fucking her. I'm pounding the ever-loving fuck out of her virgin cunt.

My cock eviscerates her little pussy as I take what's mine. Every savage thrust rips a desperate cry from her throat. But her cries only crash into my palm. They only seep in through my skin and urge me to go harder. To give her what she deserves.

All of me.

"This is all for you, baby," I growl, covering every inch of her with my burning body. "This is how you'll become my queen. This is how you'll become strong enough to rule by my side."

When I plunge my tongue back into her ear, the slick pink walls of her impossibly tight pussy start to tremble and convulse. It somehow makes her feel even tighter.

Fuck.

My throbbing cock is being strangled. My swollen shaft pulses like it's about to explode. Even my fucking balls begin to pulse as I increase the brutality of my thrust, pounding Bianca into fucking oblivion.

She's coming. I can feel the rest of her body tense up. Her whimpers are replaced by wails of ecstasy. Her screams crash against my palm as the orgasm takes hold. She begins to shake.

Still, I hold her tight. My tongue only digs deeper into her ear. My pelvis only smacks harder against her ass.

"There's nowhere to go, baby girl" I tell her, as she jerks and twitches beneath the searing cage of my body. "I've got you."

And then, suddenly, her ass gets free from my oppressive grip. It only moves an inch before I pound her back into submission, but the act is enough to bend the base of my cock in just the right way.

I lose control.

For a split-second, I go blind. My mind fucking empties. All I feel is the insane ecstasy of my own world-shattering orgasm as it erupts from my core, down my shaft and out of my throbbing head.

Somehow, I manage to pull myself back down to earth before I can cum in Bianca's virgin pussy.

Ripping my cock from her convulsing cunt, I jump off of her just as the first thick stream of cum explodes from the tip of my cock.

"Holy shit," I rumble, every muscle in me clenching.

"Oh my god," Bianca whimpers, her little body still quivering as I glaze her sweaty skin. "Oh my god..."

Then, just like that, it's over.

All of my wild energy drips off Bianca's back, off her bound wrists, and onto the covers.

I can only fall down onto the bed beside my cum covered captive, temporarily drained.

The force of my falling body sinks the mattress just enough to toss Bianca onto her side... and into my arms.

Neither of us fight the accidental embrace. Not at first. In fact, for an oddly blissful moment, she quietly presses her desecrated ear into my heaving chest.

My pounding heart must snap her back to reality, though, because it doesn't take long before she pulls herself away, and rolls over to her lonely side of the bed.

"Fuck," I grumble, staring up at the ceiling. The sudden absence of her warmth sends a chill over my sweaty skin. "I need a shower."

Even if part of me wants to roll over and force Bianca back into my arms, I quickly decide that I've already pushed her far enough for today. I'll let her rest. For now.

That decision only strengthens when I push myself up and look down at my still half-hard cock.

It's drenched in blood.

A blade of dread slices through me at the sight. Fucking hell. What have I done?

"Bianca," I whisper, looking over at the princess. "Are you alright?"

Her back is turned to me, but I can see that she's tucked her knees up to her chest. Blood stains the sheets just under her ass.

Guilt replaces the pulsing satisfaction of my orgasm.

"I'm fine," Bianca mumbles, as I crawl towards her. But her words aren't enough for me.

Fuck making her cum. The part of me that wanted to force her back into my arms also just wants to make sure she's alright.

That will come. First, you have to make her strong.

Placing my hand on her shoulder, I brush my lips against the back of her neck. Then, I start to undo her restraints.

"Are you hurt?" I quietly ask.

"No."

"Are you lying?"

"... No."

I don't believe her, especially not when I hear the jagged breath that escapes her lips after I've ripped the belt off from around her wrists.

Gingerly, her newly freed arms wrap around her huddled knees.

Fucking hell.

Seeing her in the fetal position like this does something evil to my cold, dead heart. Something dangerous.

It makes it fucking hurt. It makes me want to curl up in a ball around her and protect her from what *I've* done.

But I can't do that. For as little as I actually know Bianca, I'm certain that she'll just shrink further away if I try to take advantage of such a vulnerable moment.

Still, seeing her like this punches a fucking hole in my chest.

There's no fire here. Only smoldering embers. I'll have to be careful about how I stoke them, otherwise they could go out forever.

"If you're not hurt, then you won't have any problem standing up," I say, carefully toeing a line between monster and teacher.

Crawling over her, I push myself off of the bed. But even I'm wobbly on my feet. I can't even imagine how she'll handle it.

Still, I know I have to try. This moment is crucial. Either she withers away forever or she learns to be the resilient queen I could see myself ruling beside.

"Gabriel," Bianca looks up at me through those shimmering crystal blue eyes and my thawing heart twitches something fucking fierce.

"Bianca," I nod. Reaching out, I offer her my hand. "You've stained my sheets. Let's get you cleaned up before you stain anything else."

Just like that, I catch a glimpse of that patented fire flash behind her eyes.

It makes me fucking smile.

There you are.

"You asshole," she grumbles. But the insult hardly hurts, because she says it while pulling herself up to the side of the bed.

"See, getting up isn't so hard," I say, keeping my hand outstretched.

Bianca doesn't accept my help. Instead, she pushes herself off the mattress.

It doesn't go well. Not for her. But it gives me an excuse to hold her again. Because her fragile little knees immediately give out and I have to lunge forward to grab her.

"I didn't fall because I'm hurt," she immediately mumbles. Still, her nails dig into my bicep as she tries not to sink further into my embrace. "I'm just... exhausted."

"Well, you're going to have plenty of time to rest, because I have to go soon."

Those crystal blue eyes flicker with another flash of fire.

"And you're going to lock me back in here? After what we just did?"

"Don't worry, I'll wash you up and get clean sheets first."

Bending my knees, I slide my arms down Bianca's body and then quickly sweep her off her feet.

"Gabriel!" she yelps.

"I thought I told you not to call me that?"

"I'm not calling you daddy again..." she says. "That was a mistake."

"Was the sex a mistake too?"

It's just banter, but I still find myself holding my breath as I wait for a response.

But Bianca isn't in the mood.

"At least you didn't finish inside of me."

Fuck. She's right. But I was so close. Even if knocking her up is part of the plan, it needs to wait until after those stupid fucking Polish priests finally get here.

Well, they better hurry the hell up. The longer I have to wait to cum in my princess, the crazier I'm going to get.

"Is that all you're thankful for, *myszko*?" I return. "That I didn't cum inside of you?"

"*Myszko*," Bianca mutters, completely butchering the pronunciation. "You keep calling me that. What the hell does it mean?"

"Wouldn't you like to know."

"Obviously," she huffs. "That's why I asked."

"Well, you should have waited to ask it. You haven't earned the privilege of knowing yet. The answer will have to wait."

Turning away from the bed, I start to carry Bianca towards the bathroom.

"Where are you taking me?" she asks, a hint of panic lacing the sharpness of her voice.

I can feel her warm blood painting my forearms—hell, even a bit of cum rubs up against my sweaty skin—but I don't give a shit.

"I can't have you bleeding all over my fine grey rug while I'm gone," I smirk. "I'm going to wash you up."

"... In the shower?"

"Do you have a problem with that?"

"Doesn't sound like I have much of a choice."

"You're smarter than you look," I chuckle.

"Obviously I'm not."

Bianca trails off, lost in her own thoughts as I kick aside the bathroom door and carry her into the shower.

Placing her down on the counter carved into the marble wall, I try to ignore the conflict that must be tearing her insides apart right now.

She just gave in to me. The man she's supposed to hate.

And she liked it.

Nothing could be more obvious. Her shame isn't from being used. It's from wanting more.

Still, I decide to finally give her something she's been wanting.

"When I get back, I'll tell you everything," I hear myself say. "Now let's get you cleaned up."

Before I turn around to start the shower, I sneak a quick look at my captured princess. Clearly, my words have the intended effect, because her attention is ripped away from her internal battles and forced onto me.

"Why not just tell me now?" she asks, just as the hot water starts to rain down on me.

"Do you really want to learn the brutal truth while you're naked in a shower with me? While your bleeding from your pussy? After we just fucked?"

The reminder stops her for a second. But Bianca hardly ever freezes for long. Her chest puffs out as steam starts to rise all around us.

"Tell me. I can take it."

"I'm not sure you can," I sigh. For as tough as Bianca has proven herself to be, the depth of the darkness that surrounds us both might well just crush her into nothing.

"Please... Gabriel... Just tell me something. Anything."

Feeling myself give into another person is not something I'm even remotely used to. But looking at those pleading blue eyes, remembering how she just took my savage lust, fuck, it makes me weak.

In this violent world, it's dangerous to be weak. But maybe here, together, we can be safe—if even only for one precious moment.

"Fine," I say. Stepping forward, I block the hot water with my back. "But first, I want you to stand up."

"You're such an asshole," Bianca huffs, shaking her head.

"Guilty as charged."

This time, when I reach my hand out to her, she takes it. With a deep breath, my stubborn princess pushes herself to her feet.

My grip tightens as she struggles to stay upright, but once she gains her footing, I drop her hand.

She really wants to know what the hell is going on.

"That's a good girl," I say, stepping forward until her nose nearly touches my chest. "Now, let's start with some good news."

"I could really fucking use some good news," Bianca grumbles.

Lifting my hand again, I trace my fingers along the edges of the transparent bandage on her shoulder.

"This will need to be changed," I note. Finding an edge to the bandage, I begin to peel it off.

"That's not good news," Bianca stubbornly points out. But she doesn't flinch away from my touch.

"No," I agree. "But this is: your entire family is alive and well —and that includes your cousin."

"Rian survived?"

Bianca's sudden burst of relief is palpable. In fact, it's so intense that I worry I might have to reach out and keep her from collapsing again.

But the little princess is getting stronger by the second, and she hardly even wavers as I tear the rest of her bandage off.

"Apparently the lion is completely unscathed," I tell her, brushing my fingers across the raised wound.

But where relief arose from the first revelation, a new conflict appears in Bianca from what I just said.

"He let you take me while he was still alive?" Bianca asks, her pretty face twisting in confusion.

"He ordered me to," I shrug. "Not that either of us had much of a choice. My guns were empty. His weren't. He stayed behind to buy us time while I carried you to safety."

"And then you stabbed him in the back by taking me captive?"

There's the fire again. I'm glad it's back, even if it's lashing flames are focused entirely on me.

"Just because I respect the man, doesn't mean I was going to throw away my life's work just to keep him happy."

Bending down, I gently kiss Bianca's wound.

She quivers against the tender touch of my lips. Still, she refuses to wince away.

"Are you finally going to tell me what your life work is?"

"You," I say. Taking a step to the side, I finally let the hot water wash over Bianca.

A deep breath escapes her perfect pink lips as the water washes away her sweat and her blood and my cum. It all pools at her feet, before drifting down towards the drain.

"I thought I told you I don't want to hear any more of your vague bullshit," Bianca huffs, running her hands through her wet hair.

She closes her eyes and tilts her chin up to the ceiling. The image of her naked body standing before me, glistening wet, is almost enough to turn me savage again.

But instead of lust, I feel something else.

Something that stirs my thawing heart. Something that makes me give in again.

"Fine. No more vague bullshit," I agree. "Where do you want me to start?"

"At the beginning."

"Well, I already told you that my parents were murdered," I remind her, a familiar rage accompanying the memory. "But I guess I didn't tell you by who or why."

"No. You didn't," Bianca mutters, her voice suddenly becoming respectfully quiet.

"Well, here's the story." Reaching around her, I grab a bottle of body wash and empty some of the liquid soap onto my hands. "My parents weren't just any ordinary people, Bianca. No. They were mafia royalty, much like your parents."

Gesturing her forward, I wait until the pretty little princess is directly under the water before I step behind her and start to wash her glistening body.

"Your dad was a don?" Bianca asks, stunned.

"Something like that," I respond. Brushing my hands down her back, I wash away the last bits of my cum from her skin. "My father was leader of the Polish mafia. People called him *Krol Cieni*. In English that translates to Shadow King."

"I... I've never heard of the Polish mafia," Bianca sheepishly admits. "Or the shadow king."

"That's because, for the most part, we stayed in Poland. Things were good there. We had a stranglehold over the country. Politicians and Presidents kneeled at our feet. But some people wanted more. People always want more..."

The fury simmering behind my chest builds as I crouch down and begin to wash Bianca's thighs. Her toes curl when I slide my fingers over her pussy lips. But I'm too focused on my dark past to get aroused.

I'm already committed to telling her everything. There's no stopping me now. Not even with a body like hers.

"Someone usurped your father?" Bianca softly guesses, her voice trembling against my touch.

"More than that," I grumble. "They killed him, along with all of my aunts and uncles and cousins."

My grip tightens around her thigh and I have to shake my head to keep from getting lost in my anger.

"Who killed them?"

"Drug lords," I spit, rising up again. "Filthy fuckers who wanted to expand our empire to the west by spreading poison amongst the people. But my father wouldn't allow it. Poland was home. And drugs weren't our kind of evil. So he refused."

"But why did they want to come to America?"

"For the same reason anyone does. Power. And that's exactly what they got when they arrived. Those fuckers got exactly what they wanted. Twisted allies who would help them overthrow my father and massacre my family."

"But you escaped."

My heart clenches as I step back in front of Bianca and let the water wash over me.

"My mother escaped with me in tow," I explain, shutting my eyes. "She brought me to America. But America wasn't safe."

"No," Bianca's voice is just as heavy as my heart.

"They found her. Then they tore her from limb to limb, like ravenous fucking dogs."

"Gabriel..."

"But she still managed to save me. Until her dying breath she was only worried about me."

"I'm so sorry."

Running my hands through my hair, I take a deep breath. But the rage and the sorrow won't settle—at least, not until I feel Bianca's soapy hands on my back.

Her soft skin gently slides over my scars and my muscles, lathering me in a tender sympathy.

"I was given to one of my father's top advisors," I continue. "A man who also managed to escape the chaos back home and make it to America. He adopted me. Eventually, he told me what I had lost... and how I could get it all back."

Bianca's soft hands falter at that last line.

"I'm part of your plan to get it back," she understands, a dreadful realization joining her deep sympathy. "But how?"

"The kingdom my father once ruled is gone," I tell her. "... Well, it's hidden. I've been told the riches are being kept somewhere beneath the ruins of our old empire, along with a dark army ready to follow the rightful king. But only a certain group knows where and how to put it all together."

"What happened to the people who killed your father and took over?" Bianca gulps, her hands slowly beginning to wash me again.

"The Recas," I growl, my fists clenching as steam swirls around me. "They got what they deserved. It turns out your family isn't too fond of drug lords either. The Kilpatricks killed the family who wiped out mine... but only after collaborating with the fuckers to make sure the job was done right."

"So then who knows where everything they left behind is hidden?"

The growing heat of our shower seeps through my pores as I remember the stories Drago told me growing up. This all comes from him, but I've based my entire life around his teachings. This history is part of me.

"When the Recas were wiped out, there was no one powerful enough to replace them. Back in the motherland, the entire ancient order of things was thrown into chaos. So, a select few of the most dedicated clergymen did their best to hide everything away. Polish priests. Brothers of the Black Veil. But they are a stubborn type; religious zealots with their own outdated codes and rituals."

"How do you plan on appeasing them?" Bianca asks, more invested than I was expecting.

"If I want the power that was abandoned after my father's empire fell apart, I need to become king again. I obviously have the right bloodline to do it. But according to the Brotherhood, you cannot become king until you produce an heir, and you cannot produce a legitimate heir until you are married."

"Your plan is to marry me," Bianca gulps.

"That is what's going to happen, yes."

"And then you're going to force me to birth your heir?"

Her hands fall from my back and a cold gust appears somewhere through the steam.

"*Our* heir," I correct her. "It's what needs to be done."

"And the only reason you didn't do it just now—the only reason you didn't finish inside of me after what we just did... is because you're waiting for marriage?"

"It sounds strangely noble when you put it that way," I note.

Reaching forward, I turn off the shower.

I've had enough. This conversation is just a reminder of

what needs to be done. And apparently, that now includes returning to the Byrne family... and Rian Kilpatrick.

"No. It doesn't sound strangely noble," Bianca rasps. "It sounds insane."

"This world is insane."

"I... I..." she starts to stumble as I step out of the shower and grab a towel.

"It's a lot to take in, I know," I say. Moving towards her, I go to dry her off. But this time, she doesn't accept my touch. This time, she winces away like I'm about to hit her.

"Why... Why can't you just negotiate with my father? Why spend all of this time trying to take me? Fuck. Why even choose *me*? There wasn't some other mafia princess you could terrorize?"

Backing up all the way to the slick shower walls, Bianca does her best to avoid me. And I'm left to stand there with her towel in my hand, dripping wet.

Fucking hell.

Do I tell her that I won't ever negotiate with Ray fucking Byrne because the ravenous dogs who caught up to my mother all of those years ago weren't Polish? Do I tell her they were Irish?

Do I tell her that it was her father?

Do I tell her the reason we chose her was so that we could get our revenge while consolidating our power, all in one swift and ruthless act?

No. Not now.

It's too much.

She would shatter, and I would lose my queen before I could truly build her.

"I took you because I wanted you," I half-lie. "I've always wanted you. And an arranged marriage wasn't going to work. Your family doesn't negotiate, Bianca. And neither do I. In this world, you take what you want, or you risk having everything stolen."

"Just like you stole me?"

A sudden flash of frustration makes me shake my head. I don't have time for this anymore. Tossing Bianca's towel towards her, I turn and grab one of my own. Then, I wrap it around my waist and storm back into the bedroom.

I've barely even stepped foot on the soft carpet when I hear a buzz come from my discarded pants.

It's my phone. That must be a text from Bianca's new maid. She's here.

A nervous knot tightens in my gut at the thought of what I'm about to do. And it's not just anxiety about who I'm supposed to be tracking down. It's also about who I'm leaving Bianca with.

But I don't have a choice. I had to choose someone to look after her while I was gone. Because there's a good chance I might not ever come back.

Fuck.

After drying myself off some more, I grab my underwear and pants and slip them back on. Then, I do the same with my shirt.

I'm just about to check my phone when I hear Bianca in the bathroom doorway.

"Where are you going?" she asks, towel wrapped around her tight little body. She already looks stronger, but that doesn't stop her from leaning against the doorway for support.

Her legs must be sore as hell.

"If I survive, I'll tell you when I return," I say, finally checking my phone. It's exactly who I thought it was. And she's here.

"... If you survive?" Bianca gulps, a hint of dread cracking her voice. But before I can mistake her fear as concern for my safety, Bianca catches herself. "What happens to me if you die?

Do I just rot away in this cage until I die too? Is that what you want?"

"No," I say, shaking my head. "And it's why I've arranged for a very special maid to look after you."

"A maid?"

"That's right," I smirk. "Look, I'll even leave the bedroom door open, since you won't be alone."

I'm already in the hallway before Bianca can process what I've just told her. As soon as it clicks, though, I hear her tiny little footsteps pitter-patter against the bedroom carpet.

"What if I try to escape?" she calls after me, her head sticking out of the bedroom doorway.

"You'll fail," I assure her.

"You don't think I can overpower a maid?"

That stops me in my tracks. Looking back over my shoulder, I let Bianca see my Cheshire grin.

"If you overpower this maid, I will be very impressed. Hell, if you escape from under her, I might just let you have your freedom, because you'd have earned it."

"I'm not worried about impressing you," she quickly huffs, already back to her old self.

It makes me happy, and slightly less concerned about leaving her.

What a resilient queen Bianca could be.

"Oh, believe me, baby girl. You should be. If you keep impressing me, you might just earn yourself a crown."

With that, I turn and leave the dripping princess in my wake.

"I'd have a crown without you!" she yells, reminding me of who her father is. And she's right to. For a second there, I nearly forgot.

"Maybe, maybe not," I shrug, hardly raising my voice enough to make sure she's heard me.

"Wait! Who the hell is this maid?" I can hear the growing

anxiety in Bianca's voice. Despite her best intentions, I can tell she's reluctantly getting used to me; to my hard lessons; to my particular form of depravity. But letting another monster into her gilded cage?

That's cause for concern.

So, to drop a little hint, I stop one last time and turn back to my captured princess.

"She'll either become your best friend or your worst nightmare," I call back down the hall, toying with my captive one last time before I confront death head on.

"So make sure you behave, okay?"

12

Roz is waiting for me in the foyer when I get downstairs.

"How the hell did you get inside?" I ask. This place is supposed to be an invisible fortress.

"You know me," she shrugs. "Always getting into places I don't belong."

"Well, you belong here," I assure her. "So make yourself at home. But stay on guard. Bianca may look like a porcelain doll, but she can put up a hell of a fight."

"Do you know that from experience?" Roz smiles, lifting her brow at me.

"You know I don't hurt women."

"Was that not yelling I heard upstairs just a second ago?"

"That was playful banter," I assure her.

"Banter? At a time like this? I thought you were more serious about this plan than that."

"Serious enough to save my energy," I roll my eyes. "Save your taunts for Bianca. She likes that stuff."

Brushing by Roz, I jimmy open one of the foyer's closet doors. The inside is empty, but when I gently punch a wooden panel, it pops out, revealing my gun collection.

"You probably shouldn't take any of your own weapons," Roz wisely points out. "Those things you got there are too sophisticated for the poor street rat you're supposed to be."

"I'm not going back to the Byrnes unarmed," I grumble, chest thumping as the reality of what I'm about to do really settles in. "And I *am* a street rat—there's no need to pretend—or do you not remember how we grew up?"

"Sure, we spent most of our childhood in the slums," Roz shrugs. "But I hardly noticed. My mind was always on the future. And I knew I had a golden ticket in my pocket. A tried-and-true prince. The next *Krol Cieni*."

"We're still a long way from that," I huff, closing the hidden wooden panel without taking a weapon. "You're right about the weapon though, I'll have to grab one from some street goon on my way over to the Byrne compound."

"Good luck," Roz nods, her tone suddenly becoming less playful.

"Drago better not be overstating Rian Kilpatrick's importance," I grumble in response.

"Sometimes I wonder why we put so much blind faith into that man," Roz sighs.

"Because he saved us, Roz," I remind her. "He gave us hope when we had none. He made us killers when we were soft."

"Yeah, yeah, you're right. But that doesn't mean he always is. Just remember that. Now, where's the girl?"

"Upstairs," I say. Pulling my phone out of my pocket, I snap it in half with my bare hands. It can't come with me. Nothing can. In fact, I should probably get into a fight before I find Rian, just to make it look like I've had a rough fucking week.

"I can't wait to meet her," Roz smirks.

"Be careful," I warn. "I left her bedroom door open. So, she could be around any corner..."

That makes her laugh. "Doesn't look like there are many corners here. Who the hell designed this place?"

"It doesn't matter. It's your home until I return."

"If only I had known about it before. You know so I could have gotten used to it..."

"Everyone has their secrets."

"And their safe places..."

Before I open the door, I make sure to look deep into Roz's eyes. "Do you really want those to potentially be the last words you ever say to me?"

"No," she shakes her head. "Come here. I love you."

We embrace.

"I love you too."

"... But fuck, I'm glad I don't have to marry you anymore," she laughs when we pull back from each other. "Thank God for this Bianca Byrne."

"That marriage was never really going to happen," I dismiss her.

"Drago was pushing hard for it," she playfully reminds me.

"Drago doesn't always get what he wants," I grumble.

But he better get Rian Kilpatrick. Because if he doesn't, it will probably be because I was roped up the second I walked back into the Byrne compound.

"Yet we still follow him around," Roz shrugs.

"Once I'm king, he'll have to do what I say. What *we* say."

"I can't wait," Roz nods. "Now go out there and do your duty, little prince. And try not to get killed."

"Same to you," I wink, swallowing my nerves.

"I think I can handle a tiny princess."

"That's what I thought too," I smirk. Shaking my leg in her direction, I remind Roz about the shrapnel wound still healing just behind my knee. This hasn't been an easy week by any means—and Bianca's stubbornness hasn't exactly helped, not that I don't like her better for it.

Fuck.

I may never see her again...

The sudden thought rips through me as Roz studies my leg.

"I didn't see a limp on you. Does it still hurt?"

"No," I respond, shaking my head in an attempt to rid myself of the sudden onslaught of dread. "But hopefully I'll be able to use it as proof that I was shot by those fuckers Drago sent to ambush us; that I wasn't working with them."

"That ambush," Roz grumbles. "I'm still so fucking sorry about how it went down."

"Don't be sorry, be ready. Stall as long as you can on making more of those tracking devices. And look after Bianca while I'm gone. Feed her. Make sure she gets some rest, and don't tell too many embarrassing stories about me, alright?"

"No promises about the embarrassing stories, but roger on the rest of that."

An unexpected sigh escapes my chest in response.

Bianca.

Those crystal blue eyes. Fuck. To think, I was once willing to do anything to rid myself of them. Now, I regret that I didn't even think to stop and take one last long look.

I guess that means I can't allow myself to die. Not yet. Not until I can barge back in here and fuck my princess bloody again.

"Here goes nothing," I nod, tossing the shattered remnants of my phone away.

"See you on the other side," Roz nods back.

"See you on the other side."

13

BIANCA

Down the hallway, I can hear a new set of feet ascending some unseen staircase. Each step rattles through my chest, filling me with more dread.

Who the hell is this person?

Gabriel made her sound like some sort of psychopath, and I can't help but imagine a twisted beast of a woman lunging for me the second she appears in my doorway.

Shit.

It doesn't matter that my bedroom door is finally open. I'm not free. Far from it. Hell, I'm more cornered than ever.

Turning around, I shuffle back to the mattress. But there's nothing there that's going to save me, only blood-stained sheets and the thin nightgown that Gabriel ripped off my body just before he fucked my brains out.

Fucking hell. I can't believe that just happened... or how amazing it felt.

My legs quiver as I drop the damp towel from around my body, and replace it with the nightgown.

It feels like a small miracle that I'm even able to stand.

My pussy throbs with a burning soreness. My knees are

weak and my heart pounds like a jackhammer behind my chest.

But there's hardly time to dwell on the fact that Gabriel fucking Corso just popped my cherry. Not that there's any way I'm ever going to be able to forget the feeling of his huge cock spearing me over and over again... or the blood that followed.

But his brutality won't be all that I remember. No matter how savage his passion was, I'll never forget how gentle he acted afterwards.

Even if he tried to cut me with his words, I could tell it was only to keep me from falling into a numb state of shock.

Still, even his words eventually turned soft. Not only did Gabriel wash me off in the shower, he opened himself up and spilled his guts.

My pounding heart clenches at the fresh memory.

Sure, Gabriel only told me what he did so I'd understand why he could never let me go, but he didn't have to get so vulnerable about it. He didn't have to tell me about his parents. About how they were so ruthlessly murdered.

No. Don't get lost in misplaced sympathy, Bianca. Focus on the present. Focus on the next threat.

You've been captured. You're in the den of an enemy. You're being used.

Taking a deep breath, I turn myself around and wait for my new overseer to arrive.

All I know is that it will be a girl. But what kind of girl does a man like Gabriel associate with?

A disturbing flame of jealousy flashes behind my aching chest before I extinguish it with sheer force of will.

There is no way I'm doing that. No. Way.

Out in the hallway, the footsteps have disappeared. But I know that's only because the floor is carpeted. Whoever this 'maid' is, she's close, and she's getting closer by the second.

My sore body tenses as I wait to see what kind of she-devil Gabriel has sent to watch over me.

I'm not sure what I'm expecting, but it certainly isn't what suddenly appears in my doorway.

A dark vision of dangerous beauty.

"Hello, darling."

It's like I'm staring at the world's most gorgeous assassin.

"I... uh... who are you?" I stumble, subtly leaning against the mattress.

"I'm Rozalia," she smiles, dark red lips lifting her high cheekbones. "You must be Bianca."

"That's right."

The woman couldn't be much older than me, if even at all. Long and slender, with a snatched waist and perfect pale skin, she struts towards me like a cat, draped in a tight black turtle-neck and leather pants.

Her sharp green eyes study me with a ferocious intensity, as if she's trying to decide whether I'm prey or competition. All I can do to bolster my case is stand up a little straighter and wait for her to step a few feet before me.

Our eyes are nearly level, and it looks like we'd be almost the same height if the top of her shaved-sides, black-haired pixie-cut wasn't casually spiked upward.

"So, you're the one who's been giving my Gabriel so much trouble," she says. The smile not leaving her lips.

My Gabriel.

Fuck. There it is again. A little shock of unwelcomed jealousy.

"He's the one who's been causing the trouble," I assure her, my voice shaking ever-so-slightly as I try to gauge the threat standing before me.

"Well, I can see why." Those cat-like green eyes look me up and down, from head to toe, before an approving nod bounces her softly gelled hair. "You're definitely his type."

"His type?" I hear myself blurt out.

"Easy there, girl. I'm just joking around. Gabriel doesn't have types. He has obsessions. And for years now, he's only had one obsession. You."

My thighs clench as I remember just how hard Gabriel fucked me. His brutal thrusts were almost desperate, like he'd been waiting a very long time to make me bleed like that.

"I might be flattered if this all wasn't so fucked up," I snap.

"Looks like it hasn't been all bad," Roz responds, her sharp green eyes falling onto the bed behind me.

A heavy stone drops in my gut as I realize what she must see.

Looking over my shoulder, I spot the blood-stained sheets.

"I... uh..."

"I mean, unless that blood's from the wound on your shoulder... but I think I've seen enough injuries to know that yours hasn't been bleeding for a while."

Ignoring her, I turn around and rip the sheets from the mattress. Bundling them up in my arms, I turn back to Rozalia, my sore legs shaking to a dangerous degree.

"I need to clean these up," I mumble, a poor attempt at distraction. "Is there a washing machine in this place?"

"I don't actually know," Rozalia shrugs, before squinting her sharp eyes at me. "Let's go find out together."

Stepping forward, she gently, yet forcefully, rips the pile of bloody sheets from my hands, and I get a whiff of her breezy scent. Despite the dangerous energy that emanates from her, Rozalia smells like a rosy spring day.

It's somehow both threatening and disturbingly comforting.

Before I can get too lost in her conflicted scent, though, Rozalia turns on her heels and begins to carry my sheets towards the doorway.

"I... am I allowed to leave?" I ask after her, utterly bewildered by my new prison guard.

What's her deal? And why do I want to know so badly?

"Oh, sweetie, what has Gabriel done to you?" she pouts, sucking her teeth as she stops in the hallway outside. "The door is open, that means you can walk through it."

"What if I try to run away?"

An evil little laugh escapes those dark red lips. "You won't get far, not with me here, and especially not on those wobbly legs. Now come, my captive. Shuffle along after me. We'll find a washing machine—that is, if Gabriel is even civilized enough to have one."

At that, she disappears down around the doorway, leaving me in her confusing wake.

Clearly, she doesn't think much of my desire, or ability to escape.

Shit. She's not wrong. I'm not going anywhere. Not like this.

With a deep sigh, I suck in my pride and grit through the soreness gripping my legs. Maybe Rozalia can teach me more about what's really going on—like where the hell Gabriel has gone?

Shuffling over the bedroom carpet, I trip into the hallway outside.

Rozalia hasn't exactly waited around for me to follow her, but she's not moving that fast either. Up ahead, I spot her popping her head into an open doorway.

"There's a lot of nothing in this place, huh?" she notes, just as I catch up. But she shuts the door before I can see what's inside.

"You're telling me," I mumble.

"I hope Gabriel hasn't been too hard on you," Rozalia says, walking up to another door. This time, I make sure to get a good look inside.

"He's not exactly a gentle man," I respond, peering over Rozalia's shoulder to see a vast home gym stretching out before us.

But we're not looking for a home gym, and Rozalia quickly slams the door shut again.

"You should know that's not true," Rozalia says, continuing towards a staircase ahead. "We're both from the same dark world, darling. Compared to how other men in this line of work treat women, Gabriel's practically a saint."

In a way, she's right. But the reminder doesn't do much to comfort me.

"A saint is a stretch," I huff, as we come up to the staircase. "I'm not sure he'd be welcome in any church."

"Oh, hell no. The man would burn up within a hundred feet of any place of worship," Rozalia laughs. "But he mostly only hurts people who deserve it."

Grabbing onto the handrail, I gingerly follow Rozalia down the wide staircase. For the first time, I get a sense of just how big this place is.

"This house is huge," I whisper.

"Right? And it's not even Gabriel's main home."

The further we descend down the staircase the higher the ceiling seems to reach, and the wider the walls.

"Gabriel told me he'd lost his family fortune," I mention, brows furrowing in confusion. "How could he afford something like this, let alone multiple homes?"

"Ah, I see you two have been sharing secrets," Rozalia notes.

"He just told me about his family. Right before he left."

"Well, then you must know that nothing Gabriel has in America is on account of his family's lost fortune. He's built this all himself. The man is richer than some Fortune 500 CEOs. Unfortunately, that's not enough. Not for a man with his ambition."

"He wants everything," I quietly remember.

"That's right," Rozalia confirms. "And so do I."

When we hit the last step of the long staircase, I stop to lean against the landing. My legs are still weak, but there's no time to pause and rest.

Rozalia keeps moving.

And she has me hooked. So, I follow right along behind her.

Pushing myself off the newel post, I stare up at the sky-high ceiling above us. It's mostly barren, except for one huge, twisted, future art-type light fixture that hangs down from the very center—other than a nondescript white bench by the far wall, it's about the only decoration in the vast hall.

Still, there are no windows.

"So, you want Gabriel and I to get married too?" I call after Rozalia, hoping she'll slow down to answer the shocking question.

But she doesn't even flinch.

"You better believe it," she calls back, not bothering to make sure I'm following her. She knows I'm caught on her every word.

Sucking in a deep breath, I swat away as much soreness as I can and quicken my pace.

Rozalia is already opening up another door when I finally catch up to her again.

"And what will you be to the child he forces me to have?" I question.

I'm only trying to dig a little deeper into my predicament, but still, just saying it out loud sends a cruel shiver down my spine.

That's my fate, to be Gabriel's obedient little baby-maker.

That is, unless I can escape... or prove that I'm tough enough to be his queen.

"Oh, don't you worry, darling," Rozalia says. "I'll only be like an aunt. Gabriel is all yours." Stepping inside the newly opened doorway, she struts ahead before disappearing around a corner.

"I... that's not what I was getting at," I stumble over myself, entering after her.

"Here we go!" Rozalia excitedly shouts. "A washer and dryer. I knew Gabriel wasn't a complete barbarian."

Sure enough, when I turn the corner up ahead, I see the laundry room. It's tucked away in a little cove that doesn't look like it's ever been touched before.

"Really, I wasn't asking like that," I repeat, unable to shake the embarrassment from my cheeks.

"I believe you," she says. Opening up the washer, she shoves the sheets inside. "I don't see any detergent. Typical. The water will have to be enough." Closing the door, she starts the machine. It begins to rumble and she turns back around to me. "Any other questions?"

A thousand different questions swirl around my racing mind. But the despicable pool of jealousy simmering just below my surface threatens to make me sick if I don't obey its demands.

"Uh, yeah... When you said you'd be like an aunt to our... I mean his..." Shit. What would I even call the child Gabriel forced inside of me? He's so controlling. Would he even let me call the child mine? I have no idea. So I just cut straight to the point. "Are you two related in any way?"

"Not by blood," Rozalia quickly responds. "But we were both adopted by the same man—well, not officially adopted, but raised by him."

"The same man who took Gabriel in after his mother died?"

For the first time since she arrived, I sense a bit of hesitation in Rozalia's sharp green eyes.

"Gabriel told you about that?"

"Yes."

Was he not supposed to?

"How much did he tell you?"

"Enough."

"Do you know who killed his mother?"

"I..." I try to remember. "The drug lords, right?"

A stern weight drops Rozalia's lifted lips as she looks off into the distance.

"Let's not talk about such things," she mumbles. "Gabriel can clarify whatever questions you have when he returns."

"Gabriel said he might not live long enough to return," I whisper.

"That's the truth for all of us all of the time," Roz says. "Now stop being such a downer. It's been a while since I hung out with another girl. How about we take advantage of Gabriel's hospitality? For as empty as this place is, I'm sure there's at least one spot that will be filled to the brim."

"Where?"

"The fridge."

My stomach rumbles right on cue. "I mean, I guess I could eat."

"Of course you could. Girl, you're skin and bones." Brushing past me, Rozalia heads back out of the laundry room. "We'll come back in an hour and check on the sheets. Until then, we feast."

I have no choice but to follow her. And it's not just because I suddenly don't want to be alone. There's a magnetism to Rozalia that just pulls me along.

But that doesn't mean I'm not also suspicious... and still intensely curious.

"Why are you being so nice to me?" I desperately shout after her, sore thighs clenching as we walk out into the foyer and start searching for the kitchen.

"Because you haven't given me a reason not to be," Rozalia responds. "At least, not yet."

"And if I did?"

"Then, I'd have to remind you who's in charge here."

When she says that, her voice drops a register and I have

little doubt that this woman has done some seriously depraved shit in her lifetime.

That's when I realize why I find her so alluring.

She's exactly who I've always wanted to be.

A badass woman who's tough as nails and doesn't take shit from anyone.

At least, that's the impression I'm getting so far. But maybe I'm just projecting...

"Are you used to leading?" I prod deeper.

"The toughest lead the pack," she responds, turning a corner up ahead. "Ah, here we are!" When I round it behind her, I find myself in an immaculate marble kitchen.

"You don't look so tough," I challenge. Really, I just want to see another glimpse of her dangerous side. I want to see if Rozalia is the real deal—and if I could ever see myself reaching her level.

"Funny, I was just thinking the same about you," she smirks, heading straight for the massive stainless-steel fridge.

She's clearly unbothered by my comment. Do I dare push her further?

How much worse could she be than Gabriel? How much more can I handle?

I mean, I've already survived being locked away in the belly of the beast. I've survived Gabriel fucking me with so much power he made me bleed. I survived his hate. And his lust.

It all might have broken the woman I was just a month ago. But for as physically weak as I feel right now, there's a callous confidence growing inside of me.

"What if I *was* jealous of you and Gabriel?" I ask, trying to find any buttons Rozalia may have.

"Then I'd say you were wasting your time."

Pulling out an entire fucking rotisserie chicken from the fridge, Rozalia ungracefully tears its plastic casing off. Then, she finds the industrial size microwave and shoves the already-cooked bird inside.

"Well, it's a good thing I have plenty of free time. I mean, it's not like I'm going anywhere, right?."

When the microwave starts heating up, Rozalia turns around and leans forward, placing her forearms on the long marble island in the middle of the kitchen.

"Shit," she smiles. "You've got spunk. That's for sure. I can see why Gabriel likes you so much. But I'm still having a hard time wrapping my mind around how such a fragile looking princess could be giving my big bad wolf so much trouble."

"*Your* big bad wolf?" I hear myself blurt out.

There's no ignoring the flash of jealousy that whips through my chest at Rozalia's claim. But, this time, instead of running from it, I try to use it to my advantage.

"Ah, there it is," Rozalia smirks. "Don't worry. I told you. We're more like siblings—though, there was a time when we were supposed to get married."

She must be fucking with me, because when the microwave beeps behind her, she jumps up like a ballerina and twirls around, hardly phased by any of this.

"You and Gabriel were going to get married? Why?"

It doesn't make any sense, even if they're not blood related, no one would want to marry someone who's like a brother to them.

"Mostly to consolidate power," Rozalia shrugs, tearing into the steaming chicken with her bare hands. "It wasn't our idea. The man who took us in and raised us just thought it might be a good second option—you know, just in case you and Gabriel didn't work out. But hey, thanks for taking that bullet for me. Now I'm single... and ready to mingle. Know anyone that might be interested?"

Alright, she's definitely fucking with me. So much for trying to push her buttons.

"Yeah, how about you go have a chat with my cousin," I challenge her. "Rian Kilpatrick. Tell him all about your plans. I'm sure he'd just love to talk."

"I'm not a big fan of talking."

"Could have fooled me."

Another quick smile flashes across Rozalia's red lips just as she sinks her teeth into a big juicy chicken leg.

"You are quite feisty," she says, still chewing. "I can finally understand the potential Gabriel sees in you." Placing her leg down, she rips off the other one and slides it across the table towards me. "Now eat up. I promised the man I'd put some meat on you."

I hesitate before doing as she says.

Am I getting anywhere with her? It's impossible to tell.

My belly rumbles and I give in.

Leaning over the other side of the kitchen island, I pick up the chicken leg and take a bite for myself.

It's surprisingly delicious.

"So, do you know where Gabriel has gone?" I ask, after swallowing a big mouthful of the juicy meat.

I've abandoned my plans to get her angry, but that doesn't mean my curiosity has died down.

"Of course I do."

"Will you tell me?"

"Only if you promise to set me up with that hunky cousin of yours," Rozalia teases. "What was his name? Rian? I'm guessing he's an Irishman, huh?"

"He's half-Irish and half-Italian. Just like me."

"Ah, half-bloods. Well, maybe I don't want to meet this Rian boy after all."

"He's no boy," I warn her.

"He better not be, because it will take a man to handle Gabriel."

Rozalia hardly even finishes her sentence before her sharp green eyes go wide.

She just made a mistake.

I pounce. But not because I suddenly feel like there's an opening for me.

"What does that mean?" I ask, heart in my throat.

For a split-second, I swear I catch a glimpse of the black cat's vicious side as she considers how to retaliate.

But that fire quickly passes, and her shoulders relax as she takes another bite of her dinner.

"Gabriel is going to meet your cousin," she says.

"Rian?" I gasp.

That's the last thing I was expecting to hear.

"That's right."

"Why the hell is he doing that? Gabriel stabbed my cousin in the back when he took me. Rian will kill him!"

"Not if Gabriel doesn't kill him first."

"They'll tear each other apart!" My hand opens and the chicken leg falls to the marble island "We need to go stop him!"

I've barely turned around before I feel a blade at my throat.

"Ah ah ah," Rozalia whispers into my ear, her bright spring scent suddenly dark and suffocating. "We're not going anywhere."

"Please, we have to do something," I rasp. "Both of those men would kill for me."

"And one of them might just have to die for you."

"No," I choke on my own despair as Rozalia's cold blade hovers just inches away from my burning skin. "What about you? Are you willing to lose Gabriel?"

"I'm always ready to lose everything," Rozalia answers. "But it's nice to see how worried you are about my big bad wolf—or is he *our* big bad wolf now? Either way, it's about time you start to feel as strongly about him as he does about you."

"Roz..." I plead.

"Don't call me Roz," she snaps. "Only my friends call me that. And darling, you may have been growing on me. But I'm not here to be your friend. So, will you behave, or do you want your little nightgown to match those red bedsheets?"

Strangely, I'm not afraid of Rozalia's threats. Maybe it's because I actually am getting tougher, or maybe it's just because I'm more concerned about the lives of the two men who are about to clash somewhere beyond these walls. Either way, it quickly becomes clear to me that there's nothing I can do but try and remain calm.

"Those bedsheets are probably done by now," I mumble.

"We can go check on them, but only if you promise to behave. Can you promise me that, Bianca?"

"Yes."

At that, Rozalia recoils her blade and releases me from her merciless grip.

A violent breath instantly rushes down into my lungs, and I realize I'd been holding my breath.

"In through your nose, out through your mouth," Rozalia says, her footsteps already marching out of the kitchen. "Now, let's go check on those bedsheets."

Even though I know I should follow her like the obedient little captive I'm supposed to be, I can't help but pause by the marble island.

I knew there was something deadly about Rozalia. What I didn't quite understand, though, was just how *different* her ruthlessness would feel.

She isn't Gabriel.

There's no tenderness to her threats, no concern for my own safety in her warnings. She's just doing a job. I'm just a piece of meat.

Fuck. It makes me appreciate my dark wolf more than I ever thought I could.

In his own brutal way, he cares for me. It's clear now, especially when I have the cold steel of Rozalia's unflinching blade to compare it to.

She'd cut my throat just to keep me from escaping.

Gabriel, on the other hand, would kill everyone else just to keep me alive and by his side.

Shit.

A conflicted fire rises in my gut as I realize that I already miss him.

What the hell is happening to me?

Do I have Stockholm syndrome? Cabin fever? Or am I just on the verge of understanding something much more dangerous about myself.

Sure, maybe Gabriel cares for me. Fuck. Apparently, he might even *like* me.

But suddenly, I'm realizing that I might just like him back.

No. There's no maybe about it. He's the man who could help make you into the woman you want to be.

Shit. Maybe I am going crazy, after all.

Because that's a hell of a realization to have about someone who's dragged you into a cage and locked you away; about someone who's shattered your innocence so thoroughly; about someone who might already be dead.

My gut churns as I stare down the long empty kitchen.

Gabriel's going to confront Rian. In a fair fight, I don't know who wins that battle—not that either of those men will ever fight fair.

They are both ruthless, brutal, completely unhinged. Mirror images of each other. Deranged beasts who live for conflict and violence.

The only difference is that Rian has an entire empire at his back.

Gabriel has nothing—well, nothing other than me.

I just don't know if that will be enough to save his life.

14

"There he is," Tytus says, crouching down. "The lion himself."

"He looks pissed."

"As he should be."

Clenching my fists, I watch as the Irish lion stalks through the darkness below. His hulking silhouette is unmistakable.

"You say he's been at this for how long now?" I ask. Reaching under my belt, I pull out the shitty handgun I beat off some worthless pimp earlier.

"The lion's been hunting ever since you jumped in my car with the princess," Tytus tells me. "I've been trying to watch him as much as possible, but for such a big and reckless brute, he sure can be slippery."

"What's his mental state like?"

"Unstable."

That's an understatement. And it becomes clear soon enough.

On the docks below, between the rows of unloaded shipping containers, are two or so dozen men. Most are scattered about, keeping watch in strategic positions, but about half are centered around one particular cargo load.

My blood boils at just the sight of them. These are the disciples Drago was talking about. Spoiled and rotten leftovers from the Reca days. These assholes glorify the fuckers who massacred my family.

I'll gladly help Rian rip them apart.

I just have to hope the lion doesn't turn on me afterwards... or before.

"There he goes," Tytus warns.

Sure enough, we spot Rian discreetly approach two watch guards as they take a cigarette break. They have AKs slung over their shoulders, just inches away from their greedy fingers.

Those few inches give Rian all the time he needs to rip them from limb to limb. There isn't even any time for either of them to scream out for help.

In the blink of an eye, a vicious punch has cracked across the first fuckers skull, sending him tumbling down into the darkness. Before his body can hit the ground, though, Rian has slipped around to the second guard.

With a brutal efficiency, he wraps his arms around the man's face and snaps his neck.

But the lion's deranged fury isn't appeased. Not yet.

All we can do is watch as Rian crushes the two fallen skulls beneath the heel of his boot. We're too far away to hear the cracking and the squishing, but we both get the point.

"Are you sure you don't want me to stick around for back up?" Tytus asks.

Down below, Rian is already moving towards his next set of victims.

"No," I shake my head. "He won't kill me. Not right away. No matter how deranged he's become. I'm the last person to have been seen with Bianca. He'll need to know where she is before he can rip my heart out."

"I don't know if I can sit back and watch if he tries to hurt you."

"So leave. This is between me and him."

"We'll see..."

A few short, frenzied breaths get me ready for what's about to come.

Pain. Violence. Death.

All of my life, I've worshipped those three horsemen. But now, shit is different. Now, I'm not just chasing a dream. I'm working to protect what's locked up back home.

A dream in her own right.

Bianca.

I can still smell her on me. Still feel her body clenching around my cock. Hear her cries of pleasure and pain as I ripped away the last bits of innocence from her sheltered world.

She's far from being completely corrupted. But there's nothing holding her back anymore. Nothing to keep her from becoming the woman I've always fantasized about ruling beside.

My queen.

"Wish me luck," I mumble, shoving my second-hand gun back beneath my belt.

"I'm sure you'll have no trouble with those Reca worshipping fuckers..."

"It's not them I'm worried about."

"Well, I've seen you fight worse monsters than a lion before. If push comes to shove, I'm betting on you coming out of that fight alive."

"That's what I'm worried about," I grumble. "We're *both* supposed to come out of this alive."

"Well, then let's hope the lion's privileged upbringing has softened his edges."

"Bianca's disappearance may have sharpened them again."

"Yeah, maybe," Tytus sighs, taking a deep breath of his own. "I guess there's only one way to find out."

"See you on the other side, brother," I nod, before slipping down the back end of the tall shipping container we've been surveying from.

"I'll be waiting."

Tytus' voice quickly fades into the background, engulfed by the heavy shadows of the dock below.

Running a hand through my hair, I make one last mess of myself. I'm supposed to look as disheveled as possible. If this shit has any chance of working, I'm going to have to convince Rian that my last few days have been hellish.

If only he knew the truth.

I'm not on the ground for long before I hear the first shout come from up ahead. It's followed by a scream, and then an explosion of gunshots.

The shallow wound on the back of my knee flares up against the noise, but I bite through the bad memory. This needs to be done.

Why exactly? Shit. I fucking hate that I don't know. All that's certain is that this is important. Otherwise, why would Drago risk losing his golden goose?

By the time I reach the opening where the main shipping container is, the battle is already almost over. Out of the half dozen figures that were huddled there, only three remain.

It's quickly made into two.

Then one.

Then zero.

Fuck. Despite Rian's lethal reputation, I wasn't expecting him to be this hardcore. He grew up in absolute wealth, after all. The oldest son of the king of the entire American underworld, Aiden Kilpatrick.

He should be more sophisticated than this. Less brutally refined. But here we are, alone on the dark docks, surrounded by bodies he just single-handedly turned into corpses.

Well, maybe we're not completely alone. Not yet.

As Rian marches forward, towards the fresh pile of corpses,

I notice that not all of them are dead. At least one is still desperately trying to crawl away.

That was probably on purpose. Rian isn't just here to let out some rage. He's here for answers. Drago's rumors have already taken hold of the underworld. According to the wind, it's the drug smugglers who have knowledge about Bianca's whereabouts.

Rian is going to interrogate the last living fucker here. Torture him until he spills more than just his guts. And that's bad news for me.

If the questioning is already about to begin, it means I'm late. A single sound will turn the lion's gun towards me. And I doubt he'll hesitate to shoot.

His massacre happened too quickly. I have no way in...

Suddenly, out of the corner of my eye, I see a flash of darkness twitch through the shadows. Then, a glint of moonlight reflects off a raised gun.

There's no time to think. Only to act.

Ripping out my own weapon, I fire at the bleeding fucker who's just crawled from death's door to get one last shot in at the lion.

He doesn't get a chance to pull the trigger before my bullet rips through his skull.

But the danger isn't over. Hell, it's only just begun.

"You."

Rian's voice is a deep and guttural roar—it's infinite fury directed entirely at me.

"He was about to shoot—"

Before I can explain, Rian has left his half-conscious captive by the container and begun to charge my way.

His gun drops from his hand, and I know I'm in for a real fucking treat.

Tossing my own gun aside, I get ready for the carnage.

"You!" Rian repeats. He's gone completely mad. I only get a glimpse of his wild blue eyes before he lunges at me.

There's no point in stepping aside. In trying to talk to him. He's not in any state to listen. I'm going to have to snap him out of this stupor with my fists.

"Fuck," I curse, just as the lion's heavy shoulder connects with my chest. I'm thrown backwards, only stopped by the hard steel of a shipping container.

"Where is she?" Rian roars. Raising his fist, he charges again.

This time, I don't take his fury head on. Ducking aside, I let him dent the wall of steel behind me. But you don't survive these kinds of fights by being completely passive. So, I throw a punch of my own.

It lands against the lion's thick cheekbone, snapping his neck to the side.

For a moment, I think the punch might have snapped him out of it. But then I see the knife in his other hand.

"I'm not here to fight!" I yell.

But it's too late for that. All I can do to keep from being slashed across the chest is hit the ground and roll to the side. Still, the edge of Rian's blade catches my shirt, and a huge gash is ripped open.

The new flap temporarily blinds me, and I have to tear my shirt clean off just so I can see again.

I manage to regain my vision just in time to see Rian's fist connect with my temple. A sharp, violent pain cracks through my entire body as I'm tackled to the ground.

"You took her!" Rian roars, his bloody hands finding my throat. Before he can get a good grip, though, I throw a solid round of punches into his hard stomach.

It makes him flinch, if only just enough to give me the room I need to roll out from under him.

"I saved her!" I shout back at him, pushing myself to my feet as my lungs begin to burn.

"Where. Is. She?"

Rian's shirt has been ripped down both sides as well, and he takes the short break in action to tear the useless material from his body.

That's when I see all of the fresh cuts and bruises that litter his torso. Almost every inch of his exposed flesh has some kind of shallow wound jutting across it. The ones that were created tonight still bleed. But others are a little older. Two or three days old.

Shit. Rian really hasn't just been sitting around since the ambush. He's been putting his life on the line to try and find Bianca.

"She was taken from me," I lie to him, steam rising up from both our shirtless bodies.

"Then you deserve to die for failing to protect her," Rian sneers.

His knife glimmers in the moonlight as he charges forward again. Grunting away the pain, I wait until he's just close enough, then I jump to the side.

Rian's quick, though, and I just barely manage to grab his thick wrist before he can slash me across the face.

"I saw who took her," I tell him, muscles flexing as I try to keep the lion's hand under control.

"You took her," he spits. "I trusted you."

His free hand cocks back and before I can move out of the way, I feel his fist connect with my clenched stomach.

The force knocks me back, loosening my grip around his wrist just enough to let him break free.

"Listen to me!" I implore. "I want to get her back just as badly as you do!"

But Rian clearly doesn't want to believe my lies. Not even for a second. He's thirsty for blood. Anyone's blood.

"Bullshit," he growls, knife still drawn.

With our eyes locked, we begin to circle each other, blood dripping from our hands and steam rising from our shirtless bodies.

"I'm not your enemy," I lie. "But I have a description of the man who is. I know who took Bianca."

"So do I," Rian challenges. "It was you. The fucker who bullied her in high school. The sneaky fuck who used my uncle to become her body guard. The ghost who disappeared with my cousin and never returned. Uncle Ray tried to tell me you were either dead or locked up in some torture chamber—that it was the only reason you hadn't returned Bianca. But I knew better. I know who you are, Gabriel *Corso*... even if Uncle Ray won't tell me."

Rian's blue eyes turn black and I know he's about to charge again. But before I can jump out of the way, I feel a metal barrel press against the back of my skull.

The hot air freezes, and so do I.

"Enough of this."

It takes me a second to recognize the voice. But when I do, I know this fight is over.

Maksim Smolov.

He's got a gun trained to the back of my head.

"You're coming with us, son."

"Uncle... What the hell are you doing here?" Clearly, Rian wasn't expecting the Russian general to appear out of the shadows either.

He must have been too focused on me to give away his uncle's sudden presence... or was that why his blue eyes suddenly turned black?

"I heard about your plan to ambush this drug shipment," Maksim says. "It was foolish, I had to stop you."

"You're a little late for that," I point out.

"Not another word from you," Maksim warns, digging his

barrel deeper into my skull. "Rian, enough is enough. You'll be no good to anyone dead. And you'll only be a danger to those you care for if you continue with your reckless ways. Remember why you're here. And why you can't go back to New York. When's the last time you slept?"

"I'm not sleeping until I find my cousin."

"Then you might go mad before we do." Dropping his gun, Maksim keeps his barrel fixed on me, but chooses to threaten my spine instead of my life. "We have our lead now. Either Gabriel here is directly involved in all of this, or, as he said, he can give us a description of who is."

"He doesn't deserve to take another breath," Rian shouts. "At the very best, he lost the girl he was sworn to protect."

"Settle down, nephew," Maksim sighs. "We'll deal with Gabriel. One way or another, he'll tell us all we need to know. Now, do me a favor, and go pick up that half-dead body you left crawling back there."

Without daring to move, I peer out of the corner of my eye, towards the shipping container surrounded by corpses.

That same fucker is still trying to crawl away from his dead friends. He hasn't gotten far.

"Sure, I'll go fetch another witness," Rian huffs. Straightening up, he seems to briefly snap back down to earth. "But first, I have something to say to Gabriel here."

There's no point in trying to lunge aside. Maksim's gun is still dug into my back.

All I can do is clench my jaw and grit my teeth as Rian takes his hardest swing directly at my already swollen temple.

I hardly even feel any pain.

The world just goes black.

15

BIANCA

"I'm bored."

Rozalia slinks down against my bedroom wall, just beside the open door. Her eyes roll into the back of her head as she mindlessly fiddles with her switchblade.

"*You're* bored?" I ask, flabbergasted. "*I'm* the one who's been stuck inside this windowless nightmare for who knows how long now!"

"And it's made you boring," Rozalia shrugs.

"Well, you're welcome to leave anytime."

"As if it were that easy."

Quickly pushing herself back off of the floor, the black cat begins to pace back and forth. Then suddenly, she stops, just beside the bathroom door.

For seemingly no reason at all, she lifts her knife and plunges the blade into the wall.

"What the hell are you doing?" I ask, astonished by the casual destruction of Gabriel's property.

"Just trying to inject some life into this place," Rozalia chuckles, before crossing the bathroom doorway to stab the wall on the other side too.

"You don't think that might piss Gabriel off?"

"Maybe. But it's what he gets for locking me in here."

"Again, how do you think I feel?"

Rozalia thinks on that for a moment. Then, pursing her lips, she extends her arm in my direction, switchblade in palm, offering it to me.

"Take a stab for yourself then," she says. "I mean, unless you're afraid of what Gabriel might do to you when he finds out..."

A hot tingle washes over my skin as I consider what kind of punishment I would receive for putting a hole in Gabriel's wall.

Another round of spanking?

... Or maybe something even more twisted.

My toes curl into the carpet as I push myself off the bed.

"I'm not scared of him."

"You should be."

"Then why would you want me to get him mad?"

"Uh, because I'm bored. Have you not been listening?"

Rolling my eyes, I decide to accept the challenge. Hell, if the worst that happens is another spanking, then my punishment might be more of a reward than anything.

But Rozalia doesn't need to know that—not even if she probably already knows—this is me being tough. Stabbing Gabriel's wall is badass... right?

"And what if I turn the blade on you?" I ask, my hand hovering over Rozalia's outstretched palm.

"Then I'll knock you the fuck out."

A little smirk finally breaks her stony façade, but it's impossible to tell if that's because she's fucking with me, or if it's because she'd be more than happy for a little action.

"Fine," I huff, taking the switchblade. "I'll just stab an inanimate object then. Because, you know, that's not crazy at all."

"No one ever said I wasn't a little nuts," Rozalia shrugs. "Now put your pretty little ass into it."

Taking a step back, she gives me the room I need to plunge the blade into the bedroom wall.

It barely pierces the fucking paint, before bouncing back at me.

"What the fuck?" I grumble, stumbling backwards, my aching legs tensing to keep myself from falling over. "How the hell did you do it?"

"It helps not being a weak, sheltered little princess."

"I'm not weak," I quickly retort, not denying that I'm sheltered—at least, that I *was* sheltered. There's no coming back from this.

Not that I'm so sure I want to.

"Then put some fire into it, girl. Pretend it's Gabriel you're stabbing."

"I... I don't want to stab Gabriel," I sheepishly confess. *Not anymore. At least, not until he comes back. Alive and well.*

"It's okay, even I want to stab him sometimes... like right now, for example."

"Can't I think of someone else?"

"Sure. Think of someone you really hate."

To my surprise, I have a hard time doing that.

Shit. Have I really lived such a sheltered life that I don't have any true enemies? Rivals?

Hell, since high school ended, only the thought of one person has had the privilege of occupying my mind in such a spiteful manner.

Gabriel.

But now, that burning hate has turned mild. Hell, I even just admitted to myself that I might actually be starting to like him, in a weird, twisted kind of way.

But then who can I focus all of my frustration and anger towards?

Suddenly, the scar above my eyes softly flares, and I have my answer.

"Take this, you fucker," I hiss. Cocking my arm back, I plunge the blade down once more, directly into the wall.

To my surprise, this time, it slips right in.

"Thatta girl!" Rozalia cheers, her voice filled with faux-excitement.

Still, the surge of strength is intoxicating.

"I did it."

"Who did you think of?"

Pulling the knife out, a little waterfall of sawdust trickles to the floor. But the evidence of the destruction I caused only makes me even prouder.

"The asshole who gave me this scar," I say. Lifting the blade, I tap the dull side against the softly throbbing cut that slashes through my eyebrow.

"The frat boy," Rozalia knowingly nods.

"How... How did you know about that?".

"I might have helped Gabriel kill him—or at least wring his body up after the deed was done."

Taking a deep breath, I look back towards the pockmarked wall. "That's what started all of... *this*," I sigh. "My Dad thought someone was trying to frame us. The cops were on their way. We had to get out of there in a hurry. Meet up with my cousins so I could hide on some little island in the middle of nowhere. But we were ambushed. I was taken."

"Boring," Rozalia drawls. "I already know all of this—the fight you got into with the frat bitch also doomed all of your old bodyguards and got Gabriel through the door. Who cares? Stab the wall again. Now, that was fun."

Squeezing down on the handle of the knife, I let my rage bubble over..

"Take that, you wannabe rapist fucker," I shout, plunging the blade back into the wall. Another jagged socket opens up, and more sawdust spills out.

But I'm not done yet. Tears of frustration begin to well up in my eyes, blurring my vision as I start stabbing the fuck out of the wall.

Then, suddenly, something gives way.

Not in me, mind you, but in the wall.

"Oh shit, you went too far, girl," Rozalia laughs.

Wiping the tears from my eyes, I see what's happened.

I made my way to the closet, and stabbed right through one of the shuttered doors.

"I... I didn't mean to."

"Ah, just own it. Hey, what's in there?"

Brushing away the last bits of blurriness, I follow Rozalia's curiosity. Inside the fist-sized hole I just created, I can see the bright material of what can only be a dress.

"What the hell," I mumble. Dropping the knife, I reach for the closet doors.

When I open them up, a whole walk-in closet full of colorful outfits is exposed.

"Not a bad selection," Rozalia notes, crouching down to pick up her switchblade before rummaging through the closet.

"I... I didn't even know these were here."

"You mean you've been wearing that same ratty night-gown this whole time? You never thought to check the closet?"

"I didn't think it would have anything in it."

"Why the hell not?"

"Gabriel never said anything."

"He's stubborn like that. But it doesn't mean he doesn't enjoy spoiling those he's close to. Check out the handle on my switchblade."

Dangling her knife in front of my face, Rozalia shows me what she means.

"It's gorgeous," I gasp, noting the exquisite beauty carved onto the elegant handle. "How did I not notice that before?"

"Probably for the same reason you didn't notice that you

had a closet full of brand-new outfits sitting fifteen feet away from you."

"I'm not an airhead," I defend myself.

"Never said you were," Rozalia responds, turning to search through the outfits again. "You've been through a lot. I don't blame you one bit."

"Thanks," I mumble, turning to help her.

"Are these in your size?" Rozalia asks, pulling down a pretty red polka-dot summer dress.

I check the tag. "Yeah... weird."

"It's not weird at all. Like I said, for all of his faults, Gabriel can be strangely thoughtful sometimes. You just need to push through all of the shit to get to the closet."

"Some of these are really beautiful," I sigh, inspecting a more elegant violet gown.

"It's surprising, I know, but Gabriel has always had strangely good taste. Really, you should be flattered. He likes *you*, after all. That's a good sign."

"It feels more like a bad omen sometimes," I half-joke.

That draws a sincere laugh from Rozalia dark red lips.

"Here, try this one on," she says, pulling down a long, hip tie-dye t-shirt from the rack. "It looks comfy."

"Too colorful," I mumble, shaking my head.

"You want something darker?"

"I want something black."

Rozalia chuckles again. "I got you, girl." Dropping the long t-shirt to the floor, she shoves her way behind the first row of hanging dresses and shirts.

I don't follow behind her. Hell, I'm still in a semi-state of shock.

It feels like my world has been turned upside down again, if only on a much smaller scale.

Gabriel isn't who I thought he was.

Actually, maybe he is.

Fuck. I don't know.

That thoughtful nature of his, the caring streak I thought I sensed in him. It's real. The closet confirms it. Rozalia confirmed it.

For a man who can be so brutal, so ruthless, so endlessly violent and possessive, he can also be like this.

"Found something!"

Shaking my head, I try to leave behind all of the conflict raging inside of me.

Somehow, I almost manage it.

All I have to do is wade through the hanging clothes and find my way inside the walk-in closet.

There, at the far wall, stands Rozalia. She has a black tank-top and a black pair of leggings in her hands.

"It's not exactly as badass as my outfits," she shrugs. "But it should do well for you. What do you think?

"Agreed," I nod.

When I take the clothes from her, Rozalia respectfully turns to look the other way.

Gently, I slide the old nightgown off of my still aching body.

"So, I guess you don't think Gabriel is so bad anymore, huh?" Rozalia asks, filling the quiet air as I silently dress myself.

"I wouldn't go that far."

"Is he at least better now than he was in high school?"

I have to think about that for a second. "I suppose."

"Damn, he must have been really bad in school then," Rozalia laughs. "I mean, if kidnapping you and holding you hostage doesn't seem as bad?'"

My legs are sore enough that the skin-tight leggings aren't exactly easy to put on. But I struggle in silence as I consider Rozalia's question.

"Everything seems worse when you're a kid," I tell her.

"But was it really worse? Was *he*?"

"I mean, he did hit me with his car once..." I remember.

"Just before winter formal, too. I had to go to the dance with a cane. People called me Grandma Byrne all night. Those giggles still haunt me."

I'm only half joking.

Looking down at my feet, I desperately try to hide the teenage girl in me who's still hurt over the whole incident.

Fuck. I haven't thought about it in so long.

That night cemented my status as an outcast. I never recovered from the alienation. I still haven't.

Hell, the entire evening all anyone could talk about was whether or not Gabriel would show up. And when the prom king-favorite didn't grace us with his presence, I was blamed.

And it wasn't just the platinum blondes and the cheerleaders. It was the goths and the jocks and everyone in between. There wasn't a single soul at that school who wasn't mesmerized by the handsome, talented, and mysterious new kid.

They all thought they could break through his stoic exterior. They all thought they could be his friend or his lover. They all thought the winter formal was their chance to do it.

They all thought they were special.

God, they were all so stupid.

And so was I.

Because as badly as I tried to resist it, I'd had the same thoughts too.

But those naïve dreams were shattered right along with my hip bone.

Gabriel wasn't the kindred outsider I thought he was. No. He wasn't like me at all.

He was just another asshole.

"You think he hit you with his car on purpose?" Rozalia asks.

My heart sinks and my brain throbs as I try to access memories I've long since buried.

"I mean, it's not like we had a small parking lot. Sure, it was dark out when it happened—I'd spent an extra three hours at school taking courses for extra credit, just so I could graduate and get out of that hellhole by the end of junior year—but there was no missing me... or who was in the car with Gabriel when it happened, giggling along to it all."

"Some fake blondes with bad roots?" Rozalia guesses.

"Exactly—wait, how did you know that?"

"Because I can still remember when Gabriel told me about that whole mess."

With one last inelegant tug, I finally manage to pull the leggings up to my waist.

"Was he laughing while he told you?" I grumble, reaching for the black tank-top.

A familiar sinking feeling is taking over my gut.

"No. He was pissed. Our plan hasn't changed much over the years, Bianca. In a broad sense, it was the same back then as it is now. To make you his. Hitting you with his car wasn't going to help that."

"So, you're saying it wasn't on purpose?"

"No."

"Then why the hell hasn't he ever bothered to explain that to me?"

"You know full well that Gabriel isn't one to own up to his mistakes like that. He's even more stubborn than me... and you."

Sliding the tank top on, I cross my arms and lean against one of the closet shelves.

"But... but the car was filled with those cackling cheerleaders. I can still remember them scurrying out of the car, laughing as they ran from the scene. I swear I heard one of them yell 'Got her! You're telling me they weren't waiting to ambush me?"

"Look who's Ms. Self-Centered," Rozalia teases. "Why

would they wait around after school just to be there when Gabriel hit you with his car?"

"I... I don't want to say."

Shit. It seems so foolish now.

"Tell me," Rozalia demands, turning around. "Like you said, we have nothing but time."

"Fine," I huff. "But don't judge me. I was a teenager. And Westwood High had a lot of drama."

"No promises."

"Whatever," I grumble. "Well... as I remember it, one of the girls I saw stumbling from the car was someone named Mindy Tepper. Her whole crew of popular girls hated me. And they all had huge crushes on Gabriel. Mindy had walked by one day when I was talking shit about their golden bad boy—how Gabriel thought he was so cool with his tattoos and black car and devil-may-care attitude. I always figured she told her friends... and then they told him. It didn't seem so out of character for a guy like Gabriel to take that personally... to want to show off to some of the popular girls... "

"You really thought Gabriel was that depraved?" Rozalia asks, lifting a dark brow at me.

"I mean, with what I know now, was I really that off-base?"

"Yes," Rozalia sternly responds. "You should know by now that Gabriel isn't like the rest of the scum in the underworld. He may be brutal and ruthless and violent as all hell, but he's a man who lives by a strict code. There's nothing he hates more than those who hurt women and children—well, besides maybe those who push drugs."

"I was sixteen, and he hit me with his car," I remind Rozalia. "A woman and a child."

"It was an accident."

"It was an accident that he just so happened to be waiting outside the school in a car full of mean girls at the exact moment I stepped outside?"

"A crazy coincidence."

"Go ahead, defend him. Explain everything," I urge her, feeling a stubborn fire lashing up from the deep pit in my stomach.

"Fine," Rozalia replies. "Here's what really happened. Those stupid girls were somewhere they weren't supposed to be. A seedy bar run by one of our seedy associates. I guess they were extra thirsty, and extra stupid. And no one else was going to let some underage girls drink in their bar. So those underage girls went and found themselves a place that didn't care about the law. Usually, that would have ended very poorly for them, and it nearly did. But fortunately for those dumb bitches, one of our seedy associates decided to call us—just to see if we were okay with a group of high school girls getting raped and possibly killed at one of our fronts. Our boss didn't seem to care too much. In fact, he almost welcomed the idea; thought he could pin the inevitable 'tragedy' on one of our rivals. You know, drown them in police attention. But Gabriel overheard the phone call. He drove down to that bar himself. He beat the shit out of about a dozen hardened and horny thugs. And then he dragged those drunk bitches into his car and dropped them off at a familiar spot. A spot where his car wouldn't look out of place. The parking lot of your stupid high school."

My mind swirls as I try to figure out what's a lie and what's the truth. But Rozalia isn't letting anything slip. Her face is stone cold, unbreakable... and I can't help but believe her.

But my stubborn fire is still raging.

"Sounds unlikely," I mumble.

"But you know it's true. I can still remember the dent you left in his car. He wouldn't stop staring at it. At first, he said he'd hit a skunk, but I got the truth out of him quickly enough."

"A skunk?" I huff. "Tells you what he thinks of me."

"What he *thought* of you," Rozalia corrects. "Past tense. And even then, I'm not so sure..."

The implication makes me uncomfortable.

There's no way Gabriel ever really liked me, right? I was just a thorn in his side. The one kid at school who wouldn't get on her knees and worship him.

"Whatever," I try to deflect, unsure of how to feel. "I'm hungry. Let's go make dinner."

I've barely even taken a step back towards the closet door when I feel Rozalia's strong hand on my shoulder.

She yanks me back into her body. But this time, no blade reaches for my throat.

"Did you hear that?" she whispers.

"Hear what?" I ask back, not bothering to lower my voice.

"Shush," she insists.

Then, I hear it. It sounds like a door being opened up somewhere down the hall outside. Then, it's slowly closed.

It's subtle, but definitely there.

"Is that Gabriel?"

"Whisper!" Rozalia demands. "And think. Why would Gabriel be opening up every door in his own house. He'd have called out to us the second he got home."

She's right, and I can see just how serious she is by the short white hairs standing up on the back of her hand.

"What do we do?" I ask, finally lowering my voice.

"Take this."

Handing me her knife, Rozalia crouches down and seems to sniff the air.

"What about you?" I ask, studying the sharp blade. What the hell am I going to do with this? Stabbing a wall is one thing... but an intruder?

"I have another switchblade," Rozalia quietly responds. "Plus, I have this."

Reaching up under her shirt, the dark cat rips out a small pistol. Damn. Was she hiding that thing in her bra?

"Who do you think it is?" I ask, my voice cracking ever so slightly as I prepare myself for the worst.

"Trouble."

Up ahead, I hear another door slowly open and close. This one is nearer than the last.

"I think I'm used to trouble by now," I mumble. But it's a bluff. My hands are already shaking.

"If we have to fight, do you think you can use that thing?" Rozalia asks, not bothering to look back at me.

We're covered by a wall of hanging outfits, but if someone is serious about finding us, they shouldn't have any problem.

"Do I have a choice?"

"No. But that doesn't mean you're ready. Keep your ears open. If I tell you to run, you run. Understand?"

"Where do I run to? I don't even know how to get out of this—"

"Do. You. Understand?"

"Yes," I gulp.

Holding the handle of Rozalia's switchblade with both of my shivering hands, I wait for all hell to break loose.

Rozalia is right. Whoever is here, it's not Gabriel.

I'd be able to sense the dark wolf if he was this close.

But all I sense is danger.

True, dark, lethal danger.

Whatever resilience Gabriel has fucked into me, it's about to be put to the test.

Am I ready?

16

GABRIEL

Barbed wire digs into my wrists.

The sharp metal is the only thing keeping me from passing out again. Pain, and the steady tempo of the blood dripping from the cuts in my outstretched arms.

The last thing I remember, Rian Kilpatrick's fist was making contact with my temple. Then, there was darkness. And when my eyes finally ripped open, I was tied up here. Naked and alone.

Here.

Fuck.

The lights don't have to be on for me to realize where I am. I'd recognize the metallic sting in the air anywhere. I'd remember the claustrophobia. The desperate brutality.

This is Ray Byrne's cellar. In the basement of his compound.

If the police had been investigating him for the killing of that senator's son, they must be long gone now.

Because I know what's about to happen. I've been through it before. It doesn't matter how soundproofed this place is, my screams will seep through the walls.

All I'll be able to do is take it. Take it and lie through my fucking teeth. If a single ounce of truth slips from my bloody lips, then I'll never leave this basement. Not alive.

Until then, I just have to keep myself from going mad. My feet haven't been tied, and I have to continuously flex my core just to keep from swinging back and forth—if I let go for even one second, then the pain will drown me.

Taking a deep breath, I peer through the darkness and try to picture the reason I'm going through all of this.

Bianca.

By the end of this violent chess game, there needs to be little doubt in anyone's mind that she's mine. And even if my faith in Drago is faltering, only he knows how to unlock what I need to get where I belong.

On a throne, with Bianca by my side.

Whether she'll be on her knees, or in a chair of her own next to mine is yet to be seen. But I'm already desperate to return to her and figure it out.

More than anything, it's what keeps me strong as I wait in the darkness, suspended by barbed wire, shrouded in blood. Unsure of what exactly comes next.

Stay alive for her. Lie for yourself.

Those two contradicting motivations swirl around inside of me as I hear a heavy bolt unlock behind the cold darkness.

A sliver of light appears. Then, it explodes, filling the room, and blinding me.

"Wakey wakey," Rian Kilpatrick's deep voice precedes the slap he levies against my swollen cheek. "It's time to rise and feel the pain."

Spitting out a pearl of coagulated blood, I force my eyes open again. It takes a while for everything to come back into focus, but when it does, I see that Rian isn't the only one who's come to visit.

Ray Byrne is here as well.

The murderer.

"How are you feeling?" the old man asks, his tone cold... yet surprisingly sincere.

"I've never felt better," I spit again. This time, the blood lining my mouth doesn't get far. It dribbles from my lips, joining the thin pool of blood building below my dangling feet.

"There he goes, lying already," Rian says. "Let's get this fucker swinging, then we'll see just how much longer he can spew his bullshit."

My abs clench twice over as I'm gifted a heavy right-handed jab by the seething lion. The force doesn't bend my body, but it does start me swinging.

"Fuck..." I can't help but grunt. The numbness in my shoulders is being burned away. The skull-splitting pain is returning.

"Make him still again," Ray orders.

Rian hesitates before obeying. Eventually, though, he slaps his hands against my side and squeezes, holding me in place until the momentum of his punch has dissipated.

When he lets go, I've stopped moving. But the numbness is gone. All I feel is pain.

"Ready to tell the truth?" Rian asks.

"I've never done anything but tell you the truth."

It doesn't matter how convincing my lie is. The answer affords me another punch to the gut.

Before I can swing too far backwards, though, Rian grabs me around the waist and steadies my tense body once more.

"Who are you?" Rian asks, all as Ray quietly watches behind him.

"Gabriel Corso."

"Why did you want to become a bodyguard for the Byrne family?"

"Because I wanted to make something of myself."

Another punch to the gut nearly makes me puke. But I manage to spit out only blood.

"You could have done that any number of ways. Why come work for the family of the girl you grew up hating?"

"I never hated Bianca."

Another punch makes my entire body lurch. One of the barbs digging into my wrist is displaced, and the sharp angle slashes into the bottom of my palm, spilling even more blood.

"No more bullshit," Rian growls. "One more lie and I'm going to cut your fucking cock of."

I see the blade in his hand before I can process the threat. Still, I force myself to remain calm.

"I never hated Bianca," I stoically insist, even as every inch of my body burns.

"Then why was she so afraid of you?"

"Bianca isn't scared of anything."

Wrong answer.

"You think I'm bluffing, don't you?"

In the blink of an eye, Rian's fingers have closed in around the base of my soft cock. Holding my dick in a vice grip, he slides the flat side of his blade across my testicles.

"Which nut should I sever first?"

"Rian. That's enough."

Ray's voice is calm yet commanding. And it's enough to pull Rian away.

"One more lie and not even the old man will be able to stop me," Rian sneers, sheathing his knife.

"I'm not in any position to tell lies," I lie. "Please, just ask me what needs to be asked. Bianca is still out there. She's still in trouble."

In my life, I've uttered countless falsehoods. But for some reason, this is the first time I've felt even an ounce of guilt for doing so.

My chest twitches as I realize why.

Empathy. I know exactly how Rian and Ray are feeling,

because it would be precisely how I felt if someone like Drago had managed to get a hold of Bianca.

"Who took my daughter?" Ray asks.

The great don brushes past his nephew, his piercing brown eyes unflinching as they strip me down.

This is the man who killed your mother, I remind myself. *Lie, or he'll kill you too.*

A flash of ancient rage slashes through me. Before Bianca burrowed herself into my every thought, this entire plan was centered around killing this man.

Ray Byrne.

"During the chaos, I escaped with Bianca. Rian held off those fuckers who ambushed us," I start, swallowing my own blood. "But I was unarmed. I was injured. Check the back of my knee. Shrapnel shredded through my flesh. I was bleeding like crazy. I was on the verge of passing out..."

"We know," Rian interrupts. "I followed your trail of blood to the street. But that's where it ended. Almost like a car was there, waiting to sweep you away."

"There *was* a car there," I confirm. "It was filled with more men than I could handle. I tried to fight them off, but I wasn't at full strength. The next thing I knew, I was waking up in a sealed shipping container."

"A shipping container?" Ray asks, intrigued.

It's the first good sign yet.

"Down by the docks," I gingerly nod. The movement only starts me swinging again. I wince against the pain, but no one steps forward to stop me.

"How did you get out of this sealed container?" Rian asks, still suspicious.

"I made a hell of a lot of noise."

"Someone let you out?" Ray asks.

"A worker. By the time they heard me, I was already on the

ship. By some miracle, I was at the top of the pile. Otherwise, I'd be dead by now."

Letting my voice tremble against the unbearable pain, I try to sell my current helplessness.

It seems to work, because I soon feel a pair of sturdy hands around my waist. It's Ray.

The swinging stops. But the pain remains.

"He's lying," Rian insists. "We've already talked to a dozen dock workers. No one told us anything about letting a man out of a shipping container."

"The ship was on its way out to sea," I grit, desperately trying to salvage my lie. "I watched it disappear on the horizon as I tried to gather my breath on the dock."

"How convenient, that the worker who set you free just so happens to be long gone."

"I'm not lying," I try to assure him. "If I was, you don't think I could have come up with something better?"

"No. I think you're a bad liar, and it's a miracle you got through our vetting process at all."

Rian steams before me, still more than ready to cut my balls off. But Ray remains quiet. Without saying a word, he disappears behind me.

I don't know what I'm expecting, but the hair-raising sound of chair legs scraping against the cold cement ground definitely isn't it.

"You believe him?" Rian gasps, utterly shocked as I feel the weight of my dangling feet fall onto the seat of a chair.

The blinding pain shooting up my shoulders is finally eased, if only slightly.

"Thank you," I mumble, graciously.

But Ray ignores me. "I never said that I believe him."

"Then why ease his agony?"

"Because I would like him lucid for what comes next."

Any sense of relief I was just feeling is quickly singed away by that comment.

"Tell us where Bianca is!" Rian shouts, continuing his barrage.

"I already told you. I don't know," I repeat, a helpless weight filling my gut. My lies are falling on deaf ears. Fuck.

"Then tell us who took her. You said you had a description, right?"

"I do. And I have a name too. I overheard just enough before I blacked out."

"A name?" That's Ray's voice. Again, he sounds more intrigued than belligerent. Really, I should stop talking to Rian. Ray seems to be my only hope here.

But can I hide my loathing for him long enough to survive?

"Well, then let's hear it. That at least might keep you alive for a little while longer," Rian barks.

"Drago," I say, as loud and clear as I can, hardly believing that I am. Whatever my adoptive father has cooking up, it seems foolish to expose his name like this. We've all worked so hard to keep everything about us so shrouded in secrecy.

"Drago what?" Rian pushes.

"No one said his last name. But it was clear that he was in charge."

"What did he look like?" Ray asks, stepping back around to my front side.

"He was pale. With wispy black hair and a haggard, mangled face. Scarred, but clear of any tattoos."

"That's hardly helpful," Rian notes. "I know a hundred men like that just off of the top of my head."

"This one... Drago... his right eye. It had scars cutting through it. Claw marks almost. And while his left eye was endlessly black, his right eye was pale and dead. Almost completely white."

"Do you know anyone like that, nephew?" Ray asks Rian.

"No," Rian slowly responds. "Do you?"

"No."

A flash of agonizing pain quivers through my body as I desperately try to hold onto consciousness.

Believe me, you fools. Out of all I've said, that description is the only truth.

"Was he Russian?" Rian asks, suddenly more intrigued than hostile.

"I couldn't tell," I say, hearing my voice getting weaker. "But I don't think so. They spoke both English and another language. I didn't recognize the other language."

My two interrogators process that bit of information in silence, before slowly convening near the middle of the room.

"What do you think?" I hear Rian ask his uncle.

"I think you should go upstairs and tell Maksim what we just heard. Give him the description of our pale, dead-eyed suspect. Drago. Let him put out the word that it's someone we may be looking for."

"Do you believe him?" Rian grumbles, looking over at me.

"Go, nephew," Ray says, putting a reassuring hand on Rian's shoulder. "I'll handle the rest."

"Fine," Rian huffs. He gives me one last lethal look before turning to the door.

When it slams shut behind him, I'm left alone with the man who killed my mother.

But I'm too weak for anger. Too busy keeping up with my own lies to contemplate what this fucker means to me.

All that exists between my pain and my duty are lingering flashes of those crystal blue eyes. Those soft pillow lips. They give me glimpses of comfort as I face down hell, all by myself.

Oh, what I've already done to your 'innocent' daughter, old man.

"Who got to you?"

It's the first question Ray asks when we're all alone.

"What?"

His sudden accusation is jarring. Wasn't he supposed to be playing the good cop?

"Who's been pulling your strings?"

A stone drops in my gut as I realize the old man was never on my side.

Fuck. I haven't been fooling anyone.

"I... I was telling you the truth." Another lie amongst the countless I've already told.

In response, a deep, almost mournful sigh escapes Ray's lips. Stepping forward, he pulls the chair out from under my feet.

The sudden blast of pain temporarily knocks me out. A fact I'm only made aware of when I'm gently slapped awake.

"This is what I get for trying to do the right thing." Ray's deep voice is filled with regret, and his words pry my eyes the rest of the way open as he uses my chair as a seat for himself.

His words throw me right into a raging fire.

"Right thing?" I hear myself blurt out. My brain is so scrambled from the ever-growing agony, from my cacophony of lies, that I can hardly keep my true feelings bottled up.

This man killed my mother. He doomed me to this life. To this path. To this cellar.

Who the hell is he to talk about what's right and what's wrong?

"I understand your confusion," Ray says, his voice dropping as he runs a hand over his jaw. "Men like us don't really ever consider doing what's right. Only what's in our best interest."

"I'm nothing like you," I spit. *Woman killer.* Fuck. I almost want to throw aside my veil and tell Ray everything. To let him know who he is to me, and what his daughter will give me. What she has already given me.

But before I can break, I snap myself awake.

"I'm just a lowly street urchin," I mumble, trying to save myself—after all, it's the only way I'll ever get out of here. The only way I'll get to see Bianca again. "Not a king. Not a Great Don."

"I wasn't always a great don," Ray responds, seemingly waving aside my first rage-filled comment. "Once, I was just like you. A talented, hard-nosed kid from the gutter who would do whatever it took to make a name for myself."

"Then you know I would never throw away the opportunity you've given me."

"No. I don't know that," Ray shrugs. "When I was around your age, the Kilpatricks took me in. Hell, it was Rian's grandfather who gave me my first job. He helped lift me out of poverty, out of the sewers. He gave me the most precious gift of all. Opportunity. At first, I was resentful of that opportunity. All I could see was how much he already had. Slowly, though, I learned that the man hadn't been handed a damned thing. He'd worked his ass off for all he built. That's when I truly understood what I had been given. Not an opportunity to be handed my dreams. But a chance to work for them. That's not an opportunity many people get. But it's one that I was given. And it's one I wanted to give to you."

Even through the blaring pain pulsing through every inch of my body, the sincerity in Ray's voice is shockingly clear.

It doesn't sound like he's just speaking to some fresh recruit from an underprivileged background. It sounds like he's talking to someone he knows.

But how could he know me?

"Why would you do that for me?" I ask, my voice weak.

"Guilt."

The word rips through me like a scythe.

"Guilt for what?"

Say it, you bastard. Tell me that you know exactly who I am.

Tell me that you feel bad for killing my mother. Tell me that it eats away at your insides. That it cripples you.

"For making you an orphan."

My head drops right along with my heart.

The confession is heavier than any physical pain could ever be.

"You killed my mother."

"I did."

"Why?"

"Because I didn't have a choice."

"We always have a choice." My voice trembles.

"You're right," Ray admits. "And I made mine. I chose to take your mother's life so that I could protect the love of mine."

That rips my head back up.

"What?"

"Your mother was... a complicated woman," Ray explains, meeting my gaze head on. "But in her last moments, she crossed a line. Gun in her hand, she aimed death at the only person who'd ever made me feel the true glory of love... and not just the pain of it. If I hadn't shot Sonia first, then I would have lost everything. It was a hard decision. But it was the only one."

My chest burns and my skull aches, but through it all, my brain is desperately trying to make sense of what I'm hearing.

"...Sonia?"

Did Ray just say what I think he said?

"Sonia Caruso," Ray sighs. "Your mother."

It's like a noose has been tightened around my throat. Despite all I've been through, this is what stops my lungs from working.

My mother's name.

Finally.

But just as quickly as my breath is taken, it returns, soaked in dreadful confusion.

"Sonia Caruso," I mumble. Immediately, the name feels wrong on my lips.

That's not a Polish name. Not even fucking close.

"I'm sorry I didn't tell you before."

"I... I..." Fuck. I don't know what to say. "Are you sure?"

"The truth has haunted me for years, Gabriel. But try to understand, I wasn't made aware of your existence until long after your mother's death. By then, it was far too late to give you the upbringing you deserved. You had already grown up an orphan. Whoever your father was, he'd left long before your birth. And you were born just after Sonia decided that there was more opportunity to be had without a child than there was with one. You were hardly even a year old before she left you for the wolves. Abandoned you so she could marry some slimy Italian mob boss—it's part of the reason it took me so long to find out about you. Because she hardly ever told anyone about how she gave you up."

This is the worst torture of all. I can't believe this. I won't.

"No... My mother saved me..."

"Your mother wasn't a good person, Gabriel. I know it's cruel to say—especially now—but it must be said."

"You just want to feel better about murdering her," I hear myself growl.

"No. I'm long past that. The only guilt I feel is about not knowing of your existence sooner. I should have known to dig deeper into Sonia's past. She had so many secrets. But the memory of her death was too painful. Too fresh."

"You murdered a woman!" I shout, pain be damned.

"She was much more than a woman," Ray says, every word filled with a depth I can hardly grasp.

"She was a queen."

Pursing his lips, Ray looks up at me. Pity lines his gaze.

It disgusts me. I don't need his fucking sympathy. I hardly even care what I've just let slip.

She was a queen.

But Ray doesn't push the matter.

"Whatever you've heard about your mother, it doesn't appear to be true. She wasn't a good person, Gabriel. And no matter how hard she tried to be one, she never became a queen."

"How the hell do you know all of this?" I accuse, desperate for everything to be a lie.

"For all of her faults, your mother meant a great deal to me. She was the first girl I ever—" Ray catches himself before he can finish that thought. "Let's just say we grew up together. She taught me a lot. Including how to survive."

"Grew up where?" I ask, fists clenching despite the blood dripping from my palm and my wrists.

"New York."

Fucking hell. That seals it. Whoever Ray is talking about, it's a completely different person than who Drago has always painted for me.

There's no connecting the dots. Someone is lying. Someone is playing me for a fucking fool.

But who?

"Why are you telling me all of this?" I demand to know— not that I'm in any position to demand anything.

"Because I want you to know that you're different, Gabriel. You aren't just some orphan I can ignore. Not just some failed bodyguard that I can mindlessly toss into a shallow grave. I've committed a section of my soul to assuring you have an opportunity to succeed. From getting you into the same private school as my daughter, to pushing you through the vetting process so that you could take a prestigious job under my tutelage, I thought I could force away the guilt by providing you with untold opportunities. By opening a path not usually afforded to people like you—to people like *us*."

Every word digs deeper into my chest, until that last sentence twists the knife into my heart.

People like me.

I'm supposed to be royalty. A lost prince in exile. Not the street rat I grew up pretending to be. That was just a necessity. An unfortunate circumstance to grit through until I was strong enough to take what rightfully belonged to me.

But now I'm not sure what's mine.

Not that Ray has destroyed everything. Not yet. Even if he is telling the truth. There's still hope.

I latch onto that tiny slice of hope.

My father.

Half-bloods can still rule. Haff-bloods can still inherit empires.

"Did you know my father?" I hear myself ask. The desperation in my voice must be clear, but I'm beyond caring about any façade.

"No. And I still don't," Ray admits. Putting his hands on his knees, he stands up from his chair.

Still, even as he approaches, stern brown eyes turning back to stone, I don't feel any fear—only relief.

What I think I know of my father is still safe... for now. And along with that, my identity as an exiled prince can continue to exist.

All is not lost. Not yet.

But as Ray walks behind me again, I can't help but sneer through the agony, and through the relief.

An infinite rage begins to course through my burning body.

Drago.

I swear to God, if he's been lying to me this entire time, using me...

Suddenly, without warning, the barbed wire holding up my right arm gives out. The right part of my body collapses, before catching on the barbed wire that's wrapped around my left wrist. The pain is so sharp and stinging that I can't help but scream.

A second later, my left arm is freed as well, and I fall to the hard cement floor below.

Immediately, I keel over, stomach convulsing as I'm reintroduced to a life that isn't pure, constant suffering.

Ray let me go.

But why?

"El Blanco," Ray says. "That name is the closest I've ever gotten to finding your father. Perhaps, if you survive this whole ordeal, you can use that information to go looking for him yourself."

I hardly hear him over the hoarse, bloody coughs tearing up through my throat.

But I've been through worse. This suffering is what makes a man strong.

Ray's problem is that he hasn't suffered enough. Same goes with his daughter.

I'll have to change that.

But first...

"You're not going to kill me?" I ask, barely getting the words out.

"No," Ray says, stepping back before me. "I haven't given up on you quite yet, Gabriel. Not after all I've put in. Even if I hardly believed a word you've just said. I did hear truth in one thing. The description of the man with the dead eye. Drago. He's real. And either he paid you to betray us, or there's something else going on. Whatever the case, you're the last one to see my daughter alive. And you will help me get her back. Do you understand?"

Blood dripping from my lips, barbed wire still tied around my mangled wrists, I force myself to sit up straight.

"I understand," I nod.

Reaching out, Ray offers his hand to me.

"Good. Now, get up."

It's not like I have a choice. I take his hand. The hand of the man who just turned my entire world upside down. The hand of the man who just confessed to killing my mother.

The hand of the man whose daughter I've taken and defiled.

The same daughter I still have locked away; who I just lied to keep; who I desperately crave to see again.

Ray Byrne helps me up from a pool of my own blood, and I stand tall beside him, uneasy on my own two feet, and half-blind from pain, but full of a ruthless determination.

Because suddenly, I realize something.

Something that I've always suspected—hell, even welcomed—but which has never been so powerful or as invigorating as it is right now.

I'm the monster in this story.

Because for everything that I just learned, for all that Ray Byrne just laid bare, for all I've suffered in the face of the love shared between family members, not once did I ever think of giving in.

Bianca doesn't belong to the Byrnes anymore. Not to her parents or to her cousins.

She belongs to me.

And I'm not giving her up. Not to anyone. Not without a fight.

Drago lied to me. Ray made me an orphan. Rian Kilpatrick nearly ended my life.

No one in this dark world is innocent. Not even Bianca. Not anymore. I've tainted her. Stained her flawless skin with virgin blood. Made her crave the darkness and its depravity.

And I only want more.

Any guilt I had been feeling is burned away as I limp after her clueless father.

I know what must be done.

My fists clench. My heart hardens. I welcome the pain. I bathe in the darkness.

Royal blood be damned, I will be king.

And Bianca will be my queen—whether she likes it or not.

First, though, I need to burn everything to the fucking ground.

It's the only way to begin my reign.

17

BIANCA

The chaos is sudden and violent.

I can't tell who shoots first, but the sound of gunfire fills up the walk-in closet until I can't even hear myself think anymore.

Then, just like that, it's over.

Dead silence.

My first instinct is to look over my body. To check for wounds. But I'm clean. No blood. No pain. Nothing.

That's when I check to make sure Rozalia is alright too. Our eyes meet. The smoke from her pistol billows across the savage glint in her sharp green eyes.

Before I can speak, the black cat lifts a single finger to her lips.

Be quiet.

The knife in my hand trembles. The row of hanging outfits before us sway softly, a few of them riddled with bullet holes.

It's eerily silent... until the cursing starts.

"You fucking bitch!" The voice is coarse and phlegmy and full of hatred.

"No fucking way," Rozalia whispers in response, her sharp eyes going wide with shock.

"What's happening?" I ask, keeping my voice as low as possible.

"Stay behind me, and get ready to run."

That's all Rozalia says before blowing out the tip of her smoking pistol. Lowering the weapon again, she points it outwards and carefully starts to stalk forward.

"Shit," I mumble to myself. My heart is pounding like a jackhammer.

Still, I follow her. Jittery knife pointed outwards.

The swinging clothes are still hot from the bullets that tore through them. It's hard to say how many shots were fired, but I don't need to count. No matter the number, it was too many. It's a miracle we weren't hit.

"Oh, when Drago learns about this, he's going to—"

"Shut the fuck up, *Krol*." When I join Rozalia on the other side of the closet door, she already has her gun pointed at a man bleeding on the floor by the bed.

The man has a gun of his own pointed right back at her.

But when he sees me, the barrel shifts.

Suddenly, I'm his target.

"You're coming with me, *girl*," the man sneers. His thin white lips curl up, exposing triangle teeth, each shaved down to look like fangs. Evil emanates from him like fog from a swamp.

"I... Roz... What's happening?"

"Nothing," she spits. "Start heading towards the door. Slowly. When I say run, you start running. Understand?"

"But where—"

"Do. You. Understand?"

"Yes," I gulp. My knuckles have turned white around the handle quivering between my fingers.

"Good."

"Wrong," the man on the floor hisses. With a grunt, he clicks down on the safety of his gun. But that's all he's able to do before Rozalia shoots the weapon from his hand.

"You fucking bitch!" he shouts, grimacing.

"I heard you the first time," Rozalia snaps back. "Is that all you have to say? What the fuck are you doing here?"

"Oh no, I have much more to say, you traitorous fucking cunt. Drago will have your head for this—or maybe he'll finally let me have my way with you..."

Rozalia fires another warning shot just past the man's ear. But this time, he doesn't flinch. Not even as shards of the shredded wall fall over his bald, tattooed-crossed head.

"Start walking, Bianca," Rozalia orders again.

I do as I'm told, but my knees are like jelly.

Was that a shiver of fear I just heard in Rozalia's voice?

What the hell could scare a woman like her?

"You won't get far, *girl*," the human serpent assures me. "We have eyes in every shadow. We—"

"You're alone, aren't you?" Rozalia interrupts, the tip of her pistol quivering ever so slightly. Her voice, however, has become steady again.

"It was a mistake I won't make again," the man growls back.

"Who says I'm going to let you make any kind of decision ever again?" Rozalia asks. "I should kill you for being here. I should kill you for shooting at me. Hell, I should kill you for calling me a cunt. It's a miracle you're still alive, Krol. Count your blessings and answer my fucking questions. What the hell are you doing here?"

"I was ordered to retrieve Gabriel's special package," the man snarls. What is that Rozalia keeps calling him? Krol? Is that his name or a title? "The girl needs to be returned to us. That's what I'm doing here. Now, here's my big question: what the hell are you doing here? Because it definitely isn't what Drago ordered of you."

"I'm not doing what I was ordered to do. I'm doing what's right."

"That's the wrong answer, *girl*."

With a guttural grunt, the man pushes himself up onto his ass, revealing the wound in his spleen. I'm so prepared for the shot I'm sure is about to come from Rozalia's pistol that I pre-emptively flinch.

But nothing happens. The black cat lets the bleeding serpent get into a more comfortable position.

Still, before he can get too comfortable, Rozalia makes her way over to his fallen gun and takes it for herself.

"Bianca, this is Kuba Krol. Krol, this is Bianca," she says. New weapons in hand, she carefully starts to back away from the man. "You two get a good look at each other, because I have a feeling this is the last time you'll ever meet. Gabriel isn't going to like this, Krol. Not one bit. You've made a huge fucking mistake."

"Fuck you," Krol spits, blood trickling from his lips. "You're the one who's made the mistake. We both know Drago isn't someone you cross. Gabriel is just the prince. I'm not scared of him. And I'm definitely not scared of you, fucking cunt."

"You should be," Rozalia warns him, as we both inch closer to the doorway.

"Step out of that door and seal your fate," Krol threatens. "There's no going back. Either you come with me, or you suffer the fucking consequences."

"My choice is already made, asshole. If Drago wants to talk, then I'll get in touch."

"If you leave, there won't be anything to say. You'll be dead to him. And then I'll make sure you're just plain dead."

"Who said anything about letting you live long enough to keep that promise?"

That makes Krol laugh. At least, I think it's a laugh. It's hard to tell with him.

"You don't have the guts to kill me, Rozalia," he says, hand pressed against his bleeding wound. "Sure, you might have chosen to protect Gabriel's feelings over the fate of your family, but you'll come crawling back when you realize he only cares about the princess."

Krol's black eyes slither back onto me as I step out into the hallway. There's so much hate in his glare.

"You followed me here, didn't you?" Rozalia realizes, pistol slowly dropping as she joins me in the hallway.

"I'll never say," Krol taunts, his thin white lips twisting into a dirty smile.

"If you follow me anywhere ever again, I'll put a bullet right between your eyes."

"Not if I get you first."

There's no hiding how much Rozalia's gun is shaking now. It almost looks like she's about to lose control and drop it.

Before that can happen, though, she holsters it, right along with Krol's confiscated weapon. "See you in hell, you bastard."

"Coward! Face me like a fucking—"

That's the last thing I hear before Rozalia slams the bedroom door shut. Reaching under her shirt, she pulls out a key and shoves it into the handle, twisting until I hear the lock click.

"That won't hold him for long, but it should give us enough time to get out of here and lose the fucker. The idiot came here alone. He probably thought he could catch me snoozing. Fool. Let's start moving. Now!"

She doesn't have to tell me twice. No matter how weak my knees are, or how sore my legs, I force them forward as Rozalia and I rush down the hall.

"Who was that?" I ask, my voice trembling as I begin to realize just how close we just were to death.

"A dangerous man," Rozalia replies.

We hardly pause when we reach the stairs. Still, Rozalia unholsters her pistol again and points it forward, like she isn't quite ready to believe that Krol actually came alone.

"Why didn't you kill him?" I ask, bewildered.

"Because it's not that easy to kill a man. Especially not a man like that.

"Because he's family," I suddenly remember.

You might have chosen to protect Gabriel's feelings over the fate of your family, but you'll come crawling back when you realize he only cares about the princess.

That's what he said.

If that man is part of Rozalia's family, that means he's part of Gabriel's family too. But then what the hell was that all about?

"Fuck no," Rozalia barks. "He's not part of my fucking family. Never really was. Never really will be."

"So then who is he?"

"I'll tell you later, let's get out of here first."

Fortunately for her, my lungs are beginning to burn way harder than my curiosity, and I shut my mouth as we look for a way out of here.

To my surprise, it doesn't take long to find the front door—if only because it's been busted open, creating a howling tunnel of wind that screams out like a fucking ghoul.

We follow the wailing, stepping over the discarded door frame and into a humid night.

"What the hell?"

I'm immediately met by a face-smacking view of a sparkling skyline—as well as a strong gust that nearly knocks me off my feet.

Holy shit. We're on the top of a skyscraper.

"This way!" Rozalia calls out to me. She's heading towards what looks like a fire escape at the far end of the rooftop.

I follow her for a few steps before stopping to look back at the structure we just burst out of.

What I see doesn't seem to make any sense.

A modern mansion, baked into the rooftop. It's walls are a melted mixture of soft grey cement and sleek black glass—they somehow combine to form an almost perfect mirror.

It makes the protruding palace nearly invisible; a reflection of the skyline twinkling at my back.

"Bianca! Here! Now!"

Rozalia's voice cuts through the wind, seeping into my awestruck trance. But it's only when I remember who's still in the invisible palace that I snap back to reality.

"Coming!" I shout.

Stumbling over my own feet, I make my way across the rooftop, joining Rozalia on the fire escape.

"Are you afraid of heights?" she asks.

"... Maybe."

"Then don't look down."

With that, she takes off. The metal floor rattles against her footsteps as she disappears ahead, and I nearly drop the switch-blade still gripped between my fingers.

Don't look down. Don't look down.

Shutting my eyes, I try and force myself to concentrate.

I just survived a shoot-out at close range. I held death at knifepoint. I escaped my cage.

This is nothing.

Slowly, I can feel my shaking hands start to steady.

Fuck. Maybe I'm not so helpless after all. Even if I was terrified for every second of what just happened, I still managed to hold myself together. To do what needed to be done.

Now, I just need to keep going.

Retracting the blade on Rozalia's knife, I take a deep breath. Then, I rip my eyes back open and follow the black cat down the shaky, impossibly high fire escape.

Adrenaline pumping through my veins, I can't help the wave of pride that prickles over my skin.

I can do this.

I'm a survivor.

If only Gabriel were here to witness it.

A little pocket of disappointment appears in my gut as I struggle to catch up to Rozalia.

Gabriel.

I may have escaped my troubles, but the last time I saw him, he was about to walk into a storm of his own.

There's a chance I might not ever be able to tell him about how I handled myself under pressure. About how I escaped. About how I stabbed his walls and secretly hoped to be punished for it...

"Honey, I know you've got shaky legs, but we don't have all night. Krol could be calling for back up as we speak."

Despite the hurried pace of her words, Rozalia waits for me at a landing so that I can catch up.

"You should have killed him," I tell her, newfound courage lifting my voice—but it's mixed with a confusing anger.

I'm glad to be free, yet disturbingly hurt that my captor isn't here to see me off.

"Oh, look who thinks she's all badass now."

Even in the darkness, I can see the whites of Rozalia's eyes as she roles them at me.

"I'm serious."

"If I had held him at gun point and ordered you to cut his throat, do you think you could have done it?" I'm challenged.

"No," I sheepishly admit.

"Good. It's nice to know you haven't completely broken from reality yet. Now, enough small talk. I just texted a friend. There should be a car waiting for us down on the street any minute now. It's up to us to get there before any of Krol's backup."

Rozalia turns and I shut my mouth. Together, we continue our warpath down the black fire escape.

This is starting to feel less like a nightmare and more like an adventure. But I know that feeling won't last long.

We're descending back into hell, and I can feel the weight of the switchblade in my hand getting heavier and heavier.

Soon, I may not have a choice. If I want to survive, I might have to kill.

Fuck.

It doesn't matter that I've always wanted to become a woman who could decimate entire armies with the wave of her hand. Rozalia was right. The reality of actually taking another life fills me with dread.

... Until I remember how good the darkness can feel.

It was Gabriel who showed me just how much pleasure can be found in the heat of hell. He forced me to stare down the flames, to watch as he burned away my innocence.

I survived the pain to feel the ecstasy. The fear was part of it. So was the depravity.

Maybe, I'm not so hopeless, after all.

Maybe, all I need is his strong hand on my wrist, leading my blade as I slice the throats of those who threaten me—or maybe I'm just getting lost in the thrill of survival again.

It's hard to tell.

Still, one thing remains all too clear.

Even as I leave my cage behind, I'm not free. Not from Gabriel. Not yet.

Those hazel-green eyes follow me down the fire escape; they fill me with dread, and a wonderful, fiery darkness. But above all, they make sure I remember that there is no escape. Not without sacrifice. Not without blood. Not without death.

So, who am I going to kill?

Gabriel—or the girl I once was?

18

GABRIEL

"Hey! Don't you wander too far off now."

Rian's voice echoes through the familiar underground tunnel, but I hardly hear him.

I've barely been out of that bloody cellar for more than a few hours now, and I'm already about to be drenched in blood again.

This must be the trap Drago was talking about. We're walking right into it.

If I'm not careful, I'll die right along with everyone else—it's already clear to me that my adoptive father could care less about my safety. Hell, even my life. The ambush was clue number one.

But what I learned back in that bloody cellar, suspended from the ceiling by barbed wire, face-to-face with Ray Byrne himself, made me question more than just the worth of my life.

It made me question everything about my past too.

"Something doesn't feel right," I hear Maksim rumble. "Gabriel, stop there."

There are twenty guns at my back. I counted. And while they're all trained towards the darkness ahead of me, the implication is clear. One wrong move and I'll be shredded to bits.

So, I do as I'm told. This is no time to die. Even if my future is in doubt, one thing is clear. I need to see Bianca again. Taste her. Fuck her. Keep her.

I haven't stopped for long before Rian brushes past me. He has a tablet in his hand, and the white glow from the screen lights up his furrowed face.

"This signal doesn't make any sense," he thinks out loud. "I've hacked into both the city data base, and the private cloud used by the company that originally built this tunnel, but there's nothing about what could be causing this pattern of disruption."

Of course, I already know what he's talking about. A few years back, Roz set up a series of hi-fi signal scramblers all around Drago's underground lair. They allow him to use all of his surveillance gadgets and watch the world above without giving away his presence... or how much power he has hidden away down here.

It's part of how we've avoided detection for so long. And the invention of the scramblers were one of Roz's proudest moments.

Yet somehow, Rian hasn't just locked onto our signal. He's found the power source.

It should be impossible. Shit. Roz has said as much herself.

So, how is this brutal lion breaking through the digital haze?

I'm not knowledgeable enough about this stuff to have any idea. But one interesting thought does make me pause.

Is this the skillset that has made Drago so interested in Rian Kilpatrick?

If so, Rian's expertise must be different than Roz's, because I can't imagine anyone being better at what she does than her.

"What do you think?"

It takes me a second to realize Rian is talking to me.

"You want my opinion all of a sudden?" I ask, trying to keep as much vitriol from my voice as possible.

But it's hard. Especially with the heavy bandages wrapped around my wrists, the aching bruises on my body... and the lack of weapons I've been given.

If we're really walking into a trap, I might be in big fucking trouble.

"We're only here because your description of this Drago fucker was corroborated by the other asshole I dragged back from the docks... and he said we might find what we're looking for down here," Rian assures me, his tone laced with warning.

My curiosity is instantly piqued.

"The drug dealer?"

"That's right," Rian nods, his gaze never leaving the screen in his hands. "The drug dealer. He knew all about this guy. Dragomir Raclaw. Polish, apparently. I thought my dad and my uncles had wiped out those fuckers long ago..."

Even if Rian's gaze is locked down at his screen, I still find it necessary to disguise my own scowl.

What the hell is going on between Drago and the Reca disciples?

If I didn't know any better, I might think he was doing more than just using them. It almost sounds like he's working *with* them.

If I didn't know any better. Fucking hell. What do I even know about my 'adoptive' father anymore?

If even one thing Ray Byrne told me was true, it means Drago's been lying to me for my entire life.

My fingers curl into fists as I think about all the betrayal I've already faced. I have a bad feeling there's so much more to come.

"So, they were speaking Polish," I mumble, still playing my part, despite everything.

"Probably," Rian sighs before finally looking up from his screen. Those wild blue eyes of his study me for what feels like an eternity before he turns around and calls out to his uncle. "Uncle Maks. Take this tablet. Keep your eyes peeled on that blinking dot. If it goes out, you let me know."

"Where are you going?" Maksim asks, reluctantly taking the tablet from his nephew.

"Just for a little walk up ahead. Gabriel, you come with me." Then, looking back over his shoulder, Rian gestures for two of his men to join us. "You two follow in the flanks. Keep your weapons ready. Someone is down here. I'm just not sure who. Not yet."

With that, the lion surges forward. There isn't much I can do but march after him.

"Where are we going?" I ask, confused by the show of trust.

Sure, there are still two guns pointed at my back, but I'm led far enough away from the group that I could probably do some serious damage before anyone shoots me.

"The drug dealer from the docks said this Drago fucker had an underground lair tucked away in a series of abandoned subway tunnels. There was no public record of them, but I was able to hack into a few private servers and find the blue prints."

"Did you find where the lair is?"

"Maybe. That dot I've got my uncle watching over seems to be a source of power for whatever operation is still running down here."

"And you think it's Drago?"

"There's only one way to find out."

Running a hand through his hair, Rian cracks his neck to each side. The prince is no fool. He's just as ready for any trap as I am.

"And what if this is a trap?" I carefully suggest, trying to figure out just how much he already knows.

"Then at least I'll have a human shield to protect me."

Fuck that.

"Sounds like you don't quite trust me yet," I say, pushing my luck.

"This isn't about trust," Rian shakes his head." This is about something deeper than that. I'm not so sure I like your face, Gabriel, let alone the words that come out of your mouth. But everything seems to be falling in your favor."

"I don't know if I'd put it that way," I grumble, lifting my bandaged wrists.

To my surprise, the lion lets out a short chuckle.

"You handled the interrogation better than I expected," he stubbornly admits. "And you put up quite a fight back at the docks."

"I was holding back," I can't help but jab.

"And it cost you," Rian points out. "If this really is a trap, then I'd like to see what you're truly capable of."

"Why? After this is over, aren't you just going to put me down? I know the rules. My crew failed to protect Bianca. Everyone I trained with is dead. That means I'm next."

"Perhaps," the lion admits. "But who's to say the rules can't be tweaked?"

My fists uncurl as we come up to a fork in the tunnel.

"You don't seem so dead set on having my head, all of a sudden," I note.

Rian just shrugs. "After your interrogation, I had a chat with my uncle Ray. He let me know what was discussed when I left the room. I know why you were pushed through the vetting process, Gabriel. I know how you grew up and why."

Is that a sliver of sympathy I hear in the lion's voice?

No. It couldn't be.

"How does that change anything?" I huff, the character I'm playing slowly merging with the real me.

"If you managed to survive all of that, and still be here, stubbornly looking for a girl you didn't get along with in high school, then maybe you're not so bad. Plus, I think I've realized something that even Uncle Ray hasn't put together yet."

My fingers curl back into fists and my hackles rise at the comment. I have so many secrets to hide, and if Rian has found out the wrong one, I'm dead.

"What?"

"You killed the senator's son, didn't you?"

"I..." Shit. I wasn't expecting that. "He hurt Bianca."

The admission is a gamble. But it's one I'm forced to take.

"And your job was to protect her," Rian nods.

"It still is."

Another deep chuckle escapes the lion's lips as he chooses to lead us down the left tunnel.

Fuck. We're getting closer to Drago's lair than I expected. If this is truly a trap, we may be in big fucking trouble.

I can only hope that Roz is taking good care of Bianca.

My chest twitches at the thought of those crystal blue eyes. My cock shifts when I picture those soft pillow lips, and that flawless little body.

Shit. It's not just her body I miss, either.

It's the entire fucking package.

That fire...

"You may be a twisted fucker, Gabriel, but I can relate," Rian says, snapping me out of my dirty daydream. "I'm not on the west coast because I made a whole lot of friends back east. Sometimes, people don't understand what it means to be a protector. You do whatever it takes... no matter how savage."

"I understand," I nod.

My response is genuine.

Killing the senator's son was a lapse in judgement, but not one I regret for a single moment. He touched Bianca. He felt the blade of my knife slash through his throat. He got what he deserved.

There was no other way.

"Whatever the hell is going on between you and my cousin, whatever your history, it doesn't matter to me. All that matters is getting her back. And for all of the bullshit I heard coming out of your mouth in the cellar earlier, I could tell one thing was genuine. You're truly concerned about Bianca's safety. I Believe that, even if I don't believe much else."

"So, you don't trust me?"

"We'll see."

Stopping in his tracks, Rian turns around and calls back to his uncle.

"How's that dot looking, Uncle Maks?"

"Still beeping away!"

"I can't tell if that's a good sign or not," the lion mumbles, shaking his head. "But there's only one way to find out."

What little light there is in this dark tunnel glints off the barrel of his Glock as he pulls it out.

"You think we're close?" I ask, knowing full well that we are.

"Yeah." Reaching into his pocket, Rian pulls out a switch-blade and tosses it my way. "It's not much, but there's no way in hell I'm giving you a gun. Not yet. Trap or not, you have to earn back your firepower privileges."

The blade of the knife feels cool against my hot palm; it sends an unwelcome gust of comradery rustling through my aching bones.

Fuck, I hate that Rian is forcing me to form a begrudging respect for him. It's clear that he's a strong leader. It's clear that he cares for Bianca. It's clear that he's willing to do whatever it takes to get her back.

Shit. Maybe he can be negotiated with, after all.

"Oh, fuck."

"Shit!"

Before I can finish my thought, a flurry of panicked curses comes from the men stationed behind us.

Snapping my head around, I see the first bits of smoke

billow up from the ground. It fills the stale air with an eerie silence.

The calm before a storm.

Then, in the blink of an eye, the entire tunnel is filled with a blinding flash. It's quickly followed by a deafening round of small explosions. They seem to burst from every side as dust falls from the overgrown ceiling above and shrapnel flies past me.

"Find cover!" Rian roars through the sudden chaos. I can't see him, but his voice is already fading into the distance, racing back towards his uncle and their men.

But I don't trail after him.

It's immediately obvious that this trap hasn't been set for me. And thankfully, it doesn't seem to involve Drago at all.

The use of smoke bombs is what tips me off. Those are Tytus' favorite toys.

The monster is here.

Ahead, through the crackling tremors and thickening fog, I hear a loud heavy creak.

A door has been opened. A path for my escape.

Do I take it?

Keeping Rian's knife in my hand, I take quick glance back over my shoulder, just to make sure I'm not being watched. But there's nothing to see. Just an impenetrable mist.

For the moment, I'm all alone.

"Fucking hell," I grumble.

Tytus couldn't have picked a worse time... or a better one. I felt like I was finally getting somewhere with Rian.

"What the hell are you waiting for?" The hushed voice snakes through the smoke, landing on my ears just as I spot a sliver of blackness through the haze ahead.

I can feel Tytus' hulking presence waiting for me behind the black void.

No matter what was just going through my head, I shake it all away and chase after the voice of my old friend.

"Is this on Drago's orders?" I ask, bolting into the black doorway.

Tytus quickly slams it shut behind us.

It's too dark in here to see, but I feel the familiar scars on the monster's palm as we greet each other with a firm hand shake.

"No," Tytus growls. "This is all my own doing. Drago's trap is set up further down the way. But fuck that. Fuck him. We have a serious problem of our own."

It's not like Tytus to be so forward. For a second, my breath catches in my throat.

"You went behind Drago's back? Why?"

"Promise you won't freak out?"

My first thought is immediately on Bianca, then on Roz.

My fingers curl around the knife handle. My heart starts to pound. "You know I can't promise that. What's wrong, Tytus? Is Bianca alright? Roz?"

"They're both fine. For now. But apparently Drago sent Krol after them. I guess the snake somehow managed to follow Roz to your place..."

"He fucking what?"

Slowly, my vision readjusts to the darkness. The look of concern twisting Tytus' face punches a hole through my chest.

"He broke in."

"That fucker was in my home?"

"And now his blood is on your carpet. Don't worry, Roz managed to shoot him first. Caught him in the spleen with a bullet. But you know what that means. There's no going back now. No distracting Drago. We've drawn a line in the sand with Krol's blood."

"Is the fucker dead?"

To my disappointment, Tytus shakes his head. " Last Roz

saw him, he was laying by the bed in Bianca's room, cursing you both as she locked him in and took off with the princess."

The rage building inside of me is infinite. So is the regret.

Bianca is mine I should be the one there to protect her. That fucking seals it. I'm leaving. Rian can figure shit out on his own. Whatever Drago wants from him, he can get himself.

It no longer concerns me.

"Where did Roz and Bianca go?" I ask. "Are they alright?"

"Physically, their fine. Apparently, the Byrne girl is a little shaken up, but she's taking it on the chin."

"Bianca is tougher than she looks," I assure Tytus.

"Well, she better be, because the only place Roz could think to go was your mansion in the hills."

A bolder of dread drops in my gut.

"No. Fuck. Drago knows all about that place, Ty!"

"That's what I said when I picked Roz up. But when she asked me where else we could go, I drew a blank. Any suggestions?"

"No," I admit, after a moment of thought. The grey house was the only place I had that was truly mine. No strings attached. All of my other properties are somehow tied to my partnership with the man who suddenly seems so hellbent on screwing me over.

Drago.

What the fuck has gotten into him?

Is he losing his cool or does he simply not care about dressing this shit up anymore? It's never been more obvious to me that I'm being used.

I'm not his son. I'm just his pawn.

Fucking hell. He'll pay for it. But only after he gives me the answers I need to take what's mine. He should be expecting a visit from me.

First things first, though.

"Let's get the fuck out of here," I growl. "We'll figure out where to go after we're all together again."

"There's a chance I maybe have a line on someplace you and Bianca can hide. A place Drago doesn't know about... but I'm still waiting on confirmation."

"Do your magic," I nod. I'm already turning away when I feel Tytus' heavy hand fall onto my shoulder.

"Wait."

"What?" I ask, not even willing to turn all the way back around to look him in the eye.

Bianca is waiting for me. She needs my help.

Roz too.

We need to get the fuck out of here.

"What do you want to do about those fuckers back in the tunnel?"

For all of the burgeoning notions of begrudging respect and possible negotiations that were swirling around in my head just a few moments ago, Rian has already completely slipped my mind.

"Leave them," I grunt, before adding. "Or at least chase them back above ground. Rian can't fall into Drago's hands. Not if we're really thinking about splitting off from our 'adoptive' father."

"You don't want to kill off the competition while they're weak?" Tytus asks, an undercurrent of surprise lifting his words. "There's some nitrous oxide in the smoke. We could cut down the Kilpatrick prince in one fell swoop. He'll hardly be able to put up a fight."

"You know I like it better when they put up a fight," I remind him.

"Don't tell me you're starting to like the lion," Tytus taunts, his hand falling from my shoulder.

"I like power," I correct him. "And if Rian Kilpatrick can be useful to Drago, then he can be useful to us. We just need to find out exactly what Drago's interest in the prince is."

"And how are we going to do that if we leave them both behind?"

"We don't all have to go into hiding."

I can hear the air rush from Tytus' lungs as he realizes what I'm getting at.

"You want me to go back to Drago."

"Does he know you've chosen sides yet?"

"No. But I'm sure he's guessed which way I'm leaning, especially now that Roz has shot Krol. It'll be a huge risk for me to go back to him."

"Are you willing to take that risk?"

Tytus hardly even hesitates. "I'm willing to do whatever it takes."

"It's the only way," I nod. "Now, enough chit chat. Unless Krol is dead, there's little doubt in my mind that he's sent men to all of my properties. Roz is alone. Bianca isn't safe. I'll go help them. You stay behind and gather information. Find a place for us to hide. Then get in touch with me. Alright?"

"I'll do my best."

One last firm hand shake is all we share before going our separate ways.

Tytus stays behind. Turning back towards the doorway, he puts on a custom-made gas mask.

I storm into the darkness ahead.

My chest starts to pound, adrenaline pulses through my veins. Fuck this shit. I'm finally ready to cut off the dead weight.

Drago can go fuck himself. It was his orders that pulled me away from Bianca; that put Roz in danger. He tried to play me for a fool.

Fuck. Maybe Rian isn't even important. Maybe Drago just needed me out of the picture so he could get his hands back on Bianca.

But why?

It doesn't make any sense. None of it does. But I hardly care anymore.

Only one thing matters.

Making sure no one ever fucks with what's mine again.

I'm coming for you, Bianca.

And I'll kill anyone who gets in my way.

19

BIANCA

"Fuck, that was quick."

Ducking behind the second story window of this red brick mansion, Rozalia checks the clip on Krol's confiscated gun. Then, she quickly moves to reload her own pistol.

"What was quick?" I dare to ask, even if I already know the answer.

We're not alone.

But Rozalia isn't ready to face that reality yet. Not without preparing me first.

"Have you ever shot a gun before?" she asks, ignoring my question.

"No," I sheepishly admit.

Riding up beside the elegant French window, I peak behind the Tyrian purple drapes and peer down onto the courtyard below.

Behind the grey pines and stone statues, I spot movement. A lot of movement.

Fuck.

A stone drops in my gut and my weak fingers curl around the base of my new switchblade. It's still unsullied by blood.

But it doesn't look like that's going to last much longer. Not if I want to survive.

"Pistol or Glock?" Rozalia asks me.

She lifts her two weapons up in the air, twirling them like dolls so I can get a good look at their full figures.

"I... I don't know how to use either."

"All you do is point and shoot," she says, gesturing the motion. "Easy."

"It's not the shooting part I'm worried about," I mumble. "It's the killing part."

"It's kill or be killed, princess. Actually, it's worse than that. If you don't kill these fuckers, they're going to drag you back to the dragon's lair. Who knows what he'll do to you there..."

Her warning only adds more weight to my worries.

"What do you mean, who knows? Aren't you supposed to know these people?"

"I was supposed to," Rozalia replies, her sharp gaze trailing off. "But now, I'm not sure what we're dealing with. Gabriel's told you the plan, right? The whole idea was to wife you up, put a baby in that flat belly of yours, and then go from there. But if Drago is trying to take you from Gabriel, then it's anyone's guess as to why. You're not that much good to him alone. Just another hostage. And we've dealt with those before. It usually doesn't work out too well. Someone innocent often dies."

The implication is instantly clear—as is the revelation.

"Like Congressmen Olsen's daughter..."

"She was just supposed to be practice," Rozalia quietly confesses. "But she wouldn't play ball. Neither would her father. I can't imagine shit would go any smoother with you and your family."

"So then what would this Dragon want with me?"

Rozalia shrugs, snapping herself back to the moment. "Maybe he'll try to marry you off to his lapdog. That fucker Kuba Krol. God, I'm so glad I got to shoot him. Did you know he changed his last name so it would mean king in Polish? Idiot. I don't know who he's trying to fool. The priests would never fall for that shit. So, I guess you'd essentially just be his personal slave? I don't fucking know."

My gut twists into knots as I watch half a dozen black figures wash into the courtyard below. Their guns are twice the size of ours. Their faces are covered. It looks like we're being overrun by demons.

"What happens to you if they catch us alive?" I gulp.

"Probably some torture, then a long, drawn-out death."

"That sounds unpleasant."

"You're telling me."

Taking a deep, shaky breath, I slip my switchblade beneath the tight beltline of my leggings. Then, I reach out my hand.

"I'll take the pistol," I say, every word a struggle.

"You don't sound too confident."

"I don't have a choice. We're not dying here."

A wicked smirk lifts Rozalia's sharp cheekbones.

"Thatta girl. Gabriel would be proud. Now, take this and get ready to use it. If all else fails, you still have the knife."

"It will be just like stabbing walls, right?"

The cold metal of Rozalia's pistol pricks my skin and I almost drop it before clamping both hands tightly around the grip.

"If only taking a life were that simple."

There's no time to ponder the depth of Rozalia's statement.

A loud boom cracks from somewhere downstairs and we both flinch.

Someone's at the door. And they aren't waiting for us to answer it.

The sound of heavy wood splintering makes my skin crawl, but I put on a brave face and look over to Rozalia.

"Good luck," I whisper.

"Try not to mess up this place too badly," she smiles back up at me. "Gabriel is pretty fond of it."

"I'm sure he's fonder of you."

"And you."

With that, Rozalia lunges ahead, Glock drawn and ready to kill.

For a moment, I can't bring myself to follow after her. My heart flutters as I allow myself to gaze around the dark, gothic library we've holed ourselves up in.

In another life, this may have been where a rich, handsome gentleman brought me for a nightcap after a classy dinner date at some fancy restaurant.

Instead, it's the mansion of a man who ruthlessly kidnapped me; who savagely stole my virginity; who cruelly made me like him.

This gothic castle in the Californian foothills will either be my tomb or the place I'm forced to become what Gabriel has always desired.

A dark queen.

I still have no idea which future awaits me when I hear the first shot come from downstairs.

It's a single flashbang. One that's followed by an eerie silence.

Rozalia has her first kill.

But she can't do this alone.

Gabriel isn't the only one who wanted you to become a killer, I remind myself. *It's always been your dream too. He's just the first to take you seriously.*

Crouching down, I slip out of the musky library. The hard wooden floors creek under the tips of my toes as I keep to the shadows, barrel lifted in front of my face.

Another shot comes from downstairs. It's followed by the thud of a body hitting the floor. Fuck. I flinch so badly that I nearly drop my gun.

This time, a shout follows the execution.

"*Uwazaj na dziewcyne!*"

Whatever language that is, it's not one I'm familiar with. But it is quickly responded to in a language I understand much better.

Two quick gunshots pop off in succession. Two more thuds rattle the wooden floors.

"*Utworzyc kopie zapasowa! Potrzebujemy wspacia!*"

Ahead, I see the top of the main bifurcated staircase Rozalia and I climbed up earlier. It's steps are illuminated by two huge uncovered open windows that frame the center of the second-floor hallway. Three rows of smaller windows dot the wall beside them.

I'm already at one of the smaller windows when I first hear footsteps. They bound up the staircase, racing towards me.

They sound too heavy to belong to Rozalia.

My whole body tenses. My pounding heart slows to a snail's pace. My vision starts to tunnel—but before it can get too dark, I spot something out of the corner of my eye. Something so terrifying it rips the killer focus right out of me.

Saddled up beside the small window, I can see outside again. The half dozen men I spotted earlier have been swallowed. Joined by a veritable army.

My stomach drops.

There's got to be at least fifty killers in the courtyard below.

There's no escaping this.

"*Znalazlem ksiezniczke!*"

The yell comes from so close that it practically throws me against the wall. Ripping my gaze from the window, I quickly find the source.

A dark shadow looms atop the staircase. His giant rifle is pointed directly at me.

"Stay very still, little girl," the man hisses, his broken English full of warning.

"No," I hear myself breathlessly gasp.

I can't go out like this. Not so quickly. Not before I can put up some kind of fight. But I'm frozen in place, like a deer in the headlights. Not a single inch of me dares move.

"Give it to me?" the man demands, gesturing at the pistol dangling from my suddenly limp fingers.

"No," I quietly repeat.

This isn't courage, I quickly realize. My brain is shattering.

"Don't make me hurt—"

Suddenly, the window above my head explodes..

Glass shards rain down on me as the man ahead is flung backwards. The gun drops from my fingers. I cover my head with my hands.

Outside, a storm of deafening gunfire has erupted. Inside, deep grunts and cruses cut through my ears.

What the fuck is going on?

My body won't let me figure it out. Fear grips me like a straightjacket. I can't move. Not even to roll away from the shards of glass settling at my feet.

But then I feel a strong hand on my wrist, and I'm ripped from my cowardly little cocoon.

"Bianca!"

That's when I see those fractured hazel eyes. Their green flecks shimmer in the light that seeps through the shattered window above.

"Gabriel..."

"You're coming with me, *myszko*."

Myszko.

Somehow, the little pet name doesn't sound so bad anymore.

Hell, it's almost comforting.

But before I can get too lost in that deceptive comfort, the sinful smirk is wiped from Gabriel's thick red lips.

In the blink of an eye, he's on the ground. Behind him, I see the man who just had me at gunpoint. He's wrapped himself around Gabriel's ankle.

My right hand instantly lifts... but my gun is gone. There's little I can do to help as Gabriel lets out an earth-shaking roar.

But he hardly needs my help. Twisting around, he grabs the intruder by the hair and smashes his head into the glass covered floor, over and over again. Soon enough, the shards are stained in blood, and the intruder isn't moving anymore.

But he didn't come here alone.

Even through the shouting and the shooting outside, I can hear more footsteps racing up the staircase behind us.

Pushing himself to his feet, Gabriel takes me by the wrist again and pulls me up alongside of him.

"Are you hurt?" he asks, those blazing eyes studying me from top to bottom.

"No... I... I'm fine. Where did you come from?"

"The darkness," Gabriel smirks. "Where else?"

He may be having fun with me, but the dark wolf doesn't allow himself to get caught up in the moment.

Whipping around, he draws his gun and opens fire at the men ascending the staircase.

When their cries are hushed, I grab onto his strong shoulder and tug.

"Gabriel, there's an army outside. How are we going to get out of here?"

Reaching into his pocket, he pulls out a fresh clip and swiftly reloads his smoking weapon.

"Looks like we're going to have to sneak out."

Shoving me aside, he lunges forward, firing down the staircase at an unseen enemy.

I stumble back down the hallway.

"But how are we going to sneak out?" I ask, remembering what I just saw waiting for us outside. This place must be surrounded.

"There's a secret tunnel down in the basement," Gabriel says between gun shots. His thick forearm flexes to take the recoil of the powerful weapon. "But the main floor is flooded with these fucking Reca assholes. We're going to have to find another way down. Luckily, I know just the path."

Firing another dozen shots down the stairs, Gabriel curls back around the wall for protection. Then, those hazel-green eyes fall back onto me.

I feel my heart shiver against his intense gaze.

"Tell me what to do."

"Go to the library. On the second shelf of the middle bookcase, there's a thick, dark green spine. Pull it. That should open up the hidden doorway. I'll join you in a second."

Puckering his lips, Gabriel blows at the light cloud of smoke billowing up from his steaming barrel. I swear it drifts towards me, shaped ever so faintly like a heart.

"Please don't be too long," I hear myself quietly plead.

I've already turned my back on him when I hear that deep, chest-tugging voice call after me one last time.

"Bianca."

Immediately, I'm spun back around.

"Yes?"

"I like your new style. That black outfit will look perfect on my floor when I rip it off your body."

Those hazel-green eyes dig deep into my soul, filling me with a new confidence. Then, they're gone, ripped back towards the stairwell to kill those who threaten us.

A confusing mess of emotions swirl around inside of me, and I have to shake my head clear before I start to stumble back towards the library.

By the time I reach the bookcase, and find the thick, dark green spine I'm looking for, my cheeks are red-hot.

Through all of this frenzied chaos , one thing has become disturbingly clear.

I missed that man.

The book spine collapses against my tug, and a deep click unlocks the lines of a hidden doorway. Slipping my fingers in the cracks, I begin to pull.

But it's heavier than I thought, and I have to grit my teeth and flex as hard as I can just to move it an inch.

Still, there's no way I'm going to give up.

Blood rushes into my ears, and the harsh noise outside fades a little. I put everything I have into this one task.

Slowly but surely, the hidden doorway is pried open. The darkness inside spills out in a frigid gust, stale wind swirling around me.

The air is dry and harsh, and my lungs fill with hidden dust. But I don't care. I did it.

I'm about to turn around and look for Gabriel when something stops me.

A burning hand.

It wraps around my mouth like a wretched gag, pulling me so tightly that my neck snaps back.

My heart drops. Because I immediately know it's not my dark wolf.

"Stay quiet now, little girl," the deep voice hisses into my ear. "I would not want to hurt you... too much."

The broken English is just like that of the man who had me cornered in the hallway. But it's so much closer that I can't help but convulse against the cruelty that coats his every word.

"Let me go!" I try to shout, but my voice is caught against the man's greasy palm.

My convulsions become more desperate.

If this man was able to sneak up behind me, does that mean he got past Gabriel?

There's only one way anyone was ever going to get past Gabriel.

No.

"Thank you for showing me the way out," the man says, pushing me forward, towards the black door I just opened up. "Maybe now, you and I can spend some alone time before I hand you over to—"

The moment his fingers slip down over my lips, I know what I have to do. Despite all the dread weighing me down, I let his cold, slippery skin slide into my mouth—and then I bite into him with all my might.

That's enough to get him off of me.

"*Ty suko!*" he growls, flailing his hand out as he reaches down with the other. "You're going to pay for that."

When I see the gun in his belt, my mind goes blank.

There isn't any thought put into what I do next. My body just reacts. Reaching down under the beltline of my leggings, I find the bulge of my new knife.

The blade shimmers as it springs out from the ornamental handle. My arm swings wildly. Viciously. With an unconscious bloodlust.

I catch the man in the throat. His blood splashes against my face. He stumbles forward. But before he can touch me again, I plunge the bloody blade directly into his left eye.

The sickening squelch snaps me out of my savage daze. Dark red blood gushes from his socket as he collapses forward. My blade slips from his socket. My hand falls, fingers still gripped tightly around the ornamental handle.

Somehow, I find the strength to step aside, and he falls to the floor, face first.

The man's entire body twitches and jerks in uncontrollable spasms as his nose breaks and crunches against the hard wooden floorboards, over and over again.

A deep crimson pool leaks from his shattering face, running around the soles of my feet.

I'm frozen by the dreadful morbidity of it all.

Slowly, the adrenaline rushes away from my ears. The heaviness of the chaos rumbling outside seeps back into my world. Still, it hardly compares to the thumps of the human fish flopping before me.

I can't tell if he's screaming, or if his bloody gargles are just how it sounds to listen to someone die. Either way, I'm gripped by the icy reality of what I just did.

And then I hear the heavy set of footsteps of someone approaching from down the hall.

This isn't over.

All I want to do is drop the dripping knife from my hand; fall to my knees; wake up from this gruesome nightmare.

But my fingers won't let go of the knife. In fact, they only tighten.

That's when the true reality of what's happening hits me; when I finally understand what my body has already figured out.

There's only one way out of this endless nightmare. Only one way to escape the grim fate that Rozalia warned me about.

And it's not by fighting my way out—especially not if Gabriel is already dead.

No. I can't just go out there and kill anyone who stands in my way. I'm not made for that. My nerves have already been stretched thin. My insides scooped out. My heart hollowed.

I may never see my family again. Hell, I might never even see the light of day again. But before I'm allowed to die, I'm sure I'll be used to weaken those I love. Maybe even destroy them.

But I can still end this before it gets to that.

Lifting my bloody blade, I press it against my throat and close my eyes.

20

"Bianca!"

The scene that greets me in the library is even more horrifying than I feared.

But not for the reasons I imagined.

A mangled, flailing corpse twitches at Bianca's feet. The floor is flooded with blood. A knife is pressed against my princess's throat. Her eyes are shut. Her hands shake.

She must not have heard me, because her crystal blue eyes don't snap open until I lunge forward and rip the blade from her trembling fingers.

"Gabriel?"

It's like she's seen a ghost.

"What the hell are you doing?" I demand to know. My fingers dig into the tender skin around her wrist. But she doesn't budge.

"I... I thought you were dead," she rasps.

"I'm not letting you go that easily," I growl. Out in the hallway, I can hear gunshots slowly ascending the corpse covered stairwell.

Roz is down there somewhere, fighting for her life.

But she can take care of herself. We always have.

Bianca, obviously, cannot—even if it looks like she just got her first kill.

"That man..." she whispers, looking down at her feet. The body convulses with a vicious consistency. "He tried to take me."

"And you killed him." My gaze drifts over her shoulder, to the open window at the back of the library. Outside, I can hear orders being shouted.

This won't be the last fucker to climb in through that window. We need to leave.

"I... I didn't mean to."

"You had to."

Without looking down, I retract the blade of Bianca's knife and shove it into my pocket.

"I thought you were dead," she mindlessly repeats herself.

"You were wrong. Now, let's fucking go."

Pulling on her tiny wrist, I tug the startled princess into the dark passage behind the open bookcase.

An evil wind howls up from the descending black void. Bianca shivers beneath my strong grip.

"His blood..."

She's in shock. And her little body might as well be dead weight. Still, I toss her against the wall and drag the secret doorway shut behind us.

The moment it clicks shut, a single lightbulb pops on above us. It illuminates Bianca's pale face, spotlighting the dark blood that stains her soft skin.

I let go of her wrist and grab her by the cheeks. "You did well, *myszko*. Haven't you always wanted to be a killer? Well, now you are. You saved yourself. Let me do the rest of the work."

To my dismay, my words don't snap Bianca out of her daze.

Those crystal blue eyes are lost on some distant plane. Her body is almost entirely limp.

"I.. I... I..." Tears begin to well up in her eyes.

Behind the secret door, I hear a loud thump. It's followed by a cacophony of muffled shouts.

Enough of this shit.

Crouching down, I pick Bianca up and throw her over my shoulder. She hardly reacts.

What the hell has gotten into her?

There's no answering that question right now, so I try to ignore it as I step into the darkness and carry us both down the besieged mansion, into the underworld.

Still, no matter how far I manage to carry her away from the danger above ground, I can't shake the dreadful knot that's formed in my gut.

She was about to kill herself.

That idea sits with me like a fucking boulder as I purposely get us lost in this winding underground maze.

By the time I'm convinced we've reached a safe distance from the chaos, something even more dangerous has overcome me.

My dread has turned into a white-hot rage.

"What the hell were you doing back there?" I shout, lifting Bianca off my shoulder.

A possessive fire has erupted inside of me. It gnaws at itself, unsure of who to be angry at.

I was this close to losing Bianca... to herself.

"I... I don't know," Bianca whispers, her chin dropping to her bloody chest.

Everything about her in this moment is so fragile, so fucking dainty. It's infuriating. Where's the girl I left behind at the grey house? The girl I fucked bloody, then verbally sparred with right after?

Where the fuck is the girl who has occupied my mind for nearly every second since I left her?

"Don't lie to me!" I roar, my voice echoing through the darkness. "You were going to—"

Grabbing her chin, I force her downcast gaze back onto me. But before I can look into those crystal eyes, Bianca tears herself away.

"I know what I was going to do!" she shouts, her voice quivering as it lashes across my cheek.

"No, you didn't," I respond, refusing to believe that she would do something so cowardly. "Not really. I've trained you better than that."

"*Trained* me?" Her little state of shock has been set on fire. But she hasn't returned to herself. No. This isn't the Bianca who captivated me. This girl is frantic. Unhinged. "I just killed a man!" she sobs. "You never prepared me for that!"

"I showed you what blood looked like."

"My own blood," she scowls, shaking her head. "That's so fucking different."

My dreadful rage flickers and I find myself on her again. Bianca tries to shake me away, but even with all of her frenetic strength, she's no match for me.

Pinning her against the wall, I let the warmth of her panicked body seep beneath my skin.

"Blood is blood," I growl. "You can get pleasure from it no matter where it comes from."

"You're so wrong. There was no pleasure in that."

"So naïve," I sneer, hating that I'm losing control right along with her. "What you did was beautiful. It was strong. It was right. He was going to kill you; deprive you of all the joys in life—"

"There is no joy in life."

Her words are gasoline on my fire.

Before I know what I'm doing, my gun is out. The steel is

still warm from the shots I just fired; from the lives I just took for her. But it's not enough.

Aiming into darkness behind us, I fire. Three bullets tear through the black veil, filling the tunnel with a thunderous roar.

Beneath me, I feel Bianca tense up, her whole body going stiff with fear.

"No one is coming," I assure her. "Not to kill you... and definitely not to save you."

The barrel of my gun still smokes as I shove it between her legs. Even with my fingertips gripped tightly around the handle, I can feel Bianca's pussy lips spread against the hot steel.

"What are you doing?" Bianca gasps.

The truth is, I don't know what the fuck I'm doing. But whatever it is, it seems to be working.

The tension in her body melts away as she sinks in around the heat of my smoking gun.

"I'm showing you that there's no difference between killing and fucking. Between hate and love. Between life and death. There's pain in it all. But there's pleasure too... if you're strong enough to handle it."

Another gasp gets caught in Bianca's tender throat as I press the gun harder against her cunt.

Those wild blue eyes focus. Her black pupils widen. Her heaving chest slows.

"I'm not strong enough to handle it," she insists, her voice still quivering—but not with fear anymore.

I push myself into her, crushing that tiny body against the wall. Each deep breath she takes lifts her chest into mine. The warmth of her touch makes my blood boil. It makes my heart stir.

It makes my cock hard.

"Yes. You are. And I'll show you." Without giving her an

inch to move, I start to brush my gun up and down her pussy lips. "Do you know how many men this gun has killed? Just today? Just minutes ago?"

"No."

"Countless. It's death incarnate. It's caused more pain than you can imagine. More sorrow. But now, it's going to make you cum."

Bianca's shoulders stretch as I rub the loaded barrel faster and harder against her begging cunt.

Even through her leggings, I can feel her starting to get wet. My cock throbs and twitches in response. It fills with blood until it's thick and swollen and desperate to fuck her brains out.

But that will have to wait.

My princess is at a crossroads. Either she breaks, or she comes out of this stronger than ever... either she cums, or she withers away into nothing.

"Gabriel..." Bianca's voice is breathy and unsure. But her body has already given in.

"Let go of your sheltered life," I demand, lowering my lips to her ear. "Give in to the darkness. Let it wash over you. Find the pleasure in the pain. The ecstasy in the danger. Conquer your fears."

Bianca's entire body trembles as I slip my tongue into her ear.

Then, I feel her eager thighs clench around my gun. Her hands fall onto my arms.

"What are you going to do to me?" Bianca quietly asks.

"I'm going to kill you," I respond. Ripping down her leggings, I place the warm metal against her searing flesh. It doesn't take long before it's soaked in Bianca's pussy juices. Perfectly lubricated. "Then, I'm going to revive you into the girl of your dreams."

Every brush stroke stirs her begging clit. Her back starts to arch. Her breathing begins to deepen.

"You mean *your* dreams," she gulps.

"It's the same thing, *myszko*."

Before Bianca can respond, I slip the loaded barrel into her tight little hole.

Her gasp is so loud it echoes through the tunnels, filling up the darkness. Her nails dig into my arms. Her legs curl around my waist.

Still, I keep her pinned to the wall.

Then, I begin to fuck her with my loaded gun.

"Is the steel still warm, baby girl?" I growl into her ear.

"Yes," she moans.

"Does it feel good?"

"Yes."

"See, I told you."

The slick barrel slips in and out of her wet cunt with surprising ease. With every thrust, I push a little deeper, until the trigger is nearly inside of her as well.

When that happens, I turn the gun upside down, without removing it from her pussy, so that Bianca can feel the trigger against her clit; so that she can feel the danger with the pleasure. The ecstasy with the fear. The power in the darkness.

"Oh my god."

Each breath she takes gets deeper. Her nails dig into my arms.

I start to kiss down her neck, stopping at the tender spot where she'd held her own blade.

Just the thought of what she was about to do makes me so desperate it's infuriating. I start to fuck her even harder. The barrel of my gun curves up her slick pink walls. I bite down on the spot where the knife was held, marking it for myself.

"No one is allowed to take your life," I growl, my cock throbbing so hard I feel like I could burst at any moment. "Not even you."

"I'm sorry," Bianca rasps.

"Don't be sorry. Be strong. Cum for me, Bianca. Cum all over my gun."

"... Yes, sir."

"Promise me."

"I promise!"

That last word is punctuated by a wall-rattling cry. I'm fucking her so hard that even I'm surprised she hasn't shattered yet.

But Bianca had herself fooled. Hell, she'd almost fooled me.

She isn't just some fragile, sheltered princess. She's so much more than that. So much stronger. So much sexier. So much more dangerous.

And if I don't show her that, I'll have failed. Because I can't always be there to protect her. Not from herself. She needs to be resilient.

That's why I'm doing this. It has to be.

I don't actually ever want her to suffer. Not anymore. But the only way to truly avoid any suffering in this dark and depraved world is to grab it by the throat and squeeze. You have to conquer the fear and the dread that suffering brings.

You have to own it.

You have to find the pleasure in the pain.

To save my princess, I'll have to damn her very fucking soul.

"Do it!" I demand.

"Holy shit!"

Bianca's nails dig so deeply into my arm that I swear I can feel myself bleeding. But I don't give a shit.

Especially not when she starts to shake. Fuck. Bianca's entire body begins to violently convulse as I fuck her to orgasm with the barrel of my loaded gun.

The death throes of the man she just killed hardly compare. And he definitely didn't scream like this.

Bianca gasps and yelps and claws at me with all her might.

But I don't budge. Hell no. In fact, I only press her harder against the wall.

When she cries again, I shove my mouth around her open lips. I force my tongue down her throat. With my free hand, I grab onto her tits and squeeze. Pre-cum leaks from my cock, seeping through my underwear; through my pants.

But I'm not concerned with getting myself off. My only concern is keeping Bianca safely pinned against the wall as she shakes and squirms.

She needs to learn. There's no other way.

I can't lose her.

"Are you done, *myszko*?" I ask, when her deep breaths become short and jittery, and the last twitches slowly leave her body.

"I... I'm better now, I think," she softly sighs.

Her gaze drops to the floor as I slip my soaking gun from her dripping pussy.

"Clean it off," I tell her. "I may have to use it again to get us out of here."

Bianca's pussy juice glimmers off the slick barrel as I lift it up to her face.

Bianca's gaze rises. She bites her bottom lip. The look in her sharp blue eyes nearly makes me explode. That long, thick tongue comes out and licks my barrel.

"Swallow," I command.

My entire being vibrates as I watch the pussy juice pass down her throat. The same throat I just marked with my teeth.

"There," she whispers, her voice filled with a curious mixture of mischief and shame. "Happy?"

"No," I say, pressing my throbbing bulge between her legs. "But this isn't about me. Not now. Not until we get you to safety."

It takes all of my strength to push myself off of her. But the separation doesn't last long. The second I'm not there to prop her up, Bianca's legs give out, and I have to lunge forward again just to keep her from hitting the cold, hard ground.

"I.. I didn't mean to do... that," I hear her whisper.

Instantly, I know what she's talking about. And it's not the orgasm I just fucked out of her with my gun. It's not about falling, either.

"What were you thinking?" I ask, a dreadful emptiness threatening to engulf me. Closing my eyes, I trace a finger along the mark I just left on her throat. A very shallow cut slashes through it. Fuck. She was so close to ending it all.

"I was just trying to protect my family," she sighs. "If those men had caught me alive, I would have been used to weaken them... destroy them..."

"I'm using you against your family, too," I remind her, re-opening my eyes.

"It's different."

"Because you like me," I say, putting the words I hope to hear into her mouth.

"So what if I do?"

The sharpness in her response sends a warm arrow barreling though my chest.

There it is. The fire.

She's back.

But she's weak. This princess has been through a lot. And there's still so much more to face.

"We'll talk about that later," I force myself to say. "Let's get the hell out of here."

But even as I crouch down and pull her leggings back up, I'm not sure where we're going next.

At least, not until I feel my phone vibrate in my pocket. Holding Bianca up with one arm, I use my free hand to check the message I just received.

It's from Tytus.

Text me back if you made it out alright. I've found the perfect hideout for you and Bianca. Nice and secluded. And it comes with its very own small time drug lord for you to interrogate. I'll go ahead and prepare him for your arrival. Address is below. Delete this once you've memorized it.

The second I finish reading his text, I pull up Roz's number and send her a message.

How the fuck did I forget about her? Bianca has got me so messed up.

We're out. Are you alright?

To my surprise, Roz responds almost immediately.

Finally. Where do we meet next?

I should have known better than to worry about her—even if only for a second. With a quick reply text, I tell her to get in touch with Tytus, then I shove my phone back into my pocket.

"Is everything alright?" Bianca asks, her voice fading as she sways against my arm.

"For now," I mumble.

But the truth is, shit is more complicated than ever.

Bianca's words have reminded me of just how much is on the line. And just how little I know about how I'm going to deal with it all.

Drago. Krol. The Reca disciples. Rian. Ray. The Byrnes and the Kilpatricks.

All of my hard-set plans have been shoved into a blender. My allies are quickly becoming enemies. My enemies slowly becoming possible allies.

If it weren't for Tytus and Roz, I might be completely lost right now.

Well, maybe not completely lost.

Through all of the chaos, one thing remains clear.

I'm not letting go of Bianca. Not again. Not for anything or anyone.

"Get on my back," I tell her, crouching down. "I'll carry you the rest of the way."

"I can walk," Bianca insists, even as she sways uneasily on her feet.

But I'm not ready to play games yet. Not until we're safe and sound.

Once that happens, though, all bets are off.

My cock is still hard as fuck. It begs to be released into Bianca's tight little cunt. I'm going to fuck her so hard.

But that's not all I'll do.

Tytus said he had a drug lord for me to interrogate. Perhaps Bianca needs a little taste of torture, too. She's already gotten off on me spanking her. Why couldn't that translate to whipping some scumbag drug dealer for info?

Fuck.

My mind races with all of the depraved possibilities as I forcefully lift the stubborn princess off of her feet. Tucking her tired legs under my arms, I carry her like a backpack.

She hardly resists, and soon enough, I can hear the gentle breaths of a sleeping beauty lapping against my neck.

But even as she rests so peacefully on my shoulder, my cock remains fully erect. Every second thought I have is about how I can corrupt her further; how I can defile the remaining bits of her innocence; how I can burn away the weakness.

How I can ensure she'll survive.

Because she came way too close to dying.

Eventually, I will have to make her pay for what she nearly did to herself back in the library. No one gets that close to killing my future queen without facing some form of punishment.

First, though, I'll let her rest. I'll mend her broken body and mind.

Then, when she wakes up from her dirty dreams, she'll face my hand, my tongue, and my cock.

And she'll like it.

The only question is, how much further am I willing to push her?

All the fucking way, a greedy voice growls from somewhere deep inside me.

All. The. Way.

It's the only way to save her.

21

An endless, twisted maze of dark tunnels. The metallic tinge of blood. Rain. Moonlight. A pulsing warmth in my core. A soft leather seat. A long drive. Pine trees. The smell of water.

Everything is hazy and unreal until my head hits a soft pillow. Then, I remember nothing—at least, not until my eyelids flutter open again.

This type of situation is all too familiar to me by now. Waking up in a new place is not something I did much of growing up, but it's happened so much lately that it feels like multiple lifetimes have passed.

Still, this time doesn't feel like the others.

First off, I'm not in some skimpy nightgown. My black outfit from earlier has been replaced by comfy grey sweats.

But that's not the biggest difference.

No. The biggest difference is that, somehow, I can sense Gabriel's presence. He's nearby. And for the first time, that's not a heart-dropping realization.

Instead, it's almost comforting.

My protector.

Taking a deep breath, I sit up in my new bed. But that only dislodges the heaviness in my head.

Fuck.

Suddenly, all I can remember are the violent death throes of the man I killed. His bloody eye socket. The sound of his broken nose crunching against the hard floor, over and over again.

The memory makes me shiver... until a different memory replaces it. And the cold feeling becomes far warmer.

Gabriel.

He saved me... from that mansion and from myself. He ripped the blade from my throat. He killed to keep me safe. And then he fucked me with his weapon of choice.

A ragged breath rips down my throat.

I was so scared. So helplessly lost. But he didn't flinch. Gabriel was so harsh, but that's what I needed. He fucked some sense back into me. And he did it while teaching me a twisted lesson.

It's a lesson I can't quite remember the details of—not right now, not in this drowsy state—but I can still feel it in every fiber of my being. Because, even if I don't know where I am, even if I'm sore as fuck, one thing slowly becomes clear.

I'm not scared—or, rather, I'm not *consumed* by fear.

Sure, it's still there, pulsing gently below everything else. But it's soft enough that I can ignore it. For now.

But peace never lasts long in this world. Not when I'm around Gabriel.

In the blink of an eye, the sun-drenched bedroom is darkened by howls of pain. They come from outside, leaking through the large rounded window on the far wall.

My fear quickly spikes, before I hear something that calms it once more.

Gabriel's voice. It may be muffled, but it's loud and stern

and full of a ruthless determination. He's not the one in pain. He's the one causing the pain.

I find it strangely comforting.

And oddly arousing.

My toes curl into the soft bear rug at the foot of my bed as I prepare myself to stand up.

I can still feel the warm steel of Gabriel's gun in my pussy.

Why the hell did that feel so good?

It's not a question I'm in any state to answer, especially as I force myself onto my feet.

At first, I sway like a thin tree in a strong wind. But it doesn't take long for me to suck it up.

Maybe I am getting stronger, after all.

... Or maybe I've just been through so much that getting out of bed is practically a walk in the park now, no matter how sore I am.

The scent of fresh wood follows me to the large rounded windows at the far end of this big, but cozy bedroom. Before I can see what's happening outside, though, I catch my reflection in the glass—or more specifically, what's hanging behind me.

Mounted onto the log walls are half a dozen snarling animal heads. They range from bears and wolves to bison and elk, each bigger and more menacing than the last.

It's a completely unexpected sight.

Where the hell are we? Another one of Gabriel's eclectic properties?

For some reason, I can already tell that this place doesn't belong to him. But I'm not sure why, even as I rip my gaze away from the mounted heads behind me, and focus onto the thick wall of trees bordering this strange property.

This seems like the perfect spot for a man as secretive as Gabriel to hide out. But it's missing something. The other two places have felt like different sides of the same coin.

Not this place, though.

My dark wolf doesn't seem like the type to mount trophies of his kills on the wall. As far as I can tell, killing is a necessity to him, not a game.

The only games he seems to play are with me.

Another hair-raising wail seeps through the thick walls, prickling my skin as I snap my attention back to the matter at hand.

Gaze drifting down to the overgrown lawn below, I try to spot the source of the sound. But even as another wail causes a flock of birds to fly off, I don't notice anything out of the ordinary.

Then, suddenly, I see him.

Anything but ordinary, Gabriel walks around the corner, shirtless, sweaty skin glinting in the sunlight. His broad shoulders sway with every step, and his dark tattoos seem to slither over his muscular body as he reaches for something propped up against the trunk of a tall pine tree.

It takes me a second of squinting to see what it is.

An axe.

My stomach drops. Then, a moment later, the empty space is filled by a soft ball of pressure.

My toes curl again. My skin pimples.

This shouldn't be so fucking hot.

My little lapse of arousal doesn't last long, though. Because when Gabriel's shirtless body disappears around the corner, the begging and the screaming start again.

That's when a far more disturbing thought crosses my mind. Something that I had purposefully buried deep inside of me, because I knew there was nothing I could do about it.

it's not that Gabriel is a monster. I know that. Fuck. His beastly side is even starting to turn me on—but he doesn't play as gently with his enemies as he does with me.

And who are his enemies? Who is he at war with?

My family.

The pressure in my core instantly evaporates as I consider that those screams could very realistically be coming from someone I know; from someone I care about.

Before I can think on it any further, I find myself racing out of the bedroom. Somehow, I find the stairs and start to pound down those too, gripping onto the handrail so that my sore thighs don't give out on me.

When Gabriel last left me, he was off to see Rian.

What are the chances that meeting didn't go well?

Fucking hell. Gabriel has done such a number on me that I haven't even thought of it since that Krol guy wandered into that camouflaged rooftop palace.

Gabriel is strong, but could he really have overpowered Rian on his own? Could he have locked up a lion before he came to save me?

Is Gabriel really wicked enough to torture my own cousin right in front of me?

Doubt keeps me from keeling over as my feet hit the main floor.

Gabriel isn't that kind of monster. I'm almost certain of it.

Almost.

Maybe the meeting with Gabriel went well. Maybe Gabriel managed to convince Rian and Dad to negotiate. Or maybe, something far worse happened...

I burst out of the front door just in time to see Gabriel swing his ax towards someone tied to the trunk of a great pine tree.

"Stop!" I hear myself scream.

I can't see who the captive is, but it doesn't matter.

"... Bianca?"

Gabriel seems surprised that I'm up and on my feet so early. My presence is enough to stop his axe, mid swing.

But that doesn't stop me from suddenly feeling so light headed that I have to reach out for something to break my fall.

My vision starts to blur and I feel myself tumbling... until my hand falls on a hard, sweaty surface.

Gabriel.

"Don't hurt him," I hear myself quietly beg.

"You're delirious," Gabriel pointedly notes. "Go back to bed, I'll deal with you later."

"No," I insist, even as I fall into his hard body. "Don't hurt him."

"Hurt who?" he questions me.

"The man tied to the tree."

"Do you know who I have tied to the tree?"

"No," I gulp.

"Well, then come meet him."

Taking my arm, Gabriel pulls me alongside of him as we march across the front lawn of this modern two-story cabin. Slowly, I regain focus again, and I see just how deep in the woods we really are.

The sun is high in the sky, almost dead center, and still, the forest that surrounds us is pitch black.

"Here he is," Gabriel announces.

"Let me go, you bastard!"

Even before I turn to see who's tied to the trunk, a wave of relief washes over me. I don't recognize the nasally voice.

It gives me the strength I need to look at the captive head on.

The sight sends a shiver up my spine.

Deep black eyes glare back at me. Blood drips form an open gash in the man's forehead. His left foot is twisted nearly backwards.

"Who is that?" I hear myself asking, hoping beyond hope that it's someone who deserves this kind of treatment.

"This is Luis Falcao. A small-time drug dealer from Colombia who thinks he can just waltz onto my turf and do as he pleases."

"It's not your turf," Luis spits, blood dribbling down his lips. "Unless you've somehow managed to finesse LA from Ray Byrne..."

"... My dad gave you permission to sell drugs in our territory?" The question comes out before I can stop it.

"I don't need anyone's permission, darling," Luis sneers at me. But that sneer slowly twists into a mangled grin as he realizes what I just accidentally confessed. "I'd heard that the Byrne princess was missing," he says, looking over at Gabriel. "But who'd have thought that I'd find her all the way out here, in the cold dark woods, at my very own cabin?"

"This is your cabin?" I blurt out again.

But Gabriel isn't interested in where this conversation is heading, so he ruthlessly cuts it off.

"Enough small talk," the dark wolf growls. Lifting his axe, he swings it over his shoulder. "It's time to get to the important stuff."

"I'm not telling you shit," Luis stubbornly huffs. "But you can tell me—"

Before he can finish, Gabriel snatches the axe from his shoulder and throws it.

The sharp blade digs into the trunk just above Luis' head.

The drug dealer lets out a barely restrained yelp.

"I ask the questions," Gabriel reminds him. Marching forward, he rips the axe from the trunk and then stomps back to my side. "Now, tell me. Who is El Blanco?"

"I've never heard that name in my life."

"I don't miss twice," Gabriel warns, his axe grazing the grass as he swings it by his side.

All I can do is watch... and try to hide my growing arousal.

The pressure in my core has reappeared. My toes curl into the soft dirt below my feet.

My family is safe. For now.

And I already don't like this Luis guy. Drug dealers are scum. Mom and Dad taught me that from day one.

"You don't have the guts to—"

With another swing of his axe, Gabriel interrupts the mouthy drug dealer.

This time, the blade slashes through Luis' thigh, sticking into the muscle as a fountain of blood gushes out.

"You motherfucker!" the drug dealer squeals. But he's not acting so tough anymore. He's practically wheezing by the time Gabriel tears the blade from his leg.

"You're lucky I wasn't aiming for your throat," Gabriel says. Dropping his bloody axe to the ground, my dark wolf lifts his hands to his face.

That's when I first notice the bloody bandages wrapped around his forearms. They look dirty and worn out.

When the hell did those get there?

Unspooling the dressing from his right wrist, he motions me forward.

I do as I'm told.

I'm too aroused not to.

"Take this," Gabriel orders.

"What happened to you?" I ask, mindlessly accepting the dirty bandage.

"Nothing important. Wrap up Luis' wound for me, will you? We don't want him bleeding out before I can get my answers."

"You ain't getting shit out of me!" Luis barks.

"We'll see about that."

Stepping aside, Gabriel slaps my ass, urging me forward. But my nerves tense as I stare down the bloody drug dealer. He's in rough shape.

"Come on, doll. Fix me up," Luis taunts.

"If you talk to her again, I'll tear your cock off," Gabriel quietly threatens. "Go on, *myszko*."

"Yes, sir," I gulp.

Stepping forward, I crouch down and size up the wound. It's deep, and the mangled muscle surrounding the gash spasms uncontrollably.

"There's no need to be gentle," Gabriel reminds me.

His intention quickly becomes clear. He's trying to show me how to handle the pain of others—specifically, the pain of those who would dare disobey us.

No remorse. No tenderness.

No matter how gory his wound is, my job isn't to make Luis feel better. It's to help keep him alive until he can give us answers.

With that in mind, I begin to wrap the bandage around the throbbing lesion.

I don't get far before Luis curses out in pain. His body shakes against his restraints... and then I feel him spit on the top of my head.

Before I can even look up, I hear the crack of Gabriel's fist colliding with the fucker's jaw.

A half dozen bloody teeth tumble into the grass at my feet.

"Finish it," Gabriel growls over top of me.

Reluctantly, I comply.

Luis has the common sense to remain unconscious until I'm done. Only then does he grumble back awake.

Before he can say another word, though, Gabriel pushes me back and steps in front of Luis, lifting his axe so that it's right up in the drug dealer's shattered face.

"My shirt is over on the front steps," Gabriel tells me. "Go grab it and wash yourself off. Then return."

Again, I quietly do as I'm told, unsure of how to express just how much this is turning me on.

The scent of Gabriel's discarded shirt doesn't do much to calm me down. His earthy musk is a hundred times stronger.

Still, I somehow manage to pull myself away from it after cleaning off the top of my head.

"El Blanco is just a myth," I hear Luis grumble, when I return to Gabriel's side.

"So you have heard of him?" I hear myself say.

For all of the intensity surrounding us, the comment makes Gabriel chuckle ever so slightly.

"We see right through your lies, scumbag," he growls, quickly returning to his frightful self. "Tell me what you know about El Blanco, or I start cutting off limbs."

Gabriel already has his axe cocked when Luis finally breaks.

"There isn't much to know," he insists, the first hints of sincerity coming over his coarse voice. "Years ago, he supposedly ran cocaine from Colombia to America. He was the in-between."

"What was his real name?"

"I only ever heard him referred to as El Blanco. He wasn't Colombian, but he moved enough coke to get the nickname. He moved so much of the white stuff that they named him after it. White. Blanco. Get the it?"

"Where was he from?"

"I don't know. I swear. Why the fuck do you even want to know about this fucker? He's been out of the game for years."

"When did you last hear about him?"

"Last I heard, he was one of the unlucky fuckers killed in a government raid on a Colombian compound. Those army assholes massacred everyone and took the coke for themselves."

"If it's been so long since you last heard of him, then why risk your health by not telling me all of this right away?"

"Because you're not supposed to break under interrogation."

"But you just did," Gabriel points out. His voice is filled with a simmering fury, like he's holding it back, but just can't wait to unleash it all.

"El Blanco is dead," Luis huffs. "If that's all you get out of me, then I'll be safe."

"Safe from who?"

"None of your business."

Leaning forward, Gabriel presses the blade of his axe against Luis' throat.

My sore thighs clench. My nipples are already hard.

"It is my business," Gabriel sneers. "But don't worry, you already told my friend enough... or did you think Tytus was *your* friend?"

The drug dealer's shock is clear.

"I... I... What the fuck are you talking about?"

"You two did a little drinking last night, didn't you? Tytus told you he worked with Dragomir Raclaw, and you knew that name well enough to think you could use drunk old Tytus to put in a good word for you. You had already partnered with the Reca disciples, and you'd heard from them that they were working with Drago. So, why couldn't you... right?"

"I... I didn't say any of that."

"Oh, you did. And Tytus recorded it all. I gave it a listen on my way here. You know, after Tytus shared this address with me. But before he slipped out, letting me in so I could beat the shit out of your drunk ass and tie you up for some questioning of my own."

"He... He didn't fool me. I didn't reveal anything important," Luis tries to insist, even as the dreadful realization twists his bloody face.

But even I understand what's happening.

"I don't believe you," Gabriel says. Dropping his axe, he reaches under his beltline and pulls out a familiar looking gun. "I think I know everything that you know. Which means there's no point in keeping you alive, is there?"

"You fucking fool!" Luis wildly screeches, struggling against his restraints. "I know more than you could ever dare to imagine."

Gabriel only rolls his eyes at that claim.

"Come here, *myszko*," my dark wolf orders.

Not a word escapes my lips as I become his shadow. Together, we take ten steps away from the tree. Luis screams after us, but we don't pay him any mind.

"Take this." Handing me his gun, Gabriel grabs my shoulder and positions me so that I'm squared up perfectly with the pleading drug dealer.

The warmth of the metal immediately brings back the filthy memories of what we did in that dark tunnel.

"Is this..." I star to ask, before the words catch in my throat.

I know it's the gun he fucked me with. I can still smell myself on it. Still, I want to hear him say it—if only to stall what comes next.

Because I also know what Gabriel is about to ask of me.

"It is. Now, use it."

Luis's continued cries fall on deaf ears as I look down at the sleek black weapon. Just the sight alone makes my pussy wet.

But not even that can untangle the knots forming in my gut.

"I... I don't know if I can."

"I'll help you," Gabriel whispers. Leaning down, he rests his chin on my shoulder and lifts my wrists until the barrel is aimed at Luis.

"You fucking bitch!" the drug dealer squeals. "Don't you dare!"

"This is the world we live in, Bianca," Gabriel tells me, his voice remaining low and calm, even if I still sense the fury simmering beneath it all. But that's not all I feel. His throbbing bulge presses into the small of my back. His hot breath washes against my ear. "This is how to conquer the darkness. This is your gun now. Just like this is your cock."

Brushing his lips against my earlobe, Gabriel gently thrusts his searing bulge into my ass.

A warm shiver nearly makes me drop the gun. But my dark wolf holds me tight.

"What else is mine?" I hear myself rasp.

The pressure in my core is starting to tremble.

"What else do you want?"

"What do you mean?" I quiver, the intensity of the moment getting to me.

"What do you want out of life?"

What I want out of life is so different than what I want right now. What I right now is for Gabriel to take this gun from my hand. I want him to walk up to Luis and shoot him right between the eyes. I want him to spit on the fucker. Then I want him to pry my jaw open and spit in my mouth. I want him to bend me over right here, outside, and fuck me until I bleed again. Then I want him to lick up my blood and feed it to me.

But what do I want out of *life*?

"... To be my own woman," I mumble, shocked at the depravity of my own thoughts.

"It's too late for that. You're mine. But I can also be yours, as long as you're strong enough to handle me. Prove yourself. You want to rule one day, right? You've already killed once. But to conquer empires, you must kill hundreds. Thousands. It starts here. Now. Destroy our enemies. All of them."

"Not all of them," I hear myself whisper. "You're at war with my family."

"Yes," Gabriel quietly agrees. "But I might be able to negotiate with them."

"Why would you do that? What happened to destroying your enemies?"

"*You* happened."

My eyelids flutter as Gabriel plants the softest kiss against the back of my ear.

"Shoot him, *myszko*."

I want to pull the trigger so badly. I want to end this. I want Gabriel to fuck me. Then I want him to hold me afterwards and tell me that all of this will work out. That I can see my family again... and build something with him. Something brutal. Something ruthless. But also something pure and tender.

Something that's ours.

But Luis has started to sob. My finger twitches over the trigger. No matter how badly I want to end this, I can't bring myself to shoot.

"I can't. He's defenseless..."

"Do you want me to untie him? Give him a gun?

"No."

"This man worships the fuckers who killed my parents," Gabriel growls. "Well, my father. Do it for me, Bianca. Avenge my family."

But the talk of family has only made me weaker. What would my own parents think of me now? For as much as I've always dreamed of becoming a dark and ruthless queen, the reality of just how depraved I can truly be is terrifying.

Killing Luis like this just doesn't feel right.

"No," I rasp, devastated by my own lack of courage.

For a moment, Gabriel doesn't react. Hell, he doesn't even breathe. Neither do I.

Then, I feel a change in him.

Pushing himself off me, he tears the gun from my hands.

"Very well," he says, his voice disturbingly quiet.

Before I can even process what's happening, he's marched up to Luis and pointed the barrel of his gun between the drug dealer's eyes. The same barrel he fucked me with.

"No! Please! I have money! I can give you—"

The gunshot is sharp and stinging. At my back, I hear a flock of birds ruffle from a tree.

Ahead, Luis' neck snaps down. Blood pours from the hole in his forehead.

Gabriel tosses the gun to the ground. Then, he turns around to me.

"You failed, *myszko*," he says, his voice deeper than ever. "You need to be punished."

22

Gabriel pulls me up the stairs even faster than I stumbled down them.

His grip around my wrist is tight. His intentions are terrifying. I failed his test, and now I'm going to pay for it.

And I've never been more turned on.

My pussy is leaking like a broken fucking faucet. My nipples threaten to rip holes in my shirt. The pressure in my core is swirling like a nuclear reactor.

When we get back into the bedroom, Gabriel pulls me towards the bed and throws me over his lap. There's nothing I can do but gasp.

"Did you fail on purpose?" Gabriel asks. His hand is so big that it spreads out across my entire ass as he feels my cheeks through the baggy sweats. I'm soaking through the cotton already. "Do you want to be punished?"

Slowly, he slides his fingers between my legs, over the lips of my pussy. A ragged sigh rips up my throat.

"I didn't fail on purpose," I whisper.

In response, Gabriel rips off my pants.

"Then you're still weak, *myszko*. I gave you an easy kill, and you squandered it."

I'm not wearing any panties and Gabriel's searing touch is immediately on my skin. My back arches. My pussy begs to be taken.

"I don't want my kills to be easy," I lie. "That's not what a true queen would want."

"Silly girl," Gabriel says, clicking his tongue against the top of his mouth. "True rulers take what they're given, and they make the most of it."

Just like that, his first thick finger slides inside my slick little hole. My hands instinctively grab for the bed sheets, but the second I lift my arms, Gabriel grabs them with his free hand, hogtying me.

"Is that what I am to you?" I ask, my shoulders bending as Gabriel's finger curves up inside of me. "Just something to make the most of?"

"Oh no, you're so much more than that."

My tight little hole stretches out as Gabriel forces another finger between my soaking lips.

"Tell me what I am to you," I rasp, thigh closing in around his thick forearm.

"Haven't I already told you?"

Starting gently, Gabriel begins to pump his two fingers in and out of my pussy. The pressure in my core intensifies. My stomach sinks against the growing pleasure.

"You told me I was a useful pawn. A key to opening up the doors of your destiny."

"That's all true."

"Is that all I am to you?"

Another finger enters my pussy, and I yelp as I'm stretched out even further.

"No. And you never were only that," Gabriel says, his three fingers picking up speed.

I can hear the sloshing of my own pussy juices as I'm pounded by the giant's hand.

"Then what am I?"

I don't know why I'm suddenly so interested in cutting through all of the bullshit. Maybe I'm just so turned on by what happened outside that I need to know how Gabriel actually feels about me.

Am I growing on him like he's growing on me?

Even through the pressure building in my core, a heavy ache threatens to pierce my heart.

What if I'm the only one catching feelings here?

"You are the bane of my existence," Gabriel says, and my heart drops. "But you are also the only reason I have any hope for the future. And it's not just because of how I can use you. No. When I think of my future, you are always in it. By my side. Stronger than you are now... but forever my little sex slave."

Gabriel's thumb starts rubbing my soaking clit just as his pinky joins the rest of his fingers in my outstretched hole.

"Oh my god!" I cry out. My body has been set on fire.

This hurts so fucking good.

"What do you think about that, *myszko*? How would you like to rule with me? How would you like to be ruled by me?"

I'm too turned on to think clearly. But the heavy ache threatening my heart is erased by a flood of visions from my own future.

No matter what I see, Gabriel is there, standing tall beside me.

"And what if I get sick and tired of being ruled by you?" I ask, afraid of my own visions.

Even after all we've been through, Gabriel is still a man keeping me captive. A man who's using me for power.

"Then perhaps I will let you try to rule me right back. But not without a fight. You will have to be strong if you want to overpower me. Much stronger than you are now, *myszko*."

"*Myszko...*" I mutter.

That pet name.

No matter how much I try to convince myself that Gabriel is still the villain in my story, I can't help but notice how much softer that word has become. It leaves his thick red lips like a gentle push, rather than a sneering taunt. "Does that mean I'm not ready to learn what that pet name means?"

"Not yet," Gabriel confirms. "Not until you prove to me that you are ready."

There's no room left in my pussy. My hole already feels like it's stretched to its limits. But Gabriel isn't satisfied.

He wants me to be ready.

His thumb slides down from my clit. His four fingers curl up inside of my pussy. His thumb somehow finds a way inside.

"Gabriel!" I shout, my red-hot cheek pressing against the bedsheet.

Fuck. My stomach heaves against his thighs; against the growing heat of his rock-hard bulge. My fingers flail wildly, restrained by his powerful grip.

My dark wolf holds me in place.

His entire fists slips deeper inside of me.

When I feel his knuckles descend past my outstretched threshold, I squeal. I try to escape. This is too much. I'll be ripped apart.

But even with all of my frantic energy, I'm no match for Gabriel. Hell, the more I struggle, the bigger his fist seems to grow inside of me.

"Are you strong enough to take every last bit of my desire, no matter how depraved?"

I can barely hear him over the blood rushing into my ears.

But I can feel him. And not just his fist.

My struggle leads me just far enough up his thigh to feel the massive scale of the monster that has grown beneath his pants.

It's outline feels even thicker than his fist. And definitely longer. It twitches up into my body, cracking the swirling pressure in my core.

"How much more depraved can you get?" I dare ask.

He's already pounded me bloody. Spanked me red and raw. Fucked me with his loaded gun.

But that's just the tip of the iceberg. And we both know it.

"Would you like to find out?"

"Yes."

His fist seems to swell as it pounds my pussy, and my mind nearly goes blank from the intensity of it all.

Nearly.

Through all of the blinding ecstasy, I can still see red.

I can still picture what just happened outside.

The way Gabriel was interrogating that man tied to the tree. The way he ended his life when I wouldn't.

If we're talking about true depravity, it's got to start with that. With how turned on I was by it. By the power. By the way Gabriel dominated another man. With how I wished it was me.

I'm just as twisted as he is.

The only question that remains is this: has Gabriel made me into this monster, or has he just uncovered who I truly am?

Each thrust of his fist into my outstretched cunt makes me lean closer and closer towards the latter.

This just feels so... right.

The pain. The pleasure.

Is this what he's been talking about this whole time?

I was too panicked in that underground tunnel to truly appreciate the perverted lesson he was trying to teach me.

But now, bent over his lap, hands press against the small of my back, giant fist fucking my tiny pussy, I feel like I truly understand.

"Fuck me," I hear myself whisper. "Fuck me again, daddy."

The leviathan that is Gabriel's cock twitches beneath his pants, lifting up into my heaving belly.

"Which hole?" he asks, knuckle-deep in my cunt.

"Whichever one you want."

Before I can even take my next jittery breath, Gabriel has unsheathed his fist from my pussy and thrown me off his lap.

I fall onto the mattress, choking for air as I'm overcome by both a burning relief and a chilling emptiness.

I desperately want Gabriel back inside of me.

My hips thrust up into the air, clit begging for his tongue. Cunt begging for his cock.

Gabriel listens.

I hear his pants hit the floor. I feel the warmth of his leviathan. Then, I see it.

Thick like a fucking log, almost as long as my forearm, with veins like a river system. Gabriel's cock plunges towards my mouth.

All I can do is open wide.

Even then, he barely fits. My teeth graze against his pumping flesh. My tongue is crushed beneath his girth. My mouth is filled. My throat is smashed against his thick head.

"Choke on my cock, *myszko*. Gag for me. Squirm."

There's no mercy in his words, only an insatiable lust.

Reaching down, he grabs a fist full of my hair and starts to ruthlessly fuck my face.

Immediately, tears start streaming down my cheeks. Saliva cascades over my chin. My lips are stretched so thin they begin to hurt.

But I don't care.

This is ecstasy, in all of its depraved glory.

My choking is so loud that I can barely even hear Gabriel as he growls over me, thick thighs flexing on either side of my head.

He's caged me. Captured me on a whole new level.

And I fucking love it.

My hips thrust up into the air. My clit smacks against Gabriel's hard, muscular ass.

I can't breathe. But I don't need air.

This is all I need.

My king's cock.

The pressure in my core is about to go terminal when Gabriel rips his swollen meat out of my drooling mouth.

I gasp for air. Air that I don't want.

"I want to fuck you so badly, *myszko*," Gabriel growls down at me.

My heart flutters against the intensity of his hazel-green eyes. The hazel has never looked so primal. The green so stormy.

"So do it," I rasp.

"No," my dark wolf says, shaking his head.

"You won't fuck me?"

My tits heave as my lungs fill up with useless air. I want more cock. I need more cock.

I want to be Gabriel's queen. And his little sex slave.

"I haven't earned it yet," Gabriel says. "I haven't made you strong enough. When you become the queen I crave, then I will fill you up with my cum, I'll choke you with my seed, rip you apart with my teeth, and impale you with my cock."

His deep, untamed voice only makes me want him more. Every word is like a lash against my clit.

"Please," I quietly beg. "Fuck me."

"Not until you're ready."

But that doesn't mean Gabriel is done. Reaching back, he pries my thighs apart with his knee.

Then, both of his hands fall on my tits.

It's only then that I realize that one of them is covered in blood.

It's the hand he was fist fucking me with.

My tiny little hole throbs as I peer down below my waist. Gabriel is already lifting up my legs with his shoulders.

The inside of my thighs are covered in blood.

He's made me bleed again.

"Gabriel, what are you doing?"

"Cleaning you."

The first lash of his tongue flickers across my swollen clit, and I nearly explode.

Instantly, my hands are in his dark hair. It's all I can do to keep from erupting as he begins to play with me.

"Holy shit."

My squeals remind me of the dead man outside. The morbid memory only turns me on all the more.

When Gabriel begins to suck on my clit, I slam my bloody thighs against his ears and hold on for dear life.

The harder he licks, the crazier I get. My mind fills with blood. Visions of what I've seen. What I've done. Krol bleeding beside the bed I lost my virginity in. The man I stabbed in the library, convulsing on the floor. Luis' dead body, still outside, just feet away, his dark red blood staining the green grass and brown earth below his lifeless feet.

Something in me snaps.

The pressure in my core shatters into a million different pieces, shards that rip through my body at light speed.

I'm eviscerated by the pleasure. By the pain. By the ruthless beauty of it all.

My heart bursts behind my chest as I writhe around Gabriel's head. Somehow, I can feel his pulse through his ears. It runs up my thighs, through my pussy, across my core, straight into my chest.

I'm in love.

The thought hits me like a fucking freight train.

But just as quickly as it appears, it's gone; vanished into the

ether, leaving behind only a deep fucking concern for my own
sanity.

Slowly, I float back down to earth. But just because my
mind-blowing orgasm is fading, doesn't mean Gabriel is quite
there yet.

I'm still trying to gather my breath when my dark wolf
forces his way out from between my legs and crawls over my
body.

"It's about time you get a taste of what you do to me, *myszko*.
Are you hungry?"

"Starving," I croak.

Pinning me down with his knees, he starts to jerk his
massive cock right in front of my face.

"Good girl. Now, open wide."

The heat emanating from his balls is suffocating, yet
strangely comforting; it almost calms me as I wait for him to
finish.

That doesn't take long.

I'm almost back to breathing in regular intervals when
Gabriel pries my lips back open. His swollen cock is plunged
between my lips.

He explodes.

There's nothing I can do but swallow. Stream after stream of
thick creamy cum pours down my throat, sweet and salty and
endless.

And then it's over.

Even after he's done, Gabriel keeps his cock shoved in my
mouth.

My face is already going red from the oxygen deprivation by
the time he finally pulls out.

Without a word, he collapses down onto the bed beside me,
the massive weight of his muscular body sinking the mattress,
pulling me towards him.

Silently, Gabriel's burly arm wraps around me, his bicep pushing into my cheek, and we just lie there, peacefully.

For a moment, I can almost imagine us as a real, ordinary couple.

It doesn't matter what sick twisted things we've done—both inside the bedroom and out. A calm blanket of domestic bliss seems to flutter down over us both.

Sure, my body still twitches with involuntary spams as Gabriel's hot cum drips down my throat and into my stomach. But it's nothing compared to the fluttering in my heart; to the strange peace I feel, not just in the air around us, but deep inside of me.

What the hell is this?

I'm not lucid enough to understand. And I don't really care.

Shit. I'm hardly bothered at all as I drift off in Gabriel's arm, sandwiched between his bicep and his muscular chest.

But that doesn't mean a quiet panic isn't bubbling somewhere deep inside of me, miles below this unexpected tranquility.

That thought I had as Gabriel made me cum.

I'm in love.

It's more disturbing than anything I could have imagined.

So why does it excite me so fucking much?

My toes are already curling again when Gabriel rolls away from me.

Shit. Maybe I finally did it. Maybe the old Bianca is dead. Maybe I've killed her—with Gabriel's help.

Does that mean I've made my choice?

Did I forsake the girl I used to be? Did I choose him?

The answer floats in the air, just out of reach, as Gabriel gets up and walks around the bed.

When he picks up his pants, I hear a subtle buzzing sound coming from one of his pockets.

He rips a phone out. The pale glow lights up his blood-soaked lips, as well as the look of concern in his hazel-green eyes.

"Is everything alright?" I hear myself ask.

"Better than alright," Gabriel replies, a dark smirk creasing his dimples. "You will be my queen even sooner than I hoped."

"You think I'm ready?" I gulp, not quite sure what he means.

"You'll have to be," Gabriel nods. "The dark priests are on their way."

23

GABRIEL

"Are you sure this line is secure?"

Crouching down, I press the phone to my ear and begin to search the bedside drawers for something to rid this room of Luis' cowardly stench.

At my back, I can hear the soft sound of Bianca's hot shower drifting out from behind the half-open bathroom door.

My heart twitches at the thought of what we just did.

But it's not just what we did in that bloody bed that has me shook. It's what we did out on the front lawn too.

Bianca was my good cop. My partner as I interrogated that scumbag Luis Falcao.

She helped me get what I wanted. Answers. Even if they were vague.

El Blanco.

The mystery fucking grows.

"It better be secure," Roz's crackling voice speaks up. "Or else I'm losing my touch."

"Maybe you are losing your touch," I say, only half-joking. "After all, Rian Kilpatrick was able to break through your scramblers and latch onto the power signal you set up near Drago's lair."

"He what?" Roz hisses, before catching herself. "I mean, who's to say I didn't design it like that? Drago was trying to set up a trap. Wasn't he?"

"We don't work with Drago anymore," I remind her.

Ripping open the bottom drawer of the oakwood night-stand, I finally find what I'm looking for.

A box of matches, and a row of white candles. They smell like vanilla. It's the same fragrance I smell when I think of Bianca.

Perfect.

"We'll let's not say that too loud," Tytus pipes up, static hissing behind his voice. "At least, not yet. I still have to keep up appearances with the dragon, don't I?"

Placing the candles in strategic spots around the bedroom, I begin to light them.

The scent is invigorating, especially in the face of what I just learned.

The priests are coming.

Soon, Bianca will officially be mine—and so will all of the power that our union can bring.

But that can wait.

First, there are other matters to consider.

"Tytus, did you find out what Drago wants with Rian Kilpatrick?" I ask, keeping one ear trained towards the half open bathroom door.

My cock still gently throbs as I peek through the slit. Unfortunately, Bianca's naked figure is shrouded by the steam coating the glass shower walls.

I can still taste her sweet nectar on my lips, as well as the metallic tang of her blood.

It's almost enough to make me rock hard again.

Fuck. She tasted me too. My cum erupted down her tender

throat, and she swallowed every last drop.

But that was just the start. We'll be married soon. Then, I can reward myself, and her.

I will fuck her again. And this time, I'll finish inside of that tight little cunt.

"I didn't have time to get much out of Drago," Tytus grumbles. "But I did manage to overhear something useful."

"What?" Roz and I both ask at the same time.

"You were right, Gabriel," Tytus tells me. "It definitely has something to do with the lion's technical skills. Something about decryption."

"Fuck," Roz curses. "Decryption has always been my weak spot. But it's just because I don't like puzzles, alright?"

"I believe you," I assure her, stepping out in the hallway.

The pitter patter of Bianca's shower fades and my heart stirs.

"How's Krol doing, by the way?" Roz asks Tytus, glee lining her every word. "Is he in a lot of pain?"

"Seems like it. He was fucking pissed. Almost started a fight with me before I reminded him of how that would end."

"I wish you would have ended him," Roz snaps.

"In due time," I remind her.

"Yeah," Tytus agrees. "Before we can stage any kind of uprising, there's a wedding we all have to attend."

"Then, we'll have access to Gabriel's lost fortune... as well as his father's hidden army," Roz agrees, calming herself.

The stirring behind my chest tightens into a knot as I consider just how close I finally am to realizing my destiny.

None of this has gone according to plan. Yet, somehow I feel like it couldn't have gone any other way.

Sure, I've all but cut ties with my adoptive father. Sure, other than Tytus and Roz, I'm uncertain of who to call an ally and who to call an enemy.

But I have Bianca. And I can tell that I have more than just her body now.

My fingers clench and unclench as I pace the hallway outside the bedroom.

Something has changed between us. Something that snapped free in me while I ate out her bloody cunt.

Fucking hell. It's hard to admit, even just to myself. Even just silently.

But a four-letter word crossed my mind while she came all over my face—a word that has been all but absent from my life.

Love.

For a moment, I truly felt like I was in fucking love.

It was a dreadful, dangerous thought.

But the moment I got Tytus' text about the priests, it suddenly didn't seem so bad.

One way or another, Bianca is going to be mine. Forever.

At one point, that sounded like hell. I didn't think I could ever like her, let alone trust her with the power she would help bring me.

But now?

I can see the future in our union. I can see the light at the end of the tunnel. I can see her stunning silhouette waiting for me. Preparing for what's to come.

Shit.

Really, I should be overjoyed that I'm falling for my little mouse. I'm stuck with her, after all.

But my feelings for her are a double-edged sword.

The last thing I want is to see her get hurt. Truly hurt. I don't want to watch as she's crushed by the overbearing weight of our dark responsibilities.

She isn't ready yet. And a ring's not going to push her over the edge. So, I still have to figure out a way to break through the last bits of her soft outer shell.

And I have to do it before the ceremony.

"We're so fucking close," Roz echoes my thoughts. "Are you

sure the priests are willing to go behind Drago's back to marry Gabriel and Bianca?"

"They don't give a shit about Drago," Tytus assures us. "Gabriel is the one they've been waiting for. Hell, they almost looked relieved when I intercepted them at the airport. I'm sure they've had to deal with Krol before. And after the first time, no one ever wants to deal with that snake again."

"They didn't put up any resistance?" I ask, remembering the heart-stopping words I read in Tytus' next just minutes ago.

Call me. I have the priests. We're coming.

"No. They're just as ready for this as you are. Apparently, without a strong ruler, the Polish underworld has descended into chaos. That doesn't bode well for anyone. Not even the idiots who want a Reca on the throne. The priests are eager to return to normalcy. Everyone is."

"You're the one with royal blood," Roz reminds me. "After you put that ring on Bianca's finger, all you have to do is knock her up, and you'll be in charge of everyone and everything. Including the priests. I'm sure they only want to get on your good side."

"Let's hope," I grumble. "Will the priests be bringing everything we need for the ceremony? Or do we have to go on a scavenger hunt?"

There isn't anything here for us to wear but the clothes on our backs—well, that's not true. We could always slither into some of Luis' clothes, but there's no chance I'm doing that, and there's no way in hell I'm letting Bianca anywhere near that fucker's wardrobe.

This place already stinks of the dead man. The last thing I need is my bride smelling like anyone other than herself.

Walking back into the bedroom, I take a deep whiff of the vanilla scented candles.

This place is already starting to smell less like a dirty drug lord's woodland hideout, and more like Bianca.

My fingers curl back into fists when my gaze lands on the discarded sweats that Bianca has been wearing.

Digging my nails into my palms, I try to draw blood away from my begging cock.

Tytus picked up the outfit for Bianca on his way here. He asked if I wanted her in something skimpy or something comfortable.

She'd been through enough. Plus, I knew she'd look hot in any outfit. So, I chose the sweats.

"No need to go shopping," Tytus assures me, his voice crackling along with the background static. "We're on it."

"Yeah, I've already got the perfect wedding gown picked out for your bride," Roz says, and. I can't quite tell if she's been sincere or not. It's always hard to tell with her.

"I'll be bringing you a custom-made suit," Tytus adds. "Black as well, obviously."

Fuck. Am I actually getting excited about the prospect of finally marrying Bianca? My one-time rival. My enemy. My captive.

This isn't supposed to be exciting. Our marriage was only ever supposed to be a burden. Something I had to go through with in order to fulfill my destiny.

Bianca wasn't chosen because I thought she was special. She was chosen because she was the best option available, no matter how infuriating she was.

But she doesn't infuriate me anymore.

No. Suddenly, just the thought of her makes me feel fucking warm inside.

It's a dangerous feeling.

This is the girl I chased. The girl I returned to high school for. The girl I became a body guard for. For years, my obsession for her was fueled by hate.

But the hate is evaporating. And something else is growing in its place.

Love.

No. It's too fucking soon for that. I like her. I'm obsessed with her body and her smell and her voice and her fire. But that doesn't mean love. It just means that she's the first girl to really grab my attention... right?

Fuck. I don't know.

Even as I sit down on the edge of the bed and look over to the steamy bathroom, I'm not so sure love isn't the right word for what I'm feeling.

Whatever the case, one thing seems obvious.

Bianca will look good in black. Even more so in an elegant wedding gown than she did in that tight outfit I found her wearing back in the hills.

But we're not quite there yet.

There's so much more I need to do in preparation.

And the first thing on that list will be the most unpleasant task of them all.

"Roz. Tytus. I need to talk to Drago," I sigh, wishing that I didn't have to. "Find a secure way to make that happen."

"Why?" Roz hisses. "As far as I'm concerned, this is a clean split. He betrayed us."

"Nothing is ever clean with Drago," I remind her. "Especially not if he's sending Krol around to do his bidding. That fucker is unhinged."

"Can it wait?" Tytus asks. "We don't want to give Drago or Krol a chance to track down our location before we can go through with the ceremony."

"There are questions I need answers to," I grumble. "I need them before Bianca and I get married."

Fuck. I have so many questions for Drago. Questions about my parents. About his role in my upbringing. About his loyalty and his allegiance. About Krol. About the legitimacy of this ceremony, and about all of the hopes and dreams he filled my head with growing up.

Everything's been thrown into question.

I need to talk to my adoptive father. I need to see if I can filter the truth from the lies. At the very least, I need to try.

Back in the bathroom, I hear the shower shut off.

"Roz, if I give Drago a call, can you find a way to make sure he can't track me down?"

"I'll do my best."

"Tytus. Stay on your toes and keep those priests safe. We're so close."

"Aye aye, captain."

"I'll talk to you guys later."

With that, our conference call ends.

Slipping my phone back into my pocket, I feel the weight of something else shift.

My fingers fall onto the switchblade I confiscated from Bianca back in the library.

Pulling it out, I quickly recognize the ornate handle.

This is the knife I gave to Roz.

She must have given it to Bianca.

But Bianca wasn't ready.

Fuck. Before the priests get here, I need to prepare my bride the best I can.

But how do I do that? The only hostage we had is dead. There's no one left to kill or torture but each other...

As if on cue, one of the candles I'd set up on the nightstand flickers, drawing my gaze.

Hot wax drips down the stick as my thumb traces the blade in my hand.

Just like that, my cock is rock hard again.

I have an idea.

A dirty, depraved idea.

Bianca should love it.

But will she survive it?

24

A gentle ache pulses between my legs as I step out of the bathroom.

My skin is still soft from the heat of the shower. My mind still light and hazy.

But my heart has never been heavier.

The dark priests are on their way.

There's no ignoring what this is anymore. No losing myself in the passion. In the lust. In the darkness.

Before I waded into the bathroom to wash myself up, Gabriel spelled it all out, nice and clear.

Our wedding night is near.

A sigh escapes my lips as I shuffle towards the bed.

Gabriel isn't in the bedroom. But he's left behind a stable of flickering candles. They fill the room with a soft vanilla scent. My favorite.

Squeezing the ends of my damp hair, I drop the towel to the floor and look for the sweats he'd torn off me earlier.

They're nowhere to be found.

I don't care. I'm not uncomfortable being naked around him anymore.

It's the least of my worries.

Sitting on the edge of the bed, I begin to twirl my hair. Thick halos of light stream in through the rounded windows to my left. Snarling beasts glare down from the walls to my right.

Somehow, I feel right at home in the middle of it all. Between light and darkness.

There's beauty in both.

I know that now.

A deep breath fills my lungs as I fall back onto the mattress and stare up at the vaulted ceiling. I can still feel Gabriel's fist in my cunt; his tongue on my clit. His hands on my tits.

No matter how much hot water I swallowed in the shower, the salty sweetness of his cum still lines the inside of my throat.

The memories make me shiver. It's a warm shiver—hell, it's almost a peaceful shiver—but it doesn't lighten the load weighing down my heart.

Gabriel's plan is about to come to fruition. He's told me all about it. I know what's coming.

I should be scared. I should be worried about what this means for my family; for my future; for my body.

But I'm not scared.

Fuck. I'm almost looking forward to it.

Because even just the thought of Gabriel coming inside of pussy makes me wet.

Carrying his child would be the ultimate act of servitude.

I'd truly be his little sex slave; his submissive vessel.

Could I really live that twisted fantasy out while becoming the women I want to be?

Gabriel seems convinced that I can.

I'm not so sure.

I mean, how could I be a strong ruler when I only want to serve a single man?

My languid mind is still swirling when I hear the bedroom door creak open. Gabriel's giant presence fills the room, flickering the flames on every candle as he moves to join me on the bed.

"How are you feeling?" he asks, his deep voice lifting me up by the hips.

"Tired," I admit.

"Well, you can rest later. I have another test for you."

Before I can prop myself up, Gabriel lies down beside me. His hard, hulking body blocks the snarling heads mounted on the wall. Every muscular inch of him is bathed in fresh sunlight —including those hazel-green eyes.

They've never looked so gorgeous, or so determined.

My heart trembles towards him as he softly pinches my chin.

"I don't know if my pussy is ready for another round of... that," I sheepishly whisper.

"We won't be fucking," Gabriel says. "Not until after the ceremony."

"Then what will we be doing?"

Without looking down, Gabriel hands me something. A cold shiver churns under my skin as I recognize what it is.

Rozalia's switchblade.

"You're going to mark me," Gabriel says. "You're going to claim me like I've claimed you. But most importantly, you're going to learn how to hurt defenseless monsters. Because, clearly that's one of your weak spots."

With his hand, Gabriel closes my fingers in around the ornate handle.

"I... I don't understand?"

My sluggish brain is slowly being sharpened again... but by the dark, helpless memories of how I felt back in that dusty library... back when I lifted this very blade to my throat, ready to end it all...

"I want you to carve a B right here," Gabriel says. Lifting his forearm, he points to a particular tattoo. A dark entanglement of heavy looking chains cross over his skin. In the middle of them all is a small opening of untouched flesh—well, not completely untouched.

My stomach drops when I recognize the scar.

"... Is that..." I gulp, unable to finish.

Gabriel nods. "It's the burn mark you gave me all of those years ago."

"You covered it up in chains..."

Rozalia's knife remains tucked away in my hand as I use my other to trace the old wound.

It brings back so many memories. memories that fueled so much hate, but seem so petty and insignificant now.

"Why did we hate each other so much?" I ask, feeling the scar beneath my fingertips.

It doesn't matter that I was partially right about Gabriel— he is a liar, and he spent his time at my high school lying through his teeth, all so he could get close to me; so that he could use me. But my teenage theories were so far off. So delusional.

"Because we were foolish, and stubborn. Because we were far too similar."

Slowly, my gaze is pulled from the scar and back onto Gabriel's haunting hazel-green eyes.

"You think we're similar?"

It's shocking to hear.

This man is powerful beyond belief. And I'm... well, I'm still trying to figure out what I am.

"Neither of us know when to give up," Gabriel smiles. "And I don't think either of us really believed we deserved what we had. We always wanted more. But we wanted to earn it."

"You're so close to earning everything you've ever wanted."

"No. Not close. I already have it."

Closing his eyes, Gabriel kisses me.

It's a soft kiss. A tender kiss. But there's something intensely powerful to it.

His lips are filled with electricity. It lifts every hair on my body, and I sink even further into him.

But when my hand spreads out against his forearm, I feel more than just the raised scar I gave him all of those years ago. Something fresher dots his thick wrist.

When Gabriel pulls his lips back, I can't help but look down.

Dark indented marks hide just beneath his black tattoos. The bottom of his palm has a long shallow cut along it, barely healed.

"What are these from?" I ask, reading his wounds like brail.

"They were a gift from your father and your cousin," Gabriel grunts.

Just like that, the raised hairs on my skin fall flat again. I realize I still don't know what happened at the meeting.

My heart shrivels as I consider the worst.

No. Gabriel would have told me by now if he done something unspeakable to one of my family members... right?

I don't wait for him to confess the details to me. Lifting the ornate handle I've been given, I unsheathe the blade.

"I'll carve my initials into your arm," I surrender. "But only if you tell me what happened when you went to meet Rian."

The deep smirk that lifts Gabriel's dark red lips somehow eases the heaviness in my heart.

"Now you're learning to play the game," he says, dimples dancing in the sunlight.

"Go ahead," I urge.

"Your cousin and I fought," Gabriel admits. "But I held back. He didn't. The lion won. Knocked me the fuck out. When I woke up, I was in that same dungeon you first saw me in. The marks on my arms are from the restraints your family used on me. Barbed wire. I don't blame them. They didn't believe a word I had to say, and they shouldn't have, because I lied through my teeth."

"You didn't try to negotiate?"

"That wasn't part of the plan. But it is now."

My heavy heart twitches, and some of the lead crumbles away.

"What changed?"

Gabriel's eyes fall for a second as he remembers something unsaid. "I realized I had also been lied to," he mumbles. "And then I realized I was alone. But I didn't have to be. For all of our differences, your family and I share one thing in common."

"What?"

"We both care about you."

An avalanche of lead melts from my fluttering heart as Gabriel takes my hand and leads it to the burn mark on his forearm.

"I can do it myself," I assure him.

"Very well," Gabriel nods, his fingers falling from my skin. "Remember, right in the center of the chains, and only the letter B."

"Why only the letter B?"

"Because after our wedding your last name will change."

My steady hand shakes ever so slightly as I'm reminded of the magnitude of where we're headed.

"And what will my last name change to?" I ask.

"I still don't know."

Just like that, I remember how Gabriel had confessed to me that he didn't know his last name; about how the true identity of his parents had been hidden from him; about how I wasn't just his key to obtaining power, but also to learning the truth about who he really is.

"Well, whatever my new name will be, it can't be worse than Bianca Byrne, right?" I try to joke.

"Right," Gabriel smiles. "You should be thanking me.

Sounds like the name of some second-rate comic book character."

My eyes roll as an involuntary flash of determination makes me seize Gabriel's arm.

"Don't think I've forgotten about how you used to tease me," I remind him, wrapping my fingers around his thick wrist. But he's so broad that I barely even reach the edges. "Call this payback."

Squinting, I press the tip of my blade in the one spot of untouched flesh between all of Gabriel's tattoos.

He doesn't even flinch as I start to carve my B.

But his skin is so firm. And I hardly even make a red mark, let alone break through his skin.

"It's not working," I mumble, disappointed.

"Press harder," Gabriel insists. "Cut deeper."

"You'll bleed."

"Not any more than I've made you bleed."

"I... I don't want to hurt you. Not really."

"I do. Remember the lesson, *myszko*. Do what needs to be done."

Gritting my teeth, I push the tip of my blade deeper into his raised flesh. My hand is shaking from the pressure when the tough skin finally breaks.

To my surprise, Gabriel actually winces—if only slightly.

"Good girl," he grunts, his hand curling into a fist as a thin line of blood begins to trickle from the fresh wound. "Now, finish the job."

Following the scarlet line, I continue to push the blade down Gabriel's skin. My dark wolf becomes eerily still as I finish the first deep line, and start with the curving breasts of the B.

"There's too much blood," I note. "I can't see where I'm going."

"Then lick it up," Gabriel orders. "Clean me with your tongue, just like I cleaned you with mine."

A scorching breath squirms down my throat as I consider doing such a thing.

I've tasted Gabriel's lips. I've tasted his flesh. His cock. His cum. I'm only one step away from knowing how every part of him taste, inside and out.

What the worst that could happen?

You could love it.

Fuck it. I'm already dangerously close to loving far worse things.

Like him.

My tongue lashes across my lips as I lean forward. The smell of Gabriel's blood flagellates me with so many conflicting memories.

Flashes of fear and pain race through my mind. But so do strikes of ecstasy and passion.

This is the same scent I found waiting for me in the basement just before Gabriel erupted back into my life. It's the smell of death.

So then why does it make me feel so alive?

My first taste of his blood is unpleasant. It's sharp and metallic, just like the smell. But as it sits on my tongue, I swear it morphs into something more familiar. Something earthy. Something that reminds me exclusively of Gabriel, and all of the painful pleasure he's forced into my life.

I swallow. Then, I lap up more, until his flesh is clear enough to continue with my masterpiece.

"Does it hurt?" I ask, carving the first rounded arch into my dark wolf's skin.

"Yes," Gabriel growls. "Keep going."

A twitch in his pants temporarily draws my eyes away from my bloody canvas.

The leviathan is back. It's outline is clear against the black material barely restraining it.

A ragged breath swirls from my lips, and that familiar pressure returns to my core.

This is my man.

Ceremony or not. Marriage. Last names. None of it can be as intimate as this, right?

With the first arch finished, I move onto the second. The shadows in the bedroom have begun to stretch as the sun descends. Candles flicker in the growing pockets of darkness.

My sore pussy is already wet again.

This whole thing is so intoxicating that I almost don't want to finish the second and final arch. Still, I do my job. I carve my initial into Gabriel's forearm, right over the hard flesh that I scarred all of those years ago.

But I know this isn't the end. One day, Gabriel will learn his last name. Then, he'll give it to me, and I'll finish the job.

"Finished," I whisper, leaning back to admire my work.

"You've done well, *myszko*," Gabriel grunts, washing away what blood remains with the palm of his hand.

I lick my lips.

"Need me to carve anywhere else?"

That makes Gabriel chuckle.

"No," he says, shaking his head so that a lock of his wavy black hair falls between his stunning hazel-green eyes. "Now, it's my turn."

He's already slipped the knife from my fingers before I can process what that means.

"What?" I gulp.

"You didn't think I'd let you mark me without returning the favor, did you?"

"I... I thought it was a lesson."

"It was. And you passed. This is your reward."

Sitting up, Gabriel twists his chiselled torso to grab something on the nightstand.

"I'm starting to think there are very few differences between your punishments and your rewards," I point out.

But the pressure in my core has already started swirling. My pussy is soaking. My nipples are hard.

Whatever he has in store for me, I'm ready.

"You surprise me sometimes, *myszko*. So pretty, yet so smart."

"Obviously, I'm not that smart," I whisper, when I see what Gabriel has retrieved from the nightstand.

The flame flickering atop the candlestick lashes out as my dark wolf carries it towards me. Hot wax drifts down the shaft, pooling at the base.

"What are you going to do with that?" I ask.

"I'm going to prepare you," Gabriel says. "You're tender skin is too fragile for the process I just endured. I'll have to handle your marking much more gently. Unless you'd like me not to?"

"How is a candle going to make this any less painful?"

"I didn't say it would be any less painful."

My thighs clench together. My heart starts to thump.

"Are you going to hurt me?"

"Only a little, but it will be worth it. Now, sit up for me."

My thumping heart pulls me forward. Straightening my back, I bite down on my lip and prepare myself to be marked.

The fear of the approaching pain is indistinguishable from my arousal.

"What will you carve on me?" I ask, as Gabriel's hazel-green eyes search my naked body for the perfect canvas.

"Only one initial for now. G. The second will come as yours does, after it is learned."

Looming over me, Gabriel seems to find the perfect spot to start. I can't help but flinch when his warm fingers fall against my shoulder.

There, he traces the outline of my own raised wound. The one I got from the ambush.

"It's too fresh," I tell him. "You'll break it open if you try to carve there."

"No, I won't. That's what the wax is for. It will create a barrier."

I can only close my eyes and wait as he tilts the candlestick down towards my shoulder.

To my surprise, the first drip isn't nearly as painful as I expected. In fact, the searing heat stings in a similar fashion to Gabriel's vicious spanks—although, instead of a quick flash of pain followed by a warm wave of pleasure, the slowly spreading wax produces a more consistent burn.

The pressure in my core rumbles as the wax spreads across my wound, covering it in a soft fire, singeing away my defences.

Another splash of wax falls a little further down my shoulder, closer to my arm, and a tiny whimper escapes my parted lips.

"How does it feel?"

"It feels good," I admit.

"Savor that feeling."

Another drop falls closer to my neck. Slowly, it cascades down towards my tit. The nearer it gets to my sensitive nipple, the sharper the heat becomes. But by now, I'm used to finding the pleasure in the pain.

Not that it's hard to.

When the waxy residue flows over my hard pink nub, I'm gripped by a body-wrapping shock of gratification. It's like I've been swathed in a fiery hand. Squeezed, until the pressure in my core is nearly ready to burst.

"Oh my god," I sigh, welcoming it all.

"Stay strong," Gabriel orders. My eyes have closed, but I still feel the approaching blade.

Still, Gabriel was right. It barely even hurts as the knife is pressed down into my waxed covered wound. All I feel is a strong pressure—though, it quickly becomes stronger and stronger.

And then something breaks. It's either the wax seal, my skin, or both, because the easy throbbing is replaced by a much harsher prick.

It feels like I've been bitten, but when I open my eyes and look down, I see no teeth. Only Gabriel's blade cutting across my skin.

There isn't nearly as much blood as when I marked him— probably thanks to the wax—but I can't imagine it could hurt any more than this.

Still, it's not an irredeemable pain. And it's not just that the sharp sting is completely without pleasure.

It's that the act itself is fucking smoldering.

I don't have any tattoos. Before last month, I hardly had any markings on my entire body.

Now, I have scars. Now, I have a mafia prince carving his initial on my shoulder.

I'm being claimed. But only because I claimed him first.

A surge of power makes me shiver.

Gabriel was right, I don't have to choose between being a queen and being his little sex slave. I can be both.

And he can be more than just my king.

Wax continues to drip down my body like burning tears as Gabriel finishes off his own masterpiece.

The pressure in my core is practically jumping, begging for more. But the way I'm being teased is almost hotter than any finish line could ever be.

"There, now you are mine. And I am yours," Gabriel whispers. Slowly, the wax begins to harden and the sharp sting on my shoulder throbs into a soft ache.

"What about the wedding?" I ask, looking down at my freshly marked skin.

The skin is inflamed and red, but no blood leaks from the sharp scarlet lines that form the Gothically elegant letter G now carved into my shoulder.

"That ceremony will be about power," Gabriel says, wiping away some of the hardening wax with his finger. "This... Well, this is only about us."

The intimacy of his declaration adds to my arousal. My smoldering gaze flickers towards the massive outline throbbing beneath his tight pants.

I know exactly what I want.

"Are we done?" I ask. But I don't wait for an answer. My hand falls onto his hard cock. The leviathan twitches for me, girthy shaft practically jumping into the palm of my hand.

But Gabriel grabs my wrist and pulls me away.

"Not until after we're married," he reminds me.

"You're such a choir boy," I tease, overcome by lust.

"So, then corrupt me." My free hand is already on its way to his cock when Gabriel grabs that wrist too. "Not like that, *myszko*. The dark priests won't be long. Our wedding night will be savage. But the time between then and now will have to be filled with something else."

"Like what?" I ask, my hips swaying as I shove my ass into the mattress below. I'm turned on to the point of delirium.

"Do you remember that gun I fucked you with?" Gabriel asks, stepping back from the bed.

My pointed nipples pull me after him like fucking divining rods.

"Yes," I respond, almost angry that he's denying me the satisfaction I crave so ravenously.

You've turned me into this beast. Now feed it!

"Well, I think it's about time you learn how to use it."

Placing his dripping candle back onto the nightstand, Gabriel turns around and starts to pace towards the bedroom door.

"Where are you going?" I demand to know, pushing myself off the bed and onto my feet.

Stopping in the doorway, Gabriel looks back over his shoulder. Those hazel-green eyes sparkle in the golden sunlight. His dimples deepen as a mischievous smirk crosses his blood red lips.

"Follow me and find out."

25

My forearm brushes over Bianca's shoulder, and our fresh markings gently touch.

"Don't be scared, *myszko*," I whisper into her ear.

The sun has started its long descent towards the horizon. The thick border of black trees that surround this cabin cast long shadows. The darkness crawls towards us.

"I'm not scared," Bianca responds, and I believe her.

"Then why are you hesitating?"

"It... it just feels like overkill."

Pressing my throbbing bulge into the small of her back, I position her arms with my hands.

"You can never practice enough," I state, lining up the barrel of her gun with Luis' rotting corpse. "Aim for his heart."

"His head's in the way," she points out.

It's true, the drug dealer's neck is still cranked down from when I put a bullet between his eyes.

"Do you want me to tie his forehead to the tree, or do you want to blast through that thick skull yourself?"

Bianca's slender fingers tighten around the handle of her gun.

"Blast through it."

"That's my girl."

A quick kiss to the neck eases her nerves as she steadies her weapon.

"Ready?" she asks, the question clearly directed more towards herself than me.

"Whenever you are."

Every new breath gets deeper. My grip around her wrists gets tighter.

Then, to my surprise, she pulls the trigger.

The recoil knocks her back into me, but her arms don't drop. I keep my grip trained around her wrists as smoke rises from the barrel.

But Luis' corpse is still completely intact.

"I missed," Bianca mumbles.

"Try again."

Pushing herself off my chest, she straightens her back and flexes her forearms.

"Head?"

"Head," I nod.

Another round of deep breathing pulses through Bianca's perfect body as she aims for the dead man's skull.

"Three... Two... One..."

The crack of her gun cuts through the peaceful afternoon and the bark just above Luis' hanging neck is obliterated by the speeding bullet.

"Shit!" Bianca curses.

"You're getting closer."

I'm about to retrain her wrists when Bianca suddenly pulls the trigger again.

This time, her bullet rips into Luis' stomach, shredding through his tattered, bloody clothes.

"I hit him!"

Her excitement is addicting. My hands drop from her wrists and wrap around her waist.

"Think you can do it again?" I tease.

"Just watch me."

Three more shots tear out of her muzzle in quick succession. The first hits the ground, upending the earth at Luis' twisted foot, but the next two both hit the corpse. First, in the thigh. Then, in the bicep.

"This isn't so hard," Bianca huffs, her shoulders lifting and falling with every elevated breath.

"You still haven't hit your target yet," I gently remind her.

"What are you talking about? I just put three bullets in his body."

"But none in his head. Wasn't that what we were aiming for?"

Bianca's shoulders twitch as she re-trains her gun.

"You're right."

I feel all of the fear and hesitation drain from her as she focuses on her new goal. But before I can watch her achieve it, I feel a familiar vibration come from my pocket.

"Keep shooting, *myszko*. I've got a call to make." Reaching behind my back and under my belt, I pull out three fresh clips. "Do you think you can handle reloading that thing?"

"I'll figure it out," Bianca mumbles, without looking back. Her gaze is fixed squarely on her target.

Without saying another word, I place the clips at her feet and step away to take my call.

Pride swirls in my chest as I step around the nearest corner and press the phone to my ear.

"Yes," I answer coldly, unsure of who I'll be speaking to first.

"Are you sure this is a good idea?"

It's just Roz. Static crackles behind her voice, but I can still hear the hidden anxiety in every word.

"No. But it needs to happen. The truth has been put into

question. I need to see what Drago says when I tell him that I know about his lies."

"He'll probably just lie to you some more."

"Maybe, or maybe he'll try to salvage his relationship with me by letting the smallest bit of truth slip."

"You know Drago better than that," Roz warns.

"I thought I did."

Roz's sigh is clear even through the background static.

"I'll patch you into him now. Tytus has made sure he's expecting your call. I know I don't have to say this, but I will any way. Drago doesn't know that Tytus has chosen sides yet. He also doesn't know that Tytus is in a van driving down a dirt road right now with two dark priests in his trunk. All he knows is that you and I have drawn a line in the sand. If he crosses it, there's no saving him. Not from me."

"Not from me either," I grunt.

"Ready?"

"Do it."

The line cuts out and even the static hiss disappears as I pace a few steps backwards.

Out the corner of my eye, I see Bianca. She's back in those sweats, the ones that cover her entire perfect body. Yet she's sexier than ever.

Maybe it's the gun. Maybe it's the determination.

Or maybe it's the excitement that exudes off of her as one of her bullets rips through Luis' hanging skull.

Her little fist pump nearly makes me explode with joy— until the static returns to the phone and a familiar voice breaks through any happiness I feel.

"Where are you?"

Drago's voice barely sounds human. A devastating fury flickers through every word.

"That's not important," I bite back, turning away from my warrior princess.

Ruthless Heir

"It's not important?" Drago booms. "The priests are set to arrive any day now and I haven't heard a single word from you since you failed your last mission."

The fool. Roz was right. He really doesn't know what's going on.

"Maybe you shouldn't have sent me back to the Byrne family. Not if you had ever wanted to see me again."

"What? Did they recruit you?" he accuses.

"No. But they sure did torture me," I growl. "Not that we weren't expecting that."

"I warned you," Drago responds, unmoved. "What more do you want?"

"The truth."

A moment of silence follows my declaration.

"I've always told you the truth, *Gabryjel*."

"Bullshit," I sneer. "You were foolish to send me anywhere near Ray Byrne. Unless, of course, you thought they'd kill me."

"Why the fuck would I want that? Even if I hadn't raised you like a son. Even if I hadn't put food on your table and clothes on your back, you'd still be crucial to obtaining the power I've been chasing for decades."

"Tell me one more lie and I hang up," I spit.

"How dare you accuse me of telling lies, *boy*!"

A tsunami of rage crashes through me as I turn and punch the nearest cabin wall. The varnished log cracks and splinters against my fist. The entire structure seems to sway.

"Then why does it seem like you don't want me alive anymore? Why the fuck does it seem like you want Bianca dead? First it was that fucking reckless ambush. Then you sent Kuba fucking Krol into my inner sanctum to take my fucking girl, and you nearly got Roz killed in the process. Who among us isn't expendable to you, *Drago*? Clearly, it isn't any of your 'children', is it?"

I can hear the dragon fuming on the other end of the line.

He's not used to being challenged so brazenly—at least, not without being able to rip the motherfucker's throat out the moment they close their mouths.

"Plans change," he finally admits, viscous hate lining every word.

"I've figured that out," I snarl. "But tell me this: did you actually want Rian Kilpatrick, or did you just send me back to the Irishman to die?"

"Rian Kilpatrick is why the plan has been able to change," Drago simmers. "Dead or not, the Byrne princess can be used to draw the Irish lion to me, without having to rely on the radical whims of my treacherous subordinates."

"Why do you want the lion so badly?" I press, ignoring the jab.

"Why would I tell you?" Drago hisses. "It sounds like you've become my enemy, and you know all too well that you never reveal secrets to those who oppose you."

"That's what you think," I shoot back. "But Ray Byrne thinks differently. And when he had me hung from his cellar ceiling with fucking barbed wire, he let all kinds of secrets out of the bag."

Another wall of static lifts a veil between us, as Drago hesitates to respond again.

In the distance, I hear another round of gunfire roar through the dimming evening air.

Bianca has taught herself to reload her weapon. Good. We might be at war soon.

"What did Byrne tell you?" Drago finally asks, not sounding so confident anymore.

"Wouldn't you like to know."

"I would."

"He told me so many things."

A harsh wind creaks the thick trunks bordering this property.

"You're bluffing."

"Who is Sonia Caruso?" I growl in response.

This time, there's no hesitation.

"Don't you dare say that name with such vitriol!" Drago rages.

The rawness in his reply is so unexpected that I nearly stumble backwards. But I quickly recover.

"You don't get to tell me how to talk about my own mother," I growl, phone squeezing beneath my clenching fist.

I can practically hear the air being sucked out of Drago's lungs.

That's all it takes to confirm the truth. Ray Byrne wasn't lying. Sonia Caruso was my mother.

An Italian.

Fuck.

Does that mean he was right about her as a person too?

"Whatever Ray Byrne told you, you don't know the full story."

"Enlighten me."

"No."

"Then there's nothing else to say."

I'm about to hang up when I hear Drago roar through the receiver.

"Wait!"

There's an unfamiliar desperation in the dragon's plea.

"Are you ready to be fucking honest with me?" I reply, mercilessly.

"Only if you're ready to be honest with me, *boy*. What else did Ray Byrne tell you?"

"He told me my mom wasn't a good person."

"There are no good people in our world," Drago grumbles, clearly gritting his teeth. "Your mother did whatever it took to survive."

"But she didn't survive," I suddenly choke. "She tried to kill

Bianca's mother. That's why Ray killed her. Not because she represented the last remnants of some crumbling empire. My mother wasn't even Polish, was she? I'm a half-blood..."

"That's still enough to wear the crown."

"And that crown will be enough to crush you," I grunt. "But only if it ever gets on my head. Who is my father, Drago? Tell me, or prepare for war."

"I raised you. I am your father."

"No, you're not," I respond, unphased. "You're the man who's used me. The man who was ready to throw me aside when another young prince came along. Don't mistake my youth for stupidity, old man. You've tried to have me killed twice. No father does that. So, tell me. Who is my real father?"

"*Gabryjel*..."

"Coward," I rumble. "At least tell me what you know about El Blanco."

"El Blanco?" I can hear the shock in Drago's voice. "Who the hell told you about El Blanco?"

"That name is courtesy of Ray Byrne too. You really should have had the guts to kill me yourself. Sending me back to him was the biggest mistake you could have made. That man isn't the monster you've made him out to be. He—"

"He killed your mother!" Drago roars, so loudly that his voice distorts against the static.

"He did what he had to do," I hear myself say, not quite believing it.

On the wind, I can hear a tiny cheer. Bianca has hit her target again.

I'd kill anyone who tried to hurt her. Anyone.

Women. Children. It doesn't matter.

Ray killed my mother to protect the love of his life. I won't ever forgive him for that. But I do finally understand it.

Because I'd do the same for Bianca.

"You're losing yourself," Drago warns me. But his warning falls on deaf ears.

"No," I shake my head. "I'm finding myself."

"Are you willing to risk losing everything your owed just because of what that man told you?"

But I'm done entertaining Drago's lies.

"Tell me one truth before I hang up," I offer, ignoring his question. "Here, I'll even give you an easy one. Did you get me into Westwood High, or did Ray?"

"Why would Ray Byrne have tried to get you into Westwood?" Drago deflects.

"Because he fell for the façade I had created for myself. Because he thought I was the poor street orphan I pretended to be. Sure, if he had found out about me four years earlier, he would have been right. But you and I both know how I changed my fortunes around. You—"

"*We* changed your fortunes around," Drago interrupts. "Or have you suddenly forgotten all of the support I gave you in those lean years?"

"Don't think I don't know about your own fortune," I test him. "Don't for a fucking second think I don't understand how easy it would have been for you to actually pull me out of that squalor instead of forcing me to dredge through it for your own benefit."

"I taught you to work for your money. To seize your power!"

"Well, you did a good job, because now, I'm going to take everything from you."

My fingers are clenched so hard around the phone that it creaks and groans as I stare into the dark, swaying forest ahead.

"You will never get anything without me," Drago hisses.

"Wrong. The priests are in my possession," I reveal. "In a matter of days, I will be handed the keys to the empire that was stolen from me—that is, unless that's a lie as well?"

The air swirling around me seems to pause as I drop the hammer on all of Drago's plans.

"It's not a lie," he grits, clearly still coming to grips with what I just told him, but unwilling to show how much it's effecting him. "Your mother may not have been of royal blood, but your father ruled."

"And will you tell me my father's name now, or will I have to ask the priests?"

"They won't tell you."

"The second I put a baby in Bianca, they will do whatever I say."

"No. You still don't understand, *boy*," Drago spits, disdain flickering from his voice.

"Call me boy one more time," I snap back.

"Watch yourself... *boy*."

I've had enough.

Before I can crush the phone beneath my hand, I hang up.

I got what I wanted. Confirmation. With this marriage, I will inherit all that I was promised. For all of the lies, one thing seems to remain true.

An empire awaits me.

All I have to do is take it.

And that means marrying Bianca.

Then it means pinning her down. Fucking her raw. Filling up her tight little pussy with my seed.

It means making her the mother of my heir.

It means making her my queen.

It also means *war*.

By the time Gabriel appears behind me again, Luis' corpse is nothing more than a visceral portrait of blood and guts.

There are no defining features left, nothing to indicate that this was a human. Just gore.

Good.

Fuck drug dealers. He wasn't human anyway.

"What the fuck..." Gabriel mumbles, stopping at my side to gaze over at my artwork.

"He deserved it," I remind him, adrenaline still racing through my veins.

"He's going to be a lot harder to bury now."

"He doesn't deserve a burial."

My gun is still smoking when Gabriel grabs my wrist and turns me to face him.

"What's gotten into you?" he asks, his hazel-green eyes squinting.

"Nothing's gotten into me," I say, biting my bottom lip. "I'm the one who's been putting shit into other people. Luis' is filled with my lead..."

"Luis is long gone," Gabriel notes. "You've been shooting a corpse. There are more important matters at hand."

My body twitches against the strength of the dark wolf's grip. There's a pressure in my core that needs to be addressed; a wetness dripping from my cunt that needs to be lapped up.

Dropping my gun, I use my free hand to cup Gabriel's ever-present bulge.

"Like what?" I ask, my voice full of suggestion.

But, to my surprise, Gabriel ignores that suggestion.

"Never drop your gun, *myszko*. Who knows who could be hiding in these woods, waiting to attack."

"Could they be any more fearsome than my big bad wolf?" I ask, not giving up.

I press my body into his and I feel his cock surge.

"No, but they could be more fearsome than you," he growls.

Taking my jaw in his hand, he stares at me like I deserve a particularly savage kiss.

But that kiss never comes.

"What's wrong?" I ask, my arousal slowly fading as a prick of dread pierces the pressure in my core.

"Nothing's wrong," Gabriel assures me.

"It sounds like something is wrong."

Before he can confirm or deny my suspicion, something pulls our attention off each other.

Through the peaceful evening air, I can hear what sounds like sticks cracking beneath something heavy. It comes from behind the wall of trees surrounded us.

Gabriel obviously hears it too.

Then, we both spot the approaching light. It seeps through the trees like a false dawn, before quickly disappearing.

"Pick up your gun," Gabriel orders, his hackles rising as he steps in front of me.

I do as I'm told. The metal is still hot.

A pinprick of arousal returns through the dread and the fear. It keeps my hand steady as we creep forward.

"What is it?" I ask.

"I'm not sure. Go inside. Wait for me there."

"I can fight," I insist, perhaps a little too loudly.

Whipping around, Gabriel grabs me around the wrist and squeezes.

"Go. Inside."

Before I can fight back any more, he rips the gun from my hand.

"Hey, that's mine!"

"You'll get it back after you've listen to me," my dark wolf growls. "Now do as your told."

My heart drops a little as all of the fun of my shooting practice is swatted away.

"I can help."

"Shooting a living thing is different than eviscerating a dead body," Gabriel reminds me.

The crunch coming from the dark forest is quickly becoming a whole lot louder.

"Go," Gabriel barks, before turning back around and raising my gun.

For a moment, I just freeze and watch as he crouches forward. But when another wave of light flashes through the thick rows of trunks ahead, I know that I don't have any other choice.

If I stay out here, I'll only be a distraction. And that could put Gabriel in danger.

"Good luck," I whisper. Then, I turn and run back into the cabin.

But when I get inside, I don't go looking for some closet to hide in. No. I'm convinced that I can still help Gabriel, if even only as backup. Hell, I know what it's like to shoot a body; I know what it's like to kill a person.

Immediately, I start pillaging the drawers in the foyer. A drug lord lived here. There's got to be some weapons and ammo hidden somewhere.

"Who is it?"

Outside, I hear Gabriel's muffled voice shout into the growing darkness.

I don't hear anyone shout back.

My chest tightens as I search for anything that I could use to help.

When I whip open one of the closet doors near the far wall, I find the motherload.

The space is lined from top to bottom with guns and ammo. But there are no pistols or Glocks.

This shit looks like hunting equipment. Like the kind of weapons someone might use to kill the beasts mounted up on the bedroom walls.

They will have to do.

Stepping up on my tip toes, I reach for the nearest rifle. It has a long scope and a heavy base, but I manage to corral it.

The second I get it down, though, I realize I have no fucking clue how to work the thing. Is it loaded? If not, how the fuck do I load it?

Once more, I hear Gabriel call out into the darkness.

Once again, he gets no response.

Fuck it.

Slinging the rifle over my shoulder, I find the stairs and race up them.

When I was outside, I noticed that the strange light was coming from in front of us, which means I should be able to get a good view of the approaching threat from the bedroom window.

Sure enough, a pulsing wave of light washes through the bedroom the second I push myself inside. Immediately, I go to pry open one of the rounded windows.

I can help, Gabriel. Why won't you just let me help? Isn't this what you trained me for.

After I've managed to prop open one of the windows, I set the long barrel down on the window sill.

With the heavy stock resting on my shoulder, I can't push myself up enough to see over my own weapon. So, I have to peer through the scope to see what's happening below.

It doesn't take long before another wave of light laps through the woods. That's when I finally realize what it must be from.

A car.

Maybe multiple cars.

Fuck.

My nerves tighten, and I have to take a deep breath just to try and untangle them.

You can do this, Bianca, I tell myself, all the while trying to figure out exactly how to shoot this thing, if it comes to that.

But this rifle isn't the same beast as the gun I was using for target practice earlier. I'm in over my head, and I know it.

Strangely, though, I'm not scared. Just anxious, and worried for Gabriel.

My finger wraps around the trigger as I search for danger. I doubt this thing is loaded, but I can't just sit back and hide. Gabriel's made sure I'm not that type of girl anymore.

If shit hits the fan, I'm going to start shooting. Hopefully it won't just be blanks.

Heart in my throat, I continue to scan the dark forest.

Then, finally, I spot the source of the light—at least, one of the sources.

A single black van creeps out of a small opening in the forest, before coming to a stop under a long shadow.

Even through the powerful scope, the windows are too tinted to see through. All I can do is hold my breath and wait for something to happen.

Luckily, I don't have to wait long before the driver's door is opened.

My skin crawls as a hulking figure steps out. In the darkness of his long shadow, he appears as nothing more than a towering silhouette, but as he begins to move forward, I spot the gun in his hand.

It rests innocently by his side. But I don't take my hand off my own trigger. Because as the figure steps out of the shadows and into the light, I'm hit with an oddly visceral reaction.

... That face.

I've seen it somewhere before. Broad and chiseled like a surrealist statue, it stands atop a thick neck choked in black tattoos.

Why does he look so familiar?

It's like I can vaguely remember him from some hazy dream... or nightmare. But that's as far as my recollection goes.

I'm transfixed as the monster continues his entrance. Then, out of the corner of my scope, a new figure appears.

There's no mistaking who that is.

Gabriel.

The two beasts stop some odd five feet from each other, guns still in hand, but rested at their hips.

The sight calms me a little.

Neither of them look particularly tense.

This could be a friend.

Still, I watch intently through the scope of this oversized rifle, desperately trying to remember where I've seen this new face before...

I don't get to look much longer.

I don't know if my finger twitches involuntarily, or if I relax so much it slips down the trigger, but suddenly, a deafening roar erupts from the barrel.

The recoil flings the scope right into my eye, and I'm knocked onto my ass.

But even through the shock of what just happened, I have enough sense to curse myself to hell and back.

No. No. No.

This thing was fucking loaded. And I just shot at someone who might be on our side.

Battling through the dread, I push myself onto my knees and look back out of the window.

The second my head pops through the frame, I meet eyes with the monster I just fired at.

His gun lifts towards me.

But before he can shoot, Gabriel lunges forward, tackling the beast of a man to the ground.

Someone curses in an unknown language. The two men exchange muffled shouts. Then I hear Gabriel's voice.

"Bianca, get the hell down here! And don't you dare bring a fucking gun with you!"

His roar is so deep and angry that it rattles my bones.

Fuck. I'm in trouble.

The dread sitting in my gut twists into a whole new form... but it's also joined by the familiar heat of arousal.

I try to ignore the pressure growing in my core as I leave the gun to scurry out of the bedroom and down the stairs.

I'll be punished again.

When I burst out of the front door, I see Gabriel helping the stranger back onto his feet.

"Come here!" he bellows, spotting me.

"I'm sorry," I mutter, keeping my eyes downcast as I make my way towards them.

The closer I get, the more intimidated I become. The stranger is even bigger than Gabriel, and at least half a foot wider. Combined, their presence is nearly suffocating, but I still force myself to look up at them.

That's when I see the blood. There's a gash in the stranger's massive arm. Thankfully, it only seems to be bleeding a little bit.

I only grazed him.

"What the hell were you doing?' Gabriel demands to know.

"I... I thought we might be under attack. I was trying to help."

"I told you to go inside."

"I *was* inside!"

"You need to work on your shot, little lady," a new voice interrupts.

It's the stranger.

Up close, I can see the brutally handsome undercurrent of his monstrous appearance. His features are sharp and chiselled and dangerous, but I find no hate in his captivating eyes—at least, not any that seems to be directed towards me.

He must be one of Gabriel's friends.

"I... I'm sorry about that..." I shamefully apologize, gesturing towards his shallow wound. "It's nice to meet you."

"Oh, we've met before," the man nods. "I helped Gabriel get you away from that ambush. That feels like a lifetime ago now, though, doesn't it?"

The ambush.

That must be where I recognize him from. Did I see his face while I slipped in an out of consciousness?

"This is Tytus," Gabriel says. "He's on our side... at least, he was until you shot him."

"Still am," Tytus chuckles. "She only grazed me, but it was my fault for showing up without warning you."

"You weren't supposed to arrive until tomorrow," Gabriel sternly agrees.

"I drove a little faster than usual," Tytus shrugs. "Roz told me about your call with Drago, and I wanted to get this over with before he could get a chance to come find us."

"He won't," Gabriel snarls.

"But you'll shoot him if he does show up, ain't that right, princess?" Tytus jokes, looking my way.

"Don't call her princess," Gabriel responds for me, before moving on. "Are the priests alright?"

"Let's go find out."

My chest tightens as I follow Gabriel and Tytus to the back of the van.

The priests. They're here.

This is really happening.

It's not until Tytus rips the doors open that I realize I've been holding my breath. It all comes rushing out in a loud gasp as I see what's waiting for us inside.

"*Wszystko w porzadku?*"

That's Gabriel's voice. It's strange to hear him speak more than a word of Polish. But also strangely comforting.

Not that the comfort lasts long.

Ahead, two incredibly long, pale men sit deathly still. Their gaunt faces stare back at us, unmoving. Strange square black hats sit upon their bald heads. Their bodies are draped in black robes.

Neither of them respond to Gabriel's question with anything more than a subtle nod.

Then, they sit up.

All three of us step aside as the black priests crawl out of the back of the van.

They're disturbingly tall.

Behind them, piles of gothic accoutrements rattle and shake.

"Bianca, go upstairs and wait for me in the bedroom," Gabriel quietly orders. "I'll be up soon."

"Try to stay away from the guns," Tytus adds.

"I... I..." I'm not sure what to say. The sudden arrival of the terrifying priests has hit me like an unexpected slap.

It's a ruthless reminder of what awaits.

A cold wind wraps around me as the giant trees at my back start to creak and sway.

Then, Gabriel confirms what I already suspect.

"Go, *myszko*. Prepare yourself. The wedding happens tonight."

It's funny, I hadn't even noticed the old analogue clock until I was told the exact time I would be getting married.

Midnight.

Now, every second ticks by like a clap of thunder, so loud it overpowers the incessant pounding of my own heart.

It's all I can hear.

Tick. Tock. Your fate is nearly sealed.

"Alright. Open your eyes."

About half an hour ago, Rozalia showed up in a black van of her own. I saw her from my bedroom window. It was already dark out, and she looked like some Victorian ghost as she hustled a black laced wedding gown towards the front entrance.

She barely even stopped to admire the pile of flesh and guts that was once a man named Luis' Falcao.

Even now, I can hear the flies buzzing around his mangled body. They will still be swarming while I'm married off to Gabriel.

Opening my eyes, I look over to the eternally clicking clock above the bed.

It's almost time.

"Come on, now. Take a look at yourself."

Snapping her fingers by my ear, Rozalia pulls my gaze towards the body mirror Tytus dragged in here earlier.

"I... It's beautiful," I sigh.

Fuck. Despite the heaviness weighing down my soul, I can't deny just how gorgeous the macabre gown is.

The black skirt and train are spotted with countless sparkling silver dots, like stars in a clear night sky. The lace bodice is expertly woven. The silhouette hugs my curves like a shadow.

"Agreed," Rozalia nods, checking me out in the mirror. "And the black eye definitely adds to the charm."

Lifting my hand, I trace the swollen mark that was left around my socket after I accidentally fired that stupid rifle.

"I almost killed your friend..." I mumble.

"You aren't the first, and you definitely won't be the last," Rozalia huffs. "I'm sure he deserved it."

The old clock ticks and another second passes by.

"Have you ever been to one of these weddings?" I ask, nervously.

"Nope. As far as I know, no one has—at least, not in the last two decades. Maybe three. It's hard to say."

"Do you know what happens?"

"I suppose the same things that happen in any marriage ceremony," Rozalia shrugs. "Not that I'm sure what goes on in those either. This will be my first wedding."

"How exciting," I note, dryly.

"Oh, perk up, doll face. It's not so bad. You like Gabriel, don't you?"

I more than like him, I quietly confess to myself. But that doesn't make this any easier.

"It's not about that," I explain.

"What's it about then?"

" Isn't it obvious?"

"I guess not. Because you're going to have to tell me."

"I... I'm about to be given away. Chained to another soul for all eternity."

"Well, when you put it like that..."

A knock at the door turns our attention away from my heavy thoughts.

"Are you ready?"

It's Tytus.

He's been with Gabriel helping him prepare for this ceremony just like Rozalia has been helping me.

"Are you ready?" Rozalia asks, her tone hushed.

"I'm as ready as I'm ever going to be."

The black cat studies me for a moment before nodding.

"Tell the priests were ready!"

"Tell them yourself!" Tytus shouts back. "They're waiting downstairs with Gabriel. All that's left is you."

At my back, I hear the clock strike midnight.

There's little fanfare. No music plays. No horn trumpets. Only a soft chime twinkles through the otherwise silent room. Then, the monotone ticking starts anew.

"Let's get going then," Rozalia says. "But let's not forget this."

Circling around me, she grabs hold of my long black veil and gently places it over my head.

"I can barely see through this thing," I mumble.

"Just follow me. And walk slowly. We don't want to rip this dress. It was expensive."

"You bought it for me?" I ask, surprised.

"Well, no. But I did steal it for you. That's kind of more personal, right?"

I can't help but giggle.

"Thank you... I guess."

"No need to thank me, doll. We all benefit from this marriage. I'll be a queen one day too."

"Maybe I'll steal you a nice black gown for your wedding day."

"I won't be getting married," Rozalia assures me, opening the bedroom door. "That's not really my style."

"What is your style?"

"I'm more of a black widow."

"I always pegged you as more of a black cat."

"Can't a girl be more than one thing?"

I'm almost starting to feel better as I follow Rozalia through the cabin hallway and down the stairs.

The further we get from the secluded bedroom, the less tense I become. Especially as the smoky scent billowing from the living room slowly greets us.

It smells like eucalyptus and cinnamon. Definitely not what I was expecting.

Maybe this won't be as dark as I feared.

But that naïve hope is immediately challenged when I turn the corner into the living room.

"Shit." I mutter, involuntarily.

The scene that greets me is far more medieval than the calming scent suggests.

Black sheets cover every inch of the living room, blocking out the windows and even covering the floor. The only light comes from the dozens of flickering candles strategically placed around the perfectly still priests.

They are by far the most disturbing part of the gothic scene. With their black robes bleeding into the darkness, all I can really see are their pale glowing faces. Those gaunt faces float in a sea of blackness, following me with their sunken eyes.

Smoke from the incense shrouds everything in a thin fog. But there's nothing to run into. Nothing to stumble over.

Everything has been cleared.

It's like walking into a nightmarish void.

The dread returns.

"Go stand by the priests," Rozalia whispers, stopping in her tracks.

But I don't want to do that. Not alone.

Where is Gabriel?

Before I can ask Rozalia where my groom is, he appears out of the darkness.

Much like the priests, only his sinfully gorgeous face is visible.

Still, that's enough.

My dark wolf nods at me, his sharp hazel-green eyes shimmering in the candlelight, welcoming me to the darkness. My heart tugs after him.

"Nice of you to show up," he quietly teases when I arrive at his side, a surprising levity lifting his words.

"I only tried running away once," I blush. "But Rozalia managed to talk me out of it."

"I'm glad she did."

Reaching through the darkness, Gabriel pulls up my dark veil and cups my jaw. The warmth of his skin manages to comfort me again as he trails his thumb towards my swollen eye.

"I probably should have put some makeup on to hide that," I whisper, not daring to raise my voice.

"No. It will serve as my reminder to punish the one who did that to you."

"I did it to myself."

"Then I guess you're the one I will punish."

The familiar banter helps ease my nerves even more as one of the priests rings an unseen bell.

In response, Gabriel's hand slides down my jaw. But before he lets me go, I feel his index finger on my lips.

Hush now, myszko. This will all be over soon.

"*Zebralismy sie tu dzisiaj, aby ozywic utracone imperium,*" one of the priests starts. His voice is deep and guttural, with every word appearing to come from somewhere far down in his throat. "*Wzbudzic zatechla krew. Podbic pryszlosc...*"

I try to concentrate on Gabriel. Those hazel-green eyes keep me grounded, even when it sounds like the priest's voice is beginning to echo around the increasingly vast void surrounding us.

The chanting only becomes more ethereal as it continues. More foreign and unintelligible. It feels like I'm being lifted into the cosmos. I can't even see my body anymore. I can't see Gabriel's either.

For all I know, we could be floating in the endless vastness of space.

A chill skates up my spine from the strange intensity of it all. Then, through the cold, dark emptiness, I feel a warmth.

Gabriel has reached through the darkness below and grabbed my hands. His thick, callous fingers brush over the back of my palms, slowly pulling me back down to earth.

That's when I realize the priest has stopped talking.

The dark room is completely silent.

No one even seems prepared to take a breath.

Then, Gabriel opens his mouth.

"*Czy moge zwracac sie do niej po angielsku?*" he asks, looking briefly over at the two pale floating heads.

They both nod.

Gabriel looks back to me.

"I know this hasn't been easy on you, Bianca" he says, his fingers still brushing against the back of my palm. "But there hasn't been a single moment during these trials where you've failed to surprise me. You're a special one, *myszko*. And from the moment I first laid eyes on you, all of those years ago, I knew you were special. You weren't like the other girls. And you didn't want to be. At first, it pissed me off—after all, this marriage was always supposed to happen. But how could I steal your heart if you kept it locked so tightly away?"

"Hell, it took me way too long to realize that hating me wasn't even a personal thing with you. It was a game. Wasn't it? Know how I know that? Because you're just like me. Stubborn to the bone. Your classmates followed me through the hall, so what did you do? You made sure you swam against the current, just so you could bump into my shoulder. Just so you could make sure I knew that I didn't have you fooled. Just so I knew that I might be able to conquer the world, but I'd never win you over. Do you know how that made me feel?

"How?" I gulp, my hands shaking against the unexpected sincerity of Gabriel's speech.

"It hurt. It hurt me worse than I was willing to admit. And that made me angry. Because, even if I didn't want to admit it, I had never wanted anything as badly as I wanted you, and the fact that you didn't just fall in line and hopelessly want me back made me realize that I wasn't as invincible as I thought I was. You made me mortal, *myszko*. You made me human. And you know what? That only made you even more special. Because all of a sudden, you weren't just someone I would kill for. You were someone I could die for. And I'm just fine with that."

My heart is already in my throat, but that last line is when I feel the first tear fall down my cheek.

"Gabriel," I whisper, completely blindsided.

"I vow to always put you first," he continues. "You are my queen. You have my heart. Do I have yours?"

A thousand conflicting thoughts and emotions swirl through my head and my heart. Despite the long buildup to this moment, it still feels like it's happening so fast.

Still, a single answer rises up over the chaos.

"... Yes," I choke. "You have my heart."

Squeezing my hands, Gabriel looks over to the priests and nods.

They return the gesture, and Gabriel momentarily releases me from his grip.

"Lift your hand to your face," he tells me.

I do as I'm told.

Then Gabriel does the same, mirroring me.

A small gasp escapes my lips when I see what's suddenly being held between his fingers.

A glimmering diamond ring.

But not just any diamond ring.

I've never seen anything like it before.

Two black teardrop diamonds shimmer atop a jagged band of silver and gold.

Reaching out, Gabriel takes my hand, separating my ring finger from the rest. Despite the sharp edges crisscrossing the thorny band, the ring slides on effortlessly.

"*Doskonale dopasowanie*," says one of priests.

"A perfect fit," Gabriel repeats in English.

"What does that mean?" I manage to mutter. "Was this ring made for me?"

"Try and take it off," Gabriel responds.

"But I don't want to... It's so pretty."

I'm transfixed by the dark beauty of the jewelry. It looks like the candle flames flickering around us have been captured behind the two black diamonds.

"Try and take it off, *myszko*," Gabriel repeats. Leading my fingers, he makes me touch the smooth outer layer of the band.

But when I finally tug the ring up my finger, a surprise sharpness digs into my skin, causing me to recoil.

"It... It won't come off," I say.

"That's right," Gabriel nods. "And it won't ever come off. Not unless you're willing to bleed and suffer to get rid of it."

Twisting my hand, he forces me to take a closer look at the mesmerizing jewelry. Sure enough, I find the silver and gold thorns protruding from beneath the band. They seem to be angled perfectly so that I can hardly feel them... except when the ring is moved.

"You're mine, now," Gabriel smirks.

"What about you?" I ask, unable to take my eyes off of the macabre ring. "You don't get one?"

"No. That's not part of the ceremony."

"How will people know that you belong to me, then?"

Once more, Gabriel looks over to the priests, as if asking for permission. They both nod, their thin lips remaining closed.

In the darkness below, I can sense an exchange taking place. Then, Gabriel lifts his hand back up to his glowing face, something new pinched between his thick fingers.

"What is that?" I ask.

It looks like a long silver needle. It's sharp tip is stained black.

"This is how you're going to mark me."

Pressing the silver needle into my palm, he closes my fingers around the shaft. Immediately, I smell the ink.

"I'm going to give you a tattoo?"

"That's right," Gabriel nods.

"Where?"

"Anywhere you want."

Suddenly, the thorny ring around my finger doesn't feel so tight. I'm being given the power to show ownership over him too.

"On your throat?" I test, unsure of how far I'm actually allowed to go.

"Anywhere," Gabriel repeats.

"On your face?"

"Yes."

Lowering my voice, I lean forward so the priests can't hear.

"On your dick?"

"Yes. Though, that might be a waste of a spot. From now on, no one gets to see my cock but you."

A warm tingle washes over my skin as I lean back and try to think.

"Maybe I could fill in the carving I made on your arm..." I suggest.

"You could."

"Or maybe I could tattoo my initial right below your eye, like a tear, so everyone will know who you belong to."

"I like that idea," Gabriel smiles, unflinching.

"So do I."

Whether or not I was seriously considering etching a tattoo on his face doesn't matter anymore. Suddenly, it's all I can think about.

What could be more visible than a simple ring of thorns?

A teardrop tattoo. A tear drop in the shape of the letter B, for Bianca. His wife. His queen. His owner.

His equal.

"Then it's decided," Gabriel says. Lifting his palm into the air, he's presented with one of the flickering candles. "Put the tip into the flame."

"Will it hurt?" I ask.

"No more than your blade did."

With great caution, I tip the point of the silver needle into the candle's flame.

At first, nothing happens. Then, slowly, the blackness starts to throb with a red pulse.

"Hurry, *myszko*. Before you burn yourself."

Following Gabriel's advice, I lift the needle from the flame.

The dark wolf crouches down and tilts his head, presenting his chiselled cheek to me.

"Don't move," I quietly plead.

My hand trembles ever so slightly as I push the needle towards Gabriel's rough skin. I can feel the eyes of the priests on me. Same goes for the watchful gazes of Gabriel's friends.

Somewhere in the darkness behind me, Rozalia and Tytus are watching.

I wonder if this is romantic to them?

Because it sure as hell feels strangely romantic to me.

An involuntary twitch temporarily closes Gabriel's eye when my hot point touches his skin.

"Quick and hard jabs, Bianca."

Grinding my teeth, I grit through the nerves and do what needs to be done. Clenching the bottom of the silver needle between my fingers, I start to poke the burning ink into the top part of Gabriel's hard cheek.

"Good girl," he grumbles, his eyes remaining closed.

To my surprise, the process doesn't take nearly as long as when I carved my initial into his forearm. And it feels like I've barely even started before my B has taken form.

But I'm not done yet. At least, I'm not ready for this to be over. There's something addicting about marking your man.

It makes me feel so powerful. So dominant.

"Are we officially married now?" I ask.

Leaning back, I place the black tip of the silver needle into the candle's flame again.

"Not until after we kiss."

"Well, I'm not waiting for that. What will my new last name be? I want to add it to your face."

Squinting his freshly marked cheek, Gabriel stands up straight again.

"*Czy mozesk mi podac moje nazwisko, ksiedzu?*" he asks, looking towards the priests once more.

They both shake their heads.

"We will figure our surname out later. Let's finish this. Hand the needle back to the priest."

A tinge of disappointment follows me as I reluctantly return the instrument.

"*Teraz potwierdz zwiazek poculunkiem,*" one of the priests says.

"Finally," Gabriel rumbles.

Before I can ask what was just said, I'm shown.

Palming my face, Gabriel holds me in place and plants the deepest, most spine-tingling kiss I've ever felt directly onto my lips.

I sink into him, my disappointment washing away.

Then, I find the strength to kiss him back.

His lips are mine now. His face is mine too. So is his body and his cock... and his heart.

The sound of a ringing bell seeps through the soft darkness of our endless kiss, and Gabriel pulls back.

But he doesn't let me go. His giant hands stay fastened on my cheeks as he looks me deep in the eyes.

The intensity of his hazel-green glare makes my heart jump.

For all of the uncertainty leading up to this moment, something about it just feels so... right.

"*Spelnij swoj oboqiazek, mlody krolu.*" The priest's words sound like a command.

"What did he say?" I ask.

"It's time to consummate our marriage," Gabriel tells me. His searing palms press into my cheeks and I feel a raspy breath drift out of my open lips.

I'm ready for him. I need him—even if I know this time won't be like the others. Because there's nothing holding my dark wolf back anymore.

"It's time to do what needs to be done in order to secure our empire."

Strangely, Gabriel's words don't inspire any dread in me, though. Whether or not I'm ready to be a mother doesn't matter. Tonight, I will be filled with Gabriel's seed. I will be bred.

And I will enjoy it.

Still, all my heart can focus on is one word.

He said *our* empire.

It's done.

We've been united into one.

Gabriel is now a king.

And I'm finally a queen.

28

BIANCA

The first kiss is divine.

There's no power play, no orders, no ruthless games.

Just endless passion.

The ceremony is over. The bedroom door has been slammed shut behind us. Pale moonlight drifts in through the windows.

Electricity fills the air.

Gabriel doesn't talk. I don't say a word.

We stumble towards the bed, drunk with lust. We tear each other out of our dark wedding outfits. We strip each other bare.

It doesn't take long before it's impossible to tell where one of us begins and the other ends. I feel his thick dark lips on my throat, then on my shoulder. His tongue outlines the initial he carved into my skin. By the time his teeth are grazing my hard nipples, he's turned around so that I can kiss his washboard abs while he devours the rest of me.

Like starving beasts, we lap at each other's flesh, desperate to remove the scars and the tattoos. All the pain melts away.

His cock slips between my lips. My throat opens. My tongue flattens, spilling down his shaft until I taste his balls.

We fall to our sides. He shoves his face between my legs. Before anything else, I feel his coarse facial hair brush against the tender skin inside my thighs. I choke on his swollen cock.

Then, I feel his tongue on my clit. Up and down, back and forth, he leads me like a naughty chaperone.

My mind goes blank. The pressure in my core is on the brink of a nuclear explosion. I'm light headed from the lack of oxygen. Clenching my thighs around Gabriel's face, I make sure he's suffocating just as much as I am.

But it's not because I want him to suffer along with me.

No. None of this comes anywhere close to suffering. I've suffered before. This is not that.

This is all fun.

"You're so fucking delicious," Gabriel growls, his hot breath lashing against my soaking pussy lips.

"Then keep licking," I try to beg, but nothing comes out of my cock-filled mouth except for more saliva; it runs down my chin, onto the tousled bedsheets twisting beneath our sweat glazed bodies.

"Enough foreplay," Gabriel growls. "Or else I'm going to blow down your throat." Unsheathing his cock from my lips, I'm overwhelmed by a sudden influx of fresh air. "From now on, I only cum inside of your cunt."

I'm not allowed to refill my lungs before Gabriel shoves his tongue down my throat. I can taste my juices on his lips. He's right. I am fucking delicious.

And so is he.

"Are you going to put a baby inside of me?" I rasp, when he pulls back.

"I'm going to fill you up until you leak, baby girl. Then I'm going to do it again. And again..."

Stroking my clit with the base of his thick throbbing shaft, Gabriel lubes himself up with my juices. Every stroke makes me wetter.

"Fuck me, daddy," I beg him, unable to take it anymore. "I need you inside of me."

"As you wish."

It doesn't matter that I've felt his cock in my pussy before, or that my tight little hole has already been stretched out by his fist, the second his bulging head slips through my slick threshold, I let out a body shaking gasp.

And so does he.

We're so in sync that our hot sighs clash in the electric air swirling between us.

"You feel so good, baby," I whimper, my back arching as Gabriel's leviathan slides deeper and deeper inside of me.

"That's because this is your cock," my dark wolf snarls. "It exists to make you squirm. So scream for my cock, baby girl. Let it know just how much you appreciate it."

"Rip me apart," I plead. "Fuck me until my organs turn to liquid. I'll do anything for you."

"And I'll do anything for you."

When Gabriel's hard stomach smacks against my pelvis, he pauses. His entire cock is inside of me. Fuck. I can practically feel it pressing up from under the skin beneath my belly button.

I've never felt so absorbed by someone else... and I've never felt like I've absorbed them so completely either.

"Hold on tight, baby girl," Gabriel warns me.

My fingers dig into the bedsheets.

"I'm ready."

Sliding his cock back, Gabriel waits until his swollen shaft is half way out of my cunt before he slams back in. The feeling is so intense I momentarily white out. When I come to, it's to the deafening rhythm of our skin smacking together.

Gabriel is fucking me harder than ever before. The solid slab that is his six pack slaps against my pelvis as I arch into him, taking it all.

The swollen head of his throbbing cock rages against the molten pressure in my core, cracking it more and more with each savage thrust.

"You're so tight, *myszko*," Gabriel grunts, his brutal strokes becoming even more powerful.

"You're so big," I gasp in return, my entire body twitching dangerously close to an orgasmic seizure.

"Tell me you belong to me," Gabriel demands.

"I'm all yours, baby. Every one of my holes belongs to you."

"Good girl. Fuck. I'm going to cum."

Gabriel's already swollen cock seems to swell even more as he collapses on top of me and roars into the mattress.

I'm so lost in the moment that I don't even think about what needs to be done. Instead, instinct takes over, and I find myself preparing to be showered in Gabriel's hot creamy cum.

Opening my lips, I close my eyes and wait for my first taste. But Gabriel doesn't pull himself out. Instead, he shoves my outreached legs together with his knees, so that my ankles click behind his powerful, thrusting ass.

I'm laid out like a plank, straight as a board. There's hardly any room left between my thighs, but Gabriel continues to pound that small hole like his life depends on it.

When he wraps his bicep around my chin and forces me to look away from him, the pressure pulsating in my core shatters into a million different pieces.

Gabriel shoves his tongue into my ear, and I explode. Then he does too.

My entire body convulses in an orgasmic fit as I feel stream after stream of his hot creamy cum rope into my cunt.

"Gabriel!" I cry out.

"Bianca!" he roars back.

I'm held so tightly beneath his massive body that it doesn't matter how much I squirm or twitch or shake. I barely move an inch as I'm dragged through a universe of ecstasy.

It doesn't take long before my pussy is so filled with Gabriel's cum that it starts to leak down his throbbing shaft. But before a single drop can slip out of my hole, Gabriel unsheathes himself.

"Don't you dare spill a drop," he grumbles down to my soaking cunt. But I've lost all control. There's nothing I can do. Cum leaks from my pussy, trickling down my thigh... until Gabriel stops it with the broad side of his index finger.

"This belongs inside of you," he orders, leading the hot semen back into my pulsing hole.

He doesn't stop until his fingers are back inside of me.

"Fuck," I gasp, unable to help myself.

When the mess has been cleaned up, Gabriel slides his free hand under my knees, pushing up until they're pressed against my chest.

"Take it all, baby girl. Filling you up with my cum is the hottest thing I've ever fucking done."

I can feel his creamy cum descending deep down into my cunt as he holds me in place.

It's so fucking hot that I hardly care why he's doing it—not that I can ignore the reason.

This wasn't just for pleasure. And it definitely wasn't just to consummate our marriage.

Gabriel is trying to impregnate me.

But I'm not scared. Hell, I'm almost kind of excited.

I've never felt so alive.

And I quickly realize why.

This time wasn't like the last.

We didn't just fuck.

We made love.

"Do you think it will work?" I gulp.

"There's only one way to find out."

When Gabriel drops my legs, they flop down to the mattress, and I immediately reach between my thighs, holding the creampie in place, just to make sure.

Fuck it.

We're in this together.

"How?" I ask.

"We wait."

Crawling off the side of the bed, Gabriel walks towards one of the windows. Pale moonlight silhouettes his impressive form.

My skin tingles at the sight.

That powerful man just came inside of me.

"How long do we have to wait?" I ask.

"Usually, it takes about two weeks," Gabriel says. "But that's with a regular pregnancy test."

"And you have a special pregnancy test?"

"Courtesy of Roz," he nods. "One of her inventions. We should be able to figure out if you're pregnant within the next few days."

"Are we allowed to have sex until then?" I ask, focusing in on Gabriel's stunning reflection. Those heart-stopping hazel-green eyes shift onto me and I'm already desperate for a second round.

"We're allowed to do whatever we want, *myszko*," Gabriel smirks. "In fact, I insist that we do."

In the blink of an eye, my dark wolf has turned around and jumped back into bed. The force of his body hitting the mattress nearly hurls me into the air. But before I can fly away, he wraps his bulging bicep around my stomach and slams be back down beside him.

"Careful!" I giggle, an unexpected wave of joy washing through me. "You could hurt the baby."

Why does this suddenly feel so right?

To be Gabriel's wife. His queen. The mother of his child. *Our* child.

The intense responsibility of it all seems to fade into the background as I'm wrestled onto my back.

"Until we get a positive pregnancy test, you're the only baby in my life."

"I'm a grown ass woman!" I smile.

Gabriel just shakes his head. "No matter how powerful you grow. No matter how mature you become. You will always be my baby girl."

Pinching my chin, he smothers me in kisses and I'm overcome by the strangest fucking sensation. It works its way through every limb in my body, crisscrossing my chest until my heart becomes so swollen it feels like it could burst.

Only then do I realize what it is.

Happiness.

Happiness at a level I never even knew existed.

I'm in love.

There's no ignoring it anymore. No cursing the very idea of it.

Gabriel is my husband. My dark king. My savage lover.

My soulmate.

For a moment, I forget about all the strings and the baggage that comes with our unholy union. For a moment, I just allow myself to be happy.

But like most things in my life, that good feeling doesn't last long.

Even as the pressure returns to my core; even as my nipples harden and my toes curl; even as Gabriel flips me onto my stomach and starts to lick my tight little asshole, I can feel the pit growing in my stomach.

This isn't over.

Whatever has happened between Gabriel and me, it doesn't change the fact that my family is still out there.

They still love me.

And I still love them.

What happens if they find me? What happens if they never do?

Both options are equally depressing.

If they do find me, it won't matter what I say, there's no way anyone will be able to understand what my heart is feeling.

There will be fighting. There will be death. There will be devastation.

And if I never see them again, I lose a piece of me forever. Not even Gabriel's love can replace the love of my family.

Fuck.

One way or another, I'm going to lose something.

This fragile happiness will be shattered. Hell, it only just appeared and I can already feel it fracturing.

But there's still hope.

As long as I can become strong enough to protect those who would die to protect me, I can hang onto what I've found.

I can hang onto him.

Gabriel.

What have you done to me?

29

GABRIEL

I've never slept so well in my entire life.

The nightmares that have plagued me since I was old enough to remember them already seem like a thing of the past as I slip out from under the covers and look down at my sleeping queen.

Last night, she protected me from the darkness.

Last night, she grabbed onto my heart and squeezed.

Last night, we became one. Over and over again.

I must have cum in her half a dozen times. Each orgasm more desperate than the last. Neither of us wanted the love making to end. The passion was too intoxicating.

But I guess we must have dozed off at one point, because sunlight now seeps in through the rounded bedroom windows.

The last thing I want to do is leave Bianca for a single second. If life was perfect, I'd slip right back under these covers and hold her until the end of time.

But life isn't perfect. Not yet.

There's still so much work to do. So many loose ends to tie up.

So many horrible decisions to make.

But all of that can wait—at least, it can for a little while.

As silently as I can, I sneak out of the bedroom and make my way downstairs.

Roz and Tytus are already up. I spot them chatting through the living room window.

All of the black covers and ceremonial implements have been taken down. There's no sign of what happened here last night.

But it all still lingers deep inside of me.

Stepping out into sunlight, I walk towards my friends.

They stop chatting the second they see me.

Tytus smirks.

"Have a good night?"

"It went well," I nod. "Thank you for your help."

"We did what we had to do," Roz shrugs.

"And we'll all be greatly rewarded for it, right?" Tytus adds.

"Of course," I respond, furrowing my brow. What a strange time to ask for assurance. "Is everything okay?"

"It will be," Tytus nods.

"Once we get the priests back to Poland, we can begin gathering your inheritance," Roz explains. "Then we'll be more than just okay. We'll be fucking royalty."

"Technically, we already are royalty," I point out.

"No. *You* are technically royalty," Roz reminds me. "The second you kissed Bianca and sealed your union, it became so. But Ty and I don't have royal blood. We don't become shit until our empire is built. And we can't start building until we get a positive pregnancy test."

"You'll have it by the time you touch down in Poland."

"You're not coming with us?" Tytus and Roz both ask in unison.

"There's work to be done here."

"So why not get us to do it?" Tytus asks. "After all of this hard work, why not go sit on your throne?"

"Because I haven't earned it yet," I sigh. "Any crown I put on right now could be ripped off my head in a heartbeat. We've made more enemies than friends in our quest for power. Something will need to be done about that."

"You don't think we can handle Drago and the Kilpatricks?"

"I'm sure you could handle Drago. And it's not the Kilpatricks I'm particularly worried about."

"Fuck," Tytus grumbles, realizing where I'm going even before Roz does. "You want to try to negotiate with Ray Byrne, don't you?"

"For Bianca's sake," I admit.

"What about us?" Roz blurts out, a sliver of hurt piercing her voice.

It's like a knife to the gut.

"Yeah," Tytus piles on. "There's only two ways that turns out. Either negotiations with the Irish go south, and we lose you, or you get everything you want, and we're left in the dust."

"Who said anything about leaving you in the dust?" I quickly bite back.

"No one has to," Tytus replies. "I may not be tech smart like Roz, but you know full well I can see three moves ahead in any game of chess."

"What are you trying to say?"

"The Byrnes, the Kilpatricks, the Barinovs, they might accept you. I mean, you've married their daughter and inherited an empire, after all. If they were smart, they'd forgive your sins and open the door for you. It'd be the only way to avoid a devastating war. But us? We'll just become rooks in their game of power. They have no loyalty to us."

"But I do," I insist. "I'm loyal to you two, for now and forever. There will be no negotiation terms that don't include giving you two everything you've ever wanted; everything you've ever worked for; everything you *deserve*."

"That won't be possible if we willingly join another entity,"

Roz sighs. "We don't want to work *for* anybody, Gabriel. We want to work with each other. With you."

"Fuck," I grumble. The domestic bliss I left upstairs is already crumbling. "I won't let you two down, I promise. I just need to figure this shit out. There has to be a way everyone can come out on top."

"There is a way," Tytus says. "You and Bianca come with us, back to Poland. The second her pregnancy is confirmed, the priests will lead us to everything. Then, we can plan our next move, together. We can conquer the entire world, together."

"I can't do that to Bianca," I sigh, pinching the bridge of my nose.

"Don't get lost in your feelings," Rozalia warns me.

"I'm not, I'm trying to be smart about this shit. We only get one chance to–"

"There's nothing smart about being in love."

I don't even try to deny it.

Fuck. Back when this entire plan was originally being formed, there wasn't any concern paid to Bianca's feelings.

She'd be ripped from her family, dragged from her homeland, and used for my benefit, whether she liked it or not. She was only ever supposed to be a pawn. A pawn that I hated. That I could find pleasure in abusing for my own power.

But even back then, I think a part of me knew I only ever hated her because I thought she hated me.

It's what I revealed in my vows.

It's the truth.

Now, I'm in love. And I can't imagine purposely hurting my queen—especially not if there are other options, no matter how risky they are.

"Do you trust me?" I ask.

Tytus and Roz both share a quick glance.

"Yes." Roz speaks first.

"Same here," Tytus agrees.

"And I trust you, with everything. That's why I'm sending you back to Poland. I'm giving you the keys to my inheritance. No supervision. My empire will be yours. Yours to prepare. To cultivate. To control. You will be royalty. No one will be able to negotiate with me without taking you two into consideration. No matter what happens, you will get what you want. You will get what you deserve. Do you understand?"

Birds chirp in the short hesitation between my question and their responses.

"I understand," Roz nods.

"You've never led us astray before," Tytus agrees, reaching out his hand.

"Fuck handshakes," I grumble.

Reaching my arms out, I embrace my lifelong friends in a bear hug.

"We'll do our best," Roz assures me, grumbling into my shoulder.

"And I'll do my best. I love you guys."

That generates a few chuckles as we pull apart again.

"Bianca's making you soft," Roz smirks. "I don't think I've ever heard you use the L word before."

"There's a first time for everything," I smile back. "Just look at us. For the first time ever, we're in control."

"Let's keep it that way," Tytus says.

"Whatever it takes."

"So then, who are you going to go after first?" Roz asks. Together, we all turn and start walking towards the van. It's already been filled, and I quickly spot the dark priests, silently sitting in the back, surrounded by their accoutrements, unflinching.

"Drago," I say. Though, I'm still unsure. "Maybe, if I can bring his head to Ray Byrne, I'll have some leverage."

"You already have leverage," Tytus notes. "You'll have an army and a fortune."

"Ray Byrne has access to a bigger army, and multiple fortunes."

"But he doesn't have us. He'll never have us. That's our advantage."

"Sure," I agree. "But one way or another, we're going to have to take Drago down. Better it be sooner than later."

"I won't argue with you there."

Opening up the driver side door, Tytus hops inside the van.

Roz has already gone around back to shut the trunk when I reach out and shake Tytus' hand.

"We're so close," I remind him. "I can hardly believe it."

"I can," Tytus nods. "We've done everything right. We've adapted to every bump in the road. There are only a few more hurdles left. We jump those, and we're there."

"Good thing my legs are fresh."

"So are mine. Be safe, Gabriel. Don't get yourself killed."

"No promises," I joke.

That makes Tytus chuckle.

When Roz jumps into the passenger seat, he starts the van.

"Say goodbye to the sleeping beauty for me," Roz shouts from the window.

"And keep us updated on the pregnancy test," Tytus adds.

"Will do."

With that, Tytus backs up and turns around. There's nothing more to do but stand and watch as the van disappears into the dense forest ahead.

Shit.

A knot has formed in my gut.

It's quickly being joined by a raging fire.

My loyalty was just called into question, and by the last people I'd ever expect.

But that doesn't mean their concerns weren't legit.

When I turn back towards the cabin, my gaze is immediately drawn up to the bedroom window.

There, standing behind the sun draped glass, wrapped in the same white bedsheets we sullied so many times last night, is an angel.

My angel.

My queen.

Bianca stares down at me with a blank look on her face. Well, not entirely blank. Even from this distance, I can spot the faintest glimmer in her crystal blue eyes, and the smallest smile lifting up the corners of her perfect pink lips.

Fuck.

Tytus and Roz were right. This is dangerous.

I'd do anything for her.

But I'd also do anything for my friends.

Goddamn. Love is such a fickle bitch.

This would be so much easier if I wasn't loyal to anyone— not that I would change this feeling for the world.

I'm willing to kill for these three people. Die for these three people.

But for as much as I love Tytus and Roz, my love for Bianca is different. It's more romantic. Fresher.

I have to be careful.

Still, my cock stirs alive as Bianca and I lock eyes.

Dropping the bedsheets from her body, she turns around and struts out of sight.

My fingers clench into fists. I bite down on my lower lip.

All of my life, I've been independent to a fault. Even Drago could only hope to steer me in the right direction through a tangled web of lies and deceit.

But Bianca?

She can control me without saying a single word.

Hell, I'm already storming back into the cabin and racing up the stairs before I can even think about how to handle what comes next.

All I want is her.

It doesn't seem to matter that my once frozen heart has been placed over a pit of fire and thawed to the bone; that, if I don't hurry, it could be burned to ashes... along with everyone I care about. My queen calls to me.

So, I go to her.

I'll make my decision while my cock is in her cunt; while I stare deep into those crystal blue eyes. That's when everything is clearest. That's when the world makes the most sense.

That's when I'll know what needs to be done. Right?

Whatever path I choose, one thing will never change.

No matter what, those I care about will be protected. They will be rewarded.

First, though, I'm going to reward myself.

Because, in order for this to all work out, I might just need to take on the entire world by my fucking self.

And that's going to be a hell of a task. Even if it will be a small price to pay to keep my friends happy... and to hold onto Bianca's love.

Whatever it takes.

I'll do whatever it fucking takes.

"Is everything alright?"

The question is the first thing out of my mouth when Gabriel bursts back into the bedroom.

It's clearly not what he wants to hear.

But it's all that's on my mind.

When I first spotted him through window, there was a troubling look about him. A look that dropped a stone in my stomach.

Sure, that troubling look quickly faded when he saw me. But the feeling it left continues to linger.

Something is wrong. And I think I know what.

"Everything is perfect," Gabriel says, and I can't help but want to believe him. "What could possibly be wrong? Everything is going according to plan. And we're alone now, so I can make you scream as loudly as I want."

"I don't think I can get any louder than I did last night," I blush, realizing that Tytus and Roz must have slept over too.

Oh shit, and the priests.

"Let's put that theory to the test," Gabriel smirks.

He steps forward, and the stone in my gut falters. But it

doesn't go away. And I know it won't until I address what's on my mind.

"Wait, Gabriel…" I whisper. It's so hard not to just sink into his embrace and let the warmth of his muscular body sooth all of my worries.

But that's what I did all of last night. I let my concerns fester. And the second Gabriel slipped out of bed this morning, it all came racing back.

I can't have that. As much as I've come to care for my dark wolf, he's taught me that I can't always rely on others to protect me from this darkness.

I'll need to face it head on.

"What's wrong, *myszko*?" Gabriel asks, when I shirk away from him.

"I… It's my family," I sigh. "They're still out there. Worried. They don't know where I am. They don't know that I'm safe with you. Every moment that goes by must be torture for them."

"I'm sure they'll be fine."

"No. They won't be. And neither will I."

"What are you saying, Bianca?"

"You need to take me back to them, Gabriel."

I can practically hear his heart drop.

Then, I can almost see the fume coming out of his ears.

"You think I'll give you up that easily?" he growls.

"No," I shake my head. "I don't want you to give me up. I want you to negotiate. Explain to them what's happened. I'll tell them everything. About how we don't hate each other anymore, about how we're married, about how we're…"

I manage to trail off before a certain four-letter word can drift from my lips.

Love.

Neither of us have said it yet—even if it feels like it follows us from room to room.

"Do you really think your family will negotiate with me?" Gabriel asks.

Those hazel-green eyes stay fixed on me as the wolf begins to circle.

Straightening my back, I stand my ground.

"They will if I'm by your side. They will if they see just how close we've become."

"They'll say you have Stockholm syndrome. That I'm threatening you to speak in my favor. That they'll never forgive the man who defiled their daughter."

"You haven't defiled me..."

"Then what have I done?"

"You've crowned me. You've empowered me."

You've loved me.

Gabriel's hot breath washes against my neck as he steps up to my back.

A ragged sigh escapes my throat, but I don't sink. I don't give in. I've been through so much. I've learned so many lessons. I'm stronger than I've ever been.

"You're my queen," Gabriel confirms, his lips brushing against my tender skin.

"And you're my king. Let's tell the world. Aren't you sick of hiding?"

"I'm sick of pretending."

"Me too. Let's stop."

"What are you pretending to be, *myszko*?" Gabriel asks, his deep voice crawling into my ear.

"I'm pretending that this is all completely consensual. That I'm not still your captive. That the ceremony that bound us together is legitimate. That this ring can't be cut off my finger."

Gabriel's long thick fingers slide over my throat as he pushes his growing bulge into the small of my back.

"What else are you pretending? Are you pretending to care for me? Are you pretending to crave me?"

"No. I could never pretend that," I confess.

"Then why should I pretend that anything else matters?"

"Because you want everything else to matter. You don't just want me to be your captive pretending to be your queen. You want me to be your queen. Period."

"And how do we do that?"

"By stepping back out into the world. By going to see my family. By negotiating with them."

"And if they kill me?"

"I won't let them," I stubbornly huff.

To my surprise, Gabriel chuckles. "You think you can hold back the Great Don and the Irish Lion?"

"I think I can convince my father and my cousin to do what's right."

"And what's right?"

"Letting me be happy. That's right. Allowing me to make my own choices, and be my own woman. That's right."

"They still think you're the fragile princess you were before I took you."

"I'll teach them how wrong they are, just like how you taught me."

"Don't teach them the exact same way," Gabriel whispers.

Nibbling on my earlobe, he cups both my breasts. A hot wave washes into me from his palms, and I'm momentarily filled with a morphine-like calm.

But I fight through it.

Taking his forearms, I push Gabriel's hands away. Then, I turn around to face him.

He's already unbuckling his belt.

"Stop," I order.

No one's going to be able to fix this situation but me. It's time to call on all that I've learned. It's time to become the dark queen I've always wanted to be.

The leader. The ruler.

"You don't want to see what I have waiting for you beneath my pants?" Gabriel smirks.

Still, he does as he's told. He stops unbuckling the belt, mid latch.

"Of course I want to see it," I respond, mind racing with a thousand conflicting thoughts. "But I want to see it on my own terms."

"And what are your terms?"

My gaze darts from Gabriel's stunning hazel-green eyes to the giant bulge begging to be released from his black pants.

"Give me your belt," I hear myself say.

Gabriel squints at me, like he's not sure where I'm going with this. But that doesn't stop him from tearing the leather strap from around his waist.

"What are you going to do with my belt?" he asks, handing it to me.

The warm leather sinks into my palm as I consider how to answer that.

"I'm going to teach you a lesson," I blurt out.

Gabriel's dark brows lift in surprise, then settle into a mischievous grin.

"Do you want to dominate me, *myszko*? Is that what you're asking?"

"I want to show you how to listen to your queen," I say, my chest puffing out as it fills with fire.

Just like that, it all becomes clear.

We're supposed to be equals now. But that doesn't mean we are. If we're going to stop pretending, then I'm going to have to whip Gabriel into shape.

"Very well," Gabriel dutifully nods. "What will you have of me, my queen?"

"I'll have you lie down on the bed. On your back."

"Pants on or off?"

"Off."

The sense of power I get from watching Gabriel obey me nearly matches the toe-curling gratification I get from the unveiling of his girthy beast.

My chin lifts at the sight of his thick, veiny cock. My fingers tighten around the belt.

That's *my* cock.

"What now?" Gabriel asks, after he's gotten onto the bed.

His hard cock twitches with excitement as I approach.

"Get me wet."

Before I can step onto the mattress and sit down on his gorgeous face, Gabriel reaches a hand out and trails two fingers over my slick cunt.

"You already are wet."

In a move that surprises even me, I whip the belt down onto his forearm.

Gabriel immediately retracts his hand.

"Make me wetter," I demand.

Without giving him a chance to respond, I pounce onto the mattress.

The moment I sit down on Gabriel's face, he starts licking. That thick tongue of his finds my swollen cunt. His lips begin to suck.

My body trembles.

Grinding my teeth, I keep my back straight and fight through the pressure growing in my core. Then, I lift the belt and lash it down onto Gabriel's finely cut six-pack.

He barely even flinches. But I still get a devilish tickle from watching the red mark fade behind his black tattoos.

"Faster," I insist. "Suck harder. Lick faster. Make me cum or I start whipping your cock."

Gabriel does exactly as I instruct. Closing his lips in around my clit, he starts to suck like a fucking vacuum, all the while swirling his tongue in manic circles around the swollen nub.

"Holy shit," I can't help but gasp.

I'm already losing control. But when I spot Gabriel reaching up to grab my thighs, I burst back into form.

"Did I say you could touch me?" I ask, whipping both of his hands with the leather belt.

"No, you didn't," Gabriel's muffled voice growls up from beneath my ass.

I can tell he's trying his hardest not to snap. I'm sure all he wants is to flip me onto my back and fuck the ever-loving hell out of me.

But he resists the urge. He obeys his queen.

The thought that I'm quelling such an untamed beast makes my skin prickle; it brings me close to my first orgasm.

"Do you want me to cum all over your face?" I ask.

"Yes, my queen," Gabriel grunts, before going right back to his duty.

"Then keep licking," I rasp. "Keep sucking. Faster... faster..."

The orgasm starts in my core; a pressure builds out from the flickering of Gabriel's tongue. Then, all of a sudden, I break.

The belt drops from my hand. My back arches so sharply I could almost snap in two. Every inch of me begins to tremble as I descend into a carnal seizure.

The pleasure is unbearable. It wants to explode out of me; rip me apart.

Usually, Gabriel is here to hold me down; to keep me in place as I experience the searing ecstasy he's torn out of me.

But now, he's clamped beneath my thighs. His nose digs into my ass. His huge cock twitches against his hard belly.

And his hands stay dutifully by his side.

There's no one to keep me in line but myself.

It takes every bit of strength I have. Hell, I must go blind from the effort, because the next thing I know, the bedroom is slowly coming back into focus, and my orgasm is already washing away.

I did it.

Biting down on my bottom lip, I spot Gabriel's hard cock. It's still twitching. And now, pre-cum drips from the tip of his bulging head.

"I'm not done with you yet, big boy," I mumble.

Grabbing the belt, I twist myself around and slide down Gabriel's impeccable body, lathering him in my juices.

"You're so fucking hot," the dark wolf growls, sucking in deep breaths of air. "Get back on my face."

My belt comes down across his chest, just catching the edge of his nipples.

"You're not in charge here," I bark. "I'm the one who gives the orders."

A sneer crosses Gabriel's blood-red lips. They glisten with my juices as he continues his struggle to give in.

"And what if I refuse to listen?" he asks.

"Then you will be punished."

Another lash across his chest pulls a grunt from his sneering lips.

But then I feel his cock twitch at my back, painting my skin with a soft glaze of pre-cum.

He's into this—even if he won't admit to it.

"What if I want to be punished?" Gabriel asks.

"Then keep acting up."

This time, when he lifts his hands to make a grab at my breasts, I know it's on purpose.

He receives two lashings for his disobedience.

I can feel his cock going crazy in response.

"Don't you cum too quickly now," I order, as I direct him into my soaking pussy.

We both gasp the second he slips inside.

Immediately, Gabriel begins to thrust upwards. His pounding cock feels so fucking good. But we're not here for that.

This time, the belt comes down across his cheek, snapping his head to the side.

"What the hell?" Gabriel grumbles.

"Did that hurt?" I ask, my question sitting somewhere between a taunt and genuine concern.

"Keep going," Gabriel demands. Biting down on his lip, he straightens his neck again. "What's next?"

"You just lay there. I'll do all the work."

And that's exactly what happens. Gabriel keeps his hard body flexed as I begin to ride him like a fucking outlaw cowgirl.

The belt doesn't leave my hand as I gyrate around his swollen cock, pushing back and forth so that I can feel all of him.

Every time I feel him throb too much, though, I whip his chest again.

"Don't you dare finish inside of me," I rasp. "Not yet."

But he can't control himself.

"I'm going to cum..." he growls.

I give his hard nipples an even harder lash.

"No. You're not," I order. "Not until I do."

Somehow, the beast manages to hold out until I'm on the brink of my own orgasm.

"Holy fuck," I gasp, when it all becomes too much. "You're so fucking big..."

This time, it all explodes in a single flash, tearing through my body in a hot blast.

"Fucking hell, *myszko*. I can't control myself any longer."

"Cum for me," I shout. "Fill me the fuck up!"

A deep guttural grunt rumbles out from behind Gabriel's gritted teeth as his already tensed body flexes even harder. His cock throbs and twitches in my tight little hole, before unleashing a typhoon of hot creamy cum.

The eruption fills every available inch of my begging cunt.

Before anything can drip out, though, I squeeze my thighs shut, impaling myself on Gabriel's gushing cock.

"Don't you dare spill a single drop," I order, gasping for air.

I don't stop riding until I'm completely exhausted.

Only then do I collapse onto my dark wolf.

His hard chest is still hot from the lashings I gave him. I press my ear against the red marks, and listen to his heart beat.

It's racing even faster than mine.

"Good boy," I whisper, finally dropping the belt from my hand.

Slowly, Gabriel's cock softens, until it slips out of my gaping cunt.

He replaces that warmth by wrapping me up in his arms and holding me closer to his steaming body.

"You did well, *myszko.*"

"So did you."

"Is there anything else?"

Even through the red-hot afterglow of that glorious fucking orgasm, I force myself to regain focus. The pit in my stomach hasn't disappeared, but I finally have it in my grasp. Invisible fingers wrap around the dread-filled stone.

But before I can get to the serious stuff, there's something else I need to know.

"Yes," I say. Digging my hands into Gabriel's hard chest, I push myself up so that I can look down into those incredible hazel-green eyes. "Tell me what it means."

"What?"

"You know what."

Gabriel bites his lip. "*Myszko,*" he whispers.

My skin tingles as a strangely comforting warmth washes over me.

"That's the one."

"It's Polish," he says. "It means '*little mouse*'."

Whatever I was expecting, it wasn't that.

"This entire time, you've been calling me *little mouse?*"

"It's a term of affection," Gabriel assures me, a smirk lifting the corners of his blood red lips, and deepening the dimples on his cheeks. "*Myszko...*"

"I am not a little mouse," I tell him, gently slapping his heaving chest.

But Gabriel just shakes his head. "No matter how ferocious you become, no matter how powerful you grow, you will always be my little mouse, *myszko.*"

My heart nearly bursts.

How could such a ruthless man be so gentle?

How could such a hard man be so tender?

It's because he's in love with you.

"Fine," I give in. "I'm your *myszko*. But what do I get to call you in return?"

"Daddy."

Fuck. I walked right into that one.

Digging my nails into Gabriel's hard chest, I try to regain control.

"I'll call you Daddy when I feel like it," I offer. "But only when I feel like it."

"Deal," Gabriel grins. "Now, is that all?"

"No," I quickly challenge. "That is not all."

There's something else on my mind. Something much more pressing than the little pet name Gabriel has given me.

"Give your orders, my queen."

"I want you to set up a meeting with my family," I demand, before I can lose the courage to. "We're going to negotiate with them. Alright?"

My overflowing heart freezes as I wait for a response.

But I tell myself not to worry.

Gabriel gave me the meaning of my pet name. That must mean he finally believes I'm ready to be his queen. And that should mean he can trust me. Right?

Still, he doesn't respond right away. And my frozen heart moves into my throat as I hold my breath and wait.

Do the right thing, my king.

"Alright," he finally grumbles. "But no matter what happens, I'm not giving you up. Understand?"

My frozen heart starts to beat again.

But despite the relief washing over me, I know this is only the beginning of a very hard road.

At least we'll walk it together.

"Just give me a chance to talk to them. We might not have to give anything up."

"You always have to give something up," Gabriel sighs. "Just know that it won't be you. It won't be *us*. Understand?"

"I understand," I whisper, the invisible fingers slipping around the stone in my gut.

I know what Gabriel means.

If push comes to shove, he's going to do whatever it takes to keep me.

By setting up this meeting, I'm not just putting my dark wolf in danger, I'm putting my family in peril too.

One wrong move by them and he'll attack. One wrong move by him and we could lose each other forever.

It'll be up to me to hold everything together.

That's a huge responsibly. But it's one that I have to take on.

Because no matter what happens, one thing is clear.

This meeting needs to happen.

Otherwise, there can be no happy ending.

31

GABRIEL

"What do we do about... that?"

Peering through the dimming dusk light, I follow Bianca's gaze to the rotting pile of guts and flesh still half tied to the tree out front.

"We leave him here," I grunt, my mind still entirely preoccupied with the task at hand.

There's no time to think about what to do with dead men.

An hour ago, I sent an encrypted message to Ray Byrne. I'm sure the old man will get Rian to decrypt it. Then, they'll both see the truth.

I spared little detail.

The only thing I couldn't quite capture in words was what Bianca and I have become. Especially after I gave myself to her upstairs.

Bianca was right. We were pretending. We were ignoring the uncomfortable reality sitting just beneath our little love and hate fest.

We may have been falling for each other, but all the while, the world was crumbling around us.

The only way we're going to get out of this intact is if I face those uncomfortable truths.

Opening the garage door, I lead Bianca to the black Land Rover I originally drove us here in. It's been sitting in the darkness this whole time, idle and ignored.

I was getting far too comfortable at this secluded little cabin. Fuck. Part of me was even starting to think of it as home.

Castles and mansions and empires somehow don't feel nearly as powerful in the face of what we've found out here, in the middle of nowhere.

That naïve little part of me withers away as I open the passenger door for my queen.

This needs to be done.

For her sake.

Shit. Bianca's become stronger than I could have ever dreamed. Hopefully, that will serve us both well in the conflict to come.

We don't share much conversation as I start the car and pull out into the pink night. We're hardly halfway through the overgrown trail that leads through the forest when the sun disappears completely.

For what feels like hours, we're surrounded by almost complete darkness. Only the headlights give me any sense of direction.

Really, we should have waited until morning to leave. But I couldn't help myself.

I want to start the rest of my life as soon as possible. And it can't begin until we deal with the ghosts of our pasts.

Bianca is asleep by the time I pull onto the highway. It's the first time I see strangers since I tied Luis Falcao to that tree.

It doesn't feel right, sharing Bianca with the world like this. That cabin was the perfect cove for our love.

But it was also fragile.

Can what we've built survive the test of the outside world?

Fuck. There's only one way to find out.

"Wake up, *myszko*, we're almost there."

My knuckles go white as I squeeze the steering wheel.

Up ahead, I can spot the twinkling warning lights of the Silver Lake reservoir. The thin bridge on top of the dam is where I decided to host this all-important meeting.

There will be no room for snipers. No hiding spots for Byrne or Kilpatrick soldiers. It will just be Ray Byrne and Rian Kilpatrick, and Bianca and me.

At least, that's what I stipulated in my message. But I almost don't want them to play by the rules.

Any excuse to drag Bianca back to that cabin in the woods; to spend the rest of our days alone there. Together. Forever.

But life doesn't work like that.

As quietly as possible, I pull into a hidden parking spot, just off the main road leading into the reservoir.

"Are you ready?"

Bianca's voice is soft, and still so sleepy. She's only been awake for a couple of minutes now, and she's worried about me.

She shouldn't be. I'm the one who should be worried about her. And I am.

And not just because I'm concerned about her safety.

Her heart is on the line too.

I only have one love to lose.

She has so much more than that.

An unwelcome pang of jealousy flutters through my chest as I help Bianca out of the passenger seat.

"I'm always ready," I lie. "The real question is, are you?" wiping some sleep from her eyes, I wonder if we shouldn't wait until she's fully awake.

This opportunity is too precious to squander.

"I'm used to not being ready by now," she smiles. But her voice is still so dozy.

I decide to wake her up with a kiss.

"What was that for?" she asks, when our lips fall apart.

"It was just to shock you awake."

"Is that all?" she teases, the faintest giggle escaping her pretty pink lips as she shakes her head.

"That's all. Now, let's go."

Taking her hand, I lead my queen towards the bridge of our destiny.

I can feel the thorny ring on her finger. It makes the mark on my forearm burn. It also makes the fresh tattoo below my eye throb ever so slightly.

We belong to each other now.

There's no going back.

The closer we get to the dam, the stronger the sound of rushing water becomes. Soon enough, it's an all-encompassing roar that only fades slightly as we take our first steps onto the bridge.

I don't see anyone up ahead.

But it's dark.

Squeezing Bianca's hand, I silently lead her forward.

With my other hand, I make sure the gun tucked under my belt is still there.

For maybe the first time in my life, I hope I don't have to shoot anyone.

"... Is that them?" Bianca suddenly gasps.

Peering through the darkness, I search for what she's referring to.

That's when I spot the silhouettes.

Three of them.

My grip tightens around Bianca's hand.

"We're leaving," I growl.

"What? Why?" she chokes. "They're right there!"

"The deal was only for Ray and Rian to show up. Do you see that third shadow?"

"I... It's so small."

Planting her feet in the ground, Bianca squints ahead,

trying to make out the figures walking towards us.

"It doesn't matter if they brought a fucking dwarf. How can we trust them if they've already decided to break the—"

"Mom!"

I have to tug Bianca back when she lunges forward. But the little whimper of surprise that leaks from her lips quickly loosens my grip.

Up ahead, I see what has caught her attention.

It's Francesca Byrne. Her mother. She's sandwiched in between two giants.

Ray Byrne and Rian Kilpatrick.

Why the hell did they bring her?

"Bianca!"

Once again, Bianca tries to go to her mother. But I'm forced to hold her back.

"Gabriel... please..." she begs.

My thawed heart fucking aches for her, but I don't let go. If I do now, I'll never get her back.

"My baby girl!"

The desperation in Francesca Byrne's voice is so clear it hurts. But I don't budge.

Before Francesca can race forward to embrace her daughter, Ray reaches out and grabs her too.

The two exchange words. Words that I can't hear over the roar of the rushing water.

But I don't need to hear anything to know what's going on.

Rian Kilpatrick's glare cuts through the darkness. He's not even looking at Bianca. All of his attention is focused on me.

He's going to be the real problem tonight.

"Are you alone?"

Ray's voice is so deep it somehow undercuts the roar.

"That was the deal," I yell back.

Slowly, we inch closer together.

"How can we trust you anymore?" Rian growls. Both of his

hands are clenched into fists.

He's ready to tackle me off the side of this bridge.

I hold onto Bianca just a little bit tighter.

"You're one to talk," I bark. "It was only supposed to be the two of you."

"How could I deny a mother's right to see her daughter?" Ray asks.

We all stop about ten feet from each other. It's close enough to hear each other talk, but far enough to give us all time to react if someone does something stupid...

"Are you alright?" Francesca rasps, her attention fixed entirely on her daughter.

"I'm fine," Bianca chokes.

"How'd you get that black eye?" Rian sneers.

"It's from the scope of a rifle," Bianca replies, sniffing back some tears. "The recoil got me good, but you should see the other guy."

Her quip eases my nerves just a little bit. She's calmer than I expected—even if the emotion of this reunion is already beginning to leak from her crystal blue eyes.

"You've been shooting people?" Ray asks, completely shocked.

Francesca looks mortified.

Rian, on the other hand, seems strangely impressed.

"I've been learning how to protect myself," Bianca insists, her fingers digging into my hand.

"What have you done to my daughter?" Ray asks, his restrained fury flickering out.

"I've been teaching her how to rule."

"Rule. Ha!" Rian spits. "That weird wedding ceremony you described in your message doesn't mean shit to us. Neither does your supposed army or your fortune. You don't know shit about ruling, asshole. And you never will."

"Oh, and you do?" I can't help but reply. "Remind me again

what a nice New York boy like you is doing all the way out here on the west coast."

"Why don't I fucking show you."

Rian and I both reach for our weapons at the same time. But we don't get far.

Before I can even touch my gun, Bianca drapes herself around me. Ahead, Francesca has grabbed onto her nephew.

"Enough!" Ray bellows. "We aren't here to trade jabs. We're here to get our daughter back."

"Are you willing to agree to my terms?" I ask.

"How could we?" Ray says, shaking his head. "Do you know how dangerous it would be to give you what you want? Every common crook from here to fucking Nantucket would immediately be after our daughters, all of my nieces, just to get a slice of the same pie."

"I'm not some common crook," I growl, a gust of shame thrashing through me at the very thought.

"Yes, I read your message Gabriel. I know everything. It checks out. But that doesn't mean you're anything special. Not without my daughter."

"He is special!" Bianca suddenly blurts out. "Dad, I know how bad this looks. Believe me, I do. But we can work through this. We all have a common enemy. We—"

"What the hell are you talking about?" Rian interrupts. Francesca is still holding him back, but only barely. "You fucking bastard, what have you done to her?"

"He's made me happy," Bianca defends me. "He's taught me how to be the woman I've always wanted to be."

"You're just a girl," Ray grumbles.

"No. Dad. I'm not. I've done things. Horrible things. Necessary things. Things that I don't regret for a second. Not anymore. And I'm stronger for it. You always said I would be a queen someday. Well, now I am. Now, I finally feel like it."

"Not like this," Ray sighs.

"It was the only way," Bianca sniffles. "I love you Dad. But you were always too scared to teach me about the real world. Gabriel wasn't."

"What the fuck does that mean?" Rian shouts. If it was anyone but his aunt trying to hold him back, I'm sure he would have already plowed through them by now.

"It means I didn't treat her like a fragile doll," I tell him. "Like some sheltered princess to handle with kid gloves. I gave her weapons, I gave her confidence, I gave her—"

"You will never be able to give her what we can," Francesca suddenly speaks up.

There's no malice in her words, but still, they cut through me like a knife.

"That's not true," I mumble. "... I can give her back to you."
"What?"

Bianca's fingers go limp in my hand.

"Go hug your mother, *myszko*. Tell her you love her and feel her love. That's not something I ever want to deprive you of again."

Bianca looks like she can't believe her ears.

"What kind of trick do you have up your sleeve, asshole?" Rian spits.

"No tricks," I shake my head. "This is a gesture of goodwill."

"Are you returning my daughter?" Ray asks. Turning to Francesca, he gently pulls her off of Rian and holds her close.

"No," I admit. "That will never happen. But I will do whatever it takes to make her happy."

Ray and Francesca share a long look.

Rian, on the other hand, doesn't take his eyes off of me.

"Very well," Ray finally nods, hesitation drawing out each syllable. "At least we agree on that. Bianca deserves nothing but happiness."

Patting his wife forward, Ray gives me a look of pure warning.

But I'm not worried. This is no trick. Bianca has suffered enough.

"Go hug your mother," I tell my queen. "But come right back to me afterwards. Alright?"

No tears have fallen down her cheeks yet, but I'd be shocked if Bianca can see straight will all the water glazing over her beautiful blue eyes.

"I promise," Bianca whispers.

Dropping her hand, I push her forward.

It doesn't take much motivating.

The two women immediately sprint forward, practically tackling each other at the midway point between us.

"I missed you so much," Francesca weeps, smothering her daughter in kisses.

"I missed you too, Mama."

The sweetness of the moment is undercut by my need to stay on guard. I hardly watch the sweet little reunion. My gaze remains glued on the two very dangerous men glowering at me from just up ahead.

Francesca and Bianca quietly talk amongst themselves as I plan my next move.

"I promise, Mama. He's not like that. We... Well, would you like to meet him?"

My gaze is immediately snapped away from Ray and Rian.

That's when I meet Francesca's glimmering hazel eyes. They study me, not with anger, but with a cautious curiosity.

They don't linger long. Before I've managed to blink again, Francesca's gaze has returned to Ray.

I don't hear the short conversation they share. But when they both nod, I realize I'm about to be formally introduced to Bianca's mother.

I'm somehow more nervous for that than I was for this meeting.

With great care Francesca approaches me. Bianca stays

wrapped up in her arm.

I straighten my back.

"So, you're supposed to be my new son-in-law?" Francesca asks, when she's close enough to not have to raise her voice.

Even as she wipes tears from her eyes, her words are strong and stable.

I see so much of Bianca in her.

"That's right," I nod.

"And what does it mean to you, to be married to my daughter?"

Bianca holds her mother's arm tightly as I consider the question.

"It means everything," I admit. "She's my world."

"Pretty words," Francesca mumbles. "But words are much easier than actions."

"Look, Mama."

I don't resist as Bianca reaches out and grabs my wrist. Her soft fingers trace the initial she carved into my forearm.

"B... For Bianca?" Francesca notes.

"That's right," Bianca nods. "I did that to him. He let me. Look what else he let me do."

I lower my head so that Bianca can reach up and touch the tattoo painted beneath my eye.

"Another B," Francesca sees. "So, you've claimed him?"

"I have," Bianca gently smiles.

"But then where's the second B?" she asks.

"We're married, Mama," Bianca whispers, dancing around the answer.

"You can get married and keep your last name, you know."

"I... I want to start anew."

"With a new last name?"

"Yes."

"Well, then what is it? Let me hear it."

"We... we don't know yet."

"You don't know your own last name?" Francesca asks, looking up at me.

"I was hoping your daughter would help me find it."

"Well, I'm not sure my husband will let you take ours."

"That isn't the plan, Mama," Bianca corrects her.

"You two seem to have so many plans," Francesca sighs, her hazel eyes looking back and forth between my tattoo and my scar.

"Will you help us?" Bianca asks.

Francesca hardly even flinches at the question.

"We'll see," she says. "But first, I need something from you, Gabriel."

"What's that?"

I'll do anything. Whatever it takes to make this work out.

"I can tell everything I need to know about a person by giving them a hug," Francesca explains. "Do I have your permission to do so?"

The request is so strange that I have to look over at Bianca just to make sure I'm hearing it right.

But Bianca just shrugs.

Could this be some kind of trick? Just how badass is Mama Byrne? With a hug at the right angle, she could slip my gun out from right under my belt.

Fuck it.

It's a risk I'm willing to take.

"You have my permission," I nod.

Francesca is slightly taller than Bianca, but her head still barely reaches past my chest, and she has to turn her cheek to me as we wrap our arms around each other.

For a moment, a strange calmness comes over us both. Everything seems to go quiet. I shut my eyes, not daring to look over at the two men I'm sure are dying to rip my head off.

"Not bad," Francesca says.

When we let each other go, the sound of rushing water

comes roaring back into my ears.

"That's enough," Ray calls out. "Come back to me, dear."

With one last curious look up into my eyes, Francesca nods. Then, she turns and gives her daughter a big long kiss on the forehead.

"We'll figure this out, honey. I promise."

"I know, Mama."

The two share a final deep hug before Francesca reluctantly pulls away.

It doesn't take long before she's back by her husband's side.

He doesn't look particularly happy with what just happened.

I can't say I blame him.

"What now?" Bianca asks me.

Reaching down, I take her hand. That's when I notice the vibrations.

Her ring is trembling.

"Do you feel that?" I ask, confused.

Immediately, I turn my attention to Ray and Rian.

But they seem just as confused as I am.

"What the hell is that?" Rian growls.

The vibrations get stronger. The roaring of the rushing water seems to amplify as well.

Even the wind appears to pick up.

Then I see the lights.

My grip tightens around Bianca's hand.

"Who's fucking helicopter is that?" I shout.

My gun is out before I can get a response.

This is an ambush.

"It's not ours, you bastard!" Rian shouts back.

"Then who the fuck—"

I don't get a chance to finish.

The air is sucked out of my lungs, and for a split second everything goes quiet.

I can hardly even hear the whirling propellers of the descending helicopter as it steadies itself just off the side of the bridge.

Then, all hell breaks loose.

I only catch the silhouette of the front-mounted machine gun before it starts firing.

"Fuck!"

Throwing my body in front of Bianca, I tackle her to the ground.

Shrapnel flies over my shoulders as the bridge is shredded to pieces.

"Gabriel!" Bianca shouts from beneath me.

"We need to get the hell out of here," I rumble.

There's no hiding from a fucking machine gun.

Keeping myself wedged between the hovering helicopter and Bianca, I pull us both to our feet.

To my surprise, though, Bianca doesn't just weightlessly follow behind me. Instead she tugs in the opposite direction.

"Mom! Dad! Rian!"

Even through the hellish roar of the dam, and the endless spit fire of the machine gun, I can hear the desperate anguish in her voice.

It slashes through my exposed heart.

But I don't linger on the pain. I can't.

"We can't save them unless we save ourselves," I shout.

Ripping her back into my body, I drag her down the bridge. She sobs in my arms. I hold her tight.

Bullets whizz past our ears.

"We'll make it out of here, Bianca. I—"

Before I can finish my promise, the cement beneath our feet begins to crumble.

Then it gives out.

"No!"

All I can do is hold onto Bianca as we fall into the darkness.

32

BIANCA

The last thing I remember, I was falling.

Falling into the darkness, wrapped in Gabriel's arms.

It didn't seem like the worst way to die.

But I'm not dead.

Not yet, anyway.

"Fuck..." I grumble, slowly coming to.

My head is pounding. My body is soaked through to the bone.

The last thing I want to do is open my eyes.

There's no way I'll be greeted by good news.

Not with what I remember.

There was a helicopter. A machine gun. There was scream-ing. We were separated from my family.

Then, we started to fall.

How the hell could anyone survive that?

My stomach lurches.

No. You survived. That means everyone else could have too.

A pitiful cough jitters from my collapsed lungs, and I just want to hang my head and drift back into unconsciousness.

Nothing hurts when you're knocked out.

But I've been hiding for too long.

Forcing my heavy eyelids open, I try to face whatever harsh reality has come crashing down on me.

But I don't see anything.

Only more darkness.

That's when I realize my face has been covered by a suffocating hood.

My heart drops.

This can't be good.

"Hello?"

My voice feels so small; so insignificant. But it doesn't matter.

I need to do something. Anything.

Mom was on that bridge. Dad. Rian.

Gabriel.

A deep despair cuts through me as I try not to imagine the worst.

The meeting was going so well.

Sure, Dad and Rian looked angrier than I'd ever seen them before, but at least I got to *see* them.

I got to hug my mother, and introduce her to my husband.

My husband.

Fuck.

That's still so weird to think. But it doesn't change what happened.

Gabriel saved me. He protected me from the chaos with his own body. He held me close as the bridge gave away.

Then what happened?

I can't remember.

It had felt like we were falling for so long. Then everything went black.

Now, I'm here. Wherever that is.

But where is Gabriel?

I don't sense his massive presence. I don't feel his warmth. I'm alone. No one I love is around to comfort me.

What if he died saving me?

What if I never get to tell him that I love him?

Those intrusive thoughts slap behind my throbbing skull as I choke back tears and try to stay strong.

I'll see him again, I promise myself. One way or another, we'll be together. Same goes with my family.

But what am I going to have to suffer through before that happens?

A cold tear cascades down my cheek, and I instinctively go to wipe it away. But even if there wasn't a thick hood draped over my head, I wouldn't be able to reach my face.

My arms and legs are tied to some kind of chair.

My heart starts to palpitate. My long sighs become short and jittery.

I'm in big fucking trouble.

Who the hell was in that helicopter?

A terrifying pang flashes across my chest when I hear a heavy metal door open, and I realize that I'm about to get my answer.

"I'm checking on her now."

The sudden appearance of the slithery voice makes my skin crawl. It's gut-wrenchingly familiar. But where do I recognize it from?

The answer escapes me.

Still, I listen closely as a muffled response comes from what sounds like a cell phone's speaker. I can't make it out, but I do understand when the call ends.

Because the voice quickly turns its attention onto me.

"Let's see how you're doing, princess."

My entire body tenses as I feel a huge body approach.

The bag is ripped off my head.

Immediately, I'm flooded with an overwhelming amount of

light. I don't even get a good look at my surroundings before my eyes slam shut again, and I flinch away from the man standing before me.

"Ah, there you are," the voice taunts. "Thought I might have to wake you up myself."

A pair of slimy hands clamp around my jaw, and I'm forced to look straight ahead.

Even with my eyes closed, I can smell the evil on my captor's putrid breath.

"Open up those baby blues now, honey. See the man who saved you from a watery grave."

"Gabriel saved me," I somehow find the strength to mutter.

I get a back handed slap to the cheek in response.

"Don't you ever say that traitor's name again!"

Another slap sends a hot sting flashing across my face. My neck is snapped in the opposite direction.

Thankfully, this time the putrid man doesn't feel the need to straighten me out again.

Hell, I almost breathe a sigh of relief when I feel him step back.

Still, my mind is reeling.

Traitor?

No one speaks about my man like that.

With great effort, I force my heavy eyelids to open once more. A ringing has invaded my ears, but the bright lights seem to dim a touch as my vision slowly comes back into focus.

"Where am I?' I hear myself ask.

This room doesn't match the dark helplessness I feel inside. It's not some empty, cement-walled prison cell. Hell, it almost looks like the kind of office my dad, or one of my uncles, might have in their home.

A red-tinted Persian rug stretches out along the floor, slipping beneath a grand mahogany desk. Oakwood bookshelves cover the walls. A red leather chair sits behind it all. Empty.

"You are in hell," the voice responds.

A dark gust envelops me as I see the back of the man who's tied me up. His shoulders are slanted, and his back looks malformed and twisted.

He grabs something from the desk, then slurps it down.

When he turns around, I first see the empty brandy glass wrapped around his sharp fingers. His nails are long and have clearly been filed down into pointy claws. His skin is a sickly pale. Deep red veins flow out from beneath his cufflinks, and it's hard to tell if they're real or tattoos.

"Who are you?" I ask, not strong enough to lift my head and look up at the monster's face.

That draws a mean-spirited laugh from the stranger. "Don't you recognize me, princess? Or did you hit your head on your way off that bridge?"

Without warning, he throws the brandy glass from his hand. It flies past my ear, missing by mere inches, before shattering against the wall ahead.

I can't help but squirm against my restraints. But there's nowhere to go. Especially not when the man grabs a fistful of my damp hair and tugs me to the floor.

I hit the ground with a loud, painful thud.

My vision blurs against the pain. But that doesn't mean I don't instantly recognize the evil face glaring down at me.

His thin white lips stretch into a mangled grin, exposing those sharp, fang-like teeth. His sunken cheeks vanish into endless darkness. His black eyes sharpen.

"You."

"Call me Krol, princess," he says, snapping his neck to the side. "Or call me daddy. Doesn't really matter."

Reaching down, he grabs another fistful of my hair and pulls my chair upright.

My stomach drops.

This is the man who tried to kill Roz and me. He's the man who betrayed Gabriel.

He reeks of evil.

"Where is Gabriel?" I demand to know. But my voice is still so weak, and my question only makes Krol laugh.

"He's just hanging out," the bastard taunts. "Waiting for death to come take him away."

"No!" I shout, my chest nearly bursting. "Liar!"

"Now, why would I lie to you, princess?"

"Don't you fucking dare call me princess," I sneer. My fingers curl into fists and I desperately try to break out of my restraints.

It's no use.

I may be stronger than I once was, but I'll never be that kind of strong.

"Oh, shut the fuck up," Krol insists, rolling his eyes. "What, you think you're a queen now because you've got that fancy ring? I can take it off just as easily as you put it on. Watch."

"Fuck off," I spit, trying to squirm away as Krol reaches for my hand.

The effort earns me another backhanded slap.

Once again, my neck snaps to the side. This time, though, I taste the familiar metallic tinge of blood on my tongue.

"Stay still, bitch," Krol growls. "I'll only be freeing you from a dreadful responsibility."

"It's not a dreadful responsibility," I mumble.

"Fuck. Gabriel sure did a number on you," Krol shrugs. His greasy fingers crawl up my hand until they're wrapped around my ring. "I guess Drago was right to keep sending him after you. It worked out almost perfectly. If only you didn't grow on him so much."

"Don't touch that!" I beg.

But Krol doesn't listen.

The thorns on my ring dig into my flesh as he tries to twist it from my finger.

"Goddamnit," he grunts.

The ring barely budges. Not even as my tearing flesh is lubricated with blood.

"It won't ever come off," I sneer. "Not for you."

"Want to bet?" Krol huffs, his pale face turning red with frustration.

Letting go of my bleeding finger, he takes a frantic step back and reaches into his pocket.

My eyes go wide when I see the switchblade he pulls out.

"Leave me alone!" I shout out at him, my voice shaky and filled with terror.

But Krol only seems to revel in my fear.

"No," he simply says. "I will not leave you alone. Unlike your treacherous little husband, I do as I'm told. And I've been ordered to watch you like a fucking hawk. But that doesn't mean I can't have my fun. Drago never said anything about keeping you in one piece. All we really have to do is keep you alive for the next nine months or so. Then, it's over for you. Until then, maybe we can get into a little body horror. Huh, princess? Fuck. It would turn me on so fucking much to amputate that tiny finger bone of yours."

Krol licks his lips as he steps forward. But suddenly, my fear isn't concentrated on the knife.

"The next nine months?" I gulp, before the words catch in my throat.

No...

"That's right, princess. You're pregnant. But it's not *your* baby growing in that perfect little stomach. No. It won't belong to you for long. That child will be my meal ticket. Want me to cut you open and show you?"

"I... I..." I don't know what to say.

There's nothing to say.

My eyes clamp shut as a fitful headache rises up behind my skull. The pain is accompanied by the strangest visions. Impossible visions.

Visions of my future. A future that's about to be torn away from me.

It's a future where Gabriel and I are together; where we raise a child, and rule an empire. A future where I'm with the man I love; where I am the woman I've always wanted to be.

A future where everyone I care about is happy.

A future where I'm happy.

It all burns away in an instant, turned to ash just as quickly it appeared.

It feels like a lifetime has been ripped from my soul and crushed before my very eyes.

I'm empty.

And then I'm furious.

Especially as I feel the broad end of Krol's blade slip beneath my chin.

His cruel laugh reverberates through my aching skull as he forces me to look up at him.

But I don't give him the look he wants.

I don't give up.

Ripping my eyes open, I sneer back at him with all the hate in the world.

Only one man is allowed to bring a knife so close to my throat. Only one man is allowed to tie me up and make me bleed.

I'll do anything to get back to that man.

"You're dead, Krol," I spit.

My bloody saliva slashes across his sunken face. But he hardly even flinches. Hell, he doesn't even move to wipe it away.

Instead, he lets it all drip down his cheeks as he leans in nice and close.

"And who's going to kill me?" he asks, his putrid breath making me retch.

Still, I force myself to meet him.

"I am."

"And how are you going to do that, princess?"

"I'll tell you exactly how. First, you're going to untie me. Then, you're going to pin me down to that desk like a fucking man and prove you're strong enough to cut this ring off my finger."

"I don't see how that will lead to my death."

"You'll see it nice and clear when I take that stupid little knife from your slimy hand and shove it between your eyes. Understand?"

A deep belly laugh crackles out of Krol's thin white lips. "How about I just cut your fucking tongue off and make this process a whole lot more peaceful for myself?"

"Because anything you do to me will be paid back to you tenfold. And if I don't get the pleasure of fucking you up myself, then don't you think for a second Gabriel won't hunt you down to the ends of the earth."

For a second, it almost looks like my threat frightens the human serpent. But just as quickly as his face turned to stone, it twists back into a taunting snarl.

"Gabriel, Gabriel, Gabriel," Krol grumbles, shaking his head. "I've got bad news for you, honey. He's not going to be around long enough to make anyone pay. Traitors get what they deserve, and he's getting exactly what he deserves at this very fucking moment.

"Whatever you give him, he can take it," I whisper.

But that assurance is more for myself than it is for Krol. My heart is on the brink of collapse.

What anguish are these bastards putting Gabriel through?

Whatever it is, it can't be pretty.

But I can't give up. For his sake.

I know he won't give up on me.

"No, he won't," Krol simply states. Then, he pulls his phone back out of his pocket and checks the screen. The glow makes his gaunt pale face look somehow even more skeletal. "Your precious Gabriel won't last until dawn. And if you keep talking, neither will your tongue. Hell, I might even start cutting off limbs just for fun, princess. In fact, we keep a hot iron nearby just for that purpose. I figure I could turn you into a stump and still keep you alive long enough to take your baby."

"You aren't taking shit," I rasp. But the strength is quickly draining from my voice.

My baby.

Fucking hell. I want to cry. I want to scream. But I can't.

Hold on, Gabriel.

For me.

For our unborn child.

"Wrong, princess," Krol snaps. "I'm taking everything. And I'm going to enjoy every last second of it. Now, shut the fuck up."

Retracting his blade, Krol cocks back his fist.

I don't even feel him make contact with my skull.

The world just goes black.

33

GABRIEL

I recognized the smell the second I came to.

At first, I thought I was dreaming. But the pain ravaging my body was too real.

Harsh rope digs into my throat. A blindfold is wrapped around my eyes. The soles of my feet barely reach the varnished wood below. My wrists are tied behind my back.

I can feel how high up I am. I can sense the cavernous aura of this place.

It's a place I haven't been in over five years.

A place I swore I'd never come back to.

My old prison.

Westwood High.

My body instinctively flinches when I hear the gymnasium doors scrape open from across the basketball court.

I remember what we did to Principal Winchester.

That's what's about to happen to me.

Only, I imagine Drago won't shoot me before I've suffered the entirety of his wrath. Hell, it's clear to me now that he killed Winchester so suddenly just to shut him up before he could spill the truth about my mother.

But now I know the truth. I see through the lies.

At least, most of them.

There are still some questions I desperately need answered. Things that I can't die without knowing.

But these questions aren't the same ones I've been chasing my whole life. No. I don't give a shit about my history anymore.

All I care about is the woman who was supposed to be my future.

Bianca.

I need to know she's alright.

"Where is she?" I ask, as Drago's footsteps echo through the cavernous hall. I don't even need to see shit to know it's him. I can sense that fucker's presence.

Just like I can sense that Bianca is alive.

She has to be.

"She's alive and safe," Drago confirms, his deep voice rising from below. "Well, relatively safe. You can never be so sure with Krol. You know what he likes to do with his women."

"She's not his," I growl, shaking with fury. "She's mine."

The rope digs deeper into my throat with every subtle movement. But I don't restrain my rage.

How could Drago leave her with that monster?

I'm going to make them both fucking pay.

But first, I somehow need to survive this shit.

"Yes. Yes. I saw the ring," Drago assures me. "Good job. You did as you were told. I just got word that Krol received a positive pregnancy test from the girl too. Thank God for Roz's little invention. It's all coming together."

My stomach drops all the way down to the gymnasium floor. My heart follows closely behind.

"She's pregnant?"

"That's right," Drago says. "Let's hope it's a boy. Although, maybe I'll have better luck raising a girl this time."

The thought of him getting anywhere near my child sets me

off. My hands clench into fists. I grit my teeth and try my hardest to pull apart the rope restraining my wrists.

But the strands are too thick. I could push and pull until I'm red in the face and get nowhere.

How the fuck am I going to get out of this?

"I'll fucking kill you," I threaten. But my threat has no teeth. Not when I'm tied up like this.

"Give it a go," Drago scoffs.

I know there's no use. My best bet is to save my energy. To get answers, so if I ever get out of this, I'll know what the hell to do next.

"How the fuck did you find me?" I ask. The idea that I could have been betrayed sinks into my gut like a heavy black stone. "How did you know we were meeting at the bridge?"

"I didn't," Drago answers. "I'd simply been trailing Ray Byrne and Rian Kilpatrick since you disappeared, hoping they'd lead me to you. And they did. The moment I saw what I was looking for, I called in the helicopter. Of course, Krol was in the cockpit, controlling that machine gun. The fool went a little wild. He wasn't supposed to disintegrate the bridge like that, only separate the lot of you. But it doesn't matter now. He did his job. We got what we came for. You... and your little wife."

I nearly explode.

It doesn't matter that I wasn't betrayed. I find no relief in the truth.

"Let her go," I demand, every inch of me on fire. My noose rattles as I shake with rage.

"Or what?" Drago taunts.

"I'll make you suffer."

"You already have, my dear boy. You broke my heart. And for what? A girl?"

"She's not just a girl," I growl. "She's mine." *She's my everything.*

"No. She's just a pawn. And now, she's just a womb. We'll

keep her alive until your heir is born. After that, it's probably best she joins you in hell."

"'This won't work out like you hope it will, Drago," I sneer. "By now, Tytus and Roz will be in Poland. The second the news gets out that Bianca is pregnant, they will be given the keys to my empire. They'll have everything and you'll have nothing. They will crush you."

"They will try," Drago agrees. "But they will fail. I will control your heir, *Gabryjel*. Thus, I will control all that the priests have to offer. Your inheritance will be mine. And so will all of the power that comes with it."

"No one will ever follow you."

"They won't have a choice."

"You piece of shit," I try not to struggle against my restraints any more, but I can't fucking help it.

The rope digs deeper into my neck.

Then, I hear Drago's footsteps approach.

He's climbing up the bleachers towards me.

"I had such high hopes for you," he practically whispers as he leans into my ear.

When he tears my blindfold off, I'm greeted by his vile face.

There's no remorse it in at all. But no pleasure either.

"You were always going to betray me," I realize. "You could never just sit back and let someone else have all the power."

"Nice to see you're finally putting the pieces of the puzzle together," Drago nods.

Turning his back on me, he heads back down the bleachers, and towards the lever that controls them.

"Not all of the pieces," I rumble.

"You still haven't figured it all out?" he scoffs.

My chest tightens as his hand falls onto the wall-mounted crowbar.

"I know enough," I spit. "You've been working with those Reca disciple fuckers behind my back for years, haven't you?

You've been secretly building up your own little syndicate filled with scum of the earth drug dealers. And you knew I wouldn't approve, so you've been plotting my death. You..." The realization hits me like a fucking tsunami. "You were trying to distract me from it all with Bianca."

"Not quite," Drago says, shaking his head. The gymnasium is dark, but I can still see his forearm flex as he pushes down on the lever.

The bleachers start to retract beneath my feet. The noose tightens around my neck. I have to push up on my tip-toes just to keep from being strangled to death.

"Why not just kill me?" I choke.

But that question isn't because I'm afraid to die. No. I'm scared of something much simpler.

I'm trapped. There's no way out of this.

And the threat of never seeing Bianca again is already tearing me apart.

I never got to tell her that I love her.

"How could I just put a bullet in your head?" Drago asks, stopping the lever for moment. "No. I raised you like a son, *Gabryjel*. You need to suffer. That's what happens when you betray your family."

"This isn't how you treat family."

"It is in our world. It is when you come from a family like yours."

"No," I grumble. "My mother may not have been the saint you painted her as, but there's no way she was this depraved."

"Ah, Sonia," Drago sighs. "She was the love of my life, you know?"

The suddenness of his massive confession nearly knocks me out. I can hardly believe my fucking ears.

"But I was never powerful enough for her," Drago continues. "Your mother had great ambitions, *Gabryjel*. And I had no way of giving her what she wanted, not back then..."

"You loved my mother?" I rasp. The arches of my feet are starting to cramp. The rope is tightening around my neck.

My heart is ready to implode.

Fuck. I can't imagine Drago loving anyone.

But he did always speak of my mother with such admiration.

"I loved her from afar," Drago admits. "I could never get too close, though. Not with your father obsessively watching over her. And then he was killed. But Sonia was never one to stay single for long. She remarried before I could make my move. It hurt—even if I knew the marriage wouldn't last. The poor fool just wasn't strong enough for your mother. So, when I saw the first cracks, I jumped in. Finally, she heard me out. Sonia Caruso. The fiercest woman I had ever met. She listened to me. We talked. We... Well, we made plans. Big fucking plans. Plans that could fill an endless void. We saw a way out. Together. We would make it. And then Ray Byrne put a fucking bullet between her eyes."

It feels like I've been hit by a fucking train. My already struggling lungs nearly collapse against the force of what I'm hearing.

It brings everything together.

After all of this time, I finally understand why Drago was so focused on pairing me with Bianca.

It had nothing to do with my inheritance.

Not really.

It was just so he could get his revenge; so he could torture Ray Byrne before he took everything from him.

"You bastard," I choke. "She was my mother. She was mine to avenge. Not yours."

"You didn't even know her," Drago spits. "Not like I did. But that shouldn't matter. You would have failed in your quest. To think, you've fallen for the daughter of the very man who murdered your mother." His words are laced with venom, and overflowing with pure disgust.

"You're a coward," I tell him. "Always hiding. Always using others to do your dirty work. No wonder she never gave you the time of day. You—"

"She was going to be mine!" Drago bellows, cutting me off. His anger fills the gymnasium like thunder.

"But only because my father died," I slash through. "A real man would have fought anyone for the love of his life. *Anyone*."

I know that's true, because there isn't anyone in this world I wouldn't destroy just to keep Bianca safe and by my side.

Fuck.

Bianca...

"You're so naïve, *Gabryjel*. Your father wasn't just anyone. He was the most vile, ruthless creature to ever walk this earth. Even a single hint of disobedience and he would have kept me alive for years, just to see me suffer endlessly through them."

"My father..."

"Yes. Your father. He was a brutal and cruel man. If he had known about the feelings I'd held for Sonia, he'd have chopped me into little pieces long ago. And then he would have revived me just to do it over again. Over and over until the end of time. That's the type of bastard he was. Hell, he poisoned your mother's first husband—a senator's son—just because Sonia hinted it might be what she wanted. I was there when he made the decision. The man didn't even think twice about killing such an important and well-connected person. One day, that poor bastard Andrew Hoeven just dropped dead. And Sonia was free. Together, they ran away, pockets lined with political blackmail, and so much leverage in the war to come..."

"What the fuck are you talking about?" I cough. The rope is riding up under my jaw now. I'm starting to see black spots.

"You still haven't figured out who your father is?" Drago asks, almost disappointed.

"He was a king," I foolishly blurt out.

But the man Drago is describing doesn't sound like any kind of king I know.

"That's right. He was," Drago replies. Looking off into the distance, he presses down on the lever again.

The bleachers sink further away from my scrambling feet.

I can feel the rope pulling at my fucking spine.

Every breath is a struggle.

"Tell me who he was!" I somehow manage to choke out.

"Everything I told you was true," Drago slowly replies. "Well, nearly everything. Obviously, I lied about your mother. But Sonia was too well known in the underworld. If I'd let that connection slip too quickly, our cover may have been blown. I had to wait until just the right moment to leak it all to Ray Byrne. That info is why he helped get you into this school, after all. It's what got you close to his daughter."

Fucking hell. Did Drago really trick Ray into getting me accepted here? Was it all actually part of his secret agenda?

I don't know what to think. Big black holes burn through my vision as I struggle for air. Everything is on fire.

Still, through it all, I can picture Bianca.

My fucking angel.

So soft and sweet.

So tough and fierce.

My perfect woman.

I can't lose her.

I need to stall Drago. Even if it only prolongs my suffering, I need to give myself a chance to figure a way out of this shit— not that there seems to be one.

"What else did you lie about?" I push out.

No matter how hard I try to break through the rope restraining my wrists, I just can't fucking do it.

"So little else," Drago says, shaking his head. "Everything I told you about the old empire is true. The king. His death. The

Reca's usurping his throne. The power struggle after they had been killed by Ray and the Kilpatricks. The priests and your inheritance. It's all true, *Gabryjel*. Though, I did lie about one small detail."

"Tell me."

The very tips of my toes are only barely scraping against the varnished wood of the bleachers. One inch more and I'm dead.

"I guess I might as well," Drago sighs. "Your father was not the first king, my boy. Not the original. Not the man I said he was. No. *Gabryjel*. Your father was Kamil Reca. The man who killed him."

With that, Drago pushes down on the lever.

The noose snaps around my neck, and the bleachers disappear beneath my feet.

But I'm not killed right away.

No.

I'm made to suffer.

I'm kept alive just long enough to realize that my entire life has been a lie.

My parents. My family. My purpose.

Lies.

It was all lies.

Except for one thing.

I was truly always meant to end up with Bianca.

My shining light.

She's all I think about as the world slowly fades to black.

34

GABRIEL

There's nothing.

No sound. No light. No pain.

Only a strange warmth that carries me forward, off into some endless void.

It's almost peaceful.

... Until the drums start.

Like mallets pounding against sheepskin, a chaotic rhythm rises up through the darkness. The beating pulse echoes off the walls of infinity.

And then, suddenly, I'm ripped from it all.

The warm current gives out beneath me.

My feet hit something solid. Something tangible.

The emptiness is replaced by a searing pain. A struggle to breath. An aching heart.

"Get him down from there!" a voice shouts.

It's barely discernible from the roar of gunshots.

A jagged breath cuts through my splintered throat. My eyes flicker halfway open.

There's no focus to my vision. Everything is blurry. My brain is foggy and distant. But even through it all, the chaos below is instantly clear.

Black silhouettes dart across the floor. Glass shatters. Something crashes to the ground.

There's more yelling.

"Fuck! He's getting away!"

Is that who I think it is?

My noose creaks and my body rotates just enough to see a new hand on that all-important lever.

It takes a second for my oxygen-deprived brain to recognize the new hulking figure now pulling on the wall-mounted crowbar, but when I do, I find myself calling to him.

"Rian..."

It hurts to speak. But the pain is nothing compared to the sudden burst of hope.

All of the near-death ethereal bullshit evaporites. My mind focuses.

Bianca is alright.

She must be. Her family wouldn't come get me before they rescued her. They just wouldn't.

But my hope falters as a bullet rips through the wall just over Rian's shoulder. He's forced to duck to the ground. The lever jerks up. The bleachers pull down. My feet are suspended in mid-air again.

The noose digs into my neck.

"Someone go after him!" I hear Rian yell.

Desperately, I try to rip apart the rope tied around my wrists. But it's impossible. Especially now. I'm so weak.

I feel myself fading again.

No.

"Choose!" I hear another voice yell. Is that Ray? "Drago or Gabriel. We can't hold them off much longer."

A frustrated roar erupts from the lion's chest as he makes a decision.

I don't see what that decision is.

All I can do to keep from dying is try to take one more breath. But I can't even manage that. The noose is too tight.

And then, suddenly, I feel relief.

Just like that, the taut rope goes limp, and I start to fall. But before I can hit the ground, someone catches me.

The restraints are cut from my wrists. The rope is torn from around my neck.

"Are you alive, you fucking bastard?"

Rian slaps me so hard that I have no choice but to wake up.

"What are you doing here?" I cough, my voice a raspy mess.

I can practically taste my internal bleeding.

"Isn't it fucking obvious? We came to save you."

"Why? Is Bianca alright? Where is she?"

"I'm only here because I don't know the answer to those last two questions. Does that answer your first question?"

My burning heart drops.

"You think I know where she is?"

Fuck. I have no fucking idea.

"You better," Rian grunts.

Digging his shoulder under my struggling ribcage, the lion lifts me up to my feet.

My head rages. My mind struggles to stay present.

I can hardly grab onto a single thought. Still, my numb fingers curl into fists.

Bianca is still in trouble. I need to focus.

"How did you find me?" I manage to ask.

"I'll explain later. You're—"

"He's fucking gone!"

Somehow, I immediately recognize Maksim's voice.

The gunfire has died down. Only a ring and a fading roar echo around the gymnasium now.

Taking a deep, slow, jagged breath, I look down onto the carnage.

The basketball court is littered with corpses. Maksim is by the double doors at the far end of the room.

He looks pissed.

"There must be some other way out of this gym," Rian grumbles. "Gabriel, tell me you know another way out of here."

"I don't," I admit. Still, I search my aching mind for an answer. "Why?"

"Drago managed to slip by us. It looks like he's escaped."

When we hit the bottom of the bleachers, Rian lets me go, and I fall to the hardwood floor.

The pain hardly concerns me.

Bianca is in danger.

Drago got away.

He'll make her pay for my insolence.

Fucking hell.

"What the fuck is going on?" I choke, blood dripping from my lips.

"My aunt slipped a tracking device on you back at the bridge," Rian says. Taking out his gun, he marches up to a body that isn't quite dead yet. Half a dozen bullets burst from the lion's muzzle. The body goes still.

I watch as my blood pools on the hardwood floor. I try to think back to the meeting on the bridge. To the hug I shared with Bianca's mother.

I don't remember feeling anything unusual. Usually, I'm pretty fucking adept at knowing when someone is trying to slip something onto me.

Was I just distracted by the emotion in Bianca's pretty blue eyes? Or is Francesca a badass after all?

Shit. I don't know. But one thing quickly becomes clear.

Bianca's mother saved my life.

If she hadn't slipped that tracking device on me, there's no way these guys would have gotten here in time.

"They're almost all dead, sir," I hear Maksim announce.

"They had this place fucking surrounded. We were too busy carving through them to keep an eye out for Drago. He must have slipped out while we were distracted."

"How is it that everyone is dead except for the one fucker who can tell us where my daughter is?"

I've never heard such unfettered rage in Ray Byrne's voice before. The whole fucking gymnasium seems to shake.

But my own fury is quickly growing too.

"Why the fuck didn't you go find Bianca first?" I heave, my chest pounding as my heart twists into one giant knot. "Why the fuck did you come save my worthless ass while she's still out there?"

In response, Rian turns around and picks me up by my tattered collar. The anger in his eyes is infinite.

"Aren't you fucking listening, asshole? We don't know where Bianca is. I only saved you because I thought you might have a clue."

"You idiot!" I roar. "You must have fucking seen me run from that helicopter and it's machine gun. You just saw the state I was in. What makes you think I'm in on this?"

"I don't think you're in on this," Rian barks. "That's *why* I chose to save you instead of going after Drago..."

Trailing off, he pushes me back.

The edge of the bleachers catch the back of my knees and I'm pulled onto my ass.

"Fuck me," I growl. "I'm useless. I don't know where the hell Bianca is. But Drago does. You should have gone after him. You should have let me fucking die!"

"You're right, I should have," Rian sneers. Turning back around, he fires six more bullets into the long-dead corpse at his feet, then he storms away.

But I'm not left to wallow in my self-pity for long.

Ray suddenly appears before me.

"You will help us find Bianca," he orders, reaching out a stiff hand.

But I don't take it.

"Why didn't you put a tracking device on her too?" I bite. "Why follow me and not your own fucking daughter?"

"We did put a tracking device on her," Ray snaps back. Despite the fire flickering through his words, his arm remains outstretched; his hand remains offered to me. "But her device obviously isn't working. It must have gotten fried in the water after you fell from the bridge. Somehow, though, yours survived. Your signal was coming in loud and fucking clear."

I don't know if my skull is cracked or what, but that doesn't make any sense to me. Most trackers I know of are water resistant—or have I just been spoiled by Roz's cutting-edge inventions?

"Show me how your following the signals," I demand, trying to push myself off the bleachers. But a skull-splitting flash of pain sends me back onto my ass. "I can call someone who could help."

Pinching my nose, I try to swat away the agony.

Roz will be able to help. Even if she's in Poland. She can give me advice.

"You don't know anyone who can deal with that shit better than I can," I hear Rian return.

"Now isn't the time to be so fucking arrogant," I grumble. "Your pride doesn't matter. Neither does mine. Bianca is in danger."

"Why do you care?" Rian yaps. Lunging up beside his uncle, he covers me in his shadow. "She's my cousin. She's his daughter. She's Maksim's goddaughter. Who the fuck are you?"

"I'm her fucking husband," I shout back. "I'm her man. Her lover. I'm... hers. Just fucking hers. And she's mine. And don't think for a second I won't tear through all of you just to make sure she's safe."

Fuck my pride.

Taking Ray's hand, I use it to pull myself up and face Rian head on.

The Irish lion looks like he wants to take me up on the challenge.

But then something seems to click, and he backs down.

"Fine," he grumbles. Reaching into his pocket, he pulls out a cell phone. "Take a look at the signal. You won't be able to figure shit out. No one will. It's all scrambled."

Even before the phone hits my hand, a light bulb goes off in my shattered skull.

"Scrambled?"

"That's right."

Fuck.

"I think I know where she is."

———

"It takes a lot of balls to bring me back down here."

Rian's deep voice echoes through the overgrown tunnel as we quietly step through the puddles and over the rusted tracks.

"If only you knew how close you were to death the last time we were here," I remember. Still, the memory is fuzzy against the agony of my throbbing skull. "I saved your ass. You were walking right into a trap. "

"And you were leading me there."

"No. I was already splitting with Drago by then," I tell him, omitting the part where I had only returned to him and Ray in the first place under Drago's orders. "I was trying to help you get rid of him."

"Then why did you run away once those fucking gas bombs hit?"

"Because a friend appeared in the shadows. He told me Bianca was in danger. I went to go save her."

"You didn't think I could fucking help?"

"It was a personal matter. You would have just gotten in the way."

"That's rich coming from a guy who would still be hanging from the rafters if I hadn't come cut him loose."

"Things have changed," I grumble. Sharp pain flashes through my body with every brittle step I take. But I bite through it. "There are no teams anymore. Just two sides. The side that cares about Bianca, and the side that wants to use her."

"Don't think I'm welcoming you onto our side so quickly," Rian huffs.

"I don't need your permission to save my girl," I reply, before posting up against one of the leaking subway walls. "Let's stop here. Check your phone. Make sure everything is in place."

"I don't need to check. I know I did everything right."

"This isn't the time to—"

"Don't fucking lecture me," Rian snarls.

Ripping his phone out of his pocket, he opens up the screen.

Looking back the way we came, I see the forty or so heavily-armed silhouettes we've brought down into the tunnels with us. Maksim is dead center among them.

Ray is above ground, directing the troops we've set up around every possible exit.

We may be walking into Drago's trap. But he's already stuck in ours.

Not that it matters.

The slippery fuck always seems to find a way to escape danger. And as much as I want to kill him tonight, I know my choice is simple.

Nothing matters except for Bianca.

My only focus is on getting her out of here, safe and sound.

Though, a close second on that list is dealing with Krol.

That fucking bastard.

My pounding heart clenches as I try not to imagine how scared Bianca must be right now.

If she's even alive.

No. I want to fucking punch myself. *How dare you think such a thought?*

She's still alive. I know she is.

I would be able to sense it if the love of my life had been ripped from this earth. I'd be able to tell that all hope was lost.

But the hope is still there. Pounding painfully behind my chest.

Bianca is alive. And she's being guarded by a monster.

We have to be careful. We have to do whatever it takes.

Hell, on our way here, I even messaged Roz, asking her how to level the playing field. She was the one who helped design most of Drago's security measures, after all.

Her reply came just in time.

I can't say I understood much of her text, and not just because my brain was still desperate for oxygen. That technological babble is just so far beyond my grasp.

But when I showed Rian the schematics, he was immediately engrossed.

"So far, so good," the lion grumbles from beside me, his face flickering in the pale glow of the phone screen. "It's not like I had a lot of time to put this program together. But it's doing its job. The files your friend sent to us are nearly decrypted."

"Then we can't push ahead yet," I curse. "If we attack too soon, Drago's going to have the jump on us. We can't have that. It's too dangerous."

"I'm not scared," Rian sneers.

"I don't mean it's too dangerous for *us.*"

"Fuck."

The lion quickly seems to understand what I'm getting at.

The first target in this battle won't be either of us.

It will be Bianca.

"We need to try to do this quietly." Lifting my hand, I give the signal for the soldiers behind us to stop.

They do as instructed.

"You're going in alone?" Maksim's voice crackles through Rian's phone.

"Just at first," I reply, leaning forward so he can hear me. "The second you hear a single shot, though, all of you come running."

"Rian?"

"Do as he says."

Rian doesn't seem to enjoy saying that, but we've both come to the same understanding.

Now is the time to put aside our differences and work together.

For Bianca's sake.

"Very well."

Rian's gaze stays glued to his screen as I turn and stare down the dark tunnels ahead. We're back at the fork. I know which way Drago should be, but I'm not willing to risk anything.

Not when Bianca is at risk.

Sure, Drago admitted that he needs her alive, but he also left her with Krol. That fucker has killed more hostages than he has teeth.

My fingers tense around the gun in my hand. A furious rage washes through me. No matter how much pain I'm in, I can't think of anything else.

Bianca is with Krol.

I know the kinds of sick and twisted games he likes to play with women.

I swear to God, if he touches a hair on her perfect body.

"Huh, that was weird," Rian suddenly mumbles.

"What?"

"Uh... nothing. Never mind. The decryption process is done. Bianca's signal has been unscrambled. I'm hacked into Drago's security system."

"Where is she?" I demand. But I lunge towards the screen a little too quickly. My head goes light and I feel like I might pass out again.

But then Rian grabs me by the collar.

"Are you sure you're alright?" he asks, holding me up in the roughest way possible.

"I'm fine," I say, shaking the heaviness away. "Where is Bianca's signal coming from?"

Rian trails his finger up the screen towards a blinking dot.

"She's right here."

My gut churns.

Drago's office. That's at the center of this twisted underground maze.

"What are all those other marks?" I ask, noting the fainter, unblinking dots slowly swimming across the screen. There are so many I can hardly count them all.

"I'm not sure," Rian admits, before pulling up the schematics. "Fuck."

"What?'

"Those are people. Patrolling soldiers, probably. This program picks up their heat signatures and turns them into tracking dots. It's almost genius." Cocking his gun, Rian tears his eyes off the screen and stares down the darkness ahead. "Looks like we're going to have to fight our way through an army."

Before he can take a step forward, I reach out and stop him.

"Let me try to sneak by first," I urge. "If we go in shooting, Drago might take the opportunity to..."

I don't even want to say it. But the implication lingers in the air.

If Drago won't kill Bianca out of spite, then Krol certainly will.

I'm the one who needs to stop that from happening, no matter what that means for me.

Bianca is *my* girl.

There is no living without her. Not for me.

"What if you try to run off like last time?"

"Then shoot me along with everyone else."

I can see Rian's defences dropping as he begins to understand just how serious I am about his cousin.

"And what happens if they catch you before I can?" he asks.

"It doesn't matter. I don't matter. All that matters is that you get Bianca out of here safe and sound. Understand?"

Rian only hesitates for a second.

"Got it," he nods

Sucking up the pain, I force myself to see through the thick fog pulsing behind my skull.

"We're only going to get one shot at this," I grumble. "Make sure Maksim and the troops are ready. Tell Ray to be on guard. I'm going to get Bianca."

Pressing my gun to my forehead, I take a flurry of deep breaths, hyping myself up for what's to come.

I've been in worse spots before. But rarely have I been this roughed up. And never have I been after more precious cargo.

I'm coming Bianca.

"Let's do this."

Lowering my gun, I take my first step into the darkness ahead.

"Good luck," Rian calls after me, before catching himself. "Asshole."

"See you on the other side," I nod back to him.

"It better be with Bianca on your arm."

"Oh, believe me," I snarl. "I'm not coming out of this without her."

35

BIANCA

"Wakey wakey."

A bead of sweat drips down my forehead as my heavy eyelids flutter open one more time.

What the hell?

It feels like my skull has ruptured. The pain is nearly blinding.

"Get it over with already," a new voice orders. It's not one I recognize. But the unmistakable stench of evil wafts off every word.

"I think it would be more fun if she was awake," Krol crackles.

A cold chill passes over my skin, even as an unbearable heat seems to burn mere inches from my face.

"This isn't for fun. This is to teach that ungrateful bastard a lesson."

"Who's to say he survived?"

Who are they talking about?

"I am. If there's one thing I taught that boy, it's how to survive."

"Maybe you should have taught him how to die."

Every time I blink, an earthquake of pain rattles through my bones. Still, even through the nearly blinding agony, my vision slowly begins to refocus.

Finally, I see what's making me sweat.

"No..."

My voice is so faint it feels like it belongs to someone else. Someone far away. Someone I wish I was. Someone who wasn't in so much danger.

But there's no escaping this nightmare.

"Ah, there you are," Krol taunts. "Now, we can begin."

The glowing face of the branding iron in his hand smells like smoke and charred flesh. He waves the flat burning metal end inches from my eyes before gesturing to someone standing just behind him.

"Cut off her finger first," the stranger orders. "Or the hand. I don't fucking care. Just separate that ring from her fucking body. Then cauterize the wound immediately. We still need her alive to carry out the pregnancy."

My stomach lurches at the careless brutality of his orders. I want to puke. But I'm not even strong enough for that.

"What do we do about this mark on her shoulder?" I hear Krol ask.

However weak my body is, it's still strong enough to flinch as the serpent traces a cold sharp nail over the G that Gabriel carved into my shoulder.

"We'll burn it off of her with the branding iron later. I want every trace of that traitor destroyed. First, though, deal with the ring."

The venom in the stranger's voice is palpable. I still can't see him, but somehow, I now understand exactly who he is.

"Drago," I feel myself sneer.

A searing flash of hate gives me the tiniest bit of strength,

"Looks like Gabriel has been talking about you," Krol chuckles. "Such a daddy's boy."

"You are not his father," I hiss, before coughing up blood.

My lungs burn. But the fire in my empty belly is slowly rising too.

"You're right," Drago says. "I may not have made him, but I certainly did end him."

My shriveled heart drops into an endless pit.

"Liar!" I screech.

But when I rip my neck up to confront the bastard, my head explodes. The pain forces my chin back down to my chest.

Gabriel can't be dead. I won't accept it.

A cold tear joins the sweat dripping from my face.

"Don't talk to your new master like that," Krol hisses. His sharp hand clamps around my throat, forcing my eyes up again.

The pain pounding behind my skull makes my vision blurry, and all I can see is Drago's dark outline as he starts to stalk around the room.

His long shadow stretches over my back as he settles behind me.

"I have no master," I rasp.

"Not even Gabriel?" Drago prods.

"He's not my master. He's just... mine."

Drago and Krol both huff at the same time.

"He's marked you," Krol points out, flicking my shoulder with his long bony finger.

"I've marked him too."

"Yes, I saw," Drago grumbles. "The tear drop tattoo, and the carving on his forearm, right over the burn mark you gave him all those years ago. It will rot away with his flesh."

"He's not dead," I insist, more for myself than for anyone else. "I would be able to feel it if he was."

"Wishful thinking on your part," Drago callously replies.

But I swear I hear some hesitation in his voice.

Is he scared? Of Gabriel?

He fucking should be.

Drago's little slip up gives me just enough energy to take a big deep breath.

There's hope. If Drago's scared that Gabriel might be coming after him, then there still must be a chance he's alive.

"You're scared," I say out loud.

Krol's sharp nails dig deeper into my throat. But I don't care. I've been strangled by a far stronger beast.

I've learned to love the pain.

"What did I fucking tell—"

"Enough, Krol," Drago interrupts. "She's just trying to make us angry. The little girl is scared. Her only way out of this nightmare is through death. She wants you to make a mistake. She wants you to sever an artery so she can peacefully bleed out on my office floor. Don't give her the satisfaction of an easy death."

In response, Krol rips his hand from my throat. A twisted grin stretches out his cracked lips as he laughs at me.

"You're the only one who should be scared here, princess."

Reaching into his pocket, he pulls out the knife he'd shown me earlier. In his other hand, the branding iron still glows, red-hot.

"Show her how we handle disobedient little sluts," Drago spits from behind me.

"With pleasure."

Gritting my teeth, I force myself to concentrate on my rage instead of my fear.

But that's easier said than done. And I can't help but wince as Krol takes his first step towards me.

He doesn't get far.

Before he can take his second step, a sound stops him in his tracks.

Everyone in the room instantly recognizes it.

A muffled gunshot.

It comes from somewhere behind the heavy office door.

"Oh sh—"

Suddenly, the front door is torn from its hinges. The heavy metal frame flies forward, crushing Krol beneath its weight.

Smoke starts to fill the room.

Outside, I can hear the sharp crackle of gunshots. They fill the air like fireworks, until there's not an inch of silence left in the world.

"Goddamnit."

Drago's growl rises from behind me. Then, I feel his icy presence lean over my back.

It takes me a second to process what's happening, but when it hits me, the pain ravaging my body is overcome by a desperate will to escape.

This is my chance. Someone has come to my rescue.

Gabriel. It has to be.

But Drago is already a step ahead of me. His blade digs under my restraints. Through the thickening smoke, I feel him cut me loose. Wrists first. Then ankles.

The moment my legs are free, I call on every ounce of my strength, and I try to lunge forward.

But Drago catches me, mid-air. His fingers wrap around my hair, and he yanks me back into him.

I hit his chest with a thud. The pain returns.

But nothing is as strong as the hope.

"Gabriel!" I shout into the ever-growing fog.

"Shut the fuck up," Drago demands.

His wretched hand clasps around my mouth. I bite down.

Drago howls as I rip the flesh from his palm.

With a violent shove, he thrusts me forward, far away from him.

But I'm not pushed into freedom. No.

Krol has pulled himself out from under the fallen door. And I collide with his chest just as I hear a heart-stopping voice call back to me through the smoke.

"Bianca!"

It's Gabriel.

He's here.

He's alive.

And he's come to save me.

"Not so fast, bitch," Krol hisses.

The sizzling branding iron flashes across my face as he presses his blade against my throat, positioning me like a human shield.

"Take her out into the tunnels," Drago barks, from somewhere in the smoke. "I'll meet you above ground."

"How the hell are you going to get out of here?"

"Don't fucking worry about it. Get the girl out of here. Now!"

"Fuck." Krol's blade is pressed so tightly against my throat that I can already feel blood trickling down my skin.

But I'm not afraid of blood. Not anymore. Not with Gabriel so close.

If anything, the taste and scent of my own blood gives me strength. It turns me the fuck on.

Some of the fear and the pain evaporates as I do whatever I can to make this as uncomfortable for Krol as I can.

"Let me go, you bastard," I spit. "If Gabriel sees you treating me like this, he'll rip your head off."

"Not if I threaten to kill you first."

Krol is trying to be tough, but I can hear the same hesitation I recognized in Drago earlier.

He's scared.

My dark wolf has been unleashed.

But I know that Gabriel isn't going to attack if I'm in the way.

There must be something I can do. Something that doesn't end with my throat getting slashed.

"Hold on tight, you bitch. This is going to be a bumpy ride."

Digging his knee into my back, Krol forces me to stumble through the open doorway, into the smoky chaos outside.

There's so much shouting, so many gunshots, I can hardly make any one thing out. Still, I desperately search the frantic silhouettes for one that looks like Gabriel.

I heard him. I swear I did.

"Gabriel!" I shout again.

Krol doesn't like that. For a split second, his blade leaves my throat. But it's only to violently bring the handle down into my stomach.

The jab knocks the wind out of me. And I'd easily crumple to the ground if it weren't for the serpent holding me close to his slimy body.

"Don't even try to do that again," Krol warns.

It's not like I could. I can hardly breathe, let alone get a word out.

His blade presses back against my throat as he feverishly begins to back us both away from the battle.

"Bianca! Where are you?"

Gabriel's roar lifts over all of the others. His voice is so fucking primal. I can practically feel the hairs rise on Krol's hands.

A shot of beautiful, savage warmth fills up my heaving belly.

I'm not imagining things. He's here.

But I still haven't caught my breath; I can't yell back to my dark wolf. I can't tell him where to find me.

Not that I have to.

No. Gabriel can sense me. He can smell me. *Feel* me.

I blink, and suddenly, there he is.

A hulking silhouette that moves like lightening through the heavy fog. His brutality is unmistakable.

His shadow flashes from enemy to enemy, snapping necks and shooting through skulls at point-blank range.

"Fuck. Fuck. Fuck." Krol panics. Clearly, he sees my approaching beast too. "Kill the traitor! Fucking kill him!" he orders.

But Gabriel is on a mission. No one is going to be able to stop him—though, they do manage to slow him down. For now.

The killing spree continues ahead as Krol desperately backs us away from the action.

"Let me go, and maybe he'll spare you," I finally manage to wheeze. I need to be going in the opposite direction. I need to be going towards Gabriel, not away from him.

"People like us don't spare shit," Kroll curses, tightening his grip around me.

The scalding end of his branding iron glows faintly in the smoke.

"He's nothing like you," I quietly gasp.

But my voice is so quiet that not even Krol can hear it.

"Where the hell is that door," he mumbles to himself.

Slowly, the smoke starts to thin. Gabriel's violent silhouette fades in the distance. I can only watch as he's forced to fight his way through an endless maze of combatants.

My hope dims. Does he even see me?

My question is answered when Gabriel's hulking shadow suddenly stops. For a single breath, the vicious rampage is put on hold.

His silhouette turns in our direction.

I can feel those hazel-green eyes on me.

"Gabriel!" The cry rips out of my throat like broken glass. "Gabriel!" I shake and I squirm and I try to break free from Krol's grip.

"Oh no you fucking don't."

This time, when Krol lifts his blade from my throat to pummel me in the stomach, I take full advantage of the opening.

Planting my foot in the ground, I push myself to the side just enough to avoid his blow. Then, I somehow manage to grab hold of the long metal rod in Krol's other hand.

He's not expecting me to move so swiftly, and I'm able to catch him by surprise. Tipping the end of the rod into the air, I force the burning flat surface directly into the bastard's face.

The iron sizzles against his melting flesh, burning a hole into his eye socket. I force it into him with all my might.

His wails slash through the fog.

And then his blade slashes through my arm.

I can feel the skin on my triceps rip open as Krol stumbles backwards. The smell of burning flesh fills the air.

I fall to the ground.

"You fucking bitch. I'm going to fucking—"

Krol is interrupted by a bullet. It shreds through his shoulder, flinging him even further away from me.

He hits the ground, hand pressed against his burning eye. The coward howls like a fucking banshee.

The branding iron glows on the ground next to me. My fingers find the rod.

This isn't over.

"You asshole!" I shout, rage bursting from my mangled body.

Dragging myself to my feet, I hold the smoldering rod out towards the snake.

"Bianca!"

Gabriel's deep voice rips me out of my blood lust.

When I turn around, he's there. Hazel-green eyes cutting through the smoke.

"Gabriel…"

For a moment, the world stands still. The chaos bleeds into the background.

Nothing exists but the two of us.

I drop the branding iron. It clanks against the hard ground below.

We run to each other.

"Get the girl! Kill the traitor!" Krol's command breaks through our little moment.

The chaos returns.

Before we can reach each other, a bullet whizzes by my ear. Gabriel has to hit the ground just to avoid it. I trip on something and join him down there.

Our reunion is shattered into a thousand little pieces.

He's so close. Yet so far.

But neither of us are ready to give up.

Gritting through the overwhelming pain, I start to drag myself towards my dark wolf. He begins to crawl towards me. Bullets thrum over our heads.

"I'm coming for you, baby girl," Gabriel growls.

We both reach out.

The tips of our fingers touch. A burst of electricity erupts from the point of contact. The sizzling warmth helps re-animate my fading corpse.

I'm so desperate to feel more of him.

But Gabriel doesn't give me his hand.

Instead, he slips a chunk of throbbing metal beneath my aching fingers.

"A gun?"

"Are you alright? Can you fight? There are too many of them. If we're going to get out of this, I'm going to need you to—"

"I can fight," I respond. "I can kill."

Even through the thinning smoke and the growing darkness, I can see those fucking heart-stopping dimples deepen as Gabriel smiles at me.

"That's my girl."

Before I can gather the strength to smile back, my dark wolf twists around. Lifting his gun above his chest, he starts to fire at our pursuers.

I'm ready to join him. But there's more than one threat here.

I twist around too. Fully prepared to shred Krol to bits.

But the snake is already back on his feet. I watch as he tries to stumble away.

"I'm going after him," I grunt.

"The fuck you are," Gabriel growls back. "Not alone. I'm coming with you."

Looking over my shoulder, I see him jump to his feet, then reaches down to take my hand, all while continually shooting back into the fog.

Every one of his shots seem to hit. Bodies fall like flies.

But there are so many enemies, and just two of us.

Fuck it. I'll take those odds.

Grabbing Gabriel's hand, I let him help me to my wobbly feet.

"I missed you," I croak.

It's all I can muster before aiming my gun under his outstretched arm. Bracing myself, I fire a volley of my own. The recoil stings like a motherfucker, but I hold the barrel straight.

Still, my aim isn't as accurate as Gabriel's, and I only manage to hit one fucker in the leg, and then another in the torso.

They both fall.

Good enough.

"It's just like shooting Luis, right?" Gabriel chuckles, backing into me as we desperately try to fend off the approaching army.

"Not quite," I sputter. "But I'll get the hang of it."

Standing shoulder to shoulder, we begin to mow down our enemies. I get to feel the warmth of Gabriel's flexing muscles as he kills for me. I get to touch my man again. Finally. And all while killing in his name.

But the longer we shoot, the less exhilarating it all becomes. We're quickly being overwhelmed. My broken body is failing. And it's not long before we both have to jump behind the nearest corner just to take a breath... and to reload our smoking weapons.

"Where the fuck are they?" Gabriel curses, as he hands me a fresh clip.

"Who?" I ask.

Even through all of the pain, reloading my gun is easy. I can still remember just how I did it back at that secluded cabin. I can remember how I figured it out all on my own. How good that felt.

My heart thumps against the inside of my chest.

This is where I belong.

If I have to die, let it be like this.

Covered in blood. Killing for love, right next to my man.

"Your cousin was supposed to be my back up," Gabriel grumbles. "But I don't see—"

Just like that, the tunnel is filled with a new roar.

Peaking around the corner, I see more bodies hit the ground. The men who were just chasing after us turn to face a new foe.

"Rian?" I ask, gazing back at my dark wolf.

It's the first good look I get at him.

My stomach drops.

He's in rougher shape than I expected.

His handsome face is stained with dark crimson splashes. There's a deep scarlet imprint wrapped around his throat. Steam rises from his every pore. Blood drips from his lips.

Still, I don't spot any pain in his features. All I can see in those stunning green eyes is relief... and a slight annoyance.

"Finally," Gabriel grunts. "Why are the Irish always so late?"

I'm not given a chance to reply.

Without hesitation, Gabriel slips a hand behind the back of my throbbing skull.

Then, he pulls me in for a kiss.

All of my pain and fear seem to evaporate as I sink into the power of his tender lips.

I kiss him back.

It's heaven in hell.

Peace in chaos.

Love in hate.

The passion of our kiss intensifies.

I thought he was dead. He must have thought I was a goner too.

We have a whole future to make up for.

With a savage thrust, Gabriel shoves me against the tunnel wall. I can feel his bulge. Taste his desire.

We're both wild with lust.

But my body is so frail right now.

I can't help but whimper into his mouth.

"Shit, sorry!" he curses, hand easing around my skull.

"Don't let go," I beg.

"I'm never letting go of you again, baby girl," Gabriel promises. "I fucking love you."

He steals the breath right out of my bruised lungs.

That's all I want to hear.

It's all I've ever wanted to hear.

"I love you too," I rasp.

Gabriel presses his bloody forehead against mine, and I swear his soul seeps through my skin.

He eases my pain. He protects me from my fears.

He makes me feel loved.

For what feels like an endless moment, we don't move. We just feel each other.

The approaching violence doesn't bother us. Neither does the encroaching darkness.

Together, we are comfortable in this world.

Together, we can conquer it.

Rule it.

Love it.

Still, something tugs at my soul.

"Drago got away," I whisper.

"I don't care," Gabriel tells me, shaking his head. "All I care about is you."

"What about Krol? He's so much closer. We could catch him."

"We'll get him another day. I don't care about him either."

But my blood lust is quickly returning.

"I care," I croak. "I want him to pay. I want to taste his blood. He..." I can hardly articulate what that snake was about to do to me. "He wanted to burn away any trace of you from my body."

"That fucking bastard," Gabriel growls. Hesitantly, he pulls away from me. But he doesn't seem convinced. "You're in rough shape, *myszko*."

"I can take it," I promise him, even if I'm not sure I can.

My body is falling apart. And we're not out of danger yet.

Just around the corner, a bloody battle is playing out—it hardly even registers.

Gabriel and I are lost in our own world.

Slowly, my dark wolf withers against my determination. I can see the protective fire burning behind his hazel-green eyes. But I also see the pride... and the blood-lust.

It's a blood-lust we share.

A panty-dropping smirk finally lifts his thick red lips. Hoisting his gun, Gabriel cocks the chamber.

"Fine. Let's go hunting, babe."

I'm instantly wet.

God. I fucking love this man.

Bianca is in no shape for this.

Shit. Neither am I.

But how could I refuse?

The savage glint in her eye when she talked about wanting to taste Krol's blood...

Fuck.

It made me hard.

I'm still erect now, even as we follow the slimy serpent's trail away from the battle and deeper into the tunnels.

"Do you hear that?"

Ahead, from somewhere in the darkness, a high pitch wheeze echoes out.

"It's him," Bianca sneers.

She takes an angry step forward. But that's one step too far. I have to lunge forward to keep her from hitting the ground.

She's been through so much. _Too_ much.

But even as she wobbles in my arms, there's no way Bianca is going to stay put. Pinching the bridge of her bloody nose, she straightens against my grip.

"Let me handle him," I tell her. "I'll make sure it's safe. Then you can come in for the kill."

"No. I... I need to do this myself."

"You don't do anything by yourself anymore," I remind her. "We do everything together. Including killing people. Alright?"

I can hear the nausea building in her every breath. We've been moving too fast. She's pushing herself too hard.

Blood drips from the gash in her arm.

The sight makes me fucking sick.

And endlessly furious.

Still, I stay focused. For her sake.

Leaning forward, I plant a soft kiss against the welt on her forehead.

No one needs to tell me who gave it to her.

I already know.

Fuck. Bianca is right, Krol needs to pay. I'd do it myself, but there's no way I'm leaving her again.

Still, if we're going to do this as a team, she's going to have to let me protect her—at least, a little bit.

"Alright," my bloody queen sighs. "You go ahead. I'll follow behind. But don't you dare kill the bastard without giving me a chance to cut him open first."

"I promise."

The wheezing ahead grows fainter by the second. There's no time to lose.

Grabbing Bianca's hand, I lead her forward.

The battle raging behind us fades into the background as we're engulfed by the darkness.

There's little light down here—at least, there isn't until we spot a faint flicker ahead.

The wheezing returns. It's joined by a cough and a curse.

"*Glupi dranie!*"

I'd recognize that voice anywhere.

"Stay alert, *myszko*. And be quiet."

But my own feet are already starting to drag. No matter how softly I try to move, each step echoes like thunder around the black tunnel walls.

The adrenaline high that led me through the initial chaos is dying down. I'm bleeding like crazy.

This needs to end soon, or else I might make a mistake.

"Is that him?"

Bianca's voice snaps my attention over to a twisted figure crouching against the tunnel wall ahead.

The mangled silhouette heaves beneath a single flickering florescent light.

It's the source of the wheezing.

It's Krol.

"It's over," I call out, pointing my gun in his direction.

But something feels off—like we're slowly nearing the edge of an endless spit. I approach with great caution. I've never been to this part of these tunnels before.

The air feels colder here. More ancient.

My aching body flexes. I make sure I'm shielding Bianca. Krol needs to die. But nothing is important as her safety.

"... It's over..." the hunchbacked silhouette croaks. "For me, maybe. But not for you. Drago escaped. You're nothing without him."

"No," I snarl. "He's nothing without *me*."

The closer I get to the cloaked figure, the clearer he becomes. Krol's gun is on the ground by his feet. An empty clip hangs half out of the magazine.

"You're out of ammo," I note, not daring to ease up.

"And out of time," Krol admits. "But that doesn't mean you've won."

"Don't you dare fucking move," I warn him, tensing as he unfurls himself.

But even I'm forced to pause when I see what's become of his face.

The horror.

Krol's eyeball has been melted out of its socket. It hangs on by a single thinning thread, drooping down against his charred cheek like a wilted flower. Purple and red veins bulge out from the blackened burn mark.

"Looks like you're not the only one that bitch has burned now," Krol chuckles. His laugh is wet and sickly and absolutely unhinged.

"Tell me where Drago is going," I demand, ignoring the monster's taunt.

"Only Drago knows that," Krol wheezes. "All I know for sure is that I'm heading straight to hell. And so are you!"

I'm just distracted enough by his mutilated face that I don't immediately react to the knife that flashes from his hand.

The blade cuts through the air like lightening... before plunging directly into my chest.

"Gabriel!"

Bianca's cry is shrill and bone-chilling, yet it sounds like it's a million miles away.

I'm in shock.

And then, I'm infuriated.

The pain is delayed. For a split-second, all I can feel is pure, unadulterated rage. It gives me enough strength to aim my gun back towards Krol.

"You fucking bastard!"

My finger pulls down on the trigger. The muzzle flashes. My knees hit the ground.

The bullet shreds through Krol's throat.

But it hardly registers.

I'm numb. Everything is muted. Sound. Pain. Sight. It all turns grey... until a shadow flickers over me, and everything blasts back into color.

Bianca's battle cry roars through the tunnel as she races

towards Krol. Her gun is raised. Her muzzle flashes over and over again. Her bullets thrash through the mutilated serpent.

"Come get me, princess," Krol gargles, blood spilling from his ruptured throat.

Even as he's filled with lead, the bastard somehow manages to open up his arms, like he's welcoming her into a deathly embrace... or a trap.

"Bianca!"

She's in danger.

A debilitating agony is already starting to pulse through my chest as I grab the handle of the knife. But I don't have a choice. Not if I want to save my girl.

I don't even try to brace myself. I just rip the fucking blade out.

The pain is so powerful I nearly keel over. Blood immediately starts to gush from the wound. The world spins.

I try to steady it by latching onto my queen.

I call out to her again.

But she doesn't hear me.

Bianca's gone deaf with rage. Blind with blood-lust.

She continues to run straight at Krol, even as his body is eviscerated by her gunfire.

My heart drops as she gets close. Too close.

And then Krol falls.

His mangled body drop backwards—but instead of hitting the ground with a thud, he's just swallowed up by the darkness.

Shit.

A hole.

There's a giant fucking hole in the ground.

That's what I felt earlier.

But Bianca doesn't seem to sense it. She's still racing blindly ahead, ready to tear Krol's fallen corpse apart with her fucking teeth.

My mind goes blank.

The blood. The pain. The heartache. The fear. It all vanishes.

When the world comes rushing back, I'm tackling Bianca to the ground.

The gun drops from her hand.

We can only watch as it skids across the ground, until it too slips over the pit's edge, disappearing into the darkness below.

We never hear it hit the ground.

"Gabriel! Are you alright?"

Bianca almost immediately seems to snap out of her violent trance.

"I'm fine," I lie, nearly choking on the blood building in my lungs. "Everything will be fine. You're safe."

"Don't leave me." Bianca's tears run down my chest as she shoves her cheek into my fresh wound. She's quickly covered in my blood. But neither of us flinch away.

Instead, I just wrap her up in my arms. I force myself to feel her—even if it means feeling all of the pain and heartache that comes with it.

"I love you," I whisper into her ear. "I love you so fucking much."

My vision flickers as Bianca squeezes me tight.

"I love you too," she rasps. "I love you. I love you. I love you..."

Her sweet, desperate voice echoes around my skull as I begin to fade.

My heart shrivels. Her tight embrace loosens.

We've both lost so much blood.

Somewhere behind us, I can hear people shouting. Footsteps echo through the endless tunnels. But I'm too far gone to make out if they're friendly or not.

It doesn't matter. They can't help me.

But they might be able to help her.

Calling on my last bits of life, I find Bianca's lips.

If this is it, I want it to end it just like it started. With a kiss. A desperate attempt to wake up my sleeping beauty before we're both engulfed by the darkness.

I might never know if it works.

The heat of her lips give me one last flash of beautiful pain before I fall into the void.

"I love you."

37

BIANCA

By now, I'm used to waking up in strange places.

I'm used to opening my eyes and not having any idea where I am or what awaits me.

That's why it's so damn shocking when I open my eyes and instantly recognize the bed I'm lying in.

Sure, it takes me a second. My vision needs time to refocus as I slowly return from the twisted landscape of my unconscious. But even before I can see, I recognize the soft scent that surrounds me.

Vanilla, with the slightest hint of lavender.

The nostalgic fragrance washes over me like a calming wave. A hot towel for my aching body.

I'm home.

The first thing I can see clearly is my overloaded bookshelf. Half open textbooks are still spread out across my messy desk. Small mounds of unfolded clothes litter the floor by my shuttered closet doors.

This is my childhood bedroom.

It doesn't look like it's been touched since I was ripped from its comforting walls. The same comforting walls I once thought were so suffocating.

My head starts to pound as I'm suddenly bombarded by a flurry of painful memories.

Gabriel.

The vanilla-scented tranquility evaporates as I remember how his tight embrace went limp as we bled out together on that dark tunnel floor, hovering on the edge of a gaping hole.

He kissed me.

The electricity in his lips shocked me awake just long enough to look under his arm. To see Rian running towards us. To feel some small sliver of hope before I joined my dark king in the blackness.

Please be alright.

My sore heart flails behind my aching chest as I try to climb out of bed and find answers. But I'm immediately caught by a spiderweb of chords, tubes and IV bag-stands.

They twist around my frail body as I cry out with a helpless frustration.

In response, my bedroom door bursts open.

"Bianca, honey. You're up!"

Mama?

My burning heart cools a little as she helps me navigate the tangled mess. When I'm free, I immediately fall into her arms.

"Mama!" I rasp. The relief of her embrace calms me right back down. But only for a moment. "Where is he? Please tell me he's alright."

My heart catches in my throat as I wait for a response.

I don't dare breathe.

"Gabriel is fine," Mama quickly assures me. "At least, he is now. That boy survived some nasty injuries. Hell, when I saw him I wasn't sure... oh well, never mind that. We put him into surgery. Auntie Elisa and her team gave him the best care anyone could ever ask for. And he's been up and about for two days now. In fact, since the moment he got out of surgery, he's been sitting by your bed side. It was only about an hour ago that Dad and Rian managed to finally pull him out of here."

Tears well up in my eyes.

"Can I see him?" I choke.

"Yes. Yes. I'll go fetch him," Mama says. "But don't you want to see your cousin and your dad too?"

"Yes, of course," I nod, wiping away the tears. "I'd like to see everyone."

It's been such a long time.

But the truth is, Gabriel is who I want to see the most. And it's not just because I'm so relieved he survived.

No. It's because right now, I'm too sore and tired to pretend. And Gabriel is the only person in this world who truly knows who I am.

My parents won't understand. And when they find out what I've become, they'll demand an explanation. So will Rian.

But I don't have to explain shit to Gabriel.

My dark wolf was there for my entire transformation. He was right by my side for the whole thing.

He was helping me. Teaching me.

Loving me.

"Sit back down, honey. Please," Mama begs. "I'll go get everyone. They're all in Dad's office."

"Dad's office?" I ask, raising a heavy brow. "Does... does that mean they're all getting along?"

Mama shrugs. "Well, they're trying—some harder than others. At the very least, they've started working together."

"On what?" I gulp, remembering Krol's words. This isn't over. Drago is still out there.

Mama just sighs. "I'll let the boys explain it. I've been too pre-occupied with looking after you to get too involved with that side of things."

"Alright," I nod.

"I love you sweetie," Mama says. Tilting her head to the side, she gives me a long deep look. A smile fills her face. "I'm so happy you're feeling better."

"So am I," I smile back, weakly. "I love you too, Mama."

"Now, you take it easy while I go herd everyone."

Mama makes sure I'm back in bed before she turns to open the door.

But she's hardly even stepped foot in the hall before a new presence suddenly appears in the doorway.

My heart stops at the sight of him.

"Gabriel!"

"Bianca?"

I've never heard my big bad wolf sound so shocked. He can only stare at me as I jump up from my bed, desperate to feel him again.

But my body is not ready for such rapid movements.

A dizzy spell quickly wraps around my skull. My knees go weak.

Gabriel springs forward, effortlessly catching me before I fall.

"You're alright," I whisper, looking up at him.

Those stunning hazel-green eyes slowly come back into focus. They're just as sharp as ever.

My heart flutters.

"I am now," Gabriel smiles, his dimples deepening.

All of my aches and pains dissolve.

"So am I."

Behind us, I hear Mama gently shut the door, leaving us alone—if even just for a moment.

"I hear you're finally getting along with my family," I whisper, tears welling up in my eyes again.

"I'm trying to."

"How brave of you."

"Anything for my queen."

Queen.

I know Gabriel is just trying to be cute, but the word serves as a stark reminder of just how much I've changed since the two of us first disappeared together.

No one in my family knows the kind of person I've become; the violence I've delivered; the lives I've taken.

They will have to learn. I'm not the fragile little princess they used to shelter.

"And what do they think about that?" I mutter. "You know, about me being a queen... and your wife."

Taking my hand, Gabriel traces his fingers over my thorny ring.

"They try to ignore it," he admits. "At the very least, I think they'd like us to have a more traditional wedding."

"Would you do that?"

"I don't need any kind of ceremony to know that you're mine," Gabriel grumbles. "But maybe you deserve to be spoiled a little, after all I've put you through."

"I've been spoiled enough in my life," I sigh, pursing my lips.

"Then what do you want to do instead of a big wedding?" Gabriel smirks.

"I want to conquer. I want to rule. I want to kill. And I want to fuck you."

"I can arrange that."

I can't help but giggle as Gabriel slips his hand down to the small of my back and dips me.

"I love you, Bianca," he says, those hazel-green eyes reaching deep into my heart.

"I love you, Gabriel."

When we kiss, the electricity of his lips jumpstarts my heart one more time. Just like that, I'm ready to do anything. I *want* to do everything.

Still, when our lips fall apart, I can't help but stare up into those hazel-green eyes for just a little bit longer.

"Have we figured out our last name yet?" I find myself asking.

Lifting my hand to Gabriel's impossibly gorgeous face, I softly trace a finger over his fading bruises, before landing on the B I tattooed beneath his eye.

To my surprise, a troubling look flashes across his face, before he erases it by kissing me again.

"Let's not worry about that right now," he whispers into my mouth. "Let's just worry about getting you back on your feet."

"I'd rather you sweep me off of them," I whisper back, biting my lower lip.

The heat of Gabriel's hard body has already seeped beneath my skin. A familiar pressure is growing in my core.

"How naughty," Gabriel growls. "You want me right here? In your childhood bedroom? Under your parents noses?"

"Feels like we're back in high school again, huh?" I giggle.

"No," Gabriel says, suddenly serious. "This is nothing like that, *myszko*. This is real life. This is real love. Fuck the past, Bianca. I say we burn it. All that matters is the future. What do you say?"

"I say yes."

"That's my girl."

Without any regard for my still fragile body, Gabriel picks me up and tackles me onto the bed.

Before I can scream with excitement or pain, he wraps his hand around my mouth.

Then, he spreads his other hand out across my stomach.

The implication is clear.

For a moment, we just stop and stare down at my belly. It represents a reality that neither of us have had the time to properly process yet—at least, not together.

I'm pregnant.

The reminder steals my breath away.

There is no greater responsibility than being a parent. Not even ruling an empire can compare.

But I'm not scared.

Because it's not just me against the world anymore.

No. I've got Gabriel backing me up now.

Well, actually, I've got more than just Gabriel backing me up.

Despite their initial—and understandable—disapproval, I know my family will always have my back too.

Hell, it already sounds like everybody's working hard to get along with each other. Sure, that might take some time, but I have hope. So much fucking hope.

And that's not even all I have.

As Gabriel peppers my neck with soft kisses, I'm filled with an overwhelming sense of happiness.

It's the same kind of happiness I found back at that hidden cabin in the woods. The one where I started to finally believe in myself.

But as my toes curl and my nipples harden, I realize something I hadn't back then.

This happiness is not as fragile as I first thought it was. Because I didn't actually find it in that cabin.

I didn't find it in the seclusion of the woods, or in the freedom of finally being free of my overbearing family. I didn't find it in the barrel of my gun or in the guts of that drug dealer.

I found it in Gabriel.

He was right there by my side the whole time.

And that's all I needed.

It's all I'll ever need.

Hell, from now on, it won't matter where I am, or even what I do. As long as we're together, I know I'll be happy.

I know I'll be supported. I know I'll be protected.

I know I'll be loved.

And with all that on my side, who's to say I can't take over the fucking world?

38

GABRIEL

By the time we've both fully recovered from our injuries, Bianca's flat stomach has turned round.

It somehow makes her even hotter.

Every time I see her naked, I can only think about how I did that to her. How that's our child stretching her skin. How it was my cum that filled her up to the brim; that helped start a new life; that made her glow and swell up like this.

It makes me so fucking hard.

And when I get hard, Bianca gets wet.

Shit. Back when I put that baby in her belly, I could have counted on one hand the amount of times I'd fucked her.

Not anymore.

Now, we've fucked more times than either of us can count—and we've made love on even more occasions.

It doesn't matter how busy we get, there's always time to give into our deepest desires and explore our wildest and darkest fantasies.

Sometimes, our pleasure even bleeds into our work.

Hell, that's what happened just last night.

My pulse quickens at the memory. My cock bulges.

Sinking into my seat, I look out the window next to me. Fluffy white clouds roll over the wings of our private jet. Across from me, Bianca is curled up into a ball, her hands on her belly, protecting our unborn child.

I watch over them both.

It's almost nice to see Bianca looking so peaceful. But I'm already halfway hard. And there's nothing I want more than to gently coax her awake, drag her to the bathroom and let the sink hold up her belly as I fuck her brains out... again.

But Bianca needs her rest.

In a few months, we'll be anointed.

Ray Byrne is stepping down.

Bianca and I are to step up in his place.

The transition will be hectic.

But then, the west coast will be ours.

Shit. It's still hard to believe.

We've been working extra hard to lay the groundwork of our future reign. And that started yesterday.

Two days ago, Bianca and I flew down to the Mexican border, where a notoriously tough biker gang had set up a blockade around some of our most profitable trade routes.

They must have thought it would be easy to pull one over on Ray as he was preparing to retire. But they didn't take Bianca and I into consideration.

No one did.

We both wanted to set the tone for our new dynasty. We wanted everyone to know what crossing us means.

I can still hear the sweet screams of our burning enemies.

I can still smell their sizzling flesh as it fills the arid desert night.

Fucking hell.

My erection fills at the memory of how Bianca and I fucked in the shadows of those flames.

And I'm not the only one who remembers.

Word of our massacre quickly spread.

By the time we got back on the plane, our phones were buzzing off the hook. Everyone was calling in to swear fealty to us. No one wanted to end up like the bikers.

I told Bianca to rest. I'd take the calls. But she wasn't having it. My queen wanted to hear the fuckers grovel.

And she knew just how to convince me.

Getting on her knees, my pregnant wife sucked my cock as I took a call from the terrified leader of a supposedly savage cartel. Then, I ate Bianca out as she discussed numbers with an important European syndicate.

The power was intoxicating. Our lust was endless.

But not even my tongue can keep a pregnant woman going for too long. When I spotted the fire fading in Bianca's beautiful blue eyes, I put my foot down.

She needed to sleep.

Because my queen isn't just learning to rule an empire, she's also growing a fucking life inside of her.

Our child.

I'll do anything to keep them both healthy.

So, I switched off all communication devices for the rest of the flight. I forced her to rest.

Now, I'm wishing I hadn't.

But it's not just because my cock is swollen at the sight of her sleeping body.

There's something else.

Something that I've been trying to ignore ever since I nearly died all those months ago, hanging from those cursed rafters in that dark gymnasium.

Something that doesn't feel like it should be as important as everything else.

But when Bianca falls asleep before I do; when there's no more work to do for the day; when I've turned off my phones and cut out the world, this troubling thought always seems to crawl back inside my mind, no matter how horny or tired or happy I've been.

"...What's wrong, baby?"

It's like Bianca can sense my restlessness. She stirs awake across from me, stretching out as a yawn drifts out from her perfect pink lips.

"Nothing, *myszko*. Go back to sleep."

"You know I can't sleep when you're like this."

"I'm always like this when you're asleep," I mumble.

"Well, that would explain why I haven't been sleeping well lately. Now, do you want me to be well-rested, or do you want to keep holding onto your secrets?"

Her lashes flutter as those crystal blue eyes take hold of my heart.

God. I love her so fucking much.

And that's such a double edge sword.

Because while I may be the only person in the world who can convince her do something she doesn't want to do, she has the exact same power over me.

"It's about my father," I admit. Leaning forward, I take Bianca's soft hand in mine.

"What about him?"

She already knows the full story. I told her everything, exactly as Drago told it to me back in the gymnasium. Then, I made sure she knew it was all true after I'd managed to corroborate every last detail myself.

Fuck. It still doesn't feel real.

"He... he was always supposed to be the villain in my story," I say, unsure of how to express what I'm feeling. "Kamil Reca—the man who I thought killed my father; the man who I believed took everything from me—he *was* my father. And I only ever had any hope at all because of his despicable actions."

"That's not true," Bianca sternly insists. "You would have

been successful no matter what... and since when have we been bothered by someone else's despicable actions?"

"Ever since they involved women and children... and drugs," I sneer, remembering all that I know about the deplorable man.

Drago may have been lying about who Kamil Reca was to me, but before that, he'd never lied about just how depraved the man really was.

I've been able to confirm nearly everything. And it's flipped my entire world on its head.

At times, Bianca's presence has been the only thing keeping me from losing sight of who I really am.

She's my rock.

"That's because you live by a code," Bianca says, pushing herself up. "Your real father didn't. But who cares? You don't have to be like him if you don't want to be. Forget the bastard. You're already better than him. More powerful. More successful. Crush him like we're going to crush the rest of our enemies. Why let him drag you down at all?"

"He's not dragging me down," I grunt.

But that's not true.

"Then what's the problem?" Bianca pushes. "And don't tell me there's no problem, Gabriel. I can tell when something's wrong with my king."

"Fine. The problem is that this whole thing is making me hesitant," I blurt out. "And I don't like to hesitate."

"Hesitate about what?" Bianca asks, tilting her head.

She's knows that I rarely ever hesitate.

"Our story isn't over yet," I remind her. Shifting up in my seat, I reach across the aisle and slip my fingers beneath her shoulder strap.

She sinks into my touch as I trace the initial I once carved into her tender skin.

"... Our last name," she whispers, immediately understanding.

"I don't want to give Kamil the satisfaction," I sneer.

"Kamil Reca is dead," Bianca reminds me. "All of the Recas are. And that includes their disciples. We made sure of that."

"And they should stay dead," I respond. "That name should be forgotten. It should be buried forever."

"No," Bianca disagrees. Her fingers find the carving she made on my forearm. Then, with her other hand, she brushes over the mark she tattooed beneath my eye. "The name shouldn't be buried. It should be conquered. Just like we're going to conquer everything else."

Fuck.

I've created a monster.

A beautiful, strong, ruthless monster.

And she's absolutely right.

"I fucking love you," I growl.

Without giving Bianca a chance to respond, I cup her jaw and pull her in for a kiss. I can feel her swollen belly brush softly against my chest as I taste her delicious lips.

"I love you too," Bianca whispers into my mouth.

"Bianca Reca..." I chuckle, pulling back to look into those otherworldly blue eyes of hers. "Don't lie, you just want to get rid of that ugly alliteration in your name once and for all."

"That depends," she giggles back. "Does Bianca Reca sound better, or does it also sound like the name of some second-class comic book character?"

"It sounds like the name of some badass bitch. It sounds like the name of a queen. *My* queen."

"And Gabriel Reca sounds like the name of a king. *My* king."

"Then so it shall be."

Bianca's crystal blue eyes flicker downwards as she chews on her tongue.

"... Does that mean I get to finish the tattoo?"

Lifting my hand, I hold her palm against my cheek.

"I think that's only right. In fact—"

Before I can finish, I'm interrupted by the harsh buzz of a ringing cellphone. It vibrates in my pocket at a frequency that makes my hackles rise.

Bianca feels it too.

My phone is supposed to be off.

But there's a failsafe.

"That's the emergency line..." she recognizes, her hand falling back onto her belly as I rip out my ringing phone.

"That can only mean trouble."

Even before I read the incoming message, I'm already sneering.

"What does it say?" Bianca asks.

It takes me a second to realize I'm looking at a series of coordinates.

"That's somewhere in Poland," I realize, handing the phone over to her.

"No... You don't think... Do you?"

My mind is already racing. Standing up from my seat, I begin to pace down the aisle.

For as troubling as the revelation about my father has been, it's really only a personal issue; a problem that has haunted me exclusively in my downtime.

But there are bigger issues at hand. Issues that I haven't been able to keep to myself.

"You think these locations could be where your inheritance is hidden?" Bianca asks.

Then, the phone vibrates again.

"Who is it?"

"Uncle Maksim," Bianca says, furrowing her brow. "He says Rian's program was finally able to decrypt that encoded message we received last month. Apparently, it contained these coordinates, and nothing else."

A knot twists in my gut as I realize what that could mean.

No way...

Last month, our private servers went down for an entire day. With Rian's help, we finally got everything back up and running... but not before the lion found a tiny digital envelope hidden behind all of the tangled wires.

He made it sound like the envelope had been hiding there for a while, and that the outage may have been purposely designed to lead us to it.

But not even the legendary Rian Kilpatrick could find a way to hack into the encrypted package right then and there. Instead, he had to create a program to slowly work its way through all of the intricate built-in locks and traps, all while safeguarding our system against any potential viruses and booby-traps.

The sophistication of the technology immediately made me think of Roz.

Shit.

Just thinking about her and Tytus makes my heart hurt.

It's been months since I last heard from either them.

In fact, the last time I heard from either of them was when Roz sent me the text that helped us expose Drago's security system.

Since then, they've been radio silent.

It's been a constant rain cloud over my happily-ever-after. But I also haven't been sitting on my ass twiddling my thumbs.

I've committed a considerable amount of resources to finding my friends—even if I'm not sure they want to be found.

But are these new coordinates going to lead me to them? Or perhaps to the inheritance they were supposed to collect on my behalf...

... Or maybe even to something else entirely...

There's only one way to find out.

"We need to go to these coordinates, now," Bianca blurts out before I can. "Even if it's not where your inheritance is, there may be clues about what's happened to Rozalia and Tytus."

Sometimes, I forget about the little bond that Roz and Bianca created.

Hell, they may have only burst into each other's lives for a quick and violent flash, but Bianca got her first ever kill with the knife Roz gave her. That has to count for something.

Still, Poland is no joke. And it's definitely not a place to drag your pregnant queen—especially not after what we've just been through.

The country's underworld remains a chaotic and volatile mess, devoid of any structure or steady leadership. And there's nothing I can do about that until I receive my inheritance—not that I plan on pushing too hard on either of those fronts.

I already have control of everything I need, as well as everything I want.

I have my queen, and an empire to rule with her.

That's more than I could have ever dreamed of.

"No," I say, shaking my head. "We need to go home. You need to rest. If not for yourself, then for the sake of our child. I'll leave first thing tomorrow morning."

But I should know better than that by now.

Even with a precious human growing inside of her, Bianca shoots onto her feet like a rocket.

"You aren't going anywhere without me," she challenges. "We can make a quick stop to refuel, but after that, we're heading straight to Poland."

Fuck.

It makes me so hard when she gets like this.

This is the ruthless queen of my wildest fantasies... and my dirtiest dreams.

And she's all mine.

"Fine," I grunt, biting down on my lower lip. "We'll go together. But Poland isn't like America. And the people there are harder and more dangerous than any of those bikers. You'll need to prepare. So, I'm taking you to bed. We can spend the rest of the flight there. End of discussion."

"You're taking me to bed, just to get some rest?" Bianca teases, a sly smirk lifting up the corners of her pretty pink lips.

My cock gets so hard it threatens to rip out of my pants.

"No. I'm not taking you to bed so you can rest, *myszko*," I respond. "You've done enough of that already. We're going to bed so that I can tire you out. There are too many fights to be had in Poland, and I don't want to leave you with enough energy to seek them out."

Pinching her chin, I lead Bianca's lips up to mine.

"Then fuck going to bed," Bianca rasps. "Take me back to the bathroom. That was so much hotter."

"Very well," I growl, slipping my thumb into her wet mouth. "I'll take you to the bathroom. And then I'll take you back to the place where this all began."

———

Bianca's grip tightens around my palm as we step into the darkness.

I would never dare to assume that my queen was scared of anything, but she hasn't held my hand this tightly in a long time.

Fuck. I don't blame her.

Even with a veritable army standing watch outside, this site feels irredeemably cursed.

"What is this place?" Bianca whispers, her breath billowing out like smoke.

Ahead, on the other side of the dark doorway, are the charred ruins of a once towering castle.

The roof has long since caved in, and the charred, crumbled remains are bathed in pale moonlight.

Collapsed stone walls rise like claws out of the rubble, casting deep shadows over the wreckage.

The deeper we roam, the colder it seems to get.

"I'm not sure," I cautiously admit.

The locals wouldn't tell us shit. Hell, they hardly even spoke at all. Threats. Bribes. None of it worked. No matter how hard we pushed, their thin cracked lips remained sealed.

And we remained in the dark.

And that's where we are now. In the dark—at least, we are until we step out of the tunneled doorway, and into the moonlit courtyard.

"What's that?"

Despite the fear I felt in her grip, Bianca's fingers quickly fall from mine as she leaves my side to investigate something glinting in the moonlight.

"Be careful," I grunt, quickly catching up to her.

The fractured floor is covered with all kinds of debris. Toppled stone statues lean precariously against the ruins, headless and splintered. Shattered stained glass litters the ground.

This is no place for a woman who's carrying such fragile cargo—though, it does feel like the exact kind of place a dark queen like Bianca might have once lived.

"What is this..." Bianca trails off as she reaches into the black rubble.

The act causes a small landslide to break out, and a pile of ancient stone comes crumbling down at her feet.

Bianca jumps back. I catch her in my chest.

But not before I see what her landslide has just unearthed.

Instantly, I recognize the black biretta... and the ghastly face gaping up from beneath it.

"The priests..." I mumble, shocked. "Well, one of them, anyway."

Dry patches of blood stain the dead man's paper white skin. His once stoic face is twisted into a look of pure horror.

He was screaming before he died.

But what the hell could make one of these dark priests scream like that?

"Gabriel," Bianca's warmth shifts against my chest as she lifts something up to her face. "This was in his hand..."

The object glints against the pale moonlight.

A bloody coin.

But not just any coin. A Slavic silver piece, with a very specific symbol engraved at the center of it.

My hackles rise and my fingers curl into fists.

I know this calling card.

"This is where it was," I dare to realize. "My fortune. And maybe my army too."

"But who took it?"

The answer looms in the back of my mind like a raging leviathan.

"Shit. Other than the priests, I can only think of three people in the entire world who would know where to find this place... and no one has seen or heard from any of them in months."

"No," Bianca gasps. "You... you think this was Drago?"

Taking the coin from Bianca's hand, I study it, hoping that I'm wrong.

I'm not.

I've left coins like this behind at so many gruesome scenes before. But only back when I worked for the dragon himself.

The same dragon who's been missing ever since we smoked him out of his underground lair.

"He's still out there," I grumble. "... But this can't be him.

Drago doesn't have the resources to cause such destruction. Not anymore. Not without me. Not without Roz and Tytus."

Before I can finish, the most dreadful fucking thought I've ever had drops down on me like a fucking guillotine.

Drago couldn't have done this.

Not alone.

"What does it mean?" Bianca asks, still stunned.

I let her take the bloody silver piece from my hand as I contemplate the unthinkable.

Without his minions, Drago has no power. No one to lead him to the treasure he's spent my entire life chasing. No one to do his bidding. No one to fight his battles.

But this doesn't have to be him.

Two other people have been missing since that battle in the tunnels.

A jagged breath rips from my lungs as I remember how we first found the coordinates to this place.

The digital envelope.

We still don't know who left it. But I have my suspicions. Strong, gut-wrenching suspicions.

"Fuck..." I curse, suddenly light headed.

No. It can't be. Not them.

Roz and Tytus would never betray me.

Would they?

EPILOGUE
BIANCA

3 months later...

I can smell the fire even before I can feel it.

The smoky scent swirls through the air like a dream; it's heat washing over me in building waves.

A lustful sigh flutters from my lips.

The powerful fragrance brings back such smoldering memories.

Even from behind my blindfold, I can see the flames Gabriel and I once lit in the desert. I can feel his cock deep inside of me. I can taste his lips and feel his passion, as well as his brutality.

We burned those bikers alive. Every last one of them. Then we made love beneath the smoky blanket of their screams.

My fingers tighten around Gabriel's big hand as he leads me forward.

I love this man so much.

"How are you feeling, *myszko?*"

Even after all of this time, Gabriel's deep voice still makes me shiver.

"I'm excited," I admit, my free hand falling onto my swollen belly.

Ahead, I can hear the crackling of a massive inferno.

I'll be giving birth in only a couple of months. And as happy as I am to meet our baby boy, there is one thing I'll sorely miss about being pregnant.

The sex.

Is that what we're here for?

Hell, I wouldn't complain.

A familiar pressure appears in my core as we come to a stop.

Gabriel drops my hand.

"Are you ready?"

We've gotten so close to the bonfire that the blackness behind my blindfold has turned red. I'm sweating. But the warmth of his body somehow manages to keep me cool.

"For anything," I nod. "As long as it's with you."

Gabriel's fingers wrap around the knot of my blindfold and he plants a soft kiss against the back of my neck.

"That's my girl."

With one swift tug, my blindfold comes untied.

At first, the orange light flickering before us is so strong that I have to cover my eyes.

But when Gabriel wraps his hands around my swollen belly, and pushes his growing bulge into the small of my back, I drop my forearm and force myself to look straight ahead.

"What do you think?" he asks.

What I see makes my throat go dry.

This isn't what I was expecting.

Westwood High, our old school, sits below.

It's completely engulfed by a raging inferno.

The angry flames thrash out into the starry night sky above. The heat is nearly overwhelming.

But the sight—well, the sight is absolutely fucking mesmerizing.

"That... That's amazing," I mutter, taking a step towards the flames.

Gabriel has brought me to the top of Overwatch Point. The rolling hill that overlooks the once great building.

"I thought you might like it," Gabriel says.

My dry throat begins to dampen again... right along with my pussy.

I can feel my toes clench. That familiar pressure in my core starts to swirl.

But that's not all that's swirling.

I'm having a hard time wrapping my mind around what this means.

"Why?" I ask, hypnotized by the blaze.

"It's a symbol," Gabriel slowly replies. Suddenly, he's at my side, holding my hand again. "Our past ends tonight, Bianca. Soon, all that will matter is our future."

"Tomorrow *is* a big day," I accept. "But I don't want to forget all about our past. It's what made me into the woman I am today. It's what made me strong. It's what made me *yours*."

"And it's what's made me *yours*," Gabriel nods. "But some things need to be forgotten. Some memories will have to burn."

His grip tightens around my fingers.

Something feels off.

All night, I've had the strangest little pit in my stomach. But I thought it was just nerves. Tomorrow is a big day, after all.

It's the day Dad officially steps down.

In less than twenty-four hours, Gabriel and I will inherit our empire. We will have everything we've ever wanted. And we will have it together.

It doesn't matter if my family doesn't completely trust him quite yet. I do. And that's what counts.

But that's not what's concerning. There's something else.

And I can feel the tension in Gabriel's pulsing palm as he holds me tight.

"What's wrong?" I ask.

"Hopefully nothing," he grumbles. "Just know this, *myszko*. No matter what happens, I'm committed to our future. To you and our child. To the empire we're building together. No one will get in our way, not even..."

Before Gabriel can finish, we both sense the appearance of a new presence.

My gun is out even before I whip around.

But Gabriel doesn't draw his weapon. And when I spot who's waiting for us, I immediately understand why.

"I've heard you've gotten pretty good at using that thing," Rozalia smirks at me. "But don't think I couldn't beat you on the draw."

"I wouldn't be so sure anymore," Gabriel mutters from beside me.

But I'm too stunned to join in on the banter.

How long has it been since I've seen Rozalia?

Fuck. I can hardly believe my eyes.

But she's just the beginning.

I've hardly managed to process her appearance before I spot another figure step up the hill behind her.

"Tytus," I gasp.

"Hello there," the tattooed giant nods. His ruggedly hand-some face flickers in the fire light. Beads of sweat drip down his sharp cheekbones. "You couldn't have picked somewhere cooler to meet?"

"I wanted to send a message," Gabriel growls. The harshness in his tone surprises me, until the shock wears off, and reality comes crashing back down on all of us.

The bloody silver piece.

"The same kind of message you sent to those bikers?" Rozalia asks, crossing her arms.

"No," Gabriel grunts, shaking his head. "I don't want to hurt you."

My stomach drops as I realize what's happening.

This isn't a reunion.

It's a showdown.

"What are you doing here?" I ask, unsure of how to feel yet.

Gabriel has been looking for these two ever since he rescued me from Drago's underground lair. But they've been impossible to find.

Now, all of a sudden, they're standing right in front of us.

"Uh oh, is there trouble in paradise?" Rozalia teases. "I thought for sure Gabriel would have told you everything by now."

"Told me what?"

"That Rozalia and Tytus haven't been missing," Gabriel sneers. "They've been hiding."

"... From us?" I gulp.

"It was the only way to keep our inheritance safe," Tytus says.

It's like an anvil has been dropped over my head.

"Gabriel... What the hell is going on?"

"Yeah, tell her, Gabe," Rozalia urges.

My dark king keeps his strong fingers wound tightly around my hand.

"Rozalia sent me a message this morning," Gabriel says, keeping one eye on his old friends as he looks down at me. "She wanted to meet with us one last time..."

"One last time??"

Despite the evidence we found that pointed towards their betrayal, I never wanted to believe that Gabriel's only two friends could do such a thing to him.

I held out hope.

But here we are.

"We have our own fortune now," Tytus says. "And our own army."

"We don't need your precious husband anymore," Rozalia adds.

"How could you say that?" I croak, emotion clogging my throat. "You three are supposed to be family!"

Behind us, a section of Westwood High collapses under the heat of the bonfire.

Not a single one of us even flinches.

"It wasn't our choice," Tytus shouts back, stepping forward. "You made your own choices, Gabe. We just forged our own path around the trail you blazed."

"You always had a choice," Gabriel says, his voice low and rumbling. "I offered you a spot by my side countless times."

"And we took that spot, until you changed the path," Rozalia counters. "Look, we have no problem with Bianca. But we will not submit to her family."

"I never asked you to submit," Gabriel roars. "I asked you to work with me. With us."

"No. You didn't ask," Tytus responds, shaking his head. "You told. It all became clear at the cabin. Bianca shot me, and you were more worried about her than you were about me. Hey, I get it. No hard feelings there. Love is love. But your love for her is far more rigid than either of us are comfortable with. We both know that if push comes to shove, you would always choose her over us."

"I don't have to choose."

"Yes. You do," Rozalia states. "We know you'll be anointed tomorrow. We wanted to give you one last chance to join us before we're severed forever"

My mind is a whirling mess, but still I manage to latch onto Rozalia's final sentence.

"One *last* chance?" I rasp, looking up at my dark king.

"Gabriel, how long have you been keeping this from me? Have you been negotiating with these two behind my back?"

But even as the words leave my mouth, I don't believe them. Gabriel wouldn't do that.

"Don't worry, darling," Rozalia quickly steps in. "Gabriel hadn't heard from us for months before I sent him that message this morning. But still, that is a good question. Why is Bianca surprised to see us, Gabe? Or are you holding out on her like you held out on us?"

"I've never held out on anyone I love!" Gabriel roars. The heat at our backs is becoming overwhelming. But we don't move. Gabriel's grip around my hand only tightens. "I've only ever asked that you trust me."

"Why should we trust you anymore?" Tytus asks.

"So that I can protect you. All I've ever cared about is protecting my family."

Gabriel pulls me closer to his side, and I can feel his heart pounding behind his powerful chest.

"And what are you trying to protect us from?" Rozalia asks stubbornly.

"Me."

Gabriel's long shadow flickers at the feet of his former friends as the flames continue to grow behind us.

"Is that so?" Rozalia whispers.

"Yes," Gabriel asserts. "I'm trying to protect you from what I'll do to protect my family. Tomorrow, I will become king of the west coast. But that doesn't mean my new power will go unchecked. There are still the Kilpatricks on the east coast, as well as the Barinovs. I'm going to work with them. I need to. But all I've ever *wanted* is to work *with* you. If you don't want to do that anymore—if you continue to cause trouble from the shadows—there may be nothing I can do to stop my new allies from hunting you down. Hell, I might even help them."

"They won't have to hunt," Tytus growls, clenching his fists.

"*You* won't have to hunt us down. Not anymore. We'll meet you head on. We have the resources now. We—"

Before Tytus can take another step forward, Rozalia cuts him off.

"We don't want to work with anyone else," she barks. "We just want to be free. And we want to conquer far more than just your measly west coast. We want everything. Isn't that what you always wanted, Gabriel?"

My heart is in my throat as I feel Gabriel's hand drop from around mine.

But then I feel his arm wrap around my waist, and his fingers fall onto my swollen belly.

"I have everything," he says. There isn't a single hint of doubt or hesitation in his deep voice.

Despite the suffocating intensity of the moment, I've never felt so loved, or so protected.

"Do we not count anymore?" Tytus asks. I can hear the conflict in his voice. The pain. But also the strength.

He's made his choice.

My poor king.

"You count more than you could know," Gabriel responds. "If you go through with this, you will break my heart. But I'm not just protecting my heart anymore. I'm protecting two hearts."

"Three," I quietly remind him.

"Yes. Three..." Gabriel agrees, his palm sinking into my swollen belly. "I'm still getting used to that. Roz. You could be an aunt. Ty. You could be an uncle..."

"Oh, we'll still be that child's aunt and uncle," Rozalia assures him. "No matter what happens. The child will be safe. The child will be loved. But that doesn't mean I'll promise the child won't grow up an orphan."

The gun I had drawn earlier has been resting by my side this entire time, but it lifts at the vile comment coming from the black widow's dark red lips.

She's crossed a line.

My heart nearly erupts as I aim the muzzle at someone I once thought of as a potential friend.

Out of the corner of my eye, I see Gabriel do the same thing.

But Rozalia was right. She's just as quick as either of us, if not quicker. Tytus too.

Behind us, another section of the burning high school collapses, and an eruption of heat bursts up into the night sky.

"I won't ever let you hurt my family," Gabriel growls. He's drawn two guns. Each one is pointed at a different friend.

No. They aren't friends anymore.

They're enemies.

My heart aches through the anger.

"*We* were supposed to be your family," Tytus shouts.

"Family doesn't betray family," Gabriel barks back.

"They do if they can see the betrayal coming first..." Tytus starts, before trailing off.

The tension between us is as thick as the black smoke billowing up from the burning school. The suffocating vapors block out the stars, shrouding us in a flame-lit darkness.

"You don't have to do this," I plead.

My gun shakes in my trembling hands. Of all the horrifying shit I've been through in the past year, this might be the worst.

Gabriel could be losing his only friends, his only surviving family, all because of his love for me.

"You're still so naïve, princess," Rozalia says, shaking her head. "And it looks like it's rubbing off on your man."

"It's time for you to go," Gabriel suddenly demands.

Stepping forward, he shields me with his body. But I'm not backing away.

With one hand on my belly, I point my gun beneath his shoulder.

Sweat trickles down my face.

"You're still just an heir," I hear Tytus clamor. "Only now, you're not even the heir of your own kingdom."

"By this time tomorrow, we'll be king and queen," I call out to him.

"Of someone else's empire," Roz replies.

"No," Gabriel growls. "It will be my empire. And I will rule it with *my* family."

To my surprise, Rozalia drops her gun. "Well, then I guess this really is goodbye," she sighs. "Maybe I was the naïve one for thinking I could sway you back to the dark side."

"I'm still on the dark side," Gabriel rumbles. "But there's more than one way to rule hell."

"To each their own," Tytus agrees, also dropping his gun.

"You don't have to go," I whisper, contradicting my king.

My heart is ready to shatter. Gabriel doesn't deserve this.

"That's not true," Rozalia says to me, before turning her attention back to Gabriel. "We've come to a crossroads. But this isn't the end, darling. No. Not if we don't think of it like that. How about we call it a new beginning? Maybe even a fresh start? Hell, I've always wondered if I could take you in a real fight. Now, I'll get the chance to find out. Silver linings, right?"

"You won't get far," Gabriel promises. "I won't let you."

"Because you'll miss us?" Rozalia teases, forcing a smirk.

But I swear I spot the faintest glimmer of a tear trickling down her beautiful cheek.

"I never said I wouldn't miss you," Gabriel admits.

"Well, then don't wait too long before you come after us," Tytus taunts, wiping away something from below his own eye.

"... And feel free to bring your new friends," Rozalia adds. "Especially that little lion boy of yours. I can't say I'm not impressed by his skills. One day, I'd really like to crack open his skull and study his pretty brains. What do you think? Would he object?"

"I think you should go," Gabriel repeats, even though I can tell his heart isn't in it.

I want to cry for him.

But that won't do us any good. So, instead, I stay strong. Stepping up beside him, I nudge my ear against his hard shoulder.

"You heard him," I say.

That makes Rozalia chuckle. But she doesn't bite back. Instead, she just lifts her hand and points a finger beneath her eye. "Glad to see you decided to embrace at least one thing about your past," she says to Gabriel.

I can't help but look up at my dark king's stony face. The initials I tattooed on his cheek almost seem to cast shadows.

GR.

Gabriel Reca.

"You knew about his last name?" I ask.

"Oh, I know so much, darling" Rozalia replies. "More than you could ever imagine. And it's the only reason we have any chance against your nation-spanning empire—but some things are more obvious than others. Those initials could only mean one thing. Just like that big bonfire behind you could only mean one thing. The message is clear. The past is over. You've conquered it. All that matters is the future. It begins tonight. Do you think you can conquer that as well? Do you think you can conquer *us*?"

Rozalia doesn't wait for a response. Instead, she takes one last long look at Gabriel. Then, she silently turns away.

"See you around," Tytus says, dipping his head in a causal salute before following Rozalia down the hill.

We don't follow them.

In fact, for what feels like an eternity, we don't move at all.

Instead, we just stand here, side by side, my head nuzzled against Gabriel's shoulder.

Westwood High burns to the ground behind us.

"Why didn't you tell me they were going to be here?" I finally ask, when I'm sure we're alone again.

"To protect you," Gabriel sighs. Wrapping his arm around my shoulder, he plants a soft kiss on my forehead.

"From what?"

"From everything. From the stress. From the heartbreak. I thought I could fix this before it ever got to you. I... I thought this might turn into more of a reunion than a goodbye."

"But the silver coin we found in Poland..."

"I know, *myszko*. I know. It was them. Rozalia and Tytus. They killed the priests. They stole my army and my fortune. And they didn't do it because Drago told them to. They did it because they wanted to. But that's all over now. They can have what they took. I don't need it. I already have what I want. I have you."

The inferno continues to crackle behind us as I'm pulled into Gabriel's massive embrace. His big heart pounds behind his solid chest, and I just want to reach inside and wrap myself around it. I want to protect him from this heartbreak. Smother him in love. Heal him.

"Let's go home," I whisper. "I've had enough of our past for tonight."

"Our past is gone," Gabriel murmurs. "It's been burned to ashes, pushed away, conquered. I know it's hard to let go. But if we're going to survive, then we must do what's hard. Do you understand?"

"I understand," I respond. "I just wish it didn't have to hurt so bad."

"So do I, *myszko*. So do I. Just know that surviving the pain is the only way to get stronger. And we will need to be strong to face what comes next."

He's right.

"I love you," I tell him. Digging my face deep into his chest,

I try to reach his heart. But I know there's no point. I already have it.

"I love you too, Bianca."

The flames of hell thrash behind us as we embrace under a blackened sky. But the scorching heat isn't painful.

No. It doesn't hurt anymore. At least, not in a bad way.

Instead, it's almost comforting.

This is where we belong. This is where we'll thrive.

Because love doesn't just mean living together in a perfect world. It can't. There's no such thing as a perfect world. But there is such a thing as perfect love.

And despite all that we've suffered together, despite all that is undoubtedly still to come, I know that Gabriel and I have the perfect love.

Sure, it might be messy, and complicated and dark, and even painful at times, but that's exactly what we need. It's what will allow us to face this imperfect world, head-on.

It's what will help us conquer it.

Because if our love can survive the brutal hate we once held for each other, what hope does anyone else have?

The answer is so sharp and clear it almost hurts.

None.

No one has any fucking hope. Not against us.

It's just a shame that Rozalia and Tytus will have to learn that the hard way.

EPILOGUE
GABRIEL

3 months later...

My heart overflows with so much fucking love as I watch them sleep.

Bianca lies flat on her stomach for the first time in months. Little Jakub rests peacefully next to her.

His hair is already coming in. Jet black. Just like mine.

But when those tiny eyes are open, they are a stunning shade of crystal blue, just like his mother's.

Goddamn.

Despite all that's been going on lately, I find myself fully encompassed by the peace emanating from them.

The pressure of the outside world fades. And I just watch the soft breaths puttering out of my baby boy's lips as he snuggles up against his mom's cheek.

All I want is to crawl back into bed and hold them so close.

... Then, I feel my phone vibrate.

Fuck.

Duty never sleeps. Especially when you're the king of the west coast underworld.

"What is it?" I ask, only answering the call after I've stepped out into the hallway and quietly clicked the bedroom door shut behind me.

"I'm here."

Rian's voice is nothing more than a growl.

Shit. This can't be good.

"I'll be downstairs in a second."

Taking one last look over my shoulder, I gaze longingly at the closed door. I can still sense the beautiful slice of domestic bliss hiding just behind it. It's intoxicating. And

the only thing that allows me to pull myself away is the confidence that it's not going anywhere. Not if I have anything to say about it.

Still, the tranquility quickly evaporates as I make my way downstairs to meet Rian—I do my best to let it go gracefully.

For as much as I enjoy that calmness, it's not something I can carry with me. Satisfaction leads to sloppiness. And when you run a mafia empire, sloppiness can get you and everyone you love killed.

I'll do anything to protect Bianca and Jakub—and that includes pushing them from my mind as I march downstairs to meet an angry lion.

Rian Kilpatrick is waiting for me in the foyer. I can practically see the smoke billowing from his flared nostrils.

"I'm guessing you finally decoded that message," I say, preparing myself for the worst.

"She's losing her touch," Ryan rumbles. "This one only took me a few days to decrypt."

"Maybe," I murmur, sincerely doubting his first claim. "Let's go out back."

Turning around, I lead Rian through my home. He follows

closely behind, a thunderous black storm cloud ready to burst at any moment.

Shit.

Rian is fucking pissed. And that's bad news. But not just because of what he's about to tell me.

It's how he's going to tell it to me.

When the lion gets angry, he also gets very fucking loud.

A year ago, I wouldn't have cared. Now, though? I can't have that in my household. Upstairs, my family is sleeping soundly, a rare occurrence these days. They need to rest.

But I never can.

This shit is too fucking important.

For the past two months, someone has been sending taunting messages to the Kilpatrick prince, desperately trying to goad him into making a foolish move.

By now, it's clear who that someone is.

Roz.

Her wicked obsession with the Irish lion is only matched by his raging obsession with her.

I'm worried their lethal game of cat and mouse is going to end in a deadly explosion. One that might take out more than just the two of them.

But how do I stop two forces of nature from colliding?

"They've turned two more of our politicians," Rian barks, the second we step out into my backyard.

"Who?" I ask, my mind already racing.

I'm trying to be the calm one here, but it's hard when we're being outmaneuvered like this.

It's infuriating.

We have the most powerful standing army in the underworld, but somehow, Roz and Tytus are managing to get their hooks in every crooked politician from here to New York.

"Christopher Housley and Jake Suter," Rian sneers.

"Those are fucking senators," I realize, immediately recognizing the names. Pinching the bridge of my nose, I try to fight back an encroaching headache. "How the fuck are they managing this?"

"The bitch's newest message explains how in painstaking detail," Rian curses.

A flash of rage eviscerates my growing headache. But I keep myself from reacting too violently towards Rian's words.

Roz is supposed to be my enemy now—but old habits are hard to kick, and I still get defensive when someone attacks my former friend.

"Tell me what she said," I grunt. Turning my back on Rian, I look out over the endless courtyard that is my backyard.

I've come so far.

But my work is never done.

"She tricked us," Rian says. "The black widow set us up when we needed her the most."

"What do you mean?"

"Back in the tunnels, when we were looking for Bianca. Remember how she sent you the schematics for Drago's security system?"

"Yeah," I nod, a knot tightening in my gut. "She sent them in encrypted files so Drago wouldn't know we were trying to breach him. Right?"

Rian shakes his head. "That's not all she hid in those files. There was something else. A digital lockbox filled with the deepest, darkest secrets of nearly every significant politician in the country."

My stomach drops.

"Blackmail?"

"That's right. Blackmail that was locked away so tightly, not even she could get to it. But I could. And she knew it. Fucking hell, I decrypted it all without even knowing it..."

Just like that, it all clicks together.

No fucking way.

This is why Drago wanted Rian so badly. He didn't just send me after the lion as a distraction. He really wanted me to capture Bianca's fearsome cousin so that we could force him to decrypt some invaluable trove of information.

But how would we have forced Rian to do anything he didn't want to do?

Easy. if we had Bianca. All we'd have to do was threaten her. Then what choice would he have?

Shit.

"Where the hell did all that blackmail come from?" I ask, still confused about how Drago would know that such a thing even existed.

"I went back and checked," Rian says. "There was the faintest digital signature carved into the bottom of the strong-box. A claim of ownership."

Turning back around, I see the scowl twisting the lion's face.

But do I also spot a sliver of sympathy in his sharp blue eyes?

"Tell me the name," I demand.

Rian only hesitates for a second.

"The blackmail belonged to Sonia Caruso. Your mother."

"What the fuck?"

I can hardly believe my ears... until a repressed memory comes rushing out from the back of my mind.

When I was hanging from the rafters in Westwood's gymnasium, Drago told me something. Something that I could have easily ignored. Something that I didn't even think twice about at the time.

But now, it's the piece that puts this entire puzzle together.

Drago said that before they'd married, Kamil had killed my mother's first husband, the son of a prominent senator. Then, they'd run away together.

Their pockets lined with political blackmail, and so much leverage in the war to come...

Fuck.

"Are you sure?" I ask, naively holding out hope that the damage isn't that devastating.

"Look for yourself."

Ripping out his phone, Rian pulls something up on his screen, then hands it over to me.

"Does she mention anything about El Blanco?" I mutter.

That name still haunts me. I feel like it must be connected to all of this, but I haven't even been able to find any crumbs yet.

"No."

Shit. That's a mystery that still needs solving. But it will have to wait for another day.

"Don't be fooled by some of the things she says," Rian warns. "She's just trying to play with our heads."

"How?" I ask, glancing through the decrypted message.

"Somewhere in there, she claims that Tytus rigged smoke bombs in the tunnels surrounding Drago's underground office. Apparently, that was supposed to help you get a jump on the small army standing watch outside. I guess they were watching the whole shitshow from afar."

Damn. I'd wondered where that smoke had come from. Without it, I'd never have had a chance to get as close as I did before taking my first shot. And who knows what Krol would have done to Bianca if he'd known I was so close...

"What else do they claim to be responsible for?" I ask, hating that I feel any gratitude towards Roz and Tytus right now.

They may have helped me save Bianca. Hell, they might have even saved my life. But that was before they broke my heart.

Still, the timeline is confusing. As far as I can tell, by that point they'd already decided to betray me.

So, why the hell did they help me?

"A whole bunch of bullshit," Rian grunts. "I've already told you the important parts."

He's right.

As I scan through the message, I recognize Roz's voice, as well as her taunting confessions.

It makes my heart clench.

Why did it have to come to this?

"Where does this link lead?" I ask, reaching the end of the script. At the bottom, there's one final sentence.

CLICK HERE!

The blue font is underlined twice over.

I'm so absorbed in my own thoughts that I find myself clicking on it.

"Don't fucking touch that!" Rian shouts.

But it's too late. The screen pixelates and distorts as he rips the phone from my hand.

"What was it?" I ask, pissed at myself for being so careless.

"I don't know, and I wasn't going to touch it until I did."

"Well, it's too late for that now. We might as well—"

"No fucking way."

Rian's eyes go wide as he glares down at the phone screen.

For a second, he's frozen in shock. Then, a blistering rage engulfs him.

"What?"

Stepping forward, I glance down at the screen.

My shaking heart fucking stops dead.

On Rian's phone, I see a crystal-clear video of Bianca and Jakub. They're still sleeping in the exact same positions I left them in earlier.

"This is a live feed," Rian growls, pointing down at the running timer near the bottom of the screen.

"Roz hacked into the nanny cam..." I realize.

That's one step too fucking far.

But before I can react any further, the video trembles and

pixelates again. Then, a black bar juts across the top of the screen. Inside that bar, a message appears.

I'm coming for you.

The threat is surrounded on each side by two smirking devil emojis.

That's fucking Roz, alright.

"I'm going to rip her fucking throat out," Rian roars. But before he can storm inside and wake the whole house up, I yank him back.

"She isn't in there," I say, my fist trembling. "Roz is just trying to get a rise out of you."

"Well, it's fucking working," Rian sneers, pointing down at the screen. "That's my nephew she's threatening. That's my cousin."

"And it's my son. And my wife," I assure him. "I know how to protect them."

The only thing keeping me from blowing my top right now is remembering the promise that Roz had made to me back at Overwatch Point, in the shadows of those raging flames.

She swore she'd leave Jakub out of this—even if she did threaten to make him an orphan some day.

Fucking hell.

"No. You don't know how to protect them," Rian charges, his blue eyes white with fire. "Look at how calm you are. You're still trapped in the past, *Gabriel*. How can I expect you to protect anything if you still think you're fighting a couple of old friends?"

The accusation cuts through me like a fucking knife.

"Don't you dare question my will to protect my family!" I snap. Grabbing Rian by the collar, I shove him against the wall.

"Then pick a fucking side already!" he shoots back, before pushing me off.

"I have! Bianca and Jakub are my side. They are all that matters."

"And what about my family, huh? What about me? Do we matter?"

"That depends," I caution him. "Do you really believe what you just said, or do you trust me to protect what's mine?"

"I'm having a hard time trusting anyone right now," Rian grumbles, fixing his collar. "Let alone someone who can't decide on whether he wants to destroy our enemies or beg them to join us."

Fuck. He's right.

For the sake of my family's safety, I can't go on like this.

But I can't go after Roz like she's just another criminal, either. That switch isn't flipped so easily.

Hell, I'll admit to myself that I've been putting more effort into looking for Drago than I have for Roz and Tytus—even though the dragon might as well be a ghost, and my two former friends are causing more trouble every day.

"What do you want me to do?" I ask, still unsure of just how the fuck I'm going to deal with this.

"Let me loose," Rian snarls. "Let me go after her. Let me do whatever it takes to neutralize this threat."

"Why do you need my permission to do that?" I ask, slightly taken off guard.

This is the notorious Irish lion I'm talking to. His father, Aiden Kilpatrick is king of everything. East coast. West coast. It all falls under his crown. Sure, I rule this side of the country with an iron fist, but only because I've gained their trust. My throne sits in the shadow of Aiden's. And someday, that throne will belong to Rian.

He doesn't need to ask me for shit.

"Because I know how important you are to Bianca..." Rian relents, white fire still thrashing behind his harsh blue eyes. "And to our empire. And while I may be reckless at times, I still don't want to jeopardize any of that. Not if I don't have to. I've learned from my past mistakes."

"How would you even find the time to go after her?" I stall. "Haven't you been called back east?"

"I have," Rian admits. "But a king can do whatever he fucking pleases."

"A king... Does that mean?"

The revelation hits me like a mac truck.

"Yes," Rian nods. "Just like Ray did for you and Bianca, my father is preparing to step down... and hand the reins over to me."

"Fuck," I curse, hardly believing it. The man I just shoved against the wall is about to become the king of all kings.

I'd be happy for him, if I wasn't so shocked.

"We can't have these distractions threatening our empire," Rian says. "But more importantly, we can't allow anyone to threaten our families. And I mean *anyone*."

He's right.

Fucking hell.

A bittersweet acceptance finally washes over me. I feel myself give in.

"Fine," I sigh. "Go after Rozalia. But what will you do if you catch her?"

It's like he's already thought about it a thousand times over, because he doesn't even hesitate.

"I'm going to use her," Rian sneers, hardly blinking. "Just like she used me."

"Use her? What does that mean?"

I can't help the protective instinct that flares up inside of me. But I quickly force myself to snuff it out.

This is the only way.

Roz made her choice.

I can't protect her anymore.

I won't.

"First, I'm going to lock her up in a tiny little cage," Rian growls, his twisted scowl morphing into a sadistic smirk. "Then, I'm going to *break* her."

I'm not quite sure how to react.

"She might not be so easy to break," I warn him. "Hell, she could be one of the few people on this planet who could break you right back."

The Irish lion only huffs at that.

Running his fingers through his dirty blonde hair, he lets those sharp blue eyes trail off into the distance, like he's already picturing what he'll do to my former friend.

"I'd like to see her try," he growls. "It will be more fun if she fights back."

CAN YOU FEEL THAT ELECTRICITY?? LETHAL KING IS WHERE RIAN AND ROZ CLASH. EVERYONE WILL GET THEIR HEA. I PROMISE!

THANK YOU SO MUCH FOR READING!

ALSO BY SASHA LEONE

The Brutal Reign Series

(Each book is an interconnected standalone with its own hea!)

Merciless Prince

Brutal Savior

Cruel Knight

Wicked Master

Twisted Lover

Savage Don